I0681957

MICHAEL ATAMANOV

WEB OF WORLDS

Wishing you safe travels on your fantasy journey,

Michael Atamanov

REALITY BENDERS
BOOK FOUR

MAGIC DOME BOOKS

All books
by Michael Atamanov:

Reality Benders LitRPG series
Countdown
External Threat
Game Changer
Web of Worlds
A Jump into the Unknown
Aces High

The Dark Herbalist LitRPG series
Video Game Plotline Tester
Stay on the Wing
A Trap for the Potentate
Finding a Body

Perimeter Defense LitRPG series
Sector Eight
Beyond Death
New Contract
A Game with No Rules

League of Losers LitRPG Series
A Cat and His Human

You're in Game!
(LitRPG Stories from Bestselling Authors)

You're in Game-2!
(More LitRPG stories set in your favorite worlds)

Table of Contents:

Introduction

Point of No Return

I VAN LOZOVSKY WAS very nervous, but he was trying not to show it. For the first time in his nascent term as leader of the Human-3 Faction, the curators of the Dome project had summoned him for a meeting. And although the young diplomat couldn't see particular reason for leadership to be displeased, it was hard to be optimistic after being yanked out of important in-game negotiations with the allied German faction and urgently flown to Moscow by military helicopter. What could have possibly happened?

1

Things were going fairly well in the faction recently thanks to the long ceasefire with their dangerous northern neighbors, which had freed up resources for development that otherwise would have gone to military needs. The faction's population was growing steadily and had just topped two thousand. New nodes had been incorporated. What was more, there was reason to believe that, in the next few days, they would be getting two more nodes to the south of the Yellow Mountains from the Centaurs. All their understandings with Phylira were still in force, and the striped mare was well on track to becoming sole ruler of a unified Centaur herd numbering in the thousands.

Sure, there had been certain snags and setbacks. But for a project as major and wide-scale as this, it was inevitable. How much had we lost to the senseless war the Germans started with the Naiads, for example? And surely they'd noticed the fact that we were three times over our resource budget for building the Karelia base. NPC's just kept attacking and setting us back. But there hadn't been any serious mistakes or blunders, and certainly no glaring failures like when Tyulenev defected to the Dark Faction, or when the enemy ambush intercepted our money from the Miyelonian pirate-merchants. The last incident, by the way, cost his predecessor Radugin this very job. So what could have been the reason for today's emergency meeting?

Ivan Lozovsky gathered his thoughts and walked into the well-familiar small hall, which could hold just thirty people. On the door he saw a warning that wireless communications were blocked inside. The hall itself had no windows, and one whole wall was occupied by a big interactive board, which was now showing the territory of the Human-3 Faction and neighboring nodes. This was the same room where, five months earlier, the curators had instructed Ivan before a space flight to the Geckho homeworld of Shikharsa. He was a complete beginner in the game that bends reality back then, but leadership had pinned enormous hopes on his diplomatic mission. It was assumed that the all-powerful Geckho would share knowledge and technology with their new vassals. And that, they reasoned, would open the floodgates for long-distance spacecraft and, in the not-so-distant future, interplanetary travel would become an everyday occurrence on par with riding the subway.

Hrmph... naive fantasies. And although the faction was fed an official story that the diplomatic mission culminated in a brilliant success, and the Geckho had shared antigravitation technology with their new vassals that was not, in fact, even close to reality. There was no personal meeting with the great and powerful ruler Krong Daveyesh-Pir. And Lozovsky never needed the traditional greeting, which he had practiced and fine-tuned for days with Geckho diplomat Kosta Dykhsh. Instead, along with a large group of three hundred if not more representatives of new vassals, colonies and populations, the lone earthling was herded into a huge circular hall in the Sovereign Palace. And there, standing behind some tall Geckho, he didn't even catch the briefest glimpse of the extraterrestrial ruler.

The Earth diplomat also didn't manage to personally convey his gift to the great Krong Daveyesh-Pir, an exact copy of the golden record from the Voyager mission with all its pictures and designs. But the famous message humanity sent into deep space in the twentieth century in hopes of meeting extraterrestrial civilizations seemed pointless if he couldn't explain its deep meaning.

So before returning home, Lozovsky sold the gold disk for scrap, netting enough crystals to purchase an old and very patched up antigrav. When he made it back, it became clear that he'd been scammed by a junk dealer. The craft was of Miyelonian production and thus incompatible with the parts and software that could be obtained in the nearby Geckho spaceport. Nevertheless, the antigrav elicited colossal interest from our scientists and allowed them to understand a few of the working principles and laws of physics behind antigravitation. And that was basically the whole real story of the supposed "gift."

"Okay, we now have a quorum and can begin," the amplified voice of a middle-aged soldier with major-general stripes brought Ivan Lozovsky back from his stroll down memory lane.

The diplomat looked around. There were no more unoccupied seats. In fact, it was the same as all the meetings he had been to as Radugin's deputy. The thirty people, most in military uniform, looked extremely concentrated and stern, awaiting a report from the head of the faction.

The diplomat took out his tablet. He'd had just enough time to copy detailed data on faction affairs over before leaving for Moscow, including resource stockpiles, construction timeframes for important buildings, road maps and the few tight spots in their logistics. There was also a complete class and level breakdown of the players and an attempt at some kind of an average "combat power" statistic, a figure the curators told his predecessor Radugin to work out at the last meeting. It was of course a shame but, for now, it was only in raw formulas, tables and dry numbers, which were hard to interpret at first glance. But Lozovsky hadn't been planning to give a report today, and there just wasn't time to make an elegant presentation.

The faction head gave a bow and started looking around for the connectors and cords to his device. But the major general leading today's meeting stopped him:

"We won't be needing that, Ivan. Your next scheduled report is still in two weeks. Now we just want answers to a couple questions. First of all, we wanted to discuss the problem with Major Filippov's character. As faction head, what do you intend to do with this peculiar situation?"

The faction head made an official report on this very recently. As a matter of fact, as soon as he heard the news, he got out of his virt pod to do just that. Still, it was not so much problem as a curiosity. Filippov was a highly experienced military specialist, who the curators sent under the Dome to work as a Strategist and counterweight to the Dark Faction's terrifying new

General Ui-Taka. The issue was that he was given a very unexpected choice of class when generating his character: Fisher or Bard. Before making his decision, Major Filippov left into the real world to inform his superiors. Nevertheless, the game had already registered him as player number 2018, so there was no going back or replacing him.

Clearly embarrassed, the Major then justified himself by saying that always had adored fishing and singing songs around the campfire. In fact he was a fairly talented guitar player and, in his circle of friends, was even known to play a few songs of his own composition. But he never imagined these hobbies were so close to his heart that they would eclipse all his professional training.

So, what were our options? Well, we could use him as a Strategist anyway and take a serious hit to effectiveness, or lose one faction member forever. As head of the H3 faction, Ivan Lozovsky preferred the former. The faction was in desperate need of manpower, and a Strategist working at half capacity was still better than nothing. Of course, there another possibility Lozovsky was keeping in the back of his mind, just letting Vasily Filippov work as a Fisher or Bard. It seemed better not to mention it directly, but he was trying very cautiously to lead someone else there to the thought:

"I was told Major Filippov is an experienced specialist. As far as I know, he was involved in the extremely difficult liberation of Aleppo. We definitely want someone like him in the faction, and his talents are welcome no matter how this shakes out. In case things get hairy, he at least knows how to hold a weapon. To my eye, whether he'll level by fishing or playing guitar is a purely technical matter and up for discussion. I would personally prefer a Bard due to the morale and stat bonuses he could give other players. What's more, our faction has no lakes or large rivers currently and, due to the war with the Naiads, the sea is currently off limits."

A pause took hold. The lights went dim, leaving just a small area around the podium brightly lit. As far as Lozovsky knew, they did this to exchange opinions in private before a vote. Finally, the chairman spoke up:

"A majority decision has been reached. Major Filippov shall remain in the Human-3 Faction with the class of Bard. We expect the directors to develop an accelerated levelling plan for his character with a slant toward combat skills and providing positive bonuses to others. Strategist skills can be ignored for now. We plan to send another candidate to fill that role shortly."

Sure, a very logical and rational decision. The diplomat was sincerely happy that he would soon have a decent Strategist, and not have to make do with "neither flesh nor fowl." All that remained unclear was what to do with the new Bard. Would he still be one of the directors or deputies? Would they relegate him to the ranks of the normal players? But that decision could easily wait. The speaker must have thought so too, because he moved on to a new topic:

"The ceasefire with the Dark Faction has

expired, as has the time for General Ui-Taka's ultimatum. Our impression of the new Dark Faction leader is that he's a no-nonsense man, someone who doesn't throw words around willy-nilly. How prepared is the H3 Faction for an escalation in this low-intensity conflict?"

Ivan Lozovsky immediately lit up because he had lots of data about that issue and therefore lots to say. Thankfully, the faction had made significant progress here. The whole chain of fortifications on the border with the Dark Faction had been rebuilt and reinforced. The distant isolated garrisons of the Eastern no longer suffered from supply issues, new roads had been built, and the faction now had plenty of ammunition, explosives and provisions. Layered, staggered defensive lines had been constructed at the most vulnerable parts. We even had true fortresses with strong garrisons and underground storage with enough supplies to keep our defenders shooting for a long time, even when fully surrounded.

Our allies were also better prepared than before. Just yesterday, six hundred of the German H6 Faction's best soldiers had been brought up an almost-completed road along the sea shore and deposited in the capital node and Eastern Swamp. Phylira said she could provide two thousand muscular Centaurs as well, although the tough and fast NPC's were going to be used for transportation, not fighting. We had even reached an agreement with the harpies, who were supposedly going to patrol and do recon from the sky. Still, we didn't put much stock into these unreliable winged allies, whose intentions shifted like the desert sands. But in any case the H3 Faction had fortified the whole border line from Karelia to the Eastern Swamp like never before. Recent tests indicated that our forces could be fully deployed in just eighteen minutes and, at the most critically dangerous points, we could ready enough troops to deflect an attack in just four.

The curators were completely satisfied with that, though there was one retort that a war could not be won by sitting back on defense. Ivan Lozovsky responded to that completely accurate remark by saying the faction had many attack plans under consideration. But each time the military experts came to the same conclusion: given the present balance of forces which was thought to be, in the best-case, two thousand of us against five or six thousand darksiders, going on the attack would be akin to suicide.

At that the Diplomat assured the military men that the situation would be changing for the better soon because we were currently developing and incorporating three southern nodes: Centaur Plateau, Rainforest, and Tropics. And in just a week, given enough resources, all three of the southern territories could be up to level two, which would allow the H3 faction to bring another five hundred twenty-two players into the game. The faction's main hope then lie in bringing the Jungles and Yellow Mountains nodes up to level three on schedule, within ten days, which would give us another one thousand players. And if, beyond that, peaceful expansion into Centaur territory continued apace, it was easily possible that we would gain two more nodes. So ideally, in ten or eleven days, the Human-3 Faction's population would be practically doubling.

"The Dark Faction must realize that," the chair commented almost immediately. "And as long as they aren't growing faster than us, an attack is inevitable in the next few days."

"If you look at it that way then of course yes. But there are other factors you aren't considering..." the Diplomat chose his words carefully because this was quite a slippery topic and he didn't want to delve into details. "I have already reported on our contacts with Emancipation from Mage Tyranny, a supposed ideological anti-mage liberation organization in the parallel world. No matter who they really are, they did their job and carried out a devastating terror attack at the funeral of Coruler Thumor-Anhu La-Fin, killing or crippling a large number of mourners. Many of the victims used to form the inner circle of the former ruler of the First Directory and were among the strongest Dark Faction players. A few were even in leadership."

The experienced speaker made a pause, allowing the curators to think over what he'd said, then continued:

"We've long known that most Dark Faction players hail from the First Directory, the historical patrimony of the La-Fin dynasty of mages and corulers. So there's no reason to be surprised that many of the mages killed or injured were subjects of the La-Fin family and part of the faction created by great mage Thumor-Anhu La-Fin. But that means there is a high likelihood the Dark Faction is now paralyzed, as it is basically headless. Many of the strongest mages died or were seriously wounded, and the laws of the parallel world allow only people with magical abilities to occupy leadership positions."

"But the new head of the Dark Faction is not a mage!" came a justified objection. Lozovsky was eager to confirm that:

"General Ui-Taka is an exception. In fact, he is the only nonmage to rule in the last eight hundred years. But that terror attack has caused many problems for the new leader of the Dark Faction, the least of which is that many of his advisors and assistants in the game that bends reality were hurt or killed. He was actually blamed for the blast himself and four of the most powerful directories have declared war on his state. So..."

Ivan Lozovsky gave a satisfied snort and said the Dark Faction strategist would soon be so wrapped up in real-world conflicts that he wouldn't have any time for the game.

After that, he heard shouts of approval, even applause. The news of the fearsome enemy's new problems was taken very positively. One of the council members even said something like, "the Dark Faction will now simply collapse. Citizens of the First Directory are already not especially loyal to him as the former ruler of a different government, and it sounds like they won't be seeing him very often." However, the others in the room did not share his optimism.

"Ivan, what does this all mean?" one of the

previously silent curators asked. "You yourself just said that only mages can rule in their world, but the last of the La-Fin dynasty passed away without a mage to succeed him. So who will be the new head of the First Directory and most powerful Dark Faction figure not in the game but the real world?"

The din immediately went silent, everyone listening attentively for Lozovsky's answer. So when the Diplomat did speak up, it sounded quite abrupt:

"The new ruler of the First Directory is Gnat! Our Gnat! Coruler Thumor-Anhu La-Fin's granddaughter, Princess Minn-O La-Fin is his junior wife and he undoubtedly possesses magical abilities. According to the laws of the magocratic world, that is all it takes to make Kirill Ignatiev a Coruler!"

The buzz picked back up. The curators were actively discussing the news. However, they immediately went quiet when they saw the doors quietly peek open. Then an agitated young officer walked toward the speaker in a quick almost running gait, holding a telephone and pointing motioning toward the corridor where the call wouldn't be jammed. The Major General apologized to everyone and hurried to the exit.

Something very extreme must have happened if they sent someone in to interrupt this secret meeting. In the quiet of the hall, everyone was whispering guesses, but the word heard most often was "war." And in fact, when the speaker came in three minutes later with a deadened face, his first word was:

"War!!! At five o'clock this morning game-world

time, our Rainforest node was attacked by the Dark Faction. Under cover of thick fog, fifteen enemy Sio-Mi-Dori assault-landing antigravs entered our node from the forest and landed right at outpost thirty-four. And although they didn't catch our soldiers completely off-guard, the battle didn't last long. Outpost thirty-four has been lost, and along with it the whole Rainforest node. And that cuts off the Tropics and its garrison from the rest of our territory. But I'm afraid the bad news doesn't end there..."

The Major General wiped the perspiration from his forehead and continued, poorly hidden notes of panic slipping through:

"Simultaneously, no less than three hundred Dark Faction soldiers disembarked a Geckho ferry on the German capital island, most of them wearing exoskeleton armor and carrying heavy weaponry. Our allies were caught completely by surprise. No one was expecting an attack on the distant island, so practically all H6 players who can hold a weapon were in our territory! The island has been captured and Dark Faction assault troops are shooting on sight any Germans that try to enter the game or respawn. And all that means..." Picking up for the speaker, Ivan Lozovsky finished:

"It means we lost our six hundred allied soldiers. The H6 Faction took a huge hit to player capacity and is no longer capable of providing any manpower. Their maximum is now three hundred forty-eight, and they will need them to defend the two coastal nodes the H6 faction has left, which are at levels one and two."

Damn, damn, damn! Ivan Lozovsky was angry at himself and all the others. Now, after the fact, it dawned on him: how could they be so blind? Why had they made strong defenses on the border and just sat on their laurels? After all, they understood perfectly that General Ui-Taka was known in his world as an unrivalled tactician. And now, instead of pushing through all the mine fields and layered defense structures, he just landed a party deep in the rear, cutting off the only way south and basically taking the German faction out of the fight. Just one move, and the situation was gasp worthy!

Without support, the Tropics node, cut off from the rest of the faction, would fall. And there were no less than fifty H3 players there, mostly just builders. Plus the Germans couldn't hold their remaining hexagons. They would fall very quickly. Sending reinforcements south would mean calling off people and weakening the northern border with the Dark Faction, which was exactly what the enemy was expecting. Basically, to put it in chess terms, the H3 faction was in check and checkmate was not far off. At the very least, the faction leader didn't see any good moves. No matter what he did or didn't do, it would only get worse.

"But how were they able to take the ferry?" came a unified cry of surprise and outrage from the curators. "The Geckho don't interfere in their vassals' conflicts!"

"And they aren't interfering," the major general replied to all these objections. "Geckho Diplomat Kosta Dykhsh has already confirmed their neutrality. In his words, the Geckho merely transported some people who paid for a ticket. And the Diplomat reminded us that our faction has used the same ferry on a number of occasions to transport humans and freight, including troops and military supplies. And I suspect that transporting three hundred landing troops along with heavy weaponry and other supplies cost our enemies a pretty penny! It must have run them at least half a million crystals! Where did the Dark Faction get that kind of money?!"

Ivan Lozovsky kept silent and lowered his head morosely. He knew perfectly well where they enemy got half a million crystals. He himself along with Gerd Tamara and a few other trusted players had handed it to a Dark Faction player as payment for the funeral bombing!

Chapter One

A Talk with the Crew

YOU STOP NOTICING the measured hum of spaceship engines after just half an hour underway. In fact, after a while, any change in their tone and you're sure to be worried. The sound becomes a comfort, a sign that everything is working just fine. My Tolili-Ukh X frigate had successfully left the Medu-Ro IV pirate station and, after building speed, entered a hyperspace jump to the Miyelonian trade hub Kasti-Utsh III. No one came to meet us at the entrance to the station or followed us, which made me happy. I had calculated right, and the repair of my starship was over before the outraged Pride of the Bushy Shadow had returned with their fleet.

The second the danger had passed, my business partner Uline Tar removed her space suit and went into her bunk, asking not to be disturbed. I knew what had my coarse-haired friend so bothered. Neither she nor I had any money left. All attempts to find shipments headed to the Miyelonian station ended in potential clients recoiling from us as if we were lepers. That was a direct consequence of Gnat's reputation for piracy! Law-abiding captains didn't want anything to do with me or my ship. Uline Tar was from an ancient house of space traders, which had earned a good reputation through many generations of hard work, so that bothered her quite a bit. How could we hope to trade if no respectable merchant would have anything to do with us?!

And there was a creeping war between outworld vassal factions on the edge of the known Universe, which her human business partner was going to go fight in. War always meant big expenses. And Uline had seen the planet and its pitiful natives with her own eyes. Its primitive natives quite simply had nothing worth a Geckho trader's while. So my furry friend had plenty of reason to be distraught.

But there was nothing to be done, we just had to go to Kasti-Utsh III empty handed. And one reason we were going there was to buy ancient Relict artifacts on a tip from a Medu-Ro IV fence. But now I only had a foggy concept of where I'd get the funds to purchase them. This Miyelonian trade hub was a place of law and order, where I couldn't simply steal artifacts, even if they once did belong to members of my team and had been taken by force. Since that time, the items had changed hands at least three times, so there was no proving they were rightfully mine now. Oh well. I'd figure it out when I got there. Maybe I'd have some ideas.

For now we had another four ummi in flight. That was approximately twenty-three hours in earth time. There was no sense hanging around on the bridge for that long, so I left Starship Pilot Dmitry Zheltov in charge and headed to a spacious room on the second deck which we had adapted into a lounge.

The furniture was a bit sparse to say the least. There was just one flying table, which was kept in the middle of the room by gyroscopes on an antigravitational base and, around it, a dozen large and soft cushions on the floor. Today, our frigate was finally all fixed so I gave the crew some leave. I had ordered various delicacies from the station restaurant which the chef assured me were edible to most races, along with juices and light alcohol. But the crew, as far as I had seen, was being strangely timid and didn't want to open the boxes of treats and drinks on the flying table. And instead of passing the time together, my crew had broken down into several distinct cliques.

The brothers Basha and Vasha Tushihh, as usual in any free time, were neck deep in a game of Na-Tikh-U, moving starship pieces around the glimmering three-dimensional board and not inviting anyone to join. Eduard Boyko and Imran had changed out of their combat armor into tracksuits and, lying down near the walls, were alternating between endurance competitions and posing for the mysterious extraterrestrial girl Valeri. The only other member of the fairer sex was my wayedda Minn-O La-Fin, and I suppose my crew was not feeling suicidal enough to flirt with their captain's wife. Valeri-Urla, meanwhile was whispering with her companion Denni Marko in the corner. I even had to fall back on my psionic abilities, which is how I found out that both of them were uncomfortable here in this alien pirate crew.

The Miyelonians then were grouped up separately and engaged in some strange activity. Ayni, Tini and Orun Va-Mart, their paws and tails tucked beneath them, were sitting right on the bare metal-ceramic floor and making a sound somewhere between singing and whining. All three of them had their eyes closed and their paws held out and touching. I had no idea what kind of mystery or rite this might be, but I was afraid to interrupt, because it may have been significant to Miyelonians.

At the other end of the large room was Supercargo Avan Toi. He was lying languidly on a cushion, which was barely visible beneath his corpulent body and carrying on a conversation with Ayukh the Navigator about what was happening on the fronts of the great space war. That I could tell with my good Perception alone. I wanted to know more, so I walked up and plopped down next to them, immediately and gratefully accepting a glass of a light alcoholic cocktail from Kirsan the repair bot, who was handing out drinks. Only after that, the two Geckho turned to the Mechanoid repair bot and also took a glass with each of their large hands.

"Well, what's the news on the war?" I asked,

taking a sip of the refreshing beverage. Both Geckho were eager to tell me:

"Captain, the Geckho base on Un-Tesh has fallen, there was a very brief story about it in the news. No details. We have no idea if it's been captured or destroyed. We also don't know the fate of the Geckho who were there."

"Ayukh, you know as well as I that the Meleyephatian horde never takes prisoners. It goes against their customs!" the gloomy Supercargo reproached the sheepish Navigator. "Even with their brothers' lives on the line, the Meleyephatians would never trade prisoners. They kill all captured enemies without exception."

Alright then, I didn't know that. I'd take it into account. That meant it was no use surrendering to these intelligent spider-like creatures — it would mean death regardless. Apparently we were extremely lucky with our last-minute escape from Un-Tesh!

"So that means we've traded systems," Avan Toi continued, thinking out loud. "The Geckho captured the Meleyephatian base Ursa-II-II, the enemy did the same with the base on Un-Tesh. Just think! So many starships destroyed, so many soldiers dead, and that includes some who will now never respawn. But the political situation is practically unchanged. So I ask, what exactly were we fighting for? Who wanted this war?"

"You can say that again! Still, I suppose the Miyelonians have gained something," Ayukh pointed his broad, clawed hand at our three fluffy crew members, who were still sitting on the floor with their eyes closed and chanting. "Their Leng Keetsie-Myau, beloved fleet commander, just waited for the Geckho and Meleyephatians to tie each other up, and easily captured two Meleyephatian star systems."

"You're writing the Geckho off too early!" I came, trying to play on their patriotic feelings and support the flagging conversation about interstellar politics. "Do you really think Kung Waid Shishish's Second Strike Fleet won't send reinforcements from the central systems? There's just one fleet there, and its badly damaged after the battle."

"Well..." Avan Toi lowered his voice to a whisper, "I've heard rumors to that effect. They say Fleet Commander Kung Waid Shishish reined in his pride and made a request to the capital for reinforcements."

Other crew members started coming up. Vasha and Basha finished their games and, dragging some cushions over, plunked down next to us and refused drinks from Kirsan. The old and wise loader brothers didn't enter the conversation, but they did open one box of food and offer it to the others. I ended up with a skewer of blue spheres with some sweet juice dripping off them. They weren't exotic fruits or berries, as you might expect either, but... I really didn't know what they were. I couldn't even tell if they came from a plant or an animal. Nevertheless they were tasty, so I reached for another.

Our athletes walked up then too, engaged in a discussion about protein diets. Neither Eduard nor Imran drank alcohol, but they didn't say no to juices and food. Minn-O La-Fin walked up. My wife looked around, couldn't find any free cushions and sat on mine, not at all ashamed to push me a bit aside. I didn't argue and moved. The Princess was slowly coming to life after all the physical and psychological trauma she had borne in the real world. That made me very glad. Finally she was back to the Minn-O I first met, proud, confident and accustomed to a special privileged role in any team.

Successful Perception check!

"Hey, wait! That was mine!" Half a minute earlier, I saw one of the skewers suddenly disappear from the flying table. And now, at the very last moment, I jerked my unfinished skewer away from the invisible, inconsiderate thief and the Shadow Panther's fanged jaws slammed shut on thin air. I gave a prompt bop of my palm to her invisible nose, which clearly took Little Sister aback because she thought no one could see her. That made her mad, so she went visible and, twitching her tail in dismay, went to complain to her master Valeri about how greedy and inconsiderate their captain was. I looked at the dangerous predator from behind. A huge panther with luxuriant silvery-white fur, she weighed at least four hundred pounds. And she was fast, deadly, and capable of turning invisible. Little Sister could easily kill a person with one swipe of her clawed paw, but still I didn't sense any danger. To her we were in the same pack now, and thus I was off limits. What an awesome and intelligent big cat!

Meanwhile, the conversation about the Geckho going to war with the Meleyephatians gradually shifted to allies. Cleopians, Esthetes, Humans, Jargs... Of all the Geckho allies the wise Ayukh told me about, I'd only heard of half. And when he turned to the Meleyephatian horde, I was completely out of my depth. Some kind of Crystallids, Psio, Dharki, Antites, Dendrids, Tailaxian Humans... Wait! Tailaxians? So Tailax was a Meleyephatian subject? But we had a Tailaxian on board!

As if sensing that I was thinking about her, Valeri-Urla stopped talking with Denni and raised her huge eyes, which looked more fit for a night creature than a person. I asked her to come closer and she did but not alone. Her companion Denni Marko, who the system said belonged to the Gilvar Syndicate Faction, came too. Okay then, all the better. I extended the panther's master a whole box of the juicy blue spheres her pet just attempted to steal and asked both new crew members to tell me about themselves.

"Why you that needing want, Gnat?" Denni, as always, was surly, and his proficiency in Geckho had not improved. "We in you team, yes. We is to do you order, that is more than enough to be enough."

I just shrugged my shoulders indefinitely. So, how could I explain my curiosity about the other human factions?

"I have just fifteen human crew members on this frigate, including myself. That is a very small number. As captain, I want my small team to come together. I want us to understand, trust and help one another. I want us to be bound together by more than a formal work relationship. I wouldn't say I want us to be one big family, that's too much. But still I don't want us to be complete strangers either."

Psionic skill increased to level seventy-three!

I didn't manage it without a bit of magic. A few of the crew members were just too hard to reach. But I did what I set out to do, and that was what mattered.

"Okay then, why is not to talking you?" Denni dropped the idiotic stubbornness and, walking over to get cushions for himself and his pretty companion, started talking. Before he made it too far though, hoping greatly that I wouldn't offend him by doing so, I asked Kirsan to hand Denni the universal translator. Thankfully, that made the Bodyguard's speech smooth and comprehensible:

"Denni Marko. Born on Farunji, the largest planet of the Gilvar Syndicate. I graduated from a military school on the same planet. I fought in the Ninth Syndicate war, and was honorably discharged after an injury. Then I worked in the Quarantine Service for a long time. Our purpose was to safeguard primordial planet ζ-Reaper from black-marketeers, slavers and headhunters. And that was where I met Valeri. She first showed up on the Quarantine Service radar as an unauthorized visitor," he said, pointing to his companion. "Just one look at her was enough to see her Tailaxian origin. And Tailax is a hundred parsecs from Zeta Reaper. What was more, Valeri had strange abilities. She was not afraid to be surrounded by deadly animals, healed dangerous creatures and rode them, even though the sky. But most importantly, she carried a blaster. And that was on a primitive planet, where the upper limit of technology was supposed to be bronze blades."

Valeri laughed happily, and her sonorous giggle was like the peal of silver bells:

"I never did suspect that I was being tracked from orbit, or that someone would think me strange! I was just living, hunting and surviving as best I could. I was kidnapped by slavers, but I escaped, taking weapons from flying people. Then a shuttle came down from the sky and my sister and I were taken for research. But seemingly they were disappointed by what they found."

"Yes, that's true," Denni confirmed. "Everything that made us think she was strange had a very simple explanation. Valeri's mother, a Tailaxian, came to the savage planet as part of a group of missionaries. Her father was a native that kidnapped her mother, but he was long dead by the time we found Valeri. We confiscated the blaster. The slaver and black-market trade base was already abandoned. We discovered that she had psionic abilities, but nothing more. Basically, to the Quarantine Service, neither Valeri or her family was of any interest. We helped her mother and younger sister get back to Tailax, but Valeri-Urla wanted to stay on her home planet. So we stopped observing the little hunter. But just half a year later, I happened to hear that Valeri-Urla had been accused of murder and would soon be executed. I intervened, and my authority as a Quarantine Service employee was enough to get her transferred to a Tailaxian court."

"The world 'Urla' in my name means 'hunter,'"

she explained in an even tone, as if this wasn't even about her. "Hunters do not have the right to kill people, doing so is punishable by death. I broke the law by siccing Little Sister against some creep who was following me and threatening to rape me. Denni saved me from the gallows. I was brought by starship to Tailax, and once there sentenced to three tongs in the game that bends reality. As I requested, Little Sister was placed in my virt pod with me. She would never have left my side anyway. Then Denni met me on the projection of Tailax in the game world and, ever since, we've been travelling together."

So the game was a method of punishing criminals? As a matter of fact, why was that surprising? I myself had been sent under the Dome as an alternative to prison time. All this information was very intriguing, but I was most interested in Tailax and the Gilvar Syndicate. I asked about their two factions in the game that bends reality. Denni answered, but quickly admitted that he was a simple man and didn't know much:

"The Gilvar Syndicate is a commonwealth of eight densely-populated and highly-developed human planets. In the game they are all vassals of the Meleyephatian race. I know less about Tailax. It is a very closed society both in the game and the real world."

"A highly developed society, governed by religious figures," Valeri-Urla continued. "It is also part of the Meleyephatian horde, but functions as a nearly independent state whose policies don't always align with those of their suzerains. Tailax is considered a leader among human governments in microelectronics and applied psionics. It's hard to get onto Tailax, they do not welcome outsiders. And they don't let their own leave either. The body of every Tailaxian citizen contains so many cleverly hidden bugs of all kinds that it is generally thought to be impossible to even find them all. And Tailaxian intelligence uses them to always keep their citizens in line no matter where they are. In the game, my overseers gather information about the world through these devices, and sometimes use painful shocks and commands in my head to alter my behavior if there's something they don't like. They usually don't care where I am or what I'm doing. But recently, I was ordered to get onto the frigate of Gnat the Listener. Something in your gameplay has the Tailaxians interested, Captain."

"You were asked to spy on us, and now you're telling us openly?!" Eduard Boyko objected.

Despite the Space Commando's outraged judgmental tone, Valeri was absolutely calm:

"We're in a hyperjump. There is no signal here, so no one can track this conversation. I figured I better just get it out there while I have the chance before Gerd Gnat reads it in my thoughts."

I activated Scanning, zoomed in, took a look and gave a surprised whistle. Yep. Valeri was speaking the truth. I detected at least eight miniature foreign objects in the Beastmaster's body. Two were in her head, one very deep in her brain. There were three in her neck, one in her left shoulder blade, one in her right lung and another inside her heart — the millimeter-sized capsule was stuck to the wall of her right atrium and could stop her pulse at any second. Clearly, this was a little bomb her jailers controlled, a guarantee that she would remain loyal and obedient. Most likely, Valeri had more implants lower in her body, but I didn't keep looking because I'd seen enough. By the way...

"Valeri, does that mean that I can use you to quickly send messages to Tailax? That might be very important! Imran, leave the game and tell our directors. They've been looking for a way to get in touch with the other human factions in space. We may have just found one!"

The Dagestani athlete didn't even go to his bunk, just sat on the floor in the common room and froze as his mind left his game body. We then kept talking. In my turn, I gave a fairly brief retelling of my story to our new crew and introduced the rest of my team. Then the Miyelonians walked over, their ritual complete, and immediately threw themselves on the snacks and alcohol. And Uline Tar, thirsting for interaction, left her bunk. Then Imran came back into the game and got up off the floor. He looked dejected.

"Well, did you tell Lozovsky?" I asked, but the Dagestani Gladiator seemingly didn't hear me.

With a heavy sigh and taking a bit of air into his lungs, Imran squeezed out:

"When I got under the dome, I didn't see any players. There was a wailing siren and a recorded message from Alexander Antipov being played over the loudspeakers saying the Dark Faction has attacked and announcing an official CtA (Call to arms). WAR!"

Chapter Two

Unrelenting Hospitality

NATURALLY, given that, we could no longer even think of staying at Kasti-Utsh III for long. We'd calculate coordinates for a new hyperspace jump, this time to Earth itself, recharge if necessary then fly off to aid the Human-3 Faction! Otherwise, soon enough, Captain Gnat would be logging out permanently alongside a third of his crew. And there would be issues with piloting the frigate, because none of the remaining crew had piloting skills, and I was controlling many ship systems directly.

None of the crew objected. Perhaps my business partner Uline Tar had a differing opinion, but if she did, she kept it to herself. Minn-O also immediately stated her position that after our marriage and the death of her grandfather, there was no longer anything to connect her with her former faction. What was more, having a mage husband was the princess's only remaining chance to survive in the hostile magocratic world. With Gnat out of the picture, Minn-O La-Fin would very quickly die "on accident" because she stood in the way of too many ruthless bloodsuckers, who were currently salivating over the riches of the La-Fin family. I could read unhidden panic in my junior wife's tone, and I assured my wayedda that it was too early to count me out. I would not allow the H3 faction to be destroyed. I was not going to force the Princess to fight against her subjects either though. The mere fact that Minn-O would not be interfering or telling the enemy our plans was enough.

And although we still had a day before things would really heat up, the rest of the party was subdued because no one was in the mood to celebrate anymore. Those who were quickly finished their cocktails and the open boxes of fancy food then left, some to their quarters, some to go on shift. The Miyelonians just went into the real world.

I called the white Kirsan over, who I considered the most senior of the three Mechanics, and finally gave the repair bot my Annihilator. Previously we lacked either the materials or time to modify my weapon and had little reason to increase its firepower. It could already shred through any barrier and chew enemies into hunks of flesh already. But increasing its accurate range seemed important because now I couldn't hit anything farther than twenty or thirty feet away. And increasing the battery capacity or even adding a special firing mode with more conservative power usage wouldn't hurt. As it was, a nuclear battery on full charge was good for thirty shots at most and the fact that I had my last one in the gun now didn't paint a pretty picture. Buying an extra battery was a big challenge. There were very few on the market and batteries for guns and Relict artifacts were not exactly available at every station. And they cost way too much. I was no Croesus nor Count of Monte Cristo to be using weapons that cost two hundred crystals per shot.

"Ideally, change it away from the disposable nuclear batteries to ones that we can recharge from the ship's power systems," I kept dreaming and Kirsan looked attentively at me with his faceted eyes. The repair bot was actively moving his many little hands both to say how long it would take and trying to get a thought across: "That might be a tall order, captain, but I'll see what I can do."

The huge metal millipede stashed the invaluable weapon in a hole in its chest and crawled nimbly off toward the supply room. Before that, I never suspected that the repair bots' chest pieces could move aside to reveal a storage compartment. For some reason I instantly realized three electromagnetic bombs could easily fit, and the thin and flexible millipede could get into even the hardest to reach places on the starship including the maintenance area behind the hyperspace drives. The white Kirsan's chest cavity was empty before he put the Annihilator in there. But I ran a scan, which showed that the other two millipedes had something in theirs. Some pieces or patches of metal. I couldn't see better, so I would have to check what my Mechanics were hiding in these secret spots when I got the chance.

At the same time, I checked up on the other two repair bots through the security cameras. One of them was lying out pieces of the destroyed relict combat drone on the floor of an empty room, thoughtfully crawling between them and, one after the next, lifting them up and carefully inspecting them with its many mechanical eyes. Apparently, repairing the Small Relict Guard Drone was going to be very difficult, so I didn't want to distract Kirsan.

The last of the metal millipedes was turning something over very quickly in its jointed hands, spinning and twisting the object every which way as if solving a Rubik's Cube. With a certain surprise, I realized that it was the Pyramid Signal Booster, although it didn't look quite as disk shaped as before. In fact, it was now an articulated fractal construction, more reminiscent of a three-dimensional asymmetrical snowflake. Yeah, that was it. I had given the ancient artifact to my Mechanics so they could remove the "only for Relicts" limitation and, the mechanoid repair bost had seemingly discovered it could unfold.

I took over for Dmitry Zheltov on the bridge and sent the Starship Pilot to get some rest. The frigate was on autopilot going through a hyperspace jump, so there was virtually no work to be done on the bridge. If nothing out of the ordinary happened, this would be a long boring shift of around an ummi and a half, after which Ayukh would take over. Still, I wasn't going to

33

just sit around for eight hours. In fact, I was planning to use that time to maximum effect, levelling Gnat's skills as much as possible, above all those connected with psionics and controlling machines. After all, when would I get a better chance to practice directly operating the various frigate systems?! With the whole crew resting, they wouldn't even notice. I could also afford to pull Astrolinguistics up a bit. Sure I was understanding Relict glyphs better all the time, but some of the messages from my Listener Energy Armor were still indecipherable.

So then, how was my little Gnat doing for abilities? What to improve first? I opened my information:

Gerd Gnat. Human. H3 Faction.
Level-74 Listener
Statistics:
Strength   14
Agility 18
Intelligence   23 + +5
Perception   27 + 2
Constitution 16
Luck modifier   +3
Parameters:
Hitpoints   1612 of 1612
Endurance points   1008 of 1209
Magic points 759 of 899
Carrying capacity   62 lbs.
Fame 66
Skills:

Electronics   61

Scanning   35

Cartography 57

Astrolinguistics   83

Rifles 51

Mineralogy   50

Medium Armor   54

Eagle Eye   70

Sharpshooter   34

Targeting   23

Danger Sense   48

Psionic   73

Mental Fortitude   54

Mysticism   24

Machine Control   66

My firearm skills were noticeably lagging. To have Rifles at just 51 and Sharpshooter at 34, with my character at seventy-four was not even funny. As far as I'd heard from the First Legion, it was considered standard to have main combat skills one point five times higher than character level. Targeting was even further behind, even though discovering and highlighting targets for others to shoot was Gnat's only effective method of long-distance combat.

Sure, here I had the excuse that I had changed class, and a Listener was more a mage that knew how to control machines than a classic gunman or scout. But that did nothing about the worrisome fact that Gnat hadn't been to the firing range in a very long time. As for my psionic abilities, things were looking a bit better, but still not exactly one point five times over character level, so I had plenty of work to do there as well.

Anyhow, I started with Scanning. I gave a mental command, activating the ship scanners and requested a complete picture of everything happening outside my frigate. I had no idea what I could get from scanning in hyperjump, or if the scanners even worked like this, but the mental command worked. The computer froze for a long time, trying to interpret the clearly unusual feedback, then it brought up some long parallel stripes and something strange — a spot of light moving quickly away. A second later, some words came on screen in Geckho:

Gravitational anomaly. Class SA-113/FF.

At the same time, my heart clenched in pain and foreboding. I was at serious risk. I felt a prick as if a needle got stuck all the way into my heart. It felt like I was squeezed in a vice for a few painful seconds, but then the feeling gradually retreated, leaving me sitting in the pilot's seat and reading a flurry of messages, my eyes open wide in fear. Apparently there had been problems with the ship:

ATTENTION!!! Gravitational scanner has gone out of order!

ATTENTION!!! Short-wave radar has gone out of order!

ATTENTION!!! Neutrino scanner has gone out of order!

In parallel with this, I saw many messages run past about changes to Gnat's statistics:

Scanning skill increased to level thirty-six!

Scanning skill increased to level thirty-seven!

Electronics skill increased to level sixty-two!

Danger Sense skill increased to level forty-nine!

Machine Control skill increased to level sixty-seven!

You have reached level seventy-five!

You have received three skill points.

If I had been out fishing, the closest analogy would be a bite from an especially feisty lunker knocking me off balance, breaking the line and making off with my tackle. What even was that??? I waited one second, decided not to sound the alarm and just called Ayukh and Dmitry Zheltov. But first to come on the bridge was my Wayedda Minn-O, running in panicked:

"Gnat, what happened? I was sleeping and it felt like someone poured a bucket of cold water on me! My Danger Sense jumped up twice!"

Ayukh the Navigator then pushed her out of the doorway and strode quickly into the control room looking disheveled. He had also been awoken. Behind him was the Starship Pilot and Uline Tar for some reason. I pointed the crew to the system malfunction messages on screen and briefly explained what caused them.

The furry gray Navigator stroked his nose with a clawed paw in thought:

"I don't understand, Gerd Gnat. Why did you run a scan in a hyperjump? Here in hyper, everything goes by too fast. The scanner pulse travels at light speed, so it will never reach a target and bounce back while we're travelling faster than light! Even a child knows that!"

It looked like my abilities as a captain had seriously fallen in the Navigator's eyes. In response I just shrugged my shoulders indefinitely, then made the same motion in Geckho body language, jutting out my lower lip and rolling my eyes. What could I have said in my defense? That I didn't know it was pointless to scan in hyper? But it worked!

After another half minute of grumbling, the Navigator took a seat and opened the astronomical body classification system. Ayukh, like all the others, was looking for the "Anomalies" section. The object I scanned was eventually found in the category "Rare, unconfirmed:"

"SA-113/FF class anomalies are found moving at faster-than-light speeds in hyperspace. They have very high mass, similar to that of planetary moons class 3B and higher. Much information about this anomaly is conjecture. Only one has ever been clearly detected two hundred eleven tongs ago in the star system 5C-678/PP by a Meleyephatian scout-research ship. They are thought to correspond to ships of Supercarrier or Titan class. However, starships of super-heavy classes have not been built by the great space-faring races for more than three hundred tongs, and the few remaining ones have long been scuttled, so the most probable explanation is that this is the signature of a starship of an unknown race. WARNING! These objects react very *poorly to detection, and are known to destroy ships shortly after discovery."*

Woah! How lucky we apparently were that this contact with hot-headed unknown aliens had merely taken a few scanning systems offline. We could easily replace the fried systems. As far as I could tell from my captain's tablet, all the required parts were already in storage. After some six or seven hours work for the repair bots, all negative consequences of this unpleasant encounter would be done with. But I couldn't get rid of the feeling that this was not random, and I would be finding out more about this mysterious object despite its clear danger and unfriendly reputation.

Wow, the last time such a thing had been seen was more than seven hundred years ago. If I could detect what this mysterious ship was and where it was based, just the location of an unknown race could be sold to interested parties for lots of money, immediately solving my financial issues. And if I could be the first to reach their planet and find some unique artifacts... I checked myself for counting my chickens before they'd hatched.

"Ayukh, is there any way to tell where the anomaly came from and where it was going?"

The experienced navigator spent a long time immersed in calculations after which he turned toward me, his furry face impossibly surprised:

"As strange as it may seem, yes captain! We spent enough time at a short distance from one another, insofar as directionality and distance mean anything in the distortion of hyperspace. So we have a few markers from our locators, that we can use to estimate a trajectory. The object was headed for star system B7670/MP, that's another arm of the galaxy altogether. At our current level of technology, it would take more than a lifetime to reach. But it started from much nearer by, although it would also be quite the long haul: two tongs minimum not counting time to stop and recharge. The Aysar Cluster. Hmm. That system must be noteworthy for some reason, seeing how they gave it a name instead of just a number. "

"The Aysar Cluster? Where even is that?" I asked, and Ayukh obediently zoomed out the star map, pointing at a point far past Meleyephatian territory and outside the bounds of known space.

I had to admit I was baffled. Why was there a name for this place, a star was hundreds of parsecs from explored space? I asked, and the Navigator opened a detailed guide and read aloud:

"The Aysar Cluster. Triple star. 3B orange dwarf, two satellites of type 7D and 11F. Six uninhabited planets. This star system became famous after one of the largest space battles in the history of the Universe took place there 2.3 tongs ago.* Current sovereignty: Swarm.

*Note: all sources are secondary and require confirmation."

The Swarm? What was this Swarm? And who was battling who in that distant star system? Unfortunately, there was no more detailed information in the database. Old Ayukh, although he had worked as a Navigator his whole life and knew the star maps and space races like the back of his hand, didn't know either.

In the end, we didn't find anything of use. Both the start and end point of the mysterious space oddity's route were so far away from anywhere we could get to that the information had no practical application. Nevertheless, I asked the Navigator and everyone else there to keep it a secret.

But I was not allowed to sit and peruse the scan in calm. Ayukh was sitting at the navigator's panel, calculating the potential risk and profit from various trade routes. My business partner was still nourishing a hope that we could work our way back up to a decent reputation and be rid of the black spot of piracy. And she had a plan to tell me. Right after the end of the war on earth we were going to take a few jobs transporting goods to distant colonies that weren't too squeamish about less than savory traders. A few successful voyages and clients would stop being so worried. Then our unsavory reputation would be washed away in short order. I didn't have much to say and especially didn't argue. Still, something was telling me that, with my restless character and talent for getting myself into trouble, that black spot wouldn't wash out quite so easy!

"LEAVING JUMP in ninety seconds!" the Starship Pilot

informed me, looking concentrated and impossibly distinguished.

"Sufficient energy for hyperjump to Earth," came the voice of our Miyelonian Engineer, Orun Va-Mart over the loudspeaker. He was now in the engine room.

"Well then, Dmmmitry, I see no reason to dock. Request an acceleration lane from the dispatchers! Vector 114:37:22, distance 4.3 units, I've still got it on my palmtop," the old Navigator from the crew of the Shiamiru had flown to Earth from Kasti-Utsh III a few times before so he had no reason to run the calculations again.

Good thing we had enough power and could go help the faction right away. As it was, Imran and Eduard were going under the Dome then back into the game regularly and, every time they came back, they had worse news. The Rainforest node had fallen. What was more, the Dark Faction had managed to reinforce there by landing just under one and a half thousand marines in three waves via Sio-Mi-Dori antigrav. And by Geckho ferry, the enemy had brought heavy armor and rocket systems to the Rainforest node as well. So now the Dark Faction had a strike force that threatened our whole territory from the undefended south. It was a critical situation. I had no idea where our directors would find the troops to fight on two fronts at once.

But that wasn't all the bad news. We had confirmation of the seemingly impossible fact that the German capital node had been lost. And now the enemy had captured the island and was using it as a base to send assault groups down our whole coastline. We lost our southernmost Tropics node without a fight. Our fifty players, all from peaceful professions, had no chance against an enemy with such vast numerical superiority. So on an order from Lozovsky, they retreated through a neutral and severely boggy node to the allied German faction's land. And now everyone already knew that our three hundred H6 players, even reinforced by Centaurs and our fifty builders, had no chance of withstanding a serious attack. The fate of the H6 faction was basically hanging by a thread.

All our hopes rested on my starship getting there as fast as possible. And from there, we could either do it the nice way, negotiating as General Ui-Taka suggested, or the mean way by ruthless orbital bombardment. Either way I was intending to stop this bloody war. It would take nine hours to fly from Kasti-Utsh III to Earth. My faction could definitely survive that long, even if it came at the cost of a few territories. But I was much less sure that my badly-beaten allies could last for nine hours.

But then, finally, we emerged from hyperspace! The local station was not a colossal spindle with one entrance to dock like Medu-Ro IV, but a basically flat metal plate five miles in diameter. And it had many entrances around the whole perimeter, which was very convenient. There was so much going on! There were thousands and thousands of starships, all of Miyelonian design.

When Ayukh suddenly fell into silent agitation, I didn't know what was going on at first. In fact, Uline

Tar came on the bridge and wasn't her usual talkative self either. Also Ayni the translator, who we invited in case the station dispatchers used any complicated terms, had crawled down off her seat and was trying to sneak out of the room. Even Dmitry Zheltov went gray in the face and turned unconfidently toward me in hopes of an explanation, or perhaps further instructions. What was wrong? Then it hit me: here among the thousands of ships, not a single one was noncombat! There were only frigates, battleships, carriers and landing ships, all fitted out for war! We had stumbled upon the Miyelonian fleet!

In the midst of the Miyelonian armada, our little Meleyephatian frigate looked like an unfortunate soul that just wandered into the wrong neighborhood. And I wasn't the only one who thought so. Our instruments showed that many ships and station systems were scanning us. And why not? I was a free and neutral captain. I hadn't done anything to the Miyelonians, so I had the complete right to visit the popular trading station. Finally, the monitor lit up, and a young fluffy Miyelonian dispatcher asked:

"Free Captain Gerd Gnat, what is the purpose of your visit to Kasti-Utsh III?"

Purpose of visit? I honestly told the kindly Miyelonian lady that I was not planning to stay here or even dock my ship. Kasti-Utsh III was only a midway point on my route and now I needed a free lane to accelerate for my next hyperjump.

"I'm afraid that won't be possible, Gerd Gnat," the cat on the screen bared its teeth predatorily and pushed down its ears, immediately losing its sweet demeanor. "The station and surrounding space are on temporary military lockdown. No starship may use long-distance communication or leave the station for the next five standard days. Such is the order of Commander Leng Keetsie-Myau. So welcome to Kasti-Utsh III, Gerd Gnat!"

Chapter Three

Kasti-Utsh III

FIVE DAYS??? But everything would be over by then! Distressed, I tore the ceramoplastic headphones off my head and threw them full force at the wall, smashing the fragile item to smithereens. Nevertheless, I had no choice. I had to obey the dispatcher's demands and bring my ship into dock. What was more, there were Miyelonian interceptors spinning tight circles around my frigate, showing that we would simply not be allowed to leave.

They did not need my help to translate. The dispatchers spoke Geckho perfectly and our Starship Pilot could directly understand their commands. I ordered Dmitry Zheltov to handle the maneuvering, and headed into my bunk. I was wound up and clearly they could sense that because, as I moved through the corridors, the crew pressed themselves into the wall in fear and lowered their eyes.

"Tini!" I called my ward and a few seconds later the little Miyelonian thief was standing in my bunk. "Go into the real world right now. Get in touch with Great Priestess Leng Amiru U-Mayaoo and explain the situation. We cannot afford to spend five days sitting around here, we have urgent business to attend to!"

The kitten nodded in comprehension and hurried off to do as I said. But before the door closed behind the Miyelonian, I saw Valeri-Urla coming in. And something important must have happened, because the usually tight-lipped and bashful Tailaxian had come on her own.

I invited her in with a gesture and sat in a big comfortable chair. The huge flying armchair was made for a Geckho and I had ordered it for my bunk on Medu-Ro IV to replace the woven Meleyephatian constructions that were here before. They were just too weird and I couldn't get used to them. The Beastmaster agreed to come in, but insisted that I lock the door first because this was going to be a somewhat delicate conversation.

"Captain, Denni is planning to desert!" The Tailaxian blew up as soon as I'd locked the door. "And he keeps telling me to do the same! He says we should go to the station together, move our respawn points to somewhere in a green zone then leave the game for five days to give you time to fly off and defend your homeworld."

"But... why?" the news really did shock me. It was not nice to find out that someone wanted to flee my crew. What was more, Denni Marko was the only one who knew how to control the ship's laser turrets. Without him, we couldn't do any shooting, becoming nothing more than an advanced artillery targeting system. "Why desert when you signed a contract for five voyages?! No captain would ever take you on again!"

Valeri ignored the question of why, but she answered the second part, getting straight to the point:

"Denni has taken all precautions, even left to the real world to consult with some friends who specialize in space law. He wants to appeal to the labor commission, saying he wasn't aware of all the conditions of the contract when he signed on. He says he thought he was being hired to work as a Bodyguard as usual. Instead, he was brought onto a pirate ship to be used as a Gunner to commit genocide against a group of fellow humans from outer space. For extreme situations like that, the labor commission usually will annul contracts, especially given that there was no advance payment."

Okay... But what could I do here? I could, of course, tell the potential deserter he was not allowed to leave the ship and place guards at the airlock. I could even lock Denni in his bunk for a few days and say he wasn't allowed to leave. But then, once we were in battle in Earth's orbit, he would have a chance to take out his frustration on his despotic captain by repeatedly missing on purpose. And really, did I even want a soldier I'd have to force to fight? No, threats and pressure alone were no way of dealing with this. What was more, before doing anything, I wanted to find out how his companion felt:

"Your jailers would probably require you to stay on the station then, yes? Nevertheless, Tailax is part of the Meleyephatian horde and I'm sure they would like to observe the enemy fleet."

Valeri-Urla looked ashamed. Clearly her espionage was something of a touchy subject, but she still answered eventually:

"Weirdly no. I was surprised, but orders haven't changed. They still want me to stay with the Listener. And therein lies the problem: Denni doesn't want to let me go and insists I leave the frigate with him. We've been together for many years now, and I'm used to having him around. From time to time he acts rude, even unbearable. Sometimes he gets jealous, but overall he's reliable and well-behaved. I'd never want to leave him alone here on the station."

Well, well! I finally figured out how I should act. If Valeri wanted to stay with me, it wouldn't be too hard to convince her companion:

"Tell Denni he's making a big mistake. His plan might work on a Geckho or Meleyephatian station, but not here, not on a Miyelonian station. You see, I am personally acquainted with a Great Priestess of the Miyelonian race and have even done her a favor. Actually, what am I telling you for?! You were on Medu-Ro IV when I was arrested on charges of killing Leng Amiru U-Mayaoo, then found not guilty and released! Anyway, I also know the leaders of a few influential prides, have proven myself a reliable partner and earned their trust. So I have a certain Fame and Authority among the Miyelonians. The labor commission will have their doubts about Denni's story. He will be subjected to Truth Seeker testing, and that is a very nasty little procedure. The lie will be uncovered, Denni will be arrested. What's more, you'll also be checked and that will surely reveal the fact that you are spying for the enemy. Is that what you want, Valeri?"

Psionic skill increased to level seventy-four!

Mental Fortitude skill increased to level fifty-six!

The pop-up messages confirmed that I was being convincing, and my reasoning was having the desired effect. But suddenly she got on guard, pressed her left-hand fingers to her forehead and frowned in dismay:

"Gerd Gnat, you could have said all that without using magic, you know. I don't like when people try to manipulate me! You can't dig around in my brains without me noticing; I'm a much more experienced and powerful psionic! It was awfully arrogant on your part to attack me like that!"

By the end of her sentence, the Beastmaster was so mad that she had basically started to scream. Looking scornful, she simply would not listen when I said it was all on accident. Valeri clenched her right fist around the green stone pendant on her necklace, took a deep sigh and looked me decisively right in the eyes. Seemingly, she'd thrown down the gauntlet.

I didn't turn my head, and our gazes met. I saw a reflection of my blue glow in her huge hazel eyes. I started feeling pressure as if I was struggling to pierce a particularly resilient piece of rubber. My thoughts grew viscous and stopped making any sense. And suddenly, I could hear distinct words in my head:

"Why is this so hard? I'm twenty-three levels higher than Gnat. And I have more mana, endurance points and experience in mental duels. Is Gnat wearing some kind of thought-blocking artifact? No, I would be able to sense that. I need to just keep pushing and not break eye contact. But he has such pretty eyes! Like shimmering blue ice. I've never seen eyes like that. You could just drown in them like a mountain lake. I just want to swim and swim in that deep blue and forget anything else exists. It's simply bliss! I wonder if Minn-O is Gnat's only wife? I've overheard the crew calling her a 'junior wife.' Does that mean he has a senior one as well? Probably. Too bad if so. He's a pretty cool guy. He hasn't been in the game long, and he's already a Gerd with his own starship, plus he knows some very Miyelonian big-wigs. They also say Gnat is the only Listener in the game. I see why Denni's going so nuts and trying to desert. He's jealous. He knows that he looks dull compared to the brilliant Gerd Gnat. Wait, what's happening? I'm running out of mana! But how?! Why?! I need to look away!!! Otherwise Gnat will be able to read my thoughts! What is this??? He's not letting go!"

A wave of fully real panic rolled over me. I couldn't say exactly how, but I stopped Valeri from breaking the mental contact. She was desperately trying to look away or close her eyes, but she just couldn't. Finally, a clear thought formed in my head:

"Gnat, I know you can hear me. I admit, I lost the duel. Let me go, please!"

With immense strain, I turned my head away, breaking eye contact. My arms were shivering, blood was dripping out of my nose. I even had to lean on the wall so I wouldn't fall over. My mana was down to zero. The last moments of the mental duel had been using Endurance instead of Magic Points. Nevertheless, I won!!! And the system sent some messages of congratulations:

Psionic skill increased to level seventy-five!

Mental Fortitude skill increased to level fifty-seven!

Authority increased to 51!

Valeri-Urla, red as a boiled lobster, was sitting in a flying chair with her hands covering her face:

"Gerd Gnat, forgive me. Oh gods, I'm so ashamed! At least tell me the first thoughts you read!"

"The first thing I heard was a bit unclear. Something like 'Denni is jealous,' then about looking dull. After that I heard some easily readable thoughts about your mana running out," I lied, wanting not to embarrass her or reveal my true powers.

The Beastmaster gave a noticeably freer sigh and even a tortured smile:

"Okay then, I'll take it as a lesson. Alright, Gerd Captain. I'll have a talk with Denni Marko. I promise he won't desert and will stay on the ship until the end of the contract. As will I."

The dark-haired flexible girl's luxurious coal-black hair was braided into a plait that came down to her belt. She jumped off the chair and headed for the door. What was more, Little Sister had been scratching outside for some time, begging to be let in. In the very doorway, the Beast Master stopped sharply and turned around:

"Captain, I will challenge you to a rematch one day when I think I'm ready. It means a lot to me. After all, I am a proud Great Huntress," Valeri pointed at three wavy lines tattooed on her cheek. "In the traditions of my people I cannot be kidnapped, bought or taken by force. I bow to no one: not to chieftains or shamans, wise men or rich ones. I will only ever submit to one person in my life, and I must first deem them worthy. Might that be you, captain?"

As soon as the doors closed behind her, Tini the kitten flew into my room, now back in the game:

"Master, I was not able to carry out your order. The living incarnation of the Great First Female Leng Amiru U-Mayaoo refused to overrule the order of Commander Leng Keetsie-Myau, who is equal to her in authority. She said: 'My friend Keetsie is somewhere on the station, deal with her yourself.'"

The Miyelonian teen was down in the dumps after failing such an important mission. I walked over to Tini. His hair was standing on end, and his ears were pressed back. In an effort to reassure my ward, I gave him a tender pat on the nape and said:

"Don't worry. Somehow I knew I'd have to visit this station. Okay then, I guess we'll have to track down the great commander on this huge station, which is teeming with Miyelonian military. Get the crew together in the lounge. I'll speak with them and pick out a team to come with me."

AIRLOCK FOURTEEN, docking bay 567, just about the very center of the huge disk-shaped station. It took the gravity cranes a whole hour to drag our ship down the two-and-a-half-mile-long corridor. The pace was impossibly slow. Then, in no hurry, the ship was turned and, literally centimeter by centimeter, placed in a tiny hangar which looked to have been intended for starships of a somewhat smaller class. It was such a tight squeeze that I worried my Tolili-Ukh X modular frigate might have its armor panels scratched or its short arrow-shaped wings broken. I even asked the wise Ayukh who would pay for repair if that happened.

But thankfully it was not necessary. Still, when I left the ship to evaluate the parking job, I couldn't hold back a select word. The sharply pointed nose tip of the frigate was less than half an inch from the rough back wall. And the tips of the stabilizer wings had anywhere from six to eight inches play off the hangar walls. Jeeze, what a pinch...

Nevertheless, I had to admit we were very lucky that the dispatchers of the Kasti-Utsh III station even found a free hangar for our frigate given the huge Miyelonian fleet stationed here. Otherwise we'd have had to spend the five days just sitting in space without the right to turn on our engines or use comms systems. I suspected that the slightly different proportions of Miyelonian ships — narrower and more elongated compared to the more triangular Meleyephatian ones — prevented any of them from fitting into this small hangar, and that was why it was left for us.

I entered the lounge, where all Team Gnat was already waiting, staring at me in anticipation. The whole crew understood the gravity of the situation. We had no reason to hide that the war on Earth was going very poorly for our faction. Imran had just come back from the Dome with alarming news, saying that the Tropics node had been abandoned by its defenders and fallen. The Dark Faction was building on their drive south, acquiring more and more territory. In fact they had forced their way quickly through the swampy forest of the two coastal nodes and already reached the border with the German Human-6 Faction. Although the attack was utterly expectable and even inevitable, neither my faction nor H6 had the forces to repel it or impact the situation in any way.

Still, it wasn't like the H3 faction was just sitting with its arms folded and waiting for the end to come. We regularly attempted counterattacks, but none had been successful. Once we attempted to launch an offensive from the Capital node toward the Graveyard to test the enemy's defenses and tie up some of their reserves, but the attack drowned in blood. It was as if they knew in advance. The First Legion fell under dense crossfire and were all sent to simultaneous respawn.

Imran also told us about fierce battles at the juncture of the Centaur Plateau and Rainforest nodes, but from his words I couldn't understand who attacked who. Imran also told us about the movement and successful deployment of rocket batteries on that section of the front, so most likely we were the aggressors. Furthermore the Dagestani told me that, on the southern front, we had shot down an enemy Sio-Mi-Dori antigrav. And he had some strange news about our new faction head Gerd Ivan Lozovsky. Apparently just after returning from Moscow and entering the game, he transferred leadership to his deputies, got in a Peresvet with a group of trusted First Legion soldiers and went on the Geckho ferry to an unknown location.

Basically, the war was really heating up. My faction was resisting with all its might, but it wasn't enough at all defensive sectors.

"Captain, I spoke with other team members and here's what I want to suggest..." Uline Tar stepped forward, drawing my attention. "There's still time for you, Immmran, Dmmmitry and Eduarrrd to change faction. Go find some fixers here on the Kasti-Utsh III station who provide such services. Sure it'll cost you, something like five crypto a head, but you have that kind of money. If you don't, I can loan you some. And in five days, you just leave your virt pods in the real world on a Miyelonian station."

"Yes captain. Why risk your lives?" Vasha Tushihh supported my business partner.

Seeing dismay on my face, Avan Toi walked forward.

"Don't be angry captain, it was my idea. No one is talking about deserting, and certainly not treason or betrayal. In five days, when the state of emergency here on Kasti-Utsh III is called off, you can go help your faction at once. You can even go back and see your friends, if your Leng allows it. We're just suggesting some insurance just in case everything goes wrong."

Their suggestion to take insurance and temporarily change faction sounded logical in every way. But it was just... somehow wrong or something... Deep down, my heart just wouldn't let me.

"Friends, it's nice to know that you care, but I'm afraid I have to say no. And not least of all because a frigate that formally belongs to a Miyelonian faction might not be allowed into exclusive Geckho space. But there's a bigger issue. After all, I am not merely your captain, I am a famous and high-profile player in my faction. My factionmates are fighting heroically against a strong and intelligent enemy. Yes they are being beaten, but they're fighting for every rock, every inch of territory. They're expecting support from space and have placed their hopes in me. So now if, instead of long-awaited help, it leaks that Gerd Gnat and his crew abandoned the faction..." I shook my head in doubt. "No matter how noble the intentions, it will be taken too negatively and be a serious blow to our soldiers' morale. So I will remain with my faction to the end and am willing to share their fate!"

Authority increased to 52!

Now that I'd answered, I had to get back to the main mission: somehow finding the commander of the Miyelonian fleet on this huge station and getting an audience with her. Leng Keetsie-Myau wasn't exactly a needle in a haystack, she shouldn't have been hard to find. Plus just think how easy it would be to find that needle with my Scanning abilities! Here on the Kasti-Utsh III station there were two technical floors, docks and two residential floors. One hundred square miles of corridors and rooms! It's square mileage was double that of Paris! What was more, there were thousands and thousands of Miyelonian soldiers here now, which was causing problems of its own. Ayni had also given me another warning. Apparently the Miyelonian predilection for dueling, which I first observed on the Medu-Ro IV pirate station, was especially widespread among the military.

So I came to a somewhat paradoxical conclusion: if I wanted to get past the plethora of Miyelonian troops, I shouldn't take anyone who knew how to fight. I could only take crew members these cantankerous tomcats wouldn't see as targets, whether because it violated their mores or they'd think it was too easy. For example, I had Ayukh or Avan Toi. Sure, not a bad idea! The old Navigator and sullen Supercargo had been on this station a few times, knew their way around and could give me some advice. What was more, neither Geckho would be of interest to young thrill-seekers looking for glory and trophies from valiant duels with worthy enemies.

How about noncombat characters then? Uline Tar asked to be left out of this. My business partner had found a shipment headed for earth and was engaged in negotiations to deliver it. Gerd Ayni obviously was out, too. Fanatically inclined Miyelonians would kill my Translator for no good reason, just because of a personal dislike. And here on the Kasti-Utsh III station, teeming with quick-tempered warriors, it would be quite a difficult task to keep the Miyelonian lady alive and well. Tini? Sure he was small, and no one would challenge a kitten to a duel. What was more, my ward was somewhat familiar with Commander Leng Keetsie-Myau, which could help.

And well... I ran my gaze over the remaining crew, trying to choose between Orun Va-Mart, Valeri and Minn-O La-Fin. There's always work for an Engineer on a ship at dock, so let Orun Va-Mart stay. Valeri-Urla? I would have taken the Beastmaster with me but I remembered the recent conversation about Denni and decided to leave her on the frigate so she could have a talk with her companion. So I decided I would bring my "travelling wife." Minn-O would have to change into a civilian dress though. Otherwise I was afraid the tall and agile cartographer, who looked impressive and fearsome in an armored space suit, would seem like a worthy opponent and get challenged to a duel by surly Miyelonians.

The fact that I myself would make quite the impressive trophy I decided to ignore for now. At the end of the day, if you're afraid of wolves, stay out of the forest! And if you're afraid of trouble of any kind, it's best to just keep your nose out of space in the first place.

Chapter Four

Volatile
Analyst

WE MADE IT through control without the slightest delay. All our documents were in order, and the Tolili-Ukh X modular frigate in long-distance raider configuration was already in the galactic ship database and registered to Free Captain Gerd Gnat. My pirate status at level two caused no questions or difficulties, so the Miyelonian sitting at the registration counter wished us a nice stay on Kasti-Utsh III and opened the transparent doors, letting us onto the station. We found ourselves in short hallway. All the walls, ceiling and even floor were plastered with advertisements for all the bizarre services available on the station. There were all kinds of hotels, stores, restaurants and...

Cartography skill increased to level fifty-

eight!

Scanning skill increased to level thirty-eight!

There's what I needed! New locations, new maps being drawn by my skills and use of scanning. Given the abundance of creatures, objects, hallways and rooms, Kasti-Utsh III was a paradise for Cartographers, Scouts and Prospectors. Minn-O looked at me with a satisfied smile and asked if her husband noticed that she just hit level seventy-one. Yes, he did.

A flood of information crashed down on me after running a scan, and I noticed a good deal of it. With my skills where they were, my scanning radius was just one hundred thirty feet, but a sphere of that size could in fact contain quite a lot! I saw a group of pickpockets in a nearby gloomy wall niche, a hidden observation system lining the whole corridor, a little snack shop or cafe a floor up and an Onuri-No V container ship docked on the other side of the nearest wall. Then I noticed a strange figure thirty steps behind us and sneaking our way. It instantly darted behind a corner when Tini turned to look in its direction. The only Listener in the game was nearly drowning in the ocean of data that was Kasti-Utsh III. Doing my best to sniff out the most valuable and important parts, I stopped and gave orders to my companions:

"Tini, go talk with the thieves hiding in that hole," I pointed the kitten to the darkened niche. "Tell them Gerd Gnat really doesn't like when he and his companions are robbed. Tell them this captain generally prefers to shoot first and pay off guards rather than to search a whole huge station for the little thief that ran off with his stuff. And you, Minn-O, there's a Jarg following us back there. Quietly go pull him into the light. He's level fifty-two, you'll manage."

"A Jarg?" Ayukh and Avan Toi shuddered at once. "Careful human, don't spook him! Jargs can explode in dangerous situations, shooting hundreds of sharp neurotoxin-coated scales and leaving behind a cloud of poison gas. That's why Jargs are not allowed on most space stations."

Well, well! This was the first creature I'd ever heard about with such a bizarre ability. So I asked the knowledgeable Geckho to tell me more about the astonishing race. Minn-O also stopped to listen, in no rush to carry out my order. Ayukh was eager to share what he'd heard about Jargs:

"A peaceful race, they were first discovered by the Geckho four hundred tongs ago. In fact, Jargs were the first Geckho vassals in the game that bends reality. Their civilization was not yet at spacefaring level when discovered, and has not reached it to the present day. Jargs have no desire to explore space, although they do possess all the necessary technologies to get there. They have no drive for expansion, instead meticulously landscaping their swampy homeworld to perfection. There has never been a war in Jarg history and, in the game, they have no combat players in the usual sense of Grenadiers, Gunners, Shocktroops and the like. In case of danger, they attack with waves of suicide troops. It's easy, because all Jargs can explode from the tiniest to the greatest. No one in the galaxy can say for sure how many of them there are. Even us Geckho, their suzerains, do not know. There might be a few million, maybe a billion, or maybe a whole trillion hidden in their endless underwater cities."

"How?" I couldn't believe my own ears. "Do the Geckho not even have a basic idea of what takes place on their vassal planets?!"

"The Jargs put up an energy shield over their homeworld, and also actively jam any attempts at scanning. They don't let foreigners to visit, so it's hard to say what exactly happens down there. Just one lone Geckho diplomat is allowed to be on the planet, and he is forbidden to leave his underwater embassy."

"But the Jargs themselves travel throughout the galaxy extensively and work for lots of races both great and not so great," the Supercargo added to the Navigator's story. "It's thought that Jargs bring good luck, so captains are eager to take them on, though they do try to keep them separated from the rest of their crew. Their race is famed for its excellent Strategists, Philosophers, Physicists, Engineers and Drafters. The services of such specialists are expensive, but even Meleyephatians hire Jargs to do those jobs despite their suspicion and lack of trust, and that says a lot."

Everything in this story was interesting, although it didn't explain why this particular Jarg was stalking us. I looked at Minn-O as she took out her laser pistol and adjusted the power output. I shook my head skeptically and decided to go with my wayedda. And although I was also armed, Paralyzer in hand, something was telling me we wouldn't have to do any shooting.

Uii-Oyeye-Argh-Eeyayo. Jarg. Level-52 Analyst.

A very strange creature, I couldn't easily imagine an analogue. He was sitting in a ventilation niche and staring at us with dozens of cloudy white eyes that lacked pupils. The Jarg came up to my waist and looked something like a frog covered in triangular scales with two pairs of back legs and two pairs of front ones and suckers instead of fingers. But he also could be compared to a pear-shaped upright armadillo with extra appendages and a strange formless head with many eyes. The Analyst wasn't even slightly afraid of me or Minn-O La-Fin. He came right out to meet us, as if expecting us. But the strange gurgling sound he issued contained zero familiar words.

"I'm sorry, I don't understand. Do you speak Miyelonian?"

The creature didn't answer, so I asked if he know Geckho. More silence. I wanted to call Ayukh over to have him use his fifty or so words of Meleyephatian on the thing, but there was no need. The many-eyed Analyst used his uppermost pair of appendages to get a universal translator out of his inventory, hung it around his neck and burbled out again:

"Good one. Glad to see. You. And you. Have offer."

Minn-O and I exchanged glances and both simultaneously holstered our guns. And that was also when I noticed that the security cameras in this section were all broken. That can't have been a coincidence.

"A deal? What kind of deal?" my companion

asked the Jarg, but the alien ignored her and kept sitting and puffing out his cheeks in silence. I had to repeat.

Successful Fame check.

"You to speak. Senior human. One. Cartographer to leave. You I to know. You I not to know."

It wasn't exactly easy to parse, but it wasn't a huge challenge either. This Jarg was suggesting we speak one on one and telling me he had heard of the man named Gnat. But such mistrust would offend my junior wife, and I was already working hard to get Minn-O back to normal after all her recent traumas. So I decided to speak up on Minn-O La-Fin's behalf:

"She is my wife. I trust her. Speak, what kind of deal do you suggest?"

The Jarg spent a long time in silence. A minute or so, if not longer. Finally, I saw a message about successful Authority check, after which the strange creature told me the essence of its offer:

"I to think. You to search Keetsie. Hard. Not to find. Much area. Secret. I to tell you where. You to take package. Bring Keetsie. I no can to do. Jarg is not to allow. Big-tail warmongers."

Uhh... As far as I could tell, this Analyst with an utterly unpronounceable name had somehow heard or intuited that I was looking for the celebrated commander of the Miyelonian fleet. The Jarg assured me that without its help, Leng Keetsie-Myau would be impossible to find on the Kasti-Utsh III station because the commander's location was a big secret and no

Miyelonian would help me. But somehow he knew where to find Keetsie, and would tell me if I agreed to take a package to the fleet commander, which he couldn't deliver because Jargs weren't allowed on the station. Plus the "big-tail warmongers" were here, by which he must have meant Miyelonian soldiers who could stop the explosive Jarg from reaching their leader.

What should I say? If I weren't in a time crunch, I would have told the Jarg to get stuffed. The earlier incident with the Great Miyelonian Priestess did plenty to teach me to be careful and stay out of political games that went over my head. I had no doubt that something mysterious was brewing, possibly with big consequences. Otherwise what was the point of the Jarg being so secretive? Why go inventing strange delivery schemes if they could simply send a package by regular mail? No, he needed this to be handed off personally and by a player Leng Keetsie-Myau would know and let near. I could smell the potential for trouble from a long way off. There, the game even confirmed with a popup:

Danger Sense skill increased to level fifty!

However, unfortunately, the Jarg had calculated right. It really was critically important for me to see Leng Keetsie-Myau as fast as possible and obtain her permission to fly to Earth. I couldn't imagine any way of doing that quickly other than accepting this strange spiny armadillo's offer. Overall, with a heavy sigh, I agreed. He immediately lit up and burbled:

"Agreement. Trust. Second floor. Sector 8-13.

Bar Supernova Shine. In a quarter ummi. Here to be package."

With those words the Jarg extended me a heavy-looking black stone disk with a polished shine. After that, the Analyst strained to squeeze itself back into the fairly narrow ventilation shaft. A half minute later, he was out of sight. And twenty seconds after that, deep inside the shaft, I heard a loud but muffled pop, telling me that the messenger had chosen to self-destruct. Hrm... Not good.

I started looking the strange package over from every angle. The large and smooth black stone weighed ten pounds. There were lighter veins in it, and in places even transparent microscopic granules. The system even identified it as nothing more than a simple stone:

Polished stone. Aegirine with augite flecks.

Mineralogy skill increased to level fifty-one!
Mineralogy skill increased to level fifty-two!

A very common mineral on earth, it was composed of everyday iron and sodium silicates. Depending on the proportions of these metals and other things mixed in, the color of aegirine could vary from black to dark green or brown. The only interesting property of aegirine, as far as I remembered from university, was that it formed beautiful elongated crystals. In fact, neither aegirine or augite were even semi-precious stones and were not often used for any purpose. I suspected that this mineral was not a rarity in the rest of the galaxy either. So if not the material, there must have been some other value.

Maybe the color? Or did these veins on the

polished stone form a pattern a knowledgeable Miyelonian could read? Just then, Tini came back from the thieves and I asked my ward whether his race had any beliefs connected with black stones. Maybe giving one as a gift to the Miyelonian commander would be a mortal offense. Or maybe it was the opposite and was a sign the messenger could be trusted.

The kitten considered it, stroked his nose comedically and honestly answered that he hadn't heard of it. Still he had another gift to brag about — a special little machine for giving color tattoos directly through fur without needing to shave the skin first.

"The local thieves gave it to me as a sign of respect! And they also promised that no thief on Kasti-Utsh III would touch either Captain Gerd Gnat or any other members of his team."

Authority increased to 53!

I thanked my ward for the good work even though my authority among the local thieves was the last thing on my mind. It was much more important to get to the bottom of this stone. As soon as Scanning reloaded, its rippled icon changing color from gray to green, I activated it.

Scanning skill increased to level thirty-nine!
Electronics skill increased to level sixty-three!

There we go! As suspected, the polished stone was just a case and the real payload was inside. There were microscopic electronic chips, a power source, tensiometers along the whole inner surface to detect stress and pressure, and a large faceted crystal nearly half the size of the stone itself. And all the rest of the space was filled with... explosives! So I was holding a powerful bomb that would be sure to explode if I tried to open it recklessly. No, I definitely didn't want to bring THIS to Leng Keetsie-Myau!

I wiped the sweat off my forehead, then asked my companions to keep quiet so I could think. Most likely, this package was interesting because of the crystal, which looked like the kind often used as data drives. But I figured I'd better take the risk and open the case myself, pull out the drive and bring only it to the commander. Otherwise, if the bomb did go off, I'd be at fault in the death of the famed general. The Miyelonians would never forgive Gnat for that!

What was more, I could easily see how the package opened. When I zoomed in the mini-map, I could clearly make out a seam and carving running sideways into the stone. I could not see it on the smooth exterior, but in the scan it was hard to miss. Basically, the two halves of the case could unscrew and come apart, but it had to be done very carefully, only applying pressure in places without a sensor or tensiometer. I also had an alternative method in my back pocket: turning off all the little detonators and sensors using Machine Control. I didn't consider that seriously, though, because there were just too many of them.

Before my moment of determination passed, I traded the Intelligence rings for +1 Perception ones and took off the armored gloves from my Listener Suit so I could feel the stone with my bare fingers. Then I asked my companions to go into the corner of the hall so they wouldn't get hurt if I exploded. And I very well might have. Everyone obeyed except for Minn-O. My wayedda sat cross-legged on the floor and refused to go anywhere:

"You're my husband and, as your travelling wife, it is my right to share your fate!"

I didn't try and argue; I just didn't have the energy. If my wife wanted to stay, let her stay. She could hold the flashlight so I could see better. I compared the scan map with the real stone a few times and, adjusting my finger position just a hair, warned Minn-O:

"I can't see the groove clearly enough in the scan, it's very fine. I could easily make a mistake. So I'd say there's a fifty percent chance that we're gonna blow sky high. For that reason, I leave it up to you — clockwise or counterclockwise?"

"What? Gnat, sorry, I don't understand!"

I belatedly realized that perhaps my wife's magocratic world never had mechanical clocks like I was accustomed to, so terms like clockwise and counterclockwise were unfamiliar to Minn-O. No matter. I had already made up my mind and turned counterclockwise.

Electronics skill increased to level sixty-four!

Machine Control skill increased to level sixty-eight!

You have reached level seventy-six!

You have received three skill points (total

points accumulated: six).

How lucky! Noticing in passing that, with the six free skill points, my Electronics would already be high enough to use the ring-shaped Pyramid Signal Booster, I cautiously began unscrewing the halves of the stone. First rotation, second. There, just a little bit more. Open! I couldn't hold back the cry of disappointment. The crystal drive was so thickly wrapped in a web of fine wires that pulling it out without breaking anything seemed impossible. But what to do?

"Ayukh!" I called the Navigator over, who was cautiously peeking from around the corner. "Say, can you copy the data off this crystal? Just be careful. This thing is rigged to blow!"

The furry Geckho, extending his big hands to the dangerous package, grabbed it and held it far away from his face. Then he turned toward me in surprise:

"Captain, I have never seen such a large drive before, only read about them. I can read it, that contact edge is completely exposed. But I'm not sure our frigate has enough memory to hold everything. There's at least a yottabyte! Maybe we could stick this thing into the main ship computer temporarily until we find another swappable drive..."

"Yes, Ayukh, that's exactly what we'll do! I'll bring this dangerous item to the starship and connect it. You tell me how to do it. And Uline can try to find another gigantic drive like this, just without any explosives and wires. Let's go back to the ship!"

Pressed for time, doubting my intuition was a luxury I couldn't afford. I didn't carry the explosive item in my hands and just stashed it in my inventory. As far as I understood the game rules, no amount of shaking or walking could trigger an explosion in there. At the very least, I hoped so.

"BACK SO SOON? Did the soldiers really impose on guests to the station by challenging them to a duel?" the same registration service employee greeted our return with an acrid note.

Sensing open mockery in the Miyelonian's voice, I first got indignant and wanted to say he was wrong, but I sharply rethought. And really, why not? Let him think so! It was a great explanation for our hasty return!

"We decided to get better prepared and at least take a weapon with us," I said, fleshing out the hastily constructed story, then changed topic. "On our way back, we heard a really loud boom to the right of the corridor. Like maybe something exploded or fell. I wanted to report that and ask if everything is going alright around here."

Psionic skill increased to level seventy-six!

Mysticism skill increased to level twenty-five!

Ugh, I didn't mean to use magic. It just happened. The dispatcher wrinkled his whiskered nose, pressed his ears to his head and closed his eyes for a few seconds, which in his race meant embarrassment and uncertainty. Finally the Miyelonian admitted:

"Yes, there is a Jarg here we just can't seem to get rid of... He keeps crawling around the station even though its forbidden. Every time he dies when trying to overcome the automatic security system, but he still tries again. When I find out what ship he belongs to, I'll fine that captain and its whole crew in full measure!"

I already knew about the Jarg, though I didn't say that we'd met. My group and I returned to the frigate. Thankfully the hangar was just two hundred yards from the registration control service desk. After that I personally interfaced the rigged crystal drive with the ship's computer, not willing to entrust the sensitive operation to anyone else. Ayukh the Navigator told me how the computer was getting on:

"Captain, this is a huge file. Based on the format, I'd say it's a star map. It'll come quite in handy, we can add it to the one in our ship. And there are also some encrypted files here. Without the password, we can't get to them though."

"Copy everything!" I ordered and the Navigator quickly ran his claws over the touchscreen keyboard on the instrument panel.

A minute passed, then another. I was looking at the clock with greater and greater impatience. Finally I couldn't hold back and asked if it would take much longer. The old Navigator's answer blew me away:

"Another ummi and a half or so. Maybe two."

"Excuse me???"

I had not accounted for this. Copying such a

large amount of data would take ten hours, maybe more. But I didn't have that kind of time! In just forty minutes I was supposed to be at Supernova Shine with a package for Leng Keetsie-Myau!

"But Gerd Gnat, what did you want me to do? Just the star-map file is two yottabytes. The encrypted files are three times that! Wait, captain..." Ayukh turned to me, his face full of apprehension and even fear. I had already guessed that something bad had happened. "All the folders just permanently erased themselves! Looks like some kind of software protection. Only the star map file is still there and being copied to our ship computer. A half ummi and it'll be finished."

Damn... I guess we had just given the hug of death to six yottabytes of data. And it was probably quite valuable and secret if the Jarg had fallen back on such difficult methods of packaging and delivery. Miyelonian command was not going to like this.

Chapter Five

Big-Tail Warmongers

EVEN HALF an ummi was around two hours and forty minutes, still too long. So I had to go to meet the Miyelonian commander before the copying was finished. I left the Navigator on the frigate to watch over the transfer and installation of the star map, and make sure none of the crew accidentally touched the crystal with its mesh of wires and explosives. I also told Minn-O La-Fin she should stay on the ship. The Princess was just not in a good place after her two days of uninterrupted gaming, yawning wide constantly.

So she wouldn't get offended, I veiled my true intentions with an order to contact General Ui-Taka in the real world. That would get her out of the game, and hopefully there she could get some rest. But also, now that the military conflict with the Dark Faction had started back up, I needed to know whether the enemy Strategist's offer to meet on neutral territory remained in force. Most likely not. The greatest living commander of the parallel world would probably reach the conclusion that he could completely end the Human-3 Faction inside the ten-day-timeframe he previously offered. And that meant there was no more reason to negotiate. Minn-O's mission was to figure that out and at the same time tell our enemy about our starship's new time constraint. The earliest we could be there was six days. Not a huge difference, but I still figured it was worth reminding the enemy that harsh orbital bombardment was inevitable and could wipe all their nodes off the surface of the virtual Earth. And I decided not to mention that the Tolili-Ukh X star frigate could theoretically end up orbiting Earth much sooner than that.

Another important event was that repair bot Kirsan had given me back the disk-shaped artifact after removing the racial requirement:

Pyramid Signal Booster (Listener armor suit accessory).

+3% armor suit forcefield capacity per level.

+15% Scanning radius.

+70% more data transmitted to Pyramid.

Statistic requirements: Intelligence 26, Perception 26.

Skill requirements: Electronics 70, Machine Control 50.

Attention! Your character's Electronics level is

insufficient to equip this item.

Finally! I stuck my six free points into Electronics, raising it to seventy and stuck the bronze ring, which was covered in ancient symbols, into the special indentation in my armor's chest-piece. Also, I did have to change rings first because, without them, I didn't have enough Intelligence. I was expecting some overeager messages from my energy suit about that, but it barely seemed to notice, as if this was just a given. The Relicts must have replaced elements of their armor or added new equipment fairly regularly, so it didn't merit separate messages.

At any rate, my suit's defensive shield had changed radically. Where just a moment ago it was 3500 points, it was now 11480 in the blink of an eye. And that allowed my Gnat to survive one direct shot from a sniper rifle. If I got lucky, I might even be able to survive two. Or ten from a light blaster or laser pistol. That was exactly what I needed before entering the Kasti-Utsh III station proper, where Miyelonian troops might be itching for a fight. It was a shame the Annihilator was still being repaired and the only weapon I had on me was the nonlethal Paralyzer. Still, shooting was never Gnat's strong side and now, with the class change, I had started specializing in psionic.

After that I put the Perception rings back on because I wanted to check the crystal drive's connection to the power source. Maybe the bomb could be disarmed without undoing the many wires. But no, studying the open black stone showed that it was not so easy to detach the power source. It was fused securely to the hardened explosive. Maybe it could be extracted if the explosive was warmed and made pliable again? I didn't have the Chemistry skill at all, so I was nowhere near knowing what this was made out of or how the explosive would react to heat. In any case, there was no time to experiment. I left it as it was.

And I was already approaching the external airlock when I was called out to by Eduard Boyko, who was standing guard at the frigate exit:

"Captain, come here a minute. I've got some important things to tell you."

The Space Marine waved the armored hand of his exoskeleton suit, calling me over to some big containers waiting to be loaded onto our ship. This was the shipment Uline got for us to bring to Earth. I sent Tini and Avan Toi to the hangar exit, promising to catch up to them, then went after Eduard. Imran was there waiting for us next to the containers, having just come back from the Dome and seemingly wanting to share fresh news.

But I was wrong, they had no news from the faction. The Dagestani athlete first made sure there were no other crew around, and no one was listening to us. Then he pointed at three semi-transparent plastic containers which looked to contain some large equipment:

"Gerd Gnat, I know what these are. I've seen one before when that Dark Faction antigrav crashed. They're antigravitational thrusters for our enemies' Sio-Mi-Doris. And there are three of them, just what they need for a heavy armored assault vehicle. We just shot down one of those over the Centaur Plateau, and now the enemy is buying thrusters to build a new one and replenish their losses."

"Imran, how can you even see anything in there?" I asked in dubious surprise, walking around the big plastic boxes. Something like cubes, each side was around eight feet. "I can't see a damn thing! And there's nothing written on the packaging, just some codes I can't understand. Eduard, walk around the container and shine your flashlight from the other side so we can see shadows at least."

The plastic of the three large containers was translucent and allowed us to see the outlines of the impressively large cargo inside, but I just couldn't make anything out clearly. I had to put on my helmet, lower the IR Lens to get the +2 Perception bonus and basically press my nose into the wall before anything tripped.

Geckho Space Company GG-880E antigravity thruster.

Eagle Eye skill increased to level seventy-one.

Seemingly Imran was not wrong and inside there really was an antigravity thruster: something of a huge silvery metallic droplet with bundles of power cables and flat surfaces to attach to the wings or fuselage of a flying machine. I told my friends that at once. Imran gave a good-natured smile:

"Gnat, I don't know how to use Prospector or Listener stuff, I cannot see through objects. One side of the box slides away here." My Dagestani friend pointed at one wall of the cube and even moved the plastic panel aside, revealing the contents of the big box.

Again I had looked at a person with inflamed tonsils, and gone looking for any way to get them out but the mouth. Oh well, I didn't get myself bent out of shape over it. It may have been an unusual method, but I had accomplished my goal and seen inside the container. That was what mattered.

"Can we refuse to deliver this to our enemies?" Eduard Boyko and I both walked up and looked at the powerful machinery in its anti-shock casing.

"Unfortunately that will not be possible." I had done a lot of talking with my business partner Uline Tar, so I had an idea of how harsh the penalties were for a freight forwarder that refused to complete a contract once signed. You could forget about a positive reputation after that. No one would ever trust such an unreliable person again. And that was exactly what I tried to get through to my friends.

"What if we just take them as spoils of war? Our factions are currently fighting, so it seems reasonable. Then we can take them to the H3 Faction!" Imran seemingly didn't understand that the great space races had no interest in the little squabbles of aboriginals on a distant planet, and no one would give us the right to simply requisition a shipment that didn't belong to us.

"I've got a better idea!" Eduard took a step forward. Seeing his agitated and reddened face, I immediately realized I would be hearing something radical and shocking. "We need to blow these things to hell before we load them! No shipment, no problem! And any questions from the buyers or suppliers, we just go stone-faced and say we have no idea why they went up!"

It was of course an idiotic idea. Especially here on the Miyelonian station where Truth Seekers quickly saw through any lie and got to the bottom of any murky situation. On top of that, if we were found out, the Dark Faction would still be entitled to get what they paid for, they'd just have to wait a bit longer. Still it wouldn't be right to just do nothing here. Our faction just wouldn't understand. We needed to find a different approach...

I took a heavy sigh as if about to jump into a vortex. This might have been the stupidest thing I'd ever done, but I took three Magnetic Bombs from my inventory and handed them to Eduard and Imran:

"I warn you: if someone finds out, we'll all get screwed so bad we'll never pay it back even if we sell our kidneys and last pair of underwear. So not a word about this even to members of our faction! Look, these panels on the thrusters screw out. Inside, as far as I can tell, there is an empty space. I'm gonna set a timer on all three bombs for one ummi after the thrusters are activated, so the explosions will happen at the same time and after they're fully tested and installed. Okay, all set. Your mission is to hide the bombs inside the thrusters and make it all look like before."

"Uhh, um..." Imran tried to object, pointing at the frigate. I understood what he wanted to ask and got out ahead:

"Our loaders Basha and Vasha are out in the

real world. Supercargo Avan Toi will be going with me to the station. So no one is going to be handling this cargo for at least an hour. You've got enough time to rig the bombs and close the panels back up. If any team members try to come up to the containers, chase them off and say its an order from the captain. Everything clear?"

Authority increased to 54!

The amateur bombers nodded simultaneously. Eduard carefully set the bombs in his inventory and whispered with a predatory grin:

"Just let the Dark Faction try and use their new antigrav to attack our troops!"

I responded, trying to scare them:

"You both better hope this really is for the Dark Faction and not, let's say, Geckho scientists on some secret base. Our suzerains will be very upset if some freight antigrav of theirs crashes over the ocean while full of valuable equipment! They definitely won't forgive that. I have to imagine they'd stop at nothing to find the culprit. And they will find them sooner or later. I'm reminded that Dark Faction players were executed in the real world for less, just to protect the faction from the suzerains' rage..."

They immediately straightened up and started exchanging glances of uncertainty. Seemingly both Imran and Eduard were already slightly regretting bringing this up. But still neither of them was going to back down. Both just assured me that they acknowledged the responsibility and danger and so would be dead quiet.

Great! I went to catch up with Tini and Avan Toi, who had already made it quite far. But I held back my happy smile until I'd left the hangar. In the eyes of Imran and Eduard, their commander Gerd Gnat now looked even cooler. Beyond that, there was now a secret they would both keep even from the directors of the Human-3 Faction and everyone in it. It was seemingly a small thing, but I managed to separate the concepts of loyalty to faction and loyalty to captain, and get them leaning toward the latter. Why? Well, my actions weren't always met with approval in the faction, and I didn't want to tell the directors everything. After all, now what information and interpretation would make it under the Dome it depended directly on Dmitry, Imran and Eduard and their personal interpretation of events.

As for the bombs, there was no real danger. I didn't actually put a timer on them like I told my friends. Instead I set two identical fairly complex activation codes. If they were intended for the Geckho or one of the factions of my world, the bombs would remain hidden forever, and no one would ever guess they were there. But if the Dark Faction got them, all three thrusters would be destroyed together with whatever they ended up attached to. How? Very easy! Just broadcast a weak radio signal with the activation code a few days after coming back to Earth from Human-3 territory, one that would fade in two or three nodes. It could cover our enemy's territory, but touch nowhere else on our huge planet.

THERE WERE ONLY three of us left on our way to go meet Leng Keetsie-Myau. One was an underaged kitten, and calling the sullen shipper a combat character would sound like a joke. It was strange to my eye but advertising our harmlessness and looking like boring targets allowed us to walk past innumerable Miyelonian soldiers to the central elevators of the space station without issue. I mean, two or three big cats did try to challenge me to a ritual duel with the standard phrase: "Ah-sahntee maye-uu-u rezsh shashash-u?" But responding in a language the Miyelonians didn't know and kindly telling them to go pleasure themselves, accompanied by a polite smile and slight mind control was all it took for them to lose interest.

It should be noted that the Jarg Analyst's concern over "big-tail warmongers" was not misplaced. There were lots of Miyelonian soldiers on the station. Lots and lots. Pilots and Gunners, Gladiators and Medics, Shocktroops and Space Commandos, Snipers and Sappers. Many of them were very worked up if not to say aggressive due to drinking alcohol or various kinds of stimulants both licit and less so. Here and there I saw squabbles and fights between individuals from different squadrons, and often the outcome was lethal. In one place we even witnessed the robbing of a souvenir shop. Fluffy soldiers, both tomcats and ladies, came out of a small store barely able to move with overloaded inventories and draped in shiny jewelry like

Christmas trees.

Based on the dismembered spider-like body at the door, the owner of this shop was a Meleyephatian trader, who had been foolhardy enough to open his establishment while the big-tail warmongers were visiting Kasti-Utsh III. When my ward Tini started dashing toward the unattended shop, I sharply pulled him back and said with strain in my voice that we may have been pirates in status, but we were not looters.

Scanning skill increased to level forty!

Machine Control skill increased to level sixty-nine!

Mysticism skill increased to level twenty-six!

That was me using my skills to turn on the store's alarms, which were inactive for some reason. But although turning on the siren did surprise the fluffy-tailed marauders, it did nothing to scare them off and they all got right back to their criminal activities. What was more, the guardians of order appeared almost at once. But they didn't even try to stop the chaos, just turned off the alarm and hurried away.

Before that episode, I was still holding onto the illusion that I could visit the ancient artifact trader I heard about from the fence on the Medu-Ro IV pirate station. But now I fully appreciated that I wouldn't be finding anyone there for the next few days. Most traders at the space station were not exactly happy to see so many soldiers and, to avoid excesses, decided to temporarily close their little shops. But as I said before, the hot-headed warriors didn't touch me or my companions for a long time. Still, all good things must come to an end. It happened when we had already reached our destination sector, 8-13. I already thought we had made it...

"Ah-sahntee maye-uu-u rezsh shashash-u!" hardly able to stand after so much booze and drugs, a level-92 Miyelonian Machinegunner slurred out, standing in our way.

He was wearing heavy composite armor and holding a high-speed gun in his hands. The barrel was swaying from side to side in his shaky hands. In the Miyelonian's eyes, I could read a complete lack not only of fear but all ability to think clearly.

Danger Sense skill increased to level fifty-one!

There was a very big difference between this and the previous attempted challenges. First of all, the Machinegunner was way too high to understand what we were saying back. His only wish now was to fight and he was going to do it no matter what, even if I rejected his challenge. Second, there were ten other Miyelonian soldiers behind the Machinegunner, and they were prepared to run at me if I tried to ignore their drinking buddy. I turned around. The hallway we'd just walked down was already blocked by a dense wall of armed Miyelonians who weren't hiding their aggressive intentions.

"Gerd Gnat, you cannot run from us!" came the voice of one of the disheveled cats, and its voice was joyful, self-satisfied and utterly sober. "We recognize you and have been following you since the elevators! The Pride of the Bushy Shadow has placed a good price on your head! What's more, anyone who defeats the only Listener in the game is guaranteed a Fame boost and your appendages are rare trophies that any soldier would be proud to wear!"

It suddenly became crystal clear that they would never let me leave and the challenge from the drunken Machinegunner was just a formal pretext. These attackers were trying to use that to lend a veneer of legality to what they were doing even though this was little more than an attempt at armed robbery and murder. So now accepting the challenge was in my best interest. It was my only hope to keep this from growing out of control and having my whole group set upon by thirty bloodthirsty Miyelonians. There were rules to a duel. I activated the scanning pictogram and saw what kind of Miyelonian soldiers were around me, who was the most dangerous and who was their commander.

"So then, landing brigade one hundred forty-six..." I said, reinforcing my voice with a bit of magic so they would all grasp what I was driving at. "For some reason I don't see any trophies on you from the big war with the Meleyephatians. Not one enemy killed for the whole squadron. Your helmets are only adorned with losers like you and murdered civilians. So what's is it, snot-noses? They didn't let you fight in a real battle? Did they say you're too weak and not let you go on the front lines?"

I heard teeth scraping all around. It was so clear that even the Supercargo heard. Though he didn't understand Miyelonian he knew perfectly well that something unusual was happening. Tini was just terrified with his ears pressed back against his head. He quietly asked why I was provoking them. Lots of them heard his question, so I answered as loud as I could:

"So your kinsmen will remember that they are proud soldiers and not a band of robbers! So that Commander Leng Keetsie-Myau won't have to cover her eyes in shame for her subordinates when we talk. So the Geckho behind me will continue to see the Miyelonians as powerful and loyal allies, not some gang of drugged up lunatics!"

Psionic skill increased to level seventy-seven!

Mental Fortitude skill increased to level fifty-eight!

Mysticism skill increased to level twenty-seven!

Even without the system messages I could sense my words hitting their mark. The markers on the mini-map around me started all changing from red, meaning aggressive, to yellow for neutral. I even saw a couple of green ones. The Miyelonians stared at the ground and pressed their tails between their legs but most importantly they dispersed, letting me pass. Then the squadron commander pushed his subordinates aside and stepped out in front. This lean orange tomcat was small even for a Miyelonian:

Gerd Mauu-La Mya-Ssa. Miyelonian. Pride of the Silver Tail. Level-96 Medic.

"Harsh words. And they made my Authority fall by three points. But I agree Gerd Gnat, I deserved that.

I shouldn't have let my soldiers get so out of control. But speaking of honor and pride, I am simply obliged to challenge you to a duel because you insulted not only my subordinates and me personally, you insulted everyone in landing brigade one hundred forty-six! Ah-sahntee maye-uu-u rezsh shashash-u!"

"If you say so, bushy-tail. I'm glad to hear that Miyelonians haven't forgotten the concept of honor. I am also a man of honor, so I must warn you that you have no chance in a one-on-one duel. I could handle a Medic with my bare hands. So I propose a three-on-three. Choose any two soldiers from your squadron, I'll take the little one and the fatty from mine," I said pointing at Tini and Avan Toi, who was just listening to this conversation in an incomprehensible language.

"But he's a child!" my opponent started to object, but rethought and accepted my conditions. And immediately assured me that if I won none of his soldiers would get in my way.

So, had I gone crazy? Not at all. I just wanted to solve this problem once and for all, not get drawn into an endless string of duels. And that was sure to happen otherwise, because the fluffy soldiers would have thought it their duty to line up to fight me right after their orange commander for the honor of their squadron. Among the Miyelonians, there were some very high level and dangerous ones, although many of them weren't all that sober.

While the orange Medic chose partners, I looked aside at my friends:

"I don't expect you to fight like real soldiers. Just

don't let me get killed in the first moments of the duel. I can handle it from there. I can see they have a gladiator. Then Tini, you cover my back. Mostly likely he'll try to make a fast jump and stick his blades between my shoulders. Avan Toi, use your laser pistol and don't spare battery. Just stop that Medic from concentrating and healing his partners. And then, on my command, be prepared to lay down on enemies after I immobilize them. So, the third is a Bodyguard. How obvious! We'll leave him for dessert, he has too many hitpoints. That's all, we're expected in the arena. Good luck!"

Chapter Six

Moments from Kungdom

I PLAYED a little trick, placing markers on all three enemies and sending them out to my companions. On the one hand, there was a Priest and two Bards among the Miyelonians surrounding the arena, and the especially intense communication between them and the enemy fighters spoke to our rivals being stacked with bonuses. In fact they were doing nothing to hide that. Also the orange Medic and his two level 100+ partners, before entering the circle, started swallowing multicolored pills by the handful.

"Those are Agility and Strength boosters. They raise statistics by a few points for a short time," Tini answered. "They're generally forbidden in official tournaments, but in war they're used constantly along with boosters for Constitution, movement speed, regeneration and even immunity to pain and fear."

"But combat boosters cause addiction very quickly," the surly Supercargo said, phlegmatically and unhurriedly setting the servos of his armor into combat mode, putting on his helmet and activating his energy shield.

Combat boosters? So they were afraid of us, given they were treating this battle so seriously. Meanwhile, the three Miyelonians finally stopped taking their drugs and agreeing on tactics, entered the large circle made up of soldiers of their subdivision and stopped. Then they simultaneously melted into predatory grins, demonstrating sharp sets of fangs. Tini and Avan Toi answered in kind. But the Listener Energy Armor helmet had very dark tint on the outside, so they couldn't see my face, and I just held up a middle finger.

"Begin!" Gerd Mauu-La Mya-Ssa gave the wave.

And at that second I jumped forward with a flip, dodging the anticipated double back-stab from the Miyelonian Gladiator. Exactly right! That was the fruits of training with Fox the Morphian. We had worked on this exact scenario. Imran too, I remembered, had caught an opponent acting too predictable on Medu-Ro IV. Tini then deftly caught the Gladiator as he missed, seriously wounding the highly dangerous enemy. However, my kitten was now also caught, instantly killed by a few accurate blows from the Bodyguard and Medic. In the very first second of battle, all three enemies made a fast dash at my back, trying to take down Gnat in one fell swoop! That was unexpected. I had to admit, I had not considered that tactic, so Tini was doing the wrong thing and we lost him at the very beginning of battle.

Also... what the hell?! The orange Medic was immune to my mental attacks! And he could dodge my Paralyzer shots with ease, flipping gracefully as the toxic balls flew right past him! Did he have the Danger Sense skill? It seemed very likely. Well then, how do you like this? I tried to distance myself and not think about the nimble Miyelonian as an enemy. This was just a game, like shooting bottles at the carnival. After all, none of us was truly hated our targets or wished them ill. I tried to predict his movements and emptied a whole Paralyzer clip.

Sharpshooter skill increased to level thirty-five!

Sharpshooter skill increased to level thirty-six!

Rifles skill increased to level fifty-two!

Two of the audience standing in the first rows took balls to the forehead and fell to the floor paralyzed for a few minutes. This orange Medic was not giving himself up easy! Good thing Avan Toi didn't miss. At the same time as my pointless shooting, he made a series of blasts from the laser pistol and hit the fast-moving Miyelonian once on his left toe. It was not a severe wound, but my Supercargo had done his job, and stopped the fluffy-tailed Medic from healing the heavily wounded Gladiator.

Targeting skill increased to level twenty-four!

I stashed the emptied Paralyzer and tried to concentrate for another psionic attack. And as I did, I got a sense for the battle as a whole. The enemy Bodyguard, his blades out and snarling, was preventing me and Avan Toi from reaching the heavily wounded Gladiator, who was down on his knees. The Medic, having made a complete circle, was trying to run up from the other side to heal his comrade but was again driven off by my partner's shooting. I mentally attacked the crazily nimble Medic once again and once again it came to naught. What the hell?! What was his Intelligence if I couldn't even hit him?!

It was time to change something in this very nearly dead-end situation. I abandoned the surprisingly nimble and unhittable Gerd Mauu-La and chose a different target for my next psionic attack. And I easily took over the Bodyguard. Got him! Yes! The striped and shaggy Miyelonian swung with all his might and took off the head of his wounded comrade, who was kneeling and trying to pull Tini's blade out of his side, which was stuck in up to the hilt.

Mental Fortitude skill increased to level fifty-eight!

"Avan Toi, deal with this!" I pointed to the Bodyguard, who was frozen with a look of confusion on his face, meanwhile exerting force to keep him under control. I even grew surprised at how hard it was for me to control the big beefy soldier. In this battle, psionic actions were coming very hard to me.

The Supercargo stopped using his pistol to chase the nimble bushy-tailed Medic around the arena, stashed his useless weapon and, like a pro wrestler, got a running start and jumped high, spreading his arms wide. His nine-hundred-pound body slammed down on top of the Miyelonian Bodyguard, pressing him to the floor. The crunch of his breaking bones was so distinct that everyone watching, including me, winced in pain. Satisfied, Avan Toi gave a loud roar, tightened up and ripped the tail off his prostrated enemy with his bare hands.

"My trophy!" he shouted, raising it high above his head and demonstrating the bloodied tail. And although Avan Toi was shouting in Geckho, I don't think it was lost on anyone.

I meanwhile realized why I was having such problems with my psionic abilities. I played myself, as they say. Instead my normal +5 Intelligence rings, I was still wearing those +1 Perception ones! I quickly corrected the vexing oversight and, picking myself back up, walked unflappably toward the Medic not even trying to dodge his pistol shots.

Medium Armor skill increased to level fifty-five!

Gerd Mauu-La understood perfectly that his side had already lost, but he was in no rush to admit defeat. He hit me either five or six times, taking down two thirds of my defensive shield, then tried to run away to a safe distance. I even got the impression that the last of my enemies was planning to leave the circle and hide behind the many soldiers. Not on my watch! I sharply extended a hand and the fluffy-tailed Medic froze in a pre-jump pose. Finally! You were starting to make me worry!

Unhurriedly walking over to Gerd Mauu-La, I pulled the laser pistol from his numb fingers and looked at the weapon. A standard Miyelonian officer's laser pistol with expanded batteries, and improved damage and accuracy. Not a bad weapon. In theory, there was nothing stopping me from taking it as compensation for upsetting me and wasting my time. But I didn't do that, setting the pistol into the holster on Mauu-La's belt. Yes, he was a difficult enemy, and I found his combat abilities admirable, so I didn't take his weapon.

I raised my eyes to Gerd Mauu-La, intending to say some words of approval and even admiration, but... I drowned in his thoughts.

"They say people have no fur on their bodies. Just bare skin as if they got sick and all their hair fell out. So gross, it's nasty just to think about. But what is that glimmering deep in his helmet? Some kind of blue shade. Weird. Is this person looking at me? Spooky. Just my luck to end up against a psionic! Although I could have guessed based on how confidently Gnat acted with my goofball underlings. He had them turning tail with just a couple words. But after all, he is right. The only ones left on the station are losers, the kind who would never be put on the first wave of a landing operation. Or the second for that matter. This is deep reserves. How I wish I never would have to see these hateful constantly drunken mugs again! And why me, top graduate of the Star City medical academy? Why was I sent to command these soldiers who have no appreciation for

the knowledge and intellect of their commander?! Sure I'm not a soldier in spirit, and especially not a commander. I'm a Medic! An Astrobiologist by education! Agility and Intelligence — those are my strong suits. But I have to use my abilities to manage a squadron of dingbats who are always wobbling around like idiots with curved blades. But what's taking Gnat so long? He's already won, just take care of the one last..."

I'd heard enough to make up my mind. Extra loud so everyone would hear, I addressed the helpless captive:

"I really don't want to cut off your tail, orange cat. And not because you're an unworthy enemy, in fact quite the opposite. You did much more in battle than I was expecting. You surprised me both with your combat abilities and high resistance to magic. So in my eyes you did not lose. You won the right to keep your weapon, tail and life! You are free to go!"

Fame increased to 67.

Authority increased to 55!

The feline soldiers nearby reacted positively. Apparently, the conflict with landing brigade one hundred forty-six could be considered completely quashed. Nothing was stopping me from going further. But most importantly, as I spoke, I mentally sent a message to Gerd Mauu-La:

"You will never find understanding and respect among these cutthroats. This is no place for you. You are alien to them. And meanwhile, I just so happen to need a capable medic on my frigate. And you as an

Astrobiologist by education, may find it interesting to see new worlds and their unique creatures. Think it over. And make your choice. If you decide to go, I'm at docking bay 567, airlock number fourteen."

Psionic skill increased to level seventy-eight!

The orange Medic, shaken up after the squabble, puffed his fur out which immediately made him look twice as big, then thanked me for treating him nobly and mercifully. Then he spoke up, clearly choosing his words carefully so his subordinates and I would hear exactly what he wanted us to:

"Ah, I envy you Free Captains! Long-distance space flights, new worlds, meeting new people, so much interesting stuff! I've always dreamed of such a life and, one day, I'll definitely find work on a starship. But there's a war on, I've been drafted and, what's more, I'm a squadron commander. So I'll stay here to pay my debt to the Union of Miyelonian Prides until one of the high commanders says otherwise."

"YOU CAN'T come in! Private party!" a group of eight plainclothes guardsmen tried to stop me and my Geckho companion at the entrance to the Supernova Shine bar.

None of the security had readable names, class or level, but I could sense that they were all confident in their strength. But the main thing was that all eight of them wafted an air of danger. They didn't look like some bored bog-standard bruisers like you see at a normal bar or restaurant. And why have eight guards just at the door?

I had no doubts that I was seeing before me soldiers of the Miyelonian army. And what was more, these were not common soldiers, they were true elite. Let's check! I activated the scanning icon:

Pola Ust-Keetsie. Miyelonian Female. First Pride. Level-207 Assassin.

Gerd Deyar An-Keetsie. Miyelonian. First Pride. Level-211 Gunner.

[information hidden, insufficient skill to read]

...

Map Mo-Keetsie. Miyelonian. First Pride. Level-200 Gladiator.

Just as I thought! Not merely elite, these were First Pride, the best of the best, guarding the most important people (well, aliens) of the Union of Miyelonian Prides. And based on their names, these were Leng Keetsie-Myau's personal guard.

"I'm not used to seeing First Pride without their famous white armor," I said with a smirk. Then immediately, while the jilted guards exchanged surprised glances, I added: "I'm here to see Leng Keetsie-Myau, she knows me."

The guards didn't reach for their weapons or show aggression. But four of the Miyelonians, seemingly unrelated to us, started moving slowly, getting behind me and Avan Toi as furtively as they could. A lean black cat, the only one whose name I couldn't read with scanning, walked forward and said:

"The great commander will not be receiving guests today. She is relaxing and celebrating her fleet's brilliant victory in the Spai Cloud with her most successful captains. Petitioners will only be admitted the day after tomorrow."

"Do I look like a petitioner to you???" I managed to add a bit of humor and unfeigned surprise. "It's generally the opposite. The strong of this world ask me for unusual favors: fetch something unique, perform a miracle, win a battle that's coming together poorly. And by the way, I am also a successful captain! My group and I are responsible for the deaths of more Meleyephatians than you've seen in your life!"

"Gerd Gnat, how could you possibly know how many Meleyephatians I've seen in my life?" the black cat snorted indignantly. Nevertheless, I could sense his opinion of me changing for the better.

Successful Fame check.

Successful Authority check.

"I've heard of you, Gerd Gnat. The great commander has mentioned your name. You may enter, but without a weapon and alone. I do not know your companion, so he cannot come inside."

I really didn't want to leave Avan Toi alone on the station. But this was not the kind of situation for arguing and flexing my privileges. As it was, I was being let into a private Miyelonian party with a very restricted guestlist. That was surprising enough on its own. I turned to my Supercargo and explained what I had just talked about with the guards. The sullen Geckho bared his teeth in understanding and rumbled, which for his race was a sign of good-hearted laughter:

"Don't you worry about me, captain! I'll either make it back just fine or respawn in the dock next to the frigate. One way or another I'll get back to the ship. I've had enough adventures for one day. My fame has already gone up two points, more than enough for a day's gaming."

I slapped the Supercargo approvingly on the shoulder and handed him my Paralyzer. However the guard then scanned me with a device that looked like a thick monocle and demanded I also surrender my knife. The knife? I had never had to use blades in the game, and Gnat had no melee weapon skills. Still I didn't argue. I had personally watched the inoffensive looking Fox gut Miyelonians and Geckho with a normal knife or even just her claws, so the bodyguard's fears were not unfounded. I gave Avan Toi the knife and bid farewell to my Supercargo, then passed through a forcefield that looked solid color from one side and entered Supernova Shine.

A smell of luscious and overpowering perfume mixed with intoxicating smoke crashed down on me all at once. My eyes were spinning from the flickering of the colored bulbs, loud Miyelonian music cut into my hearing, too layered and complex for the human ear. I couldn't even distinguish the several melodies and rhythms laid atop one another. I quickly came to my senses, got my bearings and looked around.

It was a huge room made for about five hundred visitors, and it was now approximately two-thirds full. But I couldn't see any tables. The Miyelonians were sitting cross-legged on thick mattresses and pillows, and many were just lying down on soft bedding with glasses in their clawed hands. And innumerable flying robot waiters were flitting around, pouring drinks into empty glasses. At the very farthest end of the room there was a towering mountain of cushions and pillows and, at the end of it sat the nearest favorites with a proud bearing. On the top then, the Great Commander was in repose:

Leng Keetsie-Myau. Miyelonian Female. Pride of the Sharp Claw. Level-257 Strategist.

Woah! Level two hundred fifty-seven! This little kitty could leave a mark. The commander was a big Miyelonian female with very soft-looking white fur like a Persian. It covered her whole body with the exception of a mask of black hair on her face and a few small spots on her ears and neck. It looked very contrasting, and the combination of colors was very eye-catching. I had already heard from Tini that Keetsie-Myau was considered not only a brilliant fleet commander but also a reference point for Miyelonian beauty standards. Okay then, now I understood why my ward was so pleased. From the human point of view as well, this was a very cute kitty.

So, how would I get up to her? There was a whole room of hundreds of Miyelonians celebrating the shared victory. What was more, I didn't want to just ask the Great One to stop her celebration to sign some documents authorizing my ship to leave the space station. That would look very brazen. This was not the time. Keetsie would just order her subjects to throw me out so I wouldn't spoil their party. No, I needed to try something a bit different!

To the surprised gazes of hundreds, I decisively headed for the bar.

"I'll have what the Great One is drinking! In fact, I'll take two!" I said to the bushy-tailed bartender and started reaching for my wallet, but was told that in honor of the big celebration, all drinks were on the house.

Okay then, all the better. As it turned out, Leng Keetsie-Myau was drinking a strong layered cocktail that smelled of valerian and mint. Taking the two tall narrow glasses, which looked more like burettes from a chemistry lab, I decisively headed across the whole room, walking over the Miyelonians on the floor and paying no more mind to their groans of dismay. That impudence allowed me to go unimpeded to the very foot of the mountain of pillows, where one of the beautiful commander's favorites jumped up quickly to stop me:

Gerd Lekku. Miyelonian. Pride of the Sharp Claw. Level-190 Brawler.

"Stop where you are, human! Answer quickly, why are you coming this way?"

All conversations in the room went silent. Hundreds of Miyelonians set down their glasses, leaned over and cocked an ear to hear my answer over the rumbling music. Even the commander stopped talking with one of her favorites and turned in my direction. I pointed to the drinks in my hands and spoke as naturally and peaceably as possible while remaining loud enough to be heard, at the same time using psionic abilities and generously splashing out Magic Points:

"Oh, Great One! In my race, there is an ancient tradition that one should celebrate important events and victories with the most beautiful female they can find. I looked around the room. There are many gorgeous Miyelonians here, but no one is equal to you Leng Keetsie-Myau. It would be your right to punish me for audacity and give an order to your minions to get rid of me, but it would have been disingenuous on my part to walk up to any woman here. Please don't refuse me this honor, please accompany Free Captain Gerd Gnat today!" with these words, I raised one of the two glasses, offering it to the commander of the Miyelonian fleet.

To say everyone lost their minds would be to say nothing. Everyone who heard me was in complete shock. For three seconds nothing happened, then the whole room started making a racket all at once. The favorites sitting nearby then, as if on command, jumped up simultaneously, demonstrating anger and even aggression. The Brawler even pulled a glimmering blade from his bosom (I wonder how the First Pride let him in with a weapon?) and placed it to my neck:

"Human, how dare you address Leng Keetsie-Myau without being addressed first?! And to say such insolent things! Our celebrated lady, mere moments from Kungdom, is also one of the most likely claimants to the vacant seat of the Krong of all Miyelonians! And you have the cheek to approach the Great One with such an absurd and insolent proposition!"

Danger Sense skill increased to level fifty-two!

Fame increased to 68.
Authority reduced to 53!
Authority reduced to 52!

I guess I made the wrong decision. Sure I could walk up to Keetsie and draw her attention, but her subordinates were not joking around. I was surely going to respawn now...

"Leave him, Lekku!" came a dense powerful voice from above, and it seemed completely unlike the delicate sonorous voices of Ayni and other Miyelonian females I had heard before. I didn't even realize right away it belonged to Leng Keetsie-Myau. "Can I really get mad at a guest for having the gall to speak the truth?" The Brawler instantly hid his blades and took a step back from me. "But what victory of yours would you like to celebrate in my company, Gerd Gnat?"

I could hear poorly hidden mockery at the very end of the commander's question. Like, could a person really achieve something big enough that the Great One would deem it worthy of her own celebration? I gave a slight smile and started naming my achievements. I was speaking quietly so the other Miyelonians couldn't make out my words over the loud music:

"Oh Great One, I will not bore you by listing all my achievements, I will just mention the most recent ones. I discovered a Relict outpost and was among the first to enter it. A group under my command took down the defenses on the planetoid Ursa II-II, which allowed the Geckho to capture the Meleyephatian base there.

In recognition of my service, Commander of the Geckho Second Strike Fleet Kung Waid Shishish even gifted me a frigate. I already managed to accumulate significant finances, weaponry and all the equipment to remodel and modify this ship and become a Free Captain. I have escaped a few squabbles with space pirates and caused them significant losses. I managed to survive and save my starship in an encounter in space with a superheavy-class ship of an unknown race and even determined the dangerous ship's route. Well and, beyond everything I listed above, I am the only player to have turned to the Listener class and one of the very few who has studied the ancient language of the Relicts. And lots of other minor things, which are not worthy of wasting the Great One's valuable time."

"Impressive!" the Miyelonian said when I'd finished my speech. "Very impressive in fact. Well Gerd Gnat, I accept your offer. And I also invite you to join me in celebration!"

The grandiose white cat, wearing nothing but a pair of miniature shorts, came down from the huge mound of pillows. With a careless gesture of her clawed paw, she sent her favorites back to their seats at the foot of the "throne," then accepted a long transparent glass of cocktail from my hand.

Chapter Seven

After the Ball

I WAS SO messed up... I couldn't tell what time it was, where I was, or even whether I was in the game or the real world. I knew only one thing: I felt very bad! My whole body hurt, every joint, every cell of my body was sending pain signals to my brain. It even felt like my hair hurt. My head was splitting, my thoughts were muddled, it took effort to think. In fact, it was unbelievably hard to crack an eye, because the light caused searing pain...

Successful Perception check.

And meanwhile next to me was — I could feel someone else breathing on my painfully sensitive skin. It took a couple tries, but I eventually managed to unstick my eyelids. There was something big, alive and furry next to me. And it was moving! I strained enormously, focused my gaze and finally saw. It was Uline Tar.

Eagle Eye skill increased to level seventy-two!

Seeing the system messages flickering past, I realized I was in the game! And to me at that moment, that thought seemed like the pinnacle of Intelligence. At the same, it dawned on me that I was sleeping in the same bed as an alien woman. That meant I was in the game and I could have realized without any system messages. Just a bit later, I looked at the mini-map and saw my health bar down in the red zone, and my endurance and mana approaching zero. Real smart guy I was! I kept finding more and more evidence I was in the game, but I was so used to it all none of it gave me pause. Damn! It really was scary to start to perceive a virtual game as my main world. From here, it really wasn't a long trip to the nuthouse...

I gathered my will into a fist, opened an eye wider and tried to look around. Where was I? It seemed like a familiar place. Oh yeah, this was my captain's quarters! But why was I here, and wearing only my underwear? Where was my Listener armor??? I got so worried my heart just about jumped out of my chest, but I quickly discovered my things in my inventory. When and how did I get to sleep? I didn't remember... The last thing peeking up from my glitchy memory was that I was at a noisy party with lots of Miyelonians having fun around me. I felt good. I was drinking. I had lots of different drinks and no food at all. I seemed to even remember dancing, but that memory was very foggy indeed. I even remembered smoking something, although in the real world I'd never even tried the very mildest electronic cigarette...

"How... did I get here?" my throat was dry, it was hard to speak, but my business partner heard and leaned in.

"Gerd Gnat, the repair bots brought you here. All three Kirsans suddenly dashed away to the station, then dragged your senseless body back here. One of them, the white one, explained through the universal translator that the captain summoned them to come pick him up."

"Please Uline, please be quieter! My head is just humming..."

The trader heeded my request and started speaking in what she deemed to be a whisper, although all the same the words of the huge furry woman sounded like an alarm bell:

"I got you undressed and put you to sleep, because you were in no state to handle your armor and were complaining that there were too many messages going by and you couldn't read them fast enough."

"Thanks, Uline," I whispered and closed my eyes. The light was still searing.

"Oh its nothing..." my huge furry friend called back. Sitting on a fold-out table, she gave a sad chuckle: "The Geckho say someone 'drank with Miyelonians' to mean they're looking weak and beat-up. The phrase is usually used figuratively, but in your case it is quite literal. Didn't you know, human, that Miyelonians have a different metabolism? Alcohol has a lower effect on them and doesn't last long. You need Constitution twenty-five at least to drink with

Miyelonians if not thirty!"

I let her lessons go in one ear and out the other. I was trying to think. So the repair bots hauled me back to the ship. Most likely I summoned them, even though I now didn't have even a near appreciation of how I did it, especially at such a distance. The metal Mechanics accepted the order and, from the Kirsans' viewpoint, my body really did need repair because it was totally nonfunctioning. I tried to picture the three metal millipedes dragging a piss-drunk Listener through the whole space station and felt ill. Thousands of Miyelonians would have seen that. How embarrassing! Seemingly I said that out loud because the Geckho woman added:

"Yes, many saw you. It was even on the local news. And four soldiers of the elite First Pride escorted you to keep you safe," Uline seemingly decided to try and get to me with bad news.

The First Pride escorted me? Only the fleet commander could order her personal guard to do something like that. So that meant Keetsie-Myau had seen me in that unresponsive state. Wait! Keetsie-Myau. Permission to leave. Horror gripped me again. Had I even managed to ask the Great One the very question that made me seek a meeting with the influential Miyelonian in the first place? My heart aflutter, I asked my business partner.

"Yes, Gerd Gnat. You were given permission to leave the station. The frigate is ready for takeoff right now. Dmmmitry is in the pilot's seat ready to go. We're just waiting for some courier who is supposed to pick up a special delivery for Leng Keetsie."

"What?" I was still thinking groggily and missing the obvious.

"That crystal you dragged to the ship and which Ayukh is now guarding. Our Navigator, by the way, did manage to copy the data to our on-board computer. And now, panting in delight, he is immersed in studying the map. In his words, such a complete and detailed map of the known galaxy is a real treasure!"

Uline fell silent and spent a long time staring attentively at me. Then she asked compassionately:

"Gnat, you don't look so hot. Should we call the Medic?"

"Medic?" in my surprise I even unstuck an eye.

"There's a lean Miyelonian sitting alone on his bags right next to the ship. I don't understand Miyelonian, so Ayni Translator has been talking to him. The Medic told her that you invited him. But Eduwward won't let him on the starship without your confirmation. There's also a Jarg sitting at the gangway waiting for you. Gerd Ayni also talked to him, and she just happens to speak Jarg."

Jarg? I had only met one Jarg before in my life: the level-52 Analyst with an unpronounceable name. She must have been talking about him. No, I didn't want to see the Jarg yet. I just didn't want to explain why such a valuable package hadn't yet reached its destination and had now been opened and ruined. But I did ask for the Medic.

Gerd Mauu-La Mya-Ssa appeared in my cabin a few minutes later, pushing a huge levitating suitcase which resembled a coffin in shape and size. I hoped he was wrong and my condition wasn't hopeless. Meanwhile the orange doctor anchored the flying coffin in my bunk and, opening one of the sides, pulled out a whole bunch of wires twisted into a spiral and ending in suction cup contacts. Not saying a word, the Miyelonian gracefully stuck them to my temples, forehead and neck then picked up a remote and quickly typed a command.

A light buzz rang out in my head. It was somewhat unpleasant but, in comparison with the ghastly hangover, almost unnoticeable. In four seconds the Medic made a diagnosis:

"Severe alcohol intoxication complicated by general exhaustion and allergies to several components of a recently-consumed psychotropic of plant origin."

Gerd Mauu-La Mya-Ssa wrapped a bracelet on my wrist, clearly to measure my blood pressure and pulse all the while telling me off in strong terms:

"Gerd Gnat, are you not aware that the purple and green sticks you smoked are fatal to fully eleven different space races? To a human, as I'm seeing now, they are not deadly but still extremely toxic. I suspect that a serious debuff to Hitpoints and Endurance will be unavoidable for the next several days. You can see the precise numbers in your character information page. I can mitigate the effect but not completely eliminate it."

I didn't understand what he was talking about right away, what tab of the game menu to open and what exactly to look at. But unfortunately, Gerd Mauu-

La Mya-Ssa was right:

Narcotic intoxication!!!

Maximum number of Hitpoints reduced by 63%.

Maximum number of Endurance Points reduced by 70%.

Maximum number of Magic Points increased by 240%.

Regeneration speed for Hitpoints and Endurance Points reduced by 90%.

Regeneration speed for Magic Points increased by 67%.

Constitution reduced by 4 points.

Agility reduced by 3 points.

Duration: 76 hours 11 minutes 18 seconds.

Woah... I had three days of weakness ahead of me... That was some very unpleasant news, especially considering that I would have to join the fight in nine or ten hours and provide firing points from orbit. Might it be easier to kill myself and respawn in fifteen minutes with full health? But my progress bar to level seventy-seven was already more than ninety percent full. I really didn't want to die and lose that progress.

Meanwhile the Medic was checking his palmtop, probably reading about human anatomy. He opened his flying coffin and took out a pneumatic syringe. Professionally and painlessly, he gave me three shots in a vein on my left arm, a neck artery and my right shoulder. A few seconds later, the headache was gone, my health bar was slowly climbing up and I got the feeling that life was gonna be just fine. There was no need to kill myself! Nevertheless, Gerd Mauu-La asked me to lie down for a bit:

"You might experience slight disorientation, and abrupt movements will cause discomfort. But in just a quarter ummi, the sensations will be tolerable," the Miyelonian promised as he stashed tools in his levitating case, then asked me where to find his bunk.

I called Uline Tar in from the hallway and asked her to register the Medic with our crew. Thankfully she was already there to keep watch over my treatment. Only after that I made up my mind and asked the Medic if he deserted from the army. After all, an ummi and a half ago he was an official soldier! The orange Miyelonian grew sincerely offended and, his fur puffed out, removed a silver chain with a plastic card from his neck:

"Here are my documents, go ahead and check! By order from command, I was transferred from active service to the reserves. My status now is 'civilian.'"

Apologizing for the mistrust, I sent the new Medic after Uline to officially sign up on my frigate. At the same time, I called Gerd Ayni to help them understand each other.

When Uline had gone, I put on my Listener Energy Armor. I was thankfully feeling much better and, in the game, fully suiting up took only a few seconds of simply dragging the items into the proper slots. I didn't even have to get out of bed.

No, I was not going to break doctor's orders and skip my prescribed bedrest. But I did want to get to the bottom of what Uline said about me having problems with the Relict armor and saying I couldn't read the messages. What messages? And why so many all of a sudden? My armor was showing various words and messages on the inside of the helmet. They were the kind that normally referred to stat changes, but those were quite rare and the suit never just spammed me without good reason.

So I'd have to spin back through all the messages from before, which thankfully were saved. Around an ummi and a half ago. Right from here, right after the battle with the three Miyelonians. What happened next?

A few Authority drops. That was easy to understand. I started talking with Keetsie, which her subjects didn't like. Another drop in Authority, but a boost to Fame. And another Authority drop, this time by three points. What was this?! What caused it that time? Although... I had a vague memory of a sharp fall when I grabbed the Great One by her wrist and pulled her to the dancefloor, where quite a few Miyelonian couples were already spinning around. Leng Keetsie was clearly upset by that and, to my eye, even wanted to escape at first. But then she made up her mind, grinned happily and came with me. My Fame grew by two whole points! Nevertheless! My Psionic and Mysticism went up by one each, and Mental Fortitude by a whole three. Clearly, I had been using magic or mentally communicating. My Authority went up, finally! I also got a boost to Astrolinguistics. I guess I'd learned many new phrases and choice expressions. And seemingly the Great One found out the package had been opened and ruined...

That moment unexpectedly flickered up in my memory. I was holding my dance partner in an embrace and was extremely concentrated, trying to catch the rhythm and watching the other dancing couples. I can say with no false modesty, that I didn't do such a bad job either. Keetsie then, wholeheartedly giving herself to the music and dance, was clearly enjoying the moment. But the Great One, not at all hiding the fact that she was a strong psionic and Truth Seeker spoke her mind mentally:

"...sure, the star map is important too, but it's just a small part of the valuable information. The most important stuff was kept in other sections and files. Blueprints for Meleyephatian ships and new secret weapons, logistics schemes, military plans, commander lists and their real-life identities, reserves of strategic materials and production outputs... And lots of other stuff. Let me tell you a secret, this war only got started after we got the chance to get this invaluable information from our deeply embedded agent! Who could have thought handing it to us would turn out this way? Do you have any idea, Gerd Gnat, that this was the largest failure of Miyelonian intelligence in... I'm having a hard time even saying how many tongs! It might be that there has never been something like this in the whole history of my race!"

I remembered being shocked by that and tried to awkwardly justify myself, which made my dance partner start reassuring me:

"No, no Gerd Gnat. You're least of all to blame for what happened. You were chosen precisely because we *knew you'd open the package. The middleman chose that delivery method and courier with good reason. He clearly wanted the data to be lost. If you see that Jarg, kill him! That is my order! And actually..."* here Leng Keetsie sharply changed topic and squeezed tight up against me, even placing her big-eared head on my shoulder. After that a wave of messages came in about my Authority falling, *"I'm very glad you pulled me out here for a dance!"*

I couldn't exactly understand what was making the Miyelonian so happy, but Leng Keetsie-Myau easily read that question in my thoughts and answered it:

"You can't even imagine, human, how mad my favorites are right now! They're ready to eat you alive, but wouldn't dare touch you with even a claw without my permission. Let this be a lesson to them! Their depressive milieu has needed stirring up for a while now. Just imagine, I have twenty admirers in my inner circle and around fifty in the second. They're always engaging in intrigue and fights with other pretenders, trying to earn maybe not even my good favor, they're all quite far from that, but at least my attention. And here comes a person from outside and immediately gets closer to me than they even dream of! I am grateful to you! You deserve a reward for your bravery. Let me guess... Hee hee hee. Don't think so frankly, although its nice to know you like me. All your problems in your distant homeworld. Don't worry so much! Of course I'll allow your ship to leave right after one of my favorites comes to get that star map. Okay, I know what you really want! In half a tong, when your home planet is no

longer untouchable, your people don't have to worry about an invasion from the Miyelonian fleet! I promise you that as its commander!"

Now there was a reward! I wasn't even dreaming of that! Instantly, I was in seventh heaven! Humanity in my person had managed to secure a guarantee of untouchability for Earth from one of the most influential and powerful space races in this part of the galaxy! Here the dance ended and I went after Keetsie for another cocktail. And that is what they call misjudging your own strength. "A workplace accident," to quote a very famous movie...[1]

After that came many messages about failed Constitution checks, which wasn't exactly surprising. Then a successful Perception check and the Machine Control skill went up. Clearly, I managed to come to my senses for a brief instant and called a "ride home." Then my Fame went up again. That must have been while was being carried through the station. That was all clear, but as for the further messages... here I sharply shot up, because there was a big chunk of text:

Listener! In the most recent period, your share of data transmitted to the Pyramid was 42.17% An

---

[1] Translator's note: A line from classic Soviet comedy film *Kidnapping Caucasian Style*. The main character, an ethnography student, has come to the Caucasus to study their local toasting tradition. Unfortunately for him, the locals refuse to tell him their toasts, unless he follows their custom and drinks after each one. When he later causes a scene at a public event, the police conclude that it was not a criminal act but a "workplace accident," because his drinking was in pursuit of a professional endeavor.

unbelievable result! The Relict hierarchs are proud of you! From this point forward, your Energy Armor may accept level-2 modifications. You have unlocked the back slot for additional accessories and an additional drone slot.

Searching for available units...
Searching for available units...

...

Searching for available units...

The message was repeated three hundred times. I even got a bit peeved, swiping through screens of identical text. And as I did, I was trying to figure out where the Pyramid was getting the other 57.83% data. Were there still Relicts in the game? No Listeners, given the game told me I was unique, but what about other classes? Or was the data coming from ancient satellites and autonomous drones, drifting through very deep space? Or perhaps the most recent period had lasted one thousand years and the others were already long dead. I had no answers. But then came a final message after the laundry list of identical messages. And it really threw me for a loop:

Listener! We're very sorry, but no available drones were found in the nearest part of the galaxy. We recommend you get by with those you already have or order the Pyramid to send a new one.

Ugh, too bad Uline, the Geckho brothers and I had destroyed all the Small Guard Drones at the Relict outpost. I could easily have had one right now. But who knew back then that they were so rare?! In any case, I was not very upset. In fact, it was really cool! Now I could improve my armor! But I didn't have time to get happy before reading the next message, and my happiness blew away like the wind:

Equipment diagnostics underway...

Attention! Unsanctioned modifications detected. The Pyramid has been informed of your serious infraction. Listener, the hierarchs are wise and just. They shall determine your punishment.

My heart seized up. "Unsanctioned modifications" clearly meant cutting off the back part of the spacesuit, which was meant for a tail (or an abdomen, who knew with these Relicts) and the extra pairs of upper appendages. Ugh, what would happen now... Was my Energy Armor, a well-earned source of pride, and a great suit for either the vacuum of space or corrosive environments going to be somehow limited in function or even just disactivated?

Attempting to establish connection... Error!

Attempting to establish connection... Error!

...

Attempting to establish connection... Error!

I don't even know how many times the message was repeated. A few hundred at least, maybe even a few thousand. I didn't look at them all and immediately jumped to the end.

...

Attempting to establish connection... Error!

Listener, in case of military action, all public communication channels will be blocked. As such, the most probable reason the Pyramid is unreachable is WAR! Given the extraordinary situation, we recommend using an emergency channel to contact the Pyramid. (Yes/No).

...

Decision time expired.

Pyramid connection session ended. Message transmission canceled.

And was that all? Did I just get lucky and the message about the amateur refit of the Listener Energy Armor had not been sent anywhere? I ran through all possible settings of my overly self-sufficient spacesuit. The armor was working as usual. I detected no switched off elements or limitations. In fact, a new tab had appeared: "accessories," and my back oxygen tank had become removeable. Clearly it could be modernized or somehow replaced.

Electronics skill increased to level seventy-one!

Machine Control skill increased to level seventy-one!

No, I didn't detach the tank yet, I was in no position to do so now. For now, I figured it was good enough that everything worked out just fine and my armor was still in working order. Further experimenting with the ancient artifact had to stop, because Gerd Ayni appeared in my doorway:

"Gerd Gnat, a messenger has come to our hangar from the commander. He's demanding to be seen, he wants to speak with the captain. Shall we let him on board?"

"Yes, Ayni. Bring him to the lounge, I'll bring his package there right away."

I was slightly shaky and my weakness palpable. Nevertheless I managed to reach the bridge where Ayukh handed me the opened black stone with a rat's nest of wires. The Navigator was just glowing with desire to share his joy about the new map, bursting to show me our new capabilities and interesting discoveries. But I asked him to wait a minute.

Moving my disobedient legs unconfidently, I entered the largest room on the frigate, which still served as a lounge deck. It was quite crowded. The brothers Vasha and Basha, as always in their free time, were gambling on the three-dimensional board game Na-Tikh-U. Gloomy Avan Toi was lying next to them on a cushion, watching the twins play as he proudly showed everyone the trophy stuck to his helmet. Tini the kitten was talking with Imran and Orun Va-Mart was joining in, although I couldn't imagine what language they were speaking. In the opposite corner, Minn-O La-Fin was whispering something with Valeri and, when I came in, both girls gave a titter of laughter. I guessed they were making fun of me.

However, the Dark Faction princess quickly turned serious, walked up to me and said that General Ui-Taka refused to speak to her face to face. He just sent a message to her communicator saying: "Offer does not stand. In ten days your husband will only be able to negotiate for what position in my faction he can trade his space frigate for." Of course, that was about the answer I was expecting, so I wasn't mad at all and reassured my wife that everything was fine, and as it should be.

But there was good reason to think. Minn-O told him the frigate would be ready in a different timeframe: six days. I had given the ten-day timeframe only once: at the meeting of directors and high-status players under the Dome. The circle of those I suspected of spying for the Dark Faction seriously constricted.

Here I had to stop thinking because Ayni had brought a dangerous guest into our common room: a level-190 Brawler armed to the teeth and wearing combat armor.

But I knew this messenger. Gerd Lekku was the one who threatened me with a weapon during the party, putting a blade to my throat. However, I harbored no ill will towards him, because I knew perfectly that he was just putting on an act for his master. I handed the messenger the valuable package and recommended he treat it as carefully as possible, because the explosives inside were enough to blow up an apartment block. Gerd Lekku put the dangerous cargo in his inventory after which he suddenly drew his blades, which sparkled with energy:

"Gerd Gnat, you offended my master, the great Leng Keetsie-Myau when you spoke to her unaddressed! And when you touched the Great One. And when you dared to dance the Dance of Awoken Love with her. That ritual dance is only performed one time in life by a couple after they fall in love. Twelve formidable warriors of the Miyelonian race have been waiting for that honor for a long time, guessing who the Great One might choose. And you ruined it all! There is no forgiving you! I challenge you to a duel! Ah-sahntee maye-uu-u rezsh shashash-u!"

Chapter Eight

Going Home!

A DUEL? That wasn't even funny. He was a melee character specialized in duels at level-190 going against a level-76 player with shivering arms who was so weak he could barely stand. A duel between us? For such a contrived reason? To hell with this Brawler! Trying to speak evenly, without raising my voice, and praying that my dangerous guest didn't know Geckho, I said:

"Vasha, Basha, please escort that ruffian out of here! And hold him tight! Then bop him on the head a few times so he doesn't escape. It won't make things worse. Okay, okay, enough! That's enough! You don't need to give him a flat-face like a Persian. Imran, take our guest's blades so he doesn't accidentally cut himself!"

Gerd Lekku brayed, trying to escape and shouted that it was not done this way! He said that he challenged me to a duel, so I had to treat him a certain way. But I paid his whooping no mind. The powerful twin brothers were holding the hysterically flailing Miyelonian tight and weren't thinking of letting go, especially given they didn't understand his cries. The Miyelonian Gerd Ayni was watching that scene with her eyes wide in horror, and Tini and Orun Va-Mart were also pressing their ears back in fear. Clearly I really had broken the rules. But that didn't stop me:

"Tini, hand me that tattoo machine you just got!"

The kitten hurriedly handed me a small gun and even showed me how to turn it on, how to make it do one of the many ready-made patterns and how to change the color of the ink. I played with the settings and found a portrait of Leng Keetsie-Myau among the patterns. In theory, I could make this drawing right through the fur, but I didn't want to:

"Imran! I know you have a shaver. Tini steals it sometimes then puts it back to train his thief skills. Give it to me please!"

The Dagestani silently went into his bunk and quickly returned, extending me the electric battery powered shaver. I shaved a large section of fur on the Miyelonian's right thigh. Then I skeptically looked at my quaking hands and called my travelling wife over:

"Minn-O, you're a princess, right? I don't know how it is in your world, but in mine Princesses are all forced to learn to draw from a young age whether they like it or not. Were you as well?"

"My husband, you are not wrong. In that way our worlds really are similar. Those drawing classes are one of my most hated childhood memories. But in the end, my tutors were able to teach me something..." Minn-O La-Fin walked up and took the tattoo machine in her hands.

The captive Gerd, when he finally realized what I was going to do to him, started howling obnoxiously and trying to escape again.

"Don't move! Keetsie will never forgive you if her portrait turns out lopsided!"

That did the trick! Gerd Lekku froze motionless, went silent and bore it all skeptically while Minn-O quickly and professionally, as if she'd been doing this all her life, made a complicated multicolored drawing on the Miyelonian's skin. At the same time, I stood next to her and calmed the prisoner, explaining the obvious:

"Ah Lekku, you have no idea how lucky you are! Look, there are twelve of you in the first circle of favorites and another fifty in the second. To Keetsie you're all identically flawless and boring. There's no basis to choose, she told that to me herself while we danced. I'll give you the chance to stand out from this whole sad milieu. Yes, precisely! I'll guarantee that Keetsie remembers you! Gerd Lekku, you're going to be thanking me! Okay then, there you go. See look how pretty! I don't know if the tattoo will stay after death and respawn, but in your place, I would get it done again. Okay, let him go! Imran, give our guest his weapon back!"

It was a very tense moment. There was a serious risk that, after setting Gerd Lekku free, he would flare up and even break out his blades. In any case, I was prepared to mentally stun him. I had very little mana, it hadn't yet come back after the poisoning, but Valeri-Urla answered a mental call, saying she would help me. And the Tailaxian had gotten up off her cushion with both hands grasping the stone amulet around her neck. Seemingly it was what gave Valeri strength and confidence.

But the Miyelonian's reaction was unexpected. He took the blade in his right hand, cut a couple glimmering figure eights in the air and... with a sharp swipe, cut off his own fluffy dark-gray tail!

"Gerd Gnat, you had no reason to fear me. I would never attack someone weakened by illness, because there is no honor in such a victory. I just wanted to scare you and express my jealousy over the fact that you lapped me and the Great One's other favorites. But... nothing went the way I was hoping. I definitely wasn't expecting to be treated like that! At first I wanted to clobber everyone here on the ship, but then I changed my mind and decided you're right! Please, take my tail as a trophy. You've earned it! Let everyone see that you beat me and consider me a worthy opponent. Rumors to that effect will quickly reach the Great One. She will want to interrogate me, then she'll see how proudly I wear her face on my body. You're completely right Gerd Gnat, Keetsie had no real choice because all her favorites are ideal warriors who have never known defeat. We even have similar stats, skills and appearances. But now, no matter how this whole story ends, I will be different from the others and the Great One will remember me! Thank you!"

I bowed to the dangerous high-level player and extended a hand in reconciliation. The Miyelonian froze in surprise. That gesture was unknown to his race. But Ayni the translator explained the significance of my act, and Gerd Lekku cautiously touched my hand with his claws.

Authority increased to 49!

The bloody tail stump was probably hurting the Miyelonian, but he didn't show it in any way and even refused assistance from the Medic. As soon as the Brawler left the frigate with his head held high, the delighted voice of Dmitry Zheltov rolled down the halls of the starship:

"Our hangar's energy shield is down, we have been given permission to leave the station! Let's get going home!!!"

"Wait, I need another couple minutes!" I remembered that the Jarg was waiting patiently to meet with me and I wanted to finish that up before leaving, especially now that I'd received unambiguous advice or maybe even an order to kill the tricky messenger. "Minn-O, give me your laser pistol for a sec! No, no. I don't need any help. I'll handle it myself!"

I went down the stairs to the first deck and hurried to the main airlock. At the exit from the ship, Eduard Boyko was standing watch. He assured me in a whisper that my orders for the darksiders' shipment had been carried out. Great! I told the Space Commando to head to his bunk and get ready for takeoff then ran off the gangway and, looking around, discovered the many-eyed eight-armed "armadillo" sitting patiently against the wall and headed toward it. I had no weapon in my hands, but the level-54 Analyst somehow guessed my intentions and, hanging the universal translator around his neck, quickly burbled out:

"Good one. Deal is complete. Keetsie is receive. Tell to kill Jarg."

Okay then, if it had already worked out the mission the Miyelonian commander gave me, all the better. No longer hiding anything, I took out my laser pistol and, setting shot power to maximum, pressed the weapon to the Jarg's head. The alien Analyst didn't try to run or defend himself. But it did ask a question that totally baffled me:

"To speak with Keetsie. How many times must to kill Jarg?"

How many times? What kind of weird question was this? Just one time, which I honestly told the huge armored toad. The Jarg quickly lit up and burbled again:

"One fast. No shot. I to explode. Person to wait not long. Not to fly away. Then to take Jarg. Space. Flight. Crew."

What??? No, the beginning was easy to understand: this alien Analyst was assuring me that there was no need to shoot because he would just blow himself up to soothe the Great One's anger. That was just fine by me, because I really didn't want to be executioner and kill an unarmed creature. But from there the Jarg was suggesting that I not fly off and patiently await its respawn, then take him with me on the starship as a full crew member. Was he all there? Why would I want him on the frigate?

"Tell me even one reason to wait for you, and even more to take you with me," I demanded, having absolutely no idea what he could possibly offer to make me change my mind and agree to take this slippery freak on my ship.

In reply, the Jarg took a polished black stone out of his inventory, held it in his four upper sucker-hands and showed it to me. This was an exact copy of the one I was holding before. That's what I'm talking about! I quickly ran a scan on it and saw that the Jarg was not holding some mere replica, and the filling in this case was exactly the same as the one in the previous stone: a big crystal drive surrounded by wires and fused into some explosive.

Scanning skill increased to level forty-one!

"Now to know you. The true value. Information. Deal. To bring Geckho. Big commander. Waid Shishish. Help to Geckho star-war. My reward. Jarg member crew. Analyst. Lots to analyze. Benefit."

I lowered my pistol. Seemingly I had started to understand what was happening. The deeply embedded agent of the Miyelonians may have been a Jarg by race, though that was nowhere near guaranteed, and had gotten some very important information about the Meleyephatian horde. That information was of such critical importance that Miyelonians had even started a big space war so that, in the chaos, their agent would have the chance to send the crystal drive to its destination. But the package was entrusted to this Jarg messenger at some stage of the operation, who had ruined everything and decided to stage the "accidental" loss of the data by having a human named Gnat open it recklessly. Yes, the Analyst had analyzed everything correctly, considering my character and abilities, and got what he was after. However, as it was now turning out, he had a duplicate of the valuable object and was planning on sending the second one to the Geckho.

"But why the Geckho? Why not the Miyelonians?" I asked.

"No starships. Jargs have. People is just one. Suzerains protect. Geckho reinforcement. Very need. Shared goals. Otherwise destruction. By Meleyephatians. Or Miyelonians. No difference."

"Yes, you're right. We do have common goals, and both of our races need to make the Geckho stronger as they are our protectors. But do you realize how mad Leng Keetsie-Myau will get when she finds out the valuable cargo escaped and slipped out of her greedy hands?"

"Keetsie not to know. Jarg not to say. Gnat not suicidal. Miyelonians crew not to speak."

I gave a nervous chuckle. Precisely because I was not suicidal, I would not try to hide such vital information from an all-powerful Truth Seeker. And honestly, I had plenty of Miyelonians on my ship who would give me up to their vaunted commander in a second if they knew about this package. Basically, we'd play it by ear. Now, as the Jarg correctly said, we had common goals. I put the pistol in my inventory.

"Alright, have it your way. But there is no time to wait for you to commit suicide and respawn. My faction is desperately awaiting me and my frigate. Every moment's delay comes at too great a cost to my friends. Maybe you could just blow up in one of the empty bunks on the starship, then respawn on the ship?"

"Respawn point on starship. Dangerous. Must to think."

Ah yes, I had already forgotten. A foolish suggestion. Setting one's respawn point on a starship was a deadly endeavor because if the ship crashed in open space, the character and the player in the real world might die once and for all. But I didn't have time to tell the Jarg I'd changed my mind and would retract my demand before I read a successful Authority check message. After that the Jarg started burbling again, puffing out his cheek sacs:

"Agreement. To give stone after. Crew. Landing. Green zone."

After that, the black stone and universal translator put away, the many-eyed armadillo went down on all eight arms and legs and, taking short quick hops, dashed to the frigate gangway. How about that! The strange creature agreed to take a risk and move his respawn point to the ship! Clearly, he couldn't wait to get off such an unwelcoming station and saw no better way.

The Jarg promised to give me the invaluable cargo as soon as I added him to my team and brought him to a safe zone where he could change his res point.

Sure, a reasonable measure of precaution. I understood the Jarg completely and agreed to his conditions. Now I had nothing to keep me on Kasti-Utsh III and wanted to get to my star frigate, but sharply stopped. The final touch. I opened the drone control tab and summoned the Small Relict Guard Drone. I told it to fly to me and got the customary warning that this order had a high probability of error. Yes, yes, I knew. I wasn't actually going to have the drone embark on a long deadly flight. I was looking for one particular line:

Estimated time in flight: 344,802 years, 87 days, 6 hours, 58 minutes.

Much longer than the previous two. That meant I was farther away from the secret base now. I jotted down the new number, hurried back to the ship and managed to extinguish a flare up of conflict. This time Imran wasn't letting the "toad" in and threatening the explosion risk, pointing his sharp blades at the Jarg.

"Let him through Imran. He's with us! He's joining our crew! Uline Tar hire on this Analyst... Look at you, level-57 already... and issue the requisite documents. After that come to my quarters. I want to have a talk with you alone about improving our finances."

I HADN'T LEFT the game in quite some time! The last time was more than two days ago to attend a meeting of high-profile faction players and before that... I couldn't even remember right away. It was so long ago and so many different events had happened since then. I threw back the top of the virt pod and spent some time lying down and getting used to the half-forgotten sensations of my real body. The lack of a mini-map before my eyes or bars for life, hunger and exhaustion was scary at first. But anyhow I quickly came to and sat up, expecting Imran. My Dagestani friend insisted he accompany me "just in case."

I didn't argue, because some of my Human-3 Faction allies still treated me cautiously and even negatively. There had been unfortunate events before even during peace time. But now, with a war on, taking a key faction member out of play would help the Dark Faction greatly. I stood up, walked over to the glass and looked at the Dome from way up on the fourteenth floor.

"It's noon and I almost can't see anyone," Imran said as he appeared in the doorway, reacting to the unnatural quiet and emptiness under the Dome.

"Well, there's a war on. Everyone who can hold a weapon is in the game. The only time people come under the Dome is while waiting to respawn and now some commanders have been sent to rest after two and a half days of harsh battles."

We went down the spiral staircase and headed down the deserted park paths right to the administration building. Now I wanted to see Alexander Antipov. I had to tell the intelligence director that the Dark Faction knew timeframes I'd only given at our recent meeting of key players.

Fortunately, I managed to catch the fed in his office. But he wasn't alone today. He was talking with faction leader Ivan Lozovsky. What a surprise! As far as I'd heard from Imran, practically no one had seen our supreme leader for the last two days. I guess they eventually did find him. At the very least in the real world. They both turned their extremely unhappy faces toward me simultaneously. They must have been discussing secret business and this was no place for outsiders. I stopped at the threshold.

"Gnat?" the fed really seemed surprised. "What a rare treat! You have hardly been seen under the Dome at all recently. Come in, don't be ashamed. Did you have something to tell us?"

Leaving my escort in the hallway, I walked inside and closed the door behind. I immediately noticed that both directors looked gloomy and exhausted. Seemingly they had both only gotten winks of sleep in the last three days.

"I need a list of priority targets to destroy from orbit! Preferably with coordinates if they are stationary!" I blurted out, not wanting to discuss the spy in our ranks around one of the suspects.

Both directors exchanged glances, then Ivan Lozovsky asked when I would need that information.

"The Tolili-Ukh X frigate will come out of warp near earth in eight hours. We'll need another half hour or so to smooth over formalities with the Geckho and get into geostationary orbit."

"Good news has been so rare recently that it's

twice as nice to hear!" The faction leader lit up. "Yes, Kirill. You can have all that. But please stick to the plan this time. It might end very badly for all of us if you don't. I remind you that we still have an agreement with the Dark Faction not to bombard the main forts that are used to establish claim over nodes. Even this flare up of war has not cancelled that agreement, a fact which Geckho Diplomat Kosta Dykhsh has explicitly reminded us."

"To be sure... We caught hell as soon as our howitzers in the Yellow Mountains landed a volley on the citadel of the enemy Graveyard!" the fed added with a sad smirk. "We didn't do much damage to the very recently restored fortress, but now our coffers are empty and the list of goods we have to give our suzerains as compensation is a few pages long in small font..."

"And we have to gather and give up the resources on their list. Otherwise the Geckho, as guarantors of the agreement, will declare war on our faction with all the accompanying consequences..."

It was clear that Ivan Lozovsky was seriously upset. I then held back an acrid question with great effort. Still, I wanted to know how our faction Diplomat, whose job it was to remember such things, had allowed us to violate the agreement! But I kept silent. Given the tough war, it was not the right time to start a fight with leadership and accuse our main commander of incompetence. What was more, their faces were black with exhaustion, so I could see they hadn't been having a great last few days.

Nevertheless, despite the agitation and exhaustion, Antipov didn't forget the standards of hospitality and offered me coffee or something stronger. I was categorically opposed to alcohol. I hadn't yet recovered from that Miyelonian party, so in the real world the mere thought of liquor made me want to ralph. But coffee was just the thing for me, which I said. Alexander Antipov pressed the intercom button and asked someone named Anyuta to bring three coffees.

"Two coffees, I'm fine," Lozovsky quickly corrected the fed and added: "My respawn time is almost up. I need to get right back into the game. I'm afraid if I don't show up the Chinese won't know what to do."

"The Chinese?" I asked in surprise. Alexander Antipov commented with a smirk:

"Yes, our director surprised us all! He took off in a hurry and no one knew where he went. He didn't say a word. But two days later, the Dark Faction got attacked from behind by a squadron of five hundred Human-1 soldiers. The Chinese overran the few border guards and destroyed a few of the enemy's new northerly nodes. But most importantly they distracted them. And that gave our soldiers room to breathe and regroup. And we were able to go on the counterattack on the southern front! The Second Legion finally suppressed the enemy in the Rainforest and now they're tracking the darksiders through the Tropics. What is happening?! Is Anyuta asleep or something...?"

The fed again pressed the intercom button and

repeated his order for coffee. Not waiting for his secretary's answer, he slapped himself on the forehead in annoyance:

"I totally forgot! There's an active CtA. Anyuta's in the game. Okay, I'll make the coffee," the fed stood up heavily with a slap on the table and headed for the door.

"Anyuta is a pretty good targeter, by the way," Ivan Lozovsky shouted after him while Antipov was still nearby. "In many ways its thanks to her and our other artillery targeters that our 152-mm howitzers from the Yellow Mountains turned an enemy landing party into dust on Antique Beach. And the fact that the enemy retreated from the Rainforest before they could reinforce was also largely thanks to good targeting."

"So the Rainforest node has been liberated?" I asked, because this was very unexpected and pleasant news.

"The node is neutral for now," the faction leader corrected me strictly. "The enemy destroyed our claim in the first few minutes of attack, but we didn't let them fortify despite their attempts to build a base in the Rainforest. The Dark Faction lost one antigrav assault vehicle there, and we totaled another two tanks, which they extracted by sea for repair. But the main thing is that they took heavy losses, especially when our artillery started raining down thermobaric rounds on their base every fifteen minutes right where they respawned. In the end the enemy gave up and retreated further south, where our artillery can't hit them."

Ivan Lozovsky went silent and turned. He made

sure Antipov was gone, leaned in to me and, his voice lowered to a whisper, said:

"We have an incident of a totally different nature on our hands here. This is the definition of a problem coming from where we least expected. Our shared acquaintance Anna the Medic has fled the Dome!"

"How did she do that?" I couldn't believe my ears. The news was just so shocking.

"I'll tell you how. Four days ago I helped her write out a pass for leave. Her brother was getting married and, of course, we let her have a day off for that. Plus everything was going well for Anna. She was happy with things and I couldn't even see even a hint of what she was about to do. But yesterday when I was gone, she walked up to security with a signed pass. There it is on the table, take a look!" the faction head pointed to a small colored cardstock rectangle.

I picked up the thick official form. Number, date, signature. There was also a stamp and exit time written in ballpoint pen.

"The form is real. They can be obtained from the guard post. Yesterday's date is written there, but the signature is not mine! It's a very good fake, maybe Anna did it herself. The security workers were surprised. The CtA meant all players should be at their posts, but they still let her through. Then a few hours after that our curators received a photo sent to the Ministry of Defense from another Russian military agency. They clearly show Anna, accompanied by foreign diplomats and entering the Canadian embassy!"

"Canadian?" my former lover's choice wasn't

easy to understand. Traditionally, which was to say historically, all refugees and dissenters from my country chose either the British or American embassies.

"Yes, Canadian. And when we started digging, we realized that some guests at the wedding work in virtual reality at a secret facility in the Canadian province of New Brunswick. Our military intelligence has long known it as one of the three North American centers for studying the game that bends reality."

"Canada has three factions in the game?!" Today was just full of surprises. "So Canada is the most developed of all countries on earth in the 'great game' the Geckho brought us?!"

Ivan Lozovsky looked at the time, shook his head in dismay and said he had to run, but still answered:

"Kirill, I said North American, not Canadian. There's a difference. The issue is that initially the official authorities in America reacted quite skeptically to information about this new game. So at first the game that bends reality was the realm of a team of volunteer enthusiasts and employees of a few small private game developers. And among them were citizens of the USA, Canada and emigrants from a few Asian countries. As a joke they called their team Children of the Corn like in the Steven King novel. But as soon as it was proven that the space technology imported from the game could work, authorities pushed the volunteers aside and military experts took the reins. All the virt capsules were brought to a guarded military facility in the province of New

Brunswick where they instituted a strict regime of secrecy. But the first team remained. What else could they do with them? And the first station became intergovernmental, although the USA and Canada quickly built their own sets of corncobs. Okay Kirill, I'm happy we got a chance to chat and was glad to hear news from distant space, but I really don't have any time! Good luck! And be ready for unpleasant questions about Anna!"

Ivan Lozovsky hurried to leave and ran into Alexander Antipov in the doorway. He even spilled one of the cups of coffee.

"Aw damn... Okay I'll make myself another later. Here you go, Kirill. Careful, it's hot. And I have some questions about your friends."

Chapter Nine

A New Scourge

I VAN LOZOVSKY was not wrong. For the next half hour I had to recount the details my relationship with Anya from First Medical to the security director from beginning to end. Starting with the online tournament, which she and I were the last survivors of, right up to when I found her at night and without clothes in the faction head's bedroom. I suspected that most of what I said was already known to Alexander Antipov from other sources, but he still asked questions and demanded details. I hadn't done anything reprehensible, and certainly not criminal. Plus for the last week Anna and I had practically not spoken, so the fed eventually laid off.

But I felt the opposite. The more I thought over this situation, the more questions I had swarming in my head. Why flee? Anna had no access to important secrets. Yes, she had gotten as close as possible to the faction head, it wouldn't have been possible to get any closer than that. But the idea that the experienced and secretive Diplomat Lozovsky would open up in bed all of a sudden and share military and technological secrets with his lover seemed dubious at best. So the most Anna could have to tell her new masters was the coordinates of the Human-3 Faction nodes and the approximate size of our player force. That could hardly merit an emergency evacuation from the Dome and sheltering her in the embassy. I mean, where had her character even gone? Had she just picked up and ran over the border despite the war with the Dark Faction and increased security on the perimeter? I asked all that out loud.

"It's hard to say about her character. In her last session, the Medic was deployed in the Antique Beach node during our first unsuccessful counterattack on the Rainforest. To be honest, it was a huge cock-up and with the vortex of deaths and resurrections, we somehow lost track of Anna. Fourteen of our players were taken captive by the Dark Faction that day and, I have to admit, we actually got off easy. It could have been much worse if the First Legion vanguard hadn't rushed in. This wasn't the first time they'd come up against the Dark Faction, lots of players had dozens of battles behind them. But even the veterans noticed that it was like we were playing at a higher difficulty. We got the impression the enemy knew all our moves in advance and was ready with the most effective possible counter!"

The fed went silent, winced and massaged his

temples with his fingers. Clearly he had a really nasty headache. I also noticed that his eyes were red from exhaustion and lack of sleep. It was clear he was not only tired but also very wound up by the inexplicable level of information the enemy had about our faction's activity.

"I think I'm getting sick... My throat is sore, my head is splitting, aspirin is no help," Alexander Antipov commented, nevertheless continuing the conversation. "As for Anna not having much information, you're basically right. But Anna does know about our starship and is closely acquainted with its captain. And that is no small factor. She also knows the names of our high-profile players and could even describe them physically. That is more than enough to find them in the real world and determine the identities of their relatives and friends."

"But to what end? Whoever these foreign agents are after is under the Dome, so getting in touch with them would be a big problem. I mean, all high-profile and more or less significant players are already subject to round the clock surveillance, and now all the more so."

"You're wrong there, Kirill! All intelligence services the world over have ways of influencing a person indirectly. They could go through their loved ones, for example. But I'll agree that it all looks clumsy, not like the work of professionals. And the Canadian and American agencies, beyond all doubt, are professionals. As a spy, she would have been worth more in the long term if she stayed here close to the very head of the Human-3 Faction. There has to be some detail we aren't seeing. It just doesn't add up..."

We spent some time in silence, thinking over the weirdness of this whole thing. Then I asked the much better-informed director:

"Could it be that this isn't about the real world, but actually about that very North American faction? What do we know about it?"

Alexander Antipov unlocked his computer and turned the monitor so I could see:

"There are very few details. We know its number: Human-8, we know where their center is located. Take a look, your clearance level is high enough. These are satellite photos from the last six months of a military base in the province of New Brunswick. Their corncobs look just like ours, but hold one hundred fifty virt pods a piece. As you can see, three of the cobs were built a long time ago and have been working actively. They started building a fourth but for six months it remained unfinished. It looks very much like the countries involved decided to prioritize their own research centers rather than continue to share valuable information with their neighbors. So they haven't cut funding, but it isn't growing either."

"I wouldn't say that for sure! Maybe the Human-8 Faction ran into serious problems in the game," I said, trotting out another explanation for the lack of progress. "Based on the number of virt pods, they have one level-two node and two level-ones. And now they can't get more than four hundred thirty-five people, so they don't need a fourth corncob."

Antipov shrugged his shoulders indefinitely and started clicking, scrolling through the many pictures of the military base in winter and summer from outer space. But then the satellite shots ended and a video began. It was Anna in a place surrounded by a fence and coming out of a big black car with diplomatic plates and, guarded by an escort of five men of athletic build in identical suits, walking into the building. But there was one inconsistency that jumped out at me. I couldn't even believe it at first:

"Stop! Rewind five seconds. Zoom in on the face. Come on, not Anna's! See that tan security guy in dark glasses. Who's he?"

The security director traced the outline of the face, entered some command and almost immediately a brief dossier showed up, excerpts of which Alexander Antipov read aloud:

"Ahsanuddin Hussein Rahman. Citizen of Canada. Family immigrated from Bangladesh. So... education, career... Everything looks normal. At present he works at the Canadian Embassy in Moscow. What's wrong with him, Kirill?"

"What's wrong? Well we can start from the fact that this 'Hussein Rahman' is definitely not from our earth, but the parallel magocratic one!"

The security director stumbled back and looked at me, batting his red eyes in surprise and his mouth agape:

"Impossible! Are you sure, Kirill?!"

"One hundred percent. I've seen many Dark Faction people, and a few of them very close up. I mean,

I'm married to someone from that world, so I can recognize the characteristics of their race immediately! That 'native of Bengal' is wearing makeup to cover up the fact that his skin is ash-gray, but that isn't enough to stop me from recognizing a person from the magocratic world! And his dark glasses, I suspect, are for the very same purpose as mine," I said, removing the dark glasses, which I usually wore under the Dome to keep a low profile. Then I laid them on the table and finished my sentence: "to hide his glowing mage eyes!"

This was turning out much more complicated than it looked at first glance. The Dark Faction not only know a surprising amount about our plans, but had help from at least one faction from our version of Earth and had even sent agents into our world.

Antipov was alarmed and asked me to stay under the Dome for the next hour and a half or so and not disappear, then ran to the "secure room for communicating with Moscow" to tell the curators the news about the Dark Faction. But before he could leave, I asked the director to tell the Moscow bigwigs the thing I actually came here to tell him: The Dark Faction knew everything we said at the recent meeting of key players.

"The information is authentic, I got it through Princess Minn-O La-Fin from enemy leader General Ui-Taka himself. He misspoke in her presence and mentioned a timeframe he should not have known. That means someone from the very top of our faction is working for the enemy and the circle of suspects is no wider than everyone who was at that meeting!"

I thought Alexander Antipov would latch onto the new information like a tick and start sucking out more details. But his reaction caught me off guard. The fed started boring into me with his eyes, and spoke in an angered tone:

"Kirill, you must know how much I don't like all this! You're up to some behind-the-scenes negotiations with the enemy through your wife and circumventing our official Diplomat. And you're using a totally unregulated channel. No one knows what information is being sent over! What's more, you're just one person removed from a clear enemy — the leader of our enemies in fact! And let me remind you that you were present at the key-players meeting. All that, Kirill, means that you are our main suspect!"

If Alexander Antipov was trying to throw me or scare me with fearsome words and accusations, he had severely miscalculated. What was more, I could read complete bewilderment in his thoughts. Most importantly, the fed didn't himself believe I was guilty and was merely trying to scare me "just in case." What was more, I discovered that the intelligence director had an unexpectedly high opinion of me. Alexander Antipov considered my work very important and useful to the faction. So in response to his contrived allegations, I just laughed:

"Well I also know the Geckho leader Kung Waid Shishish, and not through someone else, directly. But does that make me a Geckho agent? By the way, I have requested secret one-on-one negotiations with the Kung through my business partner Uline Tar. I have something to offer the commander of the Second Geckho Strike Fleet, and I'm greatly counting on his gratitude. I don't want to predict the future, but it's possible we will repeat the trick I pulled off with the Graveyard node before. Or at the very least get rid of that penalty."

While he sat there, batting his eyes and digesting the information, I continued:

"I am also personally acquainted with the Great Prophet of the Miyelonian race Leng Amiru U-Mayaoo, as well as the commander of the Miyelonian fleet in this part of the galaxy, Leng Keetsie-Myau. Following your logic, does that make me a Miyelonian agent? And yes, just so you know, the great Miyelonian commander gave me an assurance that the fleet of the Union of Miyelonian Prides will not attack Earth after our planet's grace period is up. And although Keetsie told me that mentally, such a famous figure's promise is as valuable as an officially signed treaty covered with stamps and signatures."

"Great work!" Alexander Antipov finally stated his own position. "I imagine Ivan Lozovsky is also gonna appreciate your diplomatic success and will write you out a bonus!" the deputy faction leader assured me, but I just waved it off because a bonus was the last thing I cared about at this point.

It was actually with a certain degree of surprise that I suddenly realized I had no expectations of my faction. Or actually, not even that. The faction had nothing for me that I didn't already have or could get in the game that bends reality. Reality itself had become just a dull, faded shadow of the bright and interesting virtual world. That was frightening. I really didn't want to become some jack-off game addict, spending days and nights on end in a computer game to the detriment of real life.

As if reading my thoughts, he told me that Irina Chusovkina the psychologist really wanted me to go see her and that she had a "very tempting proposition" for me. Apparently, the leader of the Second Legion Gerd Tamara also wanted to see me and wanted me told that she was willing to meet whenever I could. Antipov again repeated his request that I not go right back into the game because the list of targets for attack from space would be ready in an hour, then declared our meeting over.

The fed clearly couldn't wait to report to Moscow that Dark Faction agents had reached our world, but still I took up another few minutes, asking him to tell me about the situation with the allied Human-6 Faction. Neither Lozovsky nor Antipov had said a word about the German faction during today's conversation, and I was seriously worried that the very worst had come to pass. But fortunately I was wrong:

"The Germans are still in control of the two coastal nodes. We have reinforced their defenses with Centaurs and our troops, but the Dark Faction hasn't attacked yet because their southern battle group has been tied up in the Rainforest and Tropics. Now the Second Legion is latched into the enemy like a bull terrier and drawing their attention while we try to figure out how long it will take the Human-6 Faction to repopulate."

"To... what? What do you mean repopulate?" I didn't understand what he said.

The security director was eager to explain:

"We gave our allies a choice of two nodes to avoid the threat of complete destruction. One is to the south east of the Yellow Mountains: Phylira the Centaur mare gifted it to us yesterday as part of a previous understanding. The other is on the opposite shore of the bay... I don't know how much you heard about Project Exodus, former faction leader Radugin's pet project. Have you even heard of it? Weird, it was meant to be top-secret. Well then you won't be surprised to hear that a level-one citadel is almost finished on the far shore of the bay to the south of the Geckho spaceport. The node is almost ready to settle, and the Germans chose it so they can get farther from this war and the Dark Faction as a whole."

NONE OF the Second Legion soldiers could find Gerd Tamara anywhere under the Dome. And no surprise: our faction was engaged in a counterattack on the southern front with battles in the swampy forests of the Tropics node. That meant the leader of the Second Legion was needed in the game. But our psychologist came and tracked me down as I was heading to the canteen with Imran. From afar, I heard rustling on the gravel path and, when I turned around I saw a middle-aged dark-haired woman wearing a track suit catching up to us.

"Kirill, what rare luck to catch you under the Dome! You got a couple minutes? I'd just like to have a chat alone, without your guard," she said, pointing to my Dagestani friend.

Slowing down, I asked Imran to go to the cafeteria alone, promising to catch up soon. Irina Chusovkina suggested we sit on a nearby bench, but I refused. I didn't feel any discomfort after all those hours in the virt pod, but still assumed my real body needed more real motion to keep my muscles in shape. And so, I suggested to the faction psychologist that we have our talk over a little run through the park. We were both already in tracksuits anyway.

"If you say so, Kirill," she agreed easily and set the pace of the run. Not wasting time, she got right to business. "It's been a fairly long time since our last conversation. I see you didn't take my advice to smooth things over with our faction. In fact, you only distanced yourself further and dove head first into the game. In the last five days, you've spent at best three hours in the real world."

"I've heard from the Geckho that you can spend up to five days in the game that bends reality without suffering negative consequences. So I have been keeping to the recommendations of our experienced and wise suzerains."

"Nevertheless, you aren't really sure they're right, which is why you decided to get a workout in, even though I've never seen you do that before," the psychologist called me out with ease. "Three hours in five days, that is nowhere near enough to understand what matters most to our people. Kirill, do you even know there's a war on?"

I didn't answer her acrid and provocative question so I wouldn't blow up in her face. I understood that the experienced psychologist was trying to draw me out, hoping to apply some of her know-how and clever tactics. Keep dreaming! We both kept quiet for a minute, just running next to one another unhurriedly before Irina understood she was mistaken and came at it another way:

"Alright, sorry, I didn't mean to offend you. I understand that your mission in the distant cosmos is important to all humanity as well. I can only guess how anxious you must be, not being able to help your friends and colleagues. Wait... I can't keep going... I'm all out of breath..." Irina slowed to a walk and I had to follow her even though I wasn't one bit tired.

My companion headed to a nearby bench and sat down, lowering her head very far and breathing heavily. I didn't sit down though, and stayed standing next to Irina Chusovkina as she tried to catch her breath.

"I guess I've really let myself go... I need to exercise more often. I'm just all out of breath, and it looks like my blood pressure is up. My head is splitting! Don't pout, Kirill!" the psychologist gave a tortured smile. "You want me to tell you a little secret? After your group of gamer students, the curators of the project deemed the experiment a success and brought another two similar groups under the Dome. Cyberathletes, professional gamers, winners of many international tournaments and championships in all kinds of online games. We even got a very famous Russian-Ukrainian team of cyberathletes to come under the Dome in its entirety."

"Yeah? And how are they doing?" I asked, my interest piqued. "We got a new levelling speed record yet?"

"If only..." she sighed grievously. "It hasn't produced the desired result. Their progress is the same as faction average, it's all within the bounds of statistical error. And that's why they keep sending me back to the issue again and again, hoping to discover just what makes you so special. You are the shining star of our faction beyond all doubt. You shine so bright that you make our faction's other high-profile players look dim by comparison. So I have to ask you, have you thought about what I said about the faction and your choice?"

Damn, this difficult conversation again...Five days ago I trembled to think about returning to this topic and giving her an answer. No matter how badly I might have wanted to ignore external problems and simply live my life like an ostrich with its head buried in sand, to my enormous pity, it was not possible.

"Irina, I thought this over five days ago. And I don't understand why they're so determined to squeeze me out of the faction. So Ivan Lozovsky can become Leng? Is that his idea? But would these new abilities make up for the potential loss of the only Listener in the game, together with his starship and all of Team Gnat?"

I thought that framing would throw her off. However, I was wrong. Irina was noticeably pleased that I was finally willing to discuss this touchy issue.

"Kirill, what makes you think Russia only has one Dome? Yes, this is the largest and has the most players, but there are others. And the First Legion even took a little trip to teach our brethren the ABC's of the game that bends reality. By and large, it makes no difference which Russian faction you, your starship and Team Gnat belong to, because in the end all new technologies, all new discoveries brought in from space will be going to the same destination. And sure the new faction has just thirty players and one level-one node. But that means the administrative requirements are minimal and, with your Fame and Authority, you will immediately become a Leng."

Here it was... I immediately realized this offer had come from above, and Ivan Lozovsky was nowhere near its original source. The curators wanted to split me from the careerist diplomat and all other key players because I was holding them back. But that didn't really mean much to me... I chose my words for a delicate refusal, but I didn't have to say anything. Irina suddenly sat back in her bench and held her head in her hands:

"Gnat... Kirill... For some reason I feel really nasty. My eyes are going dark... Help me to the medical unit. Or call a doctor."

I started freaking out and looked around, trying

to figure out where the medical unit was from there. I saw Imran running down the path in my direction. Before he got near, the Dagestani athlete shouted from the distance:

"There's something weird going on, Gnat! Two of the chefs in the cafeteria had an attack. They fell on the floor and are writhing around saying they feel sick and have a horrible headache! People are panicking, everyone is shouting that the food is severely poisoned! And some are also complaining that they feel sick."

I pointed my friend to Irina Chusovkina, who was quietly sobbing in pain and pressing her hands to her temples:

"I can see that. And Antipov the fed was also complaining of a bad headache! Pick Irina up and get her to treatment stat! Have the doctors sort out her poisoning, or whatever this is. And step to! Every second might be precious!"

Imran didn't argue, grabbed the woman by the arms and ran after me right over some bushes to the medical building. Already in the doorway of the med unit, we ran into Alexander Antipov leaving the doctor and looking displeased:

"Yeah right they don't have stronger pain killers. I'd never believe that in my life!" he started complaining about the obduracy of the medical staff. "After the information about the darksiders breaking into our world, the curators called me to an emergency meeting in Moscow, and my head is just splitting. Its unbearable. How can I possibly make a report when I'm in so much pain it's hard to speak?!"

157

"Alexander, this is very important. Did you go to the cafeteria today?" I asked the director in a strict tone.

"No, there was no time to eat breakfast or lunch today because of all the stuff going on. I just had coffee and sandwiches. Why do you ask?"

I looked at Irina, who was passed out and limp in the arms of the Dagestani athlete, then at the security director writhing with a headache in front of me unhappily, and made a decisive announcement:

"No one is flying to Moscow!!! The best-case scenario here is a mass poisoning but, most likely, this is an outbreak of a highly infectious disease! We must give an order to isolate the Dome from the outside world and strictly forbid anyone from going outside!!!"

Alexander Antipov looked at me in strain for a few seconds then nodded, took his radio off his belt and sent an order to "post one" saying not let anyone leave the Dome regardless of passes and signatures even from the top bosses. Then the fed voiced the very thought dancing on the tip of my tongue:

"I think I'm beginning to understand why Anna left the Dome in such a hurry yesterday! And what brought her back to the secret facility after her brother's wedding, even though she could have easily just fled two days earlier."

"Yes, this looks very much like the Dark Faction's payback," I agreed with a heavy sigh. "Revenge for blowing up the large number of mages at Thumor-Anhu La-Fin's funeral and the combat maneuvers spilling over into the real world from the game. And this looks like they're just showing us what they're capable of. After all, most of the people working here under the Dome don't have to fear disease. The game will heal everything. Only the auxiliary staff are at risk along with the few people connected with the game but without a character."

"Yes, like me or our psychologist," Alexander Antipov agreed thoughtfully.

"Exactly. They bet on a military victory but it didn't pay off. Our faction held out despite the suddenness and ferocity of the darksider onslaught. So now they're changing tactics. What happened here under the Dome is the Dark Faction trying to gain leverage for the upcoming peace talks. If we aren't sufficiently pliable, they may use biological weapons not just here but in Moscow with its millions of inhabitants!"

Chapter Ten

Fire from the Sky

I WAS SITTING on the bridge in front of my console, waiting for a response from the space port dispatchers and just seething with rage. Eduard, who left to the real world after Imran and me, confirmed that a biological weapon had been used under the Dome. Six of the Dome's civilian staff had died. Another twenty-seven were in quarantine in the medical unit, most in severe condition, and the medics were having a hard time making any sort of prognosis. The first to get sick and die worked in the building for high-profile players, which gave a basis to suggest that the disease had spread from there. Next were the driver of the irrigation vehicle, the old chef, and a nurse. They were also unable to save faction psychologist Irina Chusovkina.

I'd never seen Imran in such a state before. My Dagestani friend had spent a whole ummi sitting in his bunk, holding tight to his deadly blades and staring at the wall, switching the electrified edge of the finely serrated weapons on and off. The only thing Imran said in all that time was directed at me:

"Too bad there won't be any close combat and we'll just be shooting from orbit. Gnat, burn them all to hell!!!"

And Imran wasn't the only one upset. I was also very disturbed. Irina Chusovkina was a woman who looked glamorous for all her years. Her and I had talked just today, but she never came back around and died in the intensive care unit just half an hour after we brought her to the medical building. The speed with which the unknown disease progressed from initial symptoms to death was striking. So as soon as we familiarized ourselves with the list of priority targets brought by Gerd Tarasov, I ordered Imran to get quickly into the game because we had been in close contact with the recently deceased and probably were already infected with the deadly disease. What was more, my head really was starting to hurt — probably somewhat in anxiety and somewhat from the infection. I wasn't going to stick around and find out.

When Imran said "them all" he meant the Dark Faction, our main enemy beyond all doubt was behind that inhuman attack. Especially after I told Minn-O about the characteristic symptoms of the quickly spreading disease. She mentioned two horrible epidemics that swept her world seven hundred and one hundred eighty years ago. In both cases the disease was caused by single celled algae capable of quickly multiplying inside the human body. Their waste products caused a severe allergic reaction leading to death in a majority of cases. We immediately sent that information under the Dome.

By then I already knew that, in view of the crisis, Dome leadership had taken an emergency decision to fill all virt pods reserved for new players with infected nonplayers in the most severe condition. Unfortunately that left us with only eight survivors. They made one exception for the intelligence director, a valuable specialist who possessed a huge amount of secret information, who needed to be saved regardless. But Alexander Antipov said it went against his honor as an officer and he felt a share of guilt for what happened, so he refused. An hour later, his condition had deteriorated so much the doctors put him into an artificial coma.

A group of military specialists had been brought under the Dome and, wearing special hermetically sealed chemical suits, were collecting samples everywhere. In some thick grass in the park they discovered an empty thin-walled vial with spore traces inside. There were clear fingerprints on the glass as well, and they were quickly identified. They belonged to, as was not hard to guess, Anya from First Medical. With every conceivable precautionary measure, the dangerous sample was brought into a mobile laboratory set up right there under the Dome.

All members of the Human-3 Faction had been

advised to spend as long as possible in their virt pods, returning to the real world only if their character in the game that bends reality died. The disease hadn't been detected in any players yet, but it was assumed that was because the game was healing them. And the planners of this deadly attack had to have known that. But that meant the attack wasn't intended to kill our players. But then what? To sew panic in our ranks and crush our fighting spirit? If that's what they were hoping to achieve, they guessed wrong. The soldiers of the H3 faction had more determination than ever before!

Or was their goal something totally different, on a much grander scale? For example, maybe they were hoping to turn real world governments against one another. After all, if I hadn't uncovered the agent of the magocratic world by complete coincidence, the main suspect in the biological attack against Russia would have been Canadian intelligence. The potential consequences of that were not hard to predict. The Russian state had a clear defensive doctrine, and possessed plenty of thermonuclear warheads and intercontinental ballistic missiles...

The screen lit up before me showing the furry face of a Geckho dispatcher:

"All documents in order! Free Captain Gerd Gnat, your frigate is permitted to visit the star system and land in the local space port."

Fame increased to 71.

Authority increased to 50!

Right after that, a Sindirovu fighter-interceptor

stopped spinning around my frigate and descended into the atmosphere, having appeared near my starship as soon as we left hyperjump. We observed all formalities, and the Geckho wouldn't be bothering us any further. I took in some more air and, trying to look like the picture of determination for my crew, commanded:

"Dmitry, get in attack position one hundred ten miles above the central node of the Dark Faction, its coordinates are 55:476."

The frigate went into motion, gradually making a left turn and starting down to laser cannon distance. That part of the planet was already dark which was obviously not what we were hoping for. It would have been much more effective to attack in the daytime, when all targets were much easier to see. However, at night we had a decent chance of catching all enemy Sio-Mi-Dori at their base, and the Dark Faction assault antigravs were our priority target.

According to Gerd Tarasov, the fourteen heavy assault-landing antigravs, capable of unexpectedly showing up anywhere and landing four hundred troops then supporting them with heavy cannon fire, broke our whole defense system. So we were to deprive the Dark Faction of this mobile strike force then start destroying enemy infrastructure — power stations, factories, oil wells, weapon and ammunition caches, bridges and comms towers, repair shops and vehicle parking. I was told not to get distracted with reinforcements and manpower, and concentrate on destroying production facilities and reducing the mobility of enemy troops. After all, no matter how many troops the Dark Faction had, if they couldn't repair tech or make more ammunition, without heavy weaponry and the ability to quickly move around the planet, they would be easy prey for our players.

We got lucky with the weather. There was slight cloud cover, but it did nothing to stop us from seeing the surface. The sea was dark, the coastline serpentine. I was interested in a bright spot below, and mentally compared the image on the monitor with my own map. The Geckho spaceport? Yes, exactly! So many lights!

Cartography skill increased to level fifty-nine!

But then there was a peninsula jutting way out into the sea, the hilly overgrown lands to the south of the spaceport. One of the nodes there was the one the German Human-6 Faction had chosen as its new home. And that island was the former German capital node, now under Dark Faction occupation. I took a closer look from above at the enemy-occupied island. No fires or buildings were visible from one hundred miles up. Although... what was that? I could clearly see five dots starting off from the island and drifting over the sea.

Cartography skill increased to level sixty!

Eagle Eye skill increased to level seventy-three!

Despite the Eagle Eye message, I couldn't identify the flying objects. They were just too far away. So I started up the ship's lidar and scanned that part of the water's surface with other systems. I wasn't particularly surprised at what I found. It was exactly what I was expecting in fact:

Sio-Mi-Dori. Dark Faction shock-landing antigrav.

Five such flying machines were taking a course to the east from the island the Dark Faction now controlled. I couldn't say if they were going to wipe the H6 faction off their last nodes on the eastern shore or if they had other plans. No matter. They had just made themselves my priority targets.

"Dmitry! Even out the starship and head for the enemy antigravs! Denni Marko! Light them up!!! Shoot at will!!! They must not escape!!!"

Valeri's associate threw away an unfinished sandwich and, wiping the crumbs off his hands right onto his spacesuit, ran full speed to the gunner seat. Half a minute later a power surge informed me of a simultaneous shot from all three turrets at once. The first enemy Sio-Mi-Dori fell to pieces in the air, splashing down into the dark sea in a scattering of flaming debris.

Targeting skill increased to level twenty-five!

You have reached level seventy-seven!
You have received three skill points.

"Great work, Denni! Let 'em have it before they figure out what's happening!"

Targeting skill increased to level twenty-six!
Targeting skill increased to level twenty-seven!

You have reached level seventy-eight!

You have received three skill points (total points accumulated: six).

"Kap-ee-tahn! All five kill is do. But one fly-ying match-een throuuwing water resc-cue raft!" Denni's alarmed and bewildered voice in my headphones spoke to a seriously flustered state.

I looked for myself. There was a big bright orange inflatable raft capable of holding fifteen people in the midst of the stormy sea. Zooming in showed that people were swimming towards it from all sides, many of whom had taken off their heavy armor as not to be weighed down. I didn't feel hate for these people, and especially was not going to give an order to destroy their only means of salvation. My interest was more detached, like how an entomologist looks at a rare butterfly. Were Dark Faction commandos required to have the Swimming skill? After all, without it they would have all drowned instantly. Those were the rules of the game!

But that wasn't my biggest question here. To save their own skins, the soldiers had ditched heavy armor suits, which were probably expensive and hard to produce. And this was all just a game where the worst consequence of death was a fifteen-minute pause! Was their sense of self-preservation really that strong? Or had Dark Faction production capabilities allowed them to create armor suits in large quantity, and the soldiers figured they were already too ruined to be worth saving? Or was the reason something totally different, for example, a mentality we weren't accustomed to? Like for example, maybe while a warrior has even the slightest chance of completing an order, they are obliged to do so by their honor?

"Are we really gonna let them go?" the pilot's unhappy voice shook me out of my thinking. "Captain, they are enemies! They must be destroyed while we have the chance!"

"No Dmitry. Only fascists and terrorists attack downed pilots or the crews of sinking ships. We are not like them. What's more, it'll be more than an hour before they get anywhere, and that means fifteen enemy soldiers will be out of the picture all that time. Set a course for the island! Let's get back to our main mission!"

Authority reduced to 49!

Authority increased to 50!

Strange. My sharp response was heard by many and crewmembers were of two different minds about the decision. I suspected Dmitry Zheltov was among those who didn't approve of my spinelessness. Nevertheless, the pilot did not dare disobey an order and steered the frigate toward the dark craggy island.

I then called up the results of a recent scan. I wanted to see the map markers for the antigravs flying over the sea. Ah, there were their characteristic signatures. Perhaps not all the antigravs on the island were taking part in tonight's operation? Search for similar objects on the island! There we go! Completely identical signatures, although somehow shielded, the signal was weaker. Ah, now I could see. This Sio-Mi-Dori was inside a large covered hangar. It must have been damaged during recent battles and was in for repair. I studied the mesh-covered camouflage structures with my ship's powerful optics and scanning systems. Some warehouses and workshops. Hey, there were the two heavy tanks the Dark Faction brought back to the island for repair! What luck!

Cartography skill increased to level sixty-one!

Electronics skill increased to level seventy-two!

Scanning skill increased to level forty-two!

"Denni, new targets!" I set markers on the grounded antigrav and neighboring structures, as well as the two Sio-Ku-Tati tanks. "Fire!!!"

And it went up like a Roman candle! The bright flash was seen by everyone on the bridge without any optics at all. It was seemingly an ammunition storehouse. I ordered Denni to shoot the flaming tech and proper rows of military freight vehicles, now well visible in the firelight, once again.

Targeting skill increased to level twenty-eight!

Targeting skill increased to level twenty-nine!

"Okay, that's enough! Let's get back to the main mission. Set a course for the Dark Faction's main node! Actually... wait!" My attention was drawn by a large number of lights on "our" shore. It looked like there was a pitched battle underway! And we had just destroyed the reinforcements the enemy was rushing into battle! "Set a course for the Tropics node! Coordinates 60:470. Let's go help our guys!"

Ugh, I wished I could tell what was happening... One hundred miles beneath us in the swampy night, the tropical forest was host to a rampaging battle. At some sections it had even come to hand-to-hand combat. But all I could see was a barrage of flickering lights. For a minute I tried to figure out where my side was, and where to find the enemy, but I had to admit defeat.

"Dmitry, give me our faction's common channel! Twenty-five, the one for emergency messages!"

"Gnat, they changed it from twenty-five a long time ago, it's seventeen now..." the Starship Pilot started teaching me a poorly timed lesson but, seeing my gloomy gaze, sharply cut himself off. "Captain, all ready. I switched to the channel and turned on encryption."

I nodded, donned my headphones and immediately winced from an ear-piercing shout:

"...econd Legion requesting backup! We're surrounded near Putrid Ford! We've only got one Peresvet left. All our trucks have been destroyed, we cannot evacuate the cannons! We're out of ammo, and nearly out of grenades. There are less than forty of us left! Soldiers down! We need help!!!"

I recognized the voice. It belonged to Roman Pavlovich, the right hand of Gerd Tamara, leader of the Second Legion. I also knew the place the high-level Grenadier mentioned. In fact, it was me who suggested the name Putrid Ford when I first headed south to meet our potential allies from the German faction. It was a nasty place, where you had to wade up to your waist in swamp muck. Perhaps the Centaurs had built something like a road there since, but no matter what there was no way around this place. There were viscous swamps for many miles all around. An ideal place for an ambush...

"This is Filippov, over. We cannot send out reinforcements. The Dark Faction has attacked from Karelia, all our reserves are over there. Blow up your vehicle and make for the Rainforest node to get artillery support."

The Second Legion was fully surrounded, which meant the overall situation on the southern front wasn't nearly as rosy as the directors had told me a few hours earlier. Gerd Tamara's squadron was the main force holding back the enemy from the south. If they were taken out, the consequences for the whole south could be catastrophic. Plus HQ had no way to help the dying soldiers, which was an even worse sign. That meant there were no reserves in this area. What was more, the Second Legion leaving Karelia had weakened defense on the Northern front, which the darksiders quickly took advantage of.

No answer followed from the Second Legion. And what was there to really say here? I had no doubt that Major Filippov himself understood how absolutely impossible and senseless his order was. The Dark Faction hadn't gone to all the trouble of luring our elite soldiers into a trap just to let them leave afterward. I spun in my seat and turned toward the Starship Pilot, who was also listening to the negotiations:

"Dmitry, can you land this frigate in an

unprepared location?"

My friend thought for three seconds, then answered with a tight head-shake:

"It'll be hard in such a big starship. This is after all not a shuttle or some light interceptor. But even if we can set down in the swamp without busting the fuselage, we won't be able to take off again from the thick muck. Plus there's a battle down there, which means the Dark Faction might destroy or even capture our starship."

"So without all that verbal husk, you're basically saying yes?" I demanded a clear answer from the pilot.

"Yes captain. We will be able to land. But in order to be able to take back off again, we need a hard and preferably more or less even landing zone."

"I've got one," I brought up the node map on the monitor and pointed to spot on the screen. "In the middle of Putrid Ford there's a hill overgrown with bushes, the only more or less dry place. There it is. From what I can tell, our soldiers have occupied that exact high point and are defending it. Prepare to land there!"

"But captain..." it was clear the Starship Pilot was unsure it was worth breaking the rules of the game and arguing with a high-profile player, but nevertheless he was decisive: "Gnat, can I be perfectly honest? Why take such a risk? We might lose our starship. It's our only trump card in the war against the Dark Faction. And for what? Those forty players die and respawn somewhere safe, as the other Second Legion soldiers have probably already done. The vehicle? Is our last Peresvet and a few cannons worth that risk?"

I took a heavy sigh and started digesting a seemingly obvious fact:

"Good thing you wanted honesty. Did you think about why our soldiers have dug in so hard on that hill and are not retreating? Maybe they just couldn't say it on air so they wouldn't inform the enemy of their weakness, given they could easily have figured out our encryption and have been listening. Look at the map again. There are dozens of miles of swamp in every direction. And if a soldier dies with their respawn point far to the north in a safe area, they would have to spend the next day or maybe two wading through waist-deep muck to catch up to their comrades who are pursuing a retreating enemy. And the only dry land that can serve as a fulcrum point to push south..."

"The Second Legion set their respawn points there!!!" the Starship Pilot interrupted me, his eyes wide in horror. "They cannot leave!!!"

"Precisely! And that is why we will help despite the high risk. Prepare for landing!"

Dmitry Zheltov, his face bewildered, returned to his pilot's seat, closed his eyes, sat back then started stretching his fingers and whispering silently. Maybe he was repeating the steps for landing, maybe he was praying. I then turned on the microphone and went to channel seventeen:

"Gerd Gnat here number fourteen seventy, over. Second Legion! I'm in orbit directly above you. Shoot up flares to mark targets! Hold the hill and clear the brush

and vegetation from a one-hundred-by-fifty-foot landing zone. Pack all valuable equipment into the remaining Peresvet and prepare for extraction."

Authority increased to 51!

Authority increased to 52!

"Gnat!!! You can't even imagine how happy we are to hear you!!!" I don't know who's voice it was, but the young man's joy was entirely sincere. Then what followed...

"Ro'ti part Gerd Gnat La-Fin, prolo'un mi wayedde Minno-O. Avari riko inti un waye Geckho."

The strong confident voice belonged to a middle-aged man. Princess Minn-O had started teaching me the language of her people, I'd done a whole three lessons already, but my knowledge was still very far from perfect. All I could understand was an official greeting and that I had been addressed as a respected member of house La-Fin and spouse of Minn-O. Then... I had to admit I didn't understand. Something about the Geckho, but what? I covered the microphone with a hand and whispered for Dmitry Zheltov to bring my travelling wife Minn-O La-Fin here at once to help with translation.

While the pilot ran off to get Minn-O, in the complete silence of the common channel, which was thought to be basically secret and secure, I tried to address the unexpected guest:

"Ro-ti part Gerd Ui-Taka. Yenu po tim (I presume)?"

Astrolinguistics skill increased to level eighty-four!

In response came satisfied laughter, then he confirmed his identity, I was not wrong. After that came a long phrase or more like a monologue. I couldn't quite get it. Fortunately, Minn-O La-Fin came in to translate:

"Gerd Ui-Taka admits you managed to surprise him, which very, very few have done before. Now that you're here the balance of forces has changed and both sides of the conflict can inflict very severe and even irreplaceable losses, which will weaken Earth as a whole in face of an external threat. So General Ui-Taka suggests we return to an earlier offer to meet on neutral territory. For example, the Geckho spaceport in three hours. That is the fastest the General can make it there, unfortunately. If Gerd Gnat agrees to negotiate, the Dark Faction will allow the Second Legion to leave the trap unimpeded and even to evacuate their damaged vehicles. They will also cease the attack in Karelia, even though the node is already de-facto captured. And from that moment on the cease-fire shall be renewed for twenty-four hours. General Ui-Taka suggests the Geckho be brought in as guarantors."

Such weighty decisions probably warranted a chat with faction leadership. But on the other hand, I was just as much a Gerd as Ivan Lozovsky, and I was the one invited to negotiate, not him. So I answered the Dark Faction leader that I would agree to meet, but I did add some conditions:

"In the room on the second floor of the Geckho spaceport in three hours. Unarmed, and no more than three members per delegation. Also, Geckho Diplomat Kosta Dykhsh will be present as an observer."

Chapter Eleven

Crash Landing

HERE WERE a few points of view on the renewed ceasefire. Sure, the Second Legion was truly delighted. They were encircled and on the verge of dying for good, totally without ammunition. Escaping that was a small miracle, and the channel reverberated with their cries of joy for a long time. But Imran, Eduard Boyko and Dmitry Zheltov didn't understand one bit. The Starship Pilot, with all possible respect when appealing to a high-profile player, asked a logical question:

"Captain, why not first shoot down all enemy antigravs and destroy everything we can, then agree to peace negotiations?"

That was approximately the same question I was asked by faction leader Gerd Ivan Lozovsky, but he didn't even try to hold back and told me how mad he was in fairly sharp terms, calling me ambitious and overly independent. The Diplomat had one other reason to be upset, too: he couldn't get to the spaceport in three hours, so the negotiations with the Dark Faction would be taking place without him.

And I answered both my crew and the director approximately the same way. It was a great shame, but in practice the frigate proved ineffective for orbital bombardment. The enemy had no good reason to know that, but it wasn't like I had a battleship or heavy cruiser with powerful cannons. My starship had just three laser turrets, and they were not powerful enough to take out anything more stronger than a lightly armored aircraft. Even the Sio-Ku-Tati tanks had to be shot a few times before they exploded, while destroying pillboxes and reinforced concrete fortifications would take upwards of an hour. In that time the Second Legion would have been wiped out along with the loyal Centaurs and Dryads helping us on defense.

What was more, destroying the enemy antigravs was much easier said than done. Using scanning systems, I fairly quickly found three of the Dark Faction's remaining eight Sio-Mi-Doris, but they were parked... at the Geckho spaceport! The suzerains would never allow me to make an attack on their node. And no matter how hard I tried, I couldn't find the remaining five antigravs. They weren't in the Dark Faction central node, nor in the aerodrome in the Golden Valley hexagon, or any of the neighboring nodes. Perhaps they had been hidden somewhere in deep underground hangars for the night. The Dark Faction's lands were chalk full of craggy cliffs and narrow crevasses, perfect for such structures. Or maybe they were quick on their feet, had learned their lesson from their five shot-down ones and removed the rest from the conflict zone as fast as possible.

I had a third possibility in mind as well, but I didn't voice it over the airwaves. To my eye though, it was even more important than the two previous. I sent Eduard Boyko out of the game to tell our directors that the Dark Faction had levers of influence in our real world as well and the current crisis under the Dome served as a good example of it. The next vial of deadly disease could be opened anywhere, including any of Earth's mega-cities. And if peace talks were an impediment to that, we needed to take advantage of it. As the Space Marine said when he got back to the starship, although the leader of the faction was gritting his teeth in vexation, he confirmed my authority to conduct negotiations.

And I had one other reason I wasn't determined enough to tell even my closest friends. Princess Minn-O said General Ui-Taka wanted to give me control of the Dark Faction at these negotiations. And if the negotiations were a success... why destroy my own property?!

When I got confirmation from the ground that the swamp island was no longer under siege, and repair brigades were on the way from the Antique Beach with powerful all-terrain tow vehicles built on Peresvet bases, I cancelled my previous order to land in the swamp.

"And thank God!" Dmitry Zheltov breathed a sigh of clear relief. "I have never landed such a big starship on a massive planet with a dense atmosphere. There are lots of complications and nuance I couldn't predict without practical experience. It's one thing to land in a space port with a dispatcher watching, and even that can be hard. But in an unprepared landing zone..." the graduate of the Mozhaysky Space Military Academy shook his head doubtfully. "Gnat, when we practiced on the landing simulators in the Academy, at best one out of four hundred students wouldn't crash on their first try. And that was with a trainer drilling highly detailed instructions into us every day about what to do and when, and how the thrusters and control systems behaved in various conditions."

"That's all correct," I agreed with the pilot. "But also consider that psionic mages could be mind-controlling you during the landing, and that the ship would be under intensive fire from all kinds of weaponry... It was definitely lucky the Dark Faction suggested negotiations!"

My chat with Dmitry was interrupted by the Navigator. Old Ayukh removed the huge headphones, turned and reported that he had received a message from the space port. Free Captain Gerd Gnat was expected on the top floor of the dispatcher tower, where they were already preparing a secure bug-proof room to conduct negotiations with outer space.

Fame increased to 72.

"Captain, do you know anything about this?" the

furry Navigator juted out his lower jaw and squinted his eyes, demonstrating surprise.

"Yes, Ayukh, I do. As far as I understand, Commander of the Geckho Second Strike Fleet Kung Waid Shishish wants to speak with me. It seems the offer from Uline and I caught his interest. Uh... what do you want, Jarg?"

I asked, seeing the level-59 explosion-risk just stroll onto the bridge. In response the eight-armed armadillo put the Universal Translator around its thick squat neck and gave a very, very fast gurgle, inflating and deflating his throat sac:

"No can to rest. Alarm. To consider. Pirates to know home of people. Know Gnat to want going back. Pirates no can patience. They insult. Shame. Probability bad to be high. To shoot down starship for revenge. Chance attack extremely high. To jump is message."

Of course, there really wasn't anything to digest here, I knew this already. The alien Analyst, whose unpronounceable name I didn't even attempt, had come to warn me of a risk he determined in his calculations. The Miyelonian pirate Pride of the Bushy Shadow was thirsty for revenge and knew perfectly well where the person who slighted them, Gerd Gnat, came from. Obviously, one of their captains had flown to Earth for a contraband shipment of platinum, so they knew where it was. After hearing from Miyelonians on Kasti-Utsh III, or perhaps other sources, that I was going to return soon to Earth, the pirates might have put some dastardly plan into action. For example, sending high-speed starships to intercept my frigate in orbit and destroy it. In the words of the Analyst, the chance of such an event was "extremely high."

I didn't know where the new crew member had heard the little-known biographical facts he'd used to reach this conclusion. But in the best case it would have been stupid to ignore the warning from the Analyst, who had previously demonstrated a surprising ability to make far-reaching conclusions from disparate facts. So I didn't hesitate for even a second:

"Dmitry, emergency acceleration, let's get out of here! Enter the atmosphere, don't wait for permission from space port dispatchers!"

Minn-O was still on the bridge next to me and suddenly shuddered and latched her fingers painfully into my wrist. The Princess's scream was ear-piercing:

"We won't make it! Go down now! Into the dense atmosphere!"

I had already noticed that my wayedda had a much stronger Danger Sense than I did. Only two or three seconds later, a wave rolled over me as well. My heart was stinging with the presentiment of some horrible catastrophe, and it was growing stronger with every heartbeat. My eyes went dark. I wanted to repeat what Minn-O said, but noticed the pilot had already activated the thrusters and was making dodging maneuvers. So I gave a totally different order:

"Denni Marko, to the cannons!!! Turn the turrets! Risk is from the rear hemisphere! All crew! Prepare for a crash landing!"

Danger Sense skill increased to level fifty-

three!

Ow! I was too busy giving orders to care of myself. Even the grav compensators didn't help me stay on my feet when the frigate gave an especially sharp jolt, quickly gaining speed and rushing toward the planet's surface. I rolled on the floor and finished a series of painful somersaults in the corner of the room with a detached armchair and the bristly slimy Jarg.

Medium Armor skill increased to level fifty-six!

Woah! I seemed to have contusions and bruising over my whole body despite my armor. Even my Hitpoints bar had gone down fifteen percent. But the alien Analyst was unharmed, and actually quite happy:

"Human soft. Especially Cartographer."

As it turned out, I wasn't the only person in the heap of bodies and furniture. Minn-O was in the mix as well, also having fallen off her feet despite her high Agility. And though I could only be called soft conditionally, because the Jarg was protected from true impact by the ductile Listener Energy Armor forcefield, the princess in her house clothes really was "soft." Not anymore though. One second was enough for my wayedda to suit up in her armored space suit and even arm herself.

Through painful ringing in my ears, I could hear the Starship Pilot saying he had put the thrusters into emergency mode and two of the four grav compensators blew in all the force.

"There they are!" a simultaneous shout from Denni and Ayukh made me stand up, overcome the pain and grab onto hard elements to crawl to my captain's seat.

I got into the chair and buckled up. What was happening? First of all, I wanted to see the image on the external cameras. Woah! Just where our frigate was two or three seconds earlier, the bright flower of a powerful explosion blossomed, then the camera went out. The frigate gave another jolt and twist, but this time I was held down and didn't get hurt.

"Gravity torpedo," Ayukh commented unflappably. "In the very epicenter of the explosion there are really extreme forces, like what you find inside a neutron star. Hard metal tears like thin cloth. But the power falls quadratically over distance, so we were practically unaffected."

"What do you mean 'unaffected?!'" Dmitry Zheltov couldn't believe what his furry partner was saying. "It tore off our left stabilizer, and f-ed up our third grav compensator. How am I supposed to land now?!"

I quickly looked over the data on the captain's tablet. The Starship Pilot wasn't exaggerating. Our frigate's left stabilizer was damaged and split to a few layers down, but not fully detached.

But for now, landing with a damaged wing was not our biggest problem. The pirate ships were not going to let a wounded bird get away. The frigate shook from a series of blows, and Engineer Orun Va-Mart told me our forcefield was down by a third. I then, having given up hope of seeing anything through our apparently destroyed external cameras, ran a general low-distance scan and brought up the results. Three small and highly mobile aircraft were going away simultaneously and making an arc to come back for another run. And the middle starship was three times as large as the others.

Tiopeo-Myhh II Miyelonian Long-Distance Interceptor.

Big Abi. Tikon-Mra V Miyelonian long-distance scout ship.

Tiopeo-Myhh III Miyelonian Long-Distance Interceptor.

Big Abi? Well, well. The leader of the Pride of the Bushy Shadow himself, Gerd Abi Pan-Miay had deigned to fly here to Earth! I remembered the blood-thirsty pirate once boasting that he wouldn't get his ass out of his seat for less than two hundred thousand crypto. I guess he put a high value on slights against the Pride of the Bushy Shadow, because he not only came personally but brought in two other captains as well.

"Denni, new targets!" I lit up all three ships for my gunner as they were finishing their turn and coming in for another attack.

Denni tried very hard to predict the agile targets' trajectories and shot long bursts from all cannons, but they all missed. On the other hand, the pirates weren't expecting resistance from the damaged and basically falling starship and mostly also missed. Although the main reason for such poor shooting on their part was the cascade of turns and twists our pilot was carrying out, making dodging maneuvers at huge G-forces and putting our last grav compensator at risk.

"Street walking woman! They to be clever, like parasite jumping insects!" Denni Marko's emotional voice rang out in the headphone. "I alone three cannon no can hit. Gerd Gnat, for to good, need another gunner and electronic master."

"I can't find you a second gunner, so you'll have to manage there. But I can take the combat electronics systems myself! The targets are already marked, and if they come that close again, I'll try to hit one of the enemies with a stasis net."

"Forcefield at forty-seven percent..." in his turn the Engineer commented on the status of our frigate. "We may not survive another attack."

Yes, it was a very worrying situation. Although, on the other hand, it could have been much worse. If our Engineer hadn't insisted back on Medu-Ro IV that we buy only the best equipment for our frigate, not cheaping out or falling back on compromises, we would already have been shot down. But what to do? My brain was feverishly searching for a way out. Ask the spaceport for help? After all, it was strange they weren't supporting us against pirates from their terrestrial cannons. Go even lower, risking wrecking our already damaged frigate?

The answer for the most part came from our pilot, who had a better idea of starship classes. While the enemy ships were moving away, Dmitry Zheltov hurriedly clacked sliders and changed our aerodynamic configuration for increased resilience in dense atmosphere. Then he simply grumbled or explained to no one in particular:

"They attacked a wounded bird, the jackals... If we had an intact ship and full crew, we'd best these pirates for sure! Against our frigate, they've got just two weak little interceptors and a cloaker that's no better than the small fry..."

Exactly! That was exactly right! I had seen the Engineer's calculations when we selected configuration for my modular frigate! An invisibility system, which by the way worked poorly in dense atmosphere, required lots of energy to bend space. There was no way to have both cloaking and a strong energy shield. Also, apparently, the pirate leader Gerd Abi Pan-Miay had opted for maximum lightness, speed and maneuverability for his frigate, given his larger ship was only somewhat better than the interceptors in terms of speed and maneuverability.

"Denni, ignore the interceptors! Concentrate all your fire on the larger frigate! It has a weak shield!!!"

Just then I realized what seemed to be heresy at first: what if we just turned off the enemy ship's energy shield altogether, making it vulnerable? No, for real, there were a few ways! For example, my Machine Control skill. Sure, I agreed it was a stupid idea. The enemy was far away now and I couldn't catch them in a scan. Then during an attack I wouldn't have time to tell which marker I was seeing in my scan. But we could try another way, like giving an order to their pilot mentally!

And really, why not? After all, this was not a battle in open space, where there were huge distances, furious ship speeds and quickly changing situations to make a mental attack ineffective. Here in the atmosphere the speeds were lower and distances were not measured in the thousands of miles. How far was I on Kasti-Utsh III when I called the repair bots while drunk? About two miles. During each attack, the pirate starships flew at even lower distances. What was more, I personally knew the person piloting the pirate frigate, and that might help.

The issue now was the strength of mental attack and making it a surprise. Could I maybe level Psionic with the free points I had sitting around? Actually no, a different skill governed the power and range of psionic attacks: Mental Fortitude. Then all six free skill points into Mental Fortitude! Raise it to sixty-six!

But alone I still might not manage. I needed the support of the Beast Master with her strong psionic abilities. I addressed her mentally:

"Valeri, I'm going to try and stun the enemy pilot. Support me!"

I received a mental answer from the mysterious huge-eyed girl at once:

"Yes, Gnat. I will help."

Busy with my and her thoughts, I nearly missed the fact that the pirate ships had long since finished their turn and were coming back on the attack! Target them, to make shooting easier! Stasis net on the frigate, reducing his speed! But most importantly... I turned away from the monitor and concentrated. I needed the leader of the Pride of the Bushy Shadow, he was somewhere very close... There! Somewhere on the very edge of perception, I could sense the presence of another's conscience. Well, given I managed to connect, take this!

"The forcefield is eating up too much energy and stopping me from beating that horrible Gnat! He is already practically defeated and will not resist, but now I really need energy both for the cannons and so we can turn on invisibility as soon as we're done. Yes, I should have done that a long time ago!"

I very vividly imagined the tousled Miyelonian Gerd Abi Pan-Miay vexed by the drawn-out battle near the risky space port as he decisively slammed his clawed paw on the console, turning off his starship's forcefield.

Electronics skill increased to level seventy-three!

Targeting skill increased to level thirty!

Psionic skill increased to level eighty!

Mental Fortitude skill increased to level sixty-seven!

Machine Control skill increased to level seventy-two!

"Got you! I hitted!!! I hitted!!! You seen how he explode right in air?!" Denni Marko's blood-curdling scream rang out in my headphones, breaking my concentration.

You have reached level seventy-nine!

You have received three skill points.

ATTENTION!!! Gerd Abi Pan-Miay's danger rating has fallen to eight.

Gerd Gnat, you have been given a reward for

destroying the ship of a dangerous pirate!

As I read that message, I felt my wallet vibrate. Intrigued, I unlocked the screen with a finger and my lips spread into a satisfied smile: three million one hundred eighteen thousand crystals!!! That's what I'm talking about! As it turned out, shooting down pirate bigwigs was quite the profitable business!

"Only eight percent shield remaining..." the Engineer's dry commentary brought me back to harsh reality.

Our Starship Pilot answered and I heard bravado and slang in his voice, which was unusual for the generally clean and military Dmitry Zheltov:

"Don't piss yourself, tomcat, we'll push through! It's cloudy already, the interceptors are gonna get called off. Or blow up in midair. Only... Damn! I won't have time to burn enough speed! This is gonna be a hard landing! Hol-d-d ooon!!!"

Danger Sense skill increased to level fifty-four!

I was reminded then of the Shiamiru and my flights with Captain Uraz Tukhsh. After that came a severe blow, the crack of breaking equipment and partitions, and my eyes went dark...

Chapter Twelve

Medicine and Rudeness

SHARP PAIN brought me to my senses. I even howled, not able to bear it even though a muted voice, sounding as if it was coming from the other side of a wall was asking me to just hold on because I'd be getting an injection of painkillers any moment. And it did let up. The dark circles in front of my eyes dimmed and disappeared and I managed to look around.

I was on the captain's bridge, but it was no easy task to recognize the room due to the heaps of debris all around. Gerd Mauu-La Mya-Ssa the Medic was hunched over me messing with my left shoulder. And he had his "coffin" levitating next to him with tubes and wires running from it to my body. I squinted and saw a bunch of bright crimson blood streaming out of my chest and forearm and being absorbed by porous synthetic bandages. The medic, turning my head back without even asking and looking closely into my pupils, explained what he was doing:

"Broken collar bone, open fracture, large veins have been damaged. But I have already set the bone fragments and fixed them in place with medical glue. Blood loss has been compensated with perftoran. I'm finishing up with the wound. I'll just stitch it up and then cover it with a bioresorbable bandage. You've got some severed tendons, and your left shoulder was dislocated, but I've already put it back. Captain, you'll have to use a sling for a couple of days. By then the negative effect from the narcotics will have passed, your Constitution will be back and the healing will go at a quicker pace."

Just two days in a sling? For a person who had fallen from the sky at massive speed and nearly bit the dust on impact with the vile earth, that was quite encouraging. For now I had a weak idea of whether I could wear the Listener Energy Armor over my shoulder sling, but in any case I would say I got lucky. One could expect much worse than that from a starship crash, after all. I asked how the rest of my crew was doing. Were they all alive?

"Yes captain, they are all alive. Vasha Tushihh broke his right leg, his twin brother Basha broke his left. I finished up with them for the most part. They can already move slightly, and in three days they'll be back to normal. The other crew members have abrasions and contusions, but nothing serious. You were hurt worst of all, Captain. Okay, I'm done. Try not to strain your shoulder for the next few days at least."

The lean Miyelonian carefully folded all the tubes and bundles of wires back into his flying coffin and started leaving but I stopped him, grabbing him by the shoulder:

"I want to say thank you. You've been on my ship less than one standard day, but I already can't imagine how we ever got by without such a capable and experienced Medic."

The Miyelonian stretched his toothy maw into something resembling a smile. Clearly that was something he'd seen people do, because his race had nothing like that as far as I'd seen, and to them showing one's teeth was a threatening gesture.

"To me it's interesting experience and my skills are levelling fast. But if you keep getting into scrapes this often, I'll be able to write a whole thesis on human medical treatment soon enough."

That was probably just a joke, but the Medic kept a serious expression on his furry face. I carefully tried to move my shoulder and left arm and was endlessly surprised because the arm worked, and the unpleasant sensations were minimal.

"You're a wizard, Mauu-La! If you need some kind of medicine or equipment, go talk with Uline Tar. Tell her the captain approved the purchase in advance."

The thin orange Miyelonian gave a very human-like bow and walked into the hallway, pushing the levitating container in front of him. The Medic didn't get far before his place in front of me was taken by the Starship Pilot and scaly Analyst.

"Gerd Gnat, it's all my fault..." Dmitry Zheltov started excusing himself in a voice full of despair. "In the heat of battle with all these maneuvers I stopped watching height and speed. I only noticed our trajectory was near vertical right at the end, when I tried to reduce the angle. Thankfully we landed on our belly, but the speed was too high and all the landing supports broke on impact. We slid a quarter mile, stripping our chassis... Uline Tar is with Avan Toi and Ayukh now evaluating the damage."

"And where did we end up landing?" I asked, extending my good hand to my friend so he could help me up.

"At the Geckho spaceport... well, almost... We didn't hit the landing zone, broke the fence, and our fuselage is two thirds sticking out. But destruction to the spaceport was minimal. I can't imagine it'll cost too much to repair a few sections of fence and put the light masts back up. I'm prepared to compensate the Geckho with my own money!"

I just waved off the foolish offer. To my eye the Starship Pilot had done more than expected trying to save the frigate and all of our lives. He deserved rewards, not fines. The main fault for the crash was with the spaceport authorities for not providing security in their area of responsibility. And that's what

I answered to the crew.

"Yes. With Geckho to speak. Needs. To recommend you be stricture. And rude."

It was an interesting suggestion from the rough Analyst who had by the way reached level 63. Be rude to the Geckho? Be rude... Well, it was worth a shot. No, I hadn't forgotten what my faction Diplomat Ivan Lozovsky had said, recommending that I be extremely polite with the suzerains of mankind. But seemingly this was the right time to ignore that.

"Good one. Contract fulfilled. Jarg to observe."

With these words the Analyst extended me the black polished stone he promised, which I immediately stashed in my Inventory for safekeeping.

"And what about the pirate ships?" I shuddered, remembering the end of the aerial battle. "We shot down one... Where did it land?"

Dmitry Zheltov as the best informed, answered:

"The interceptors didn't come down into the dense atmosphere after the death of the pirate leader and immediately left combat. But the cloaked frigate fell somewhere in the bay... You could find out the exact place from Ayukh. He was tracking all that. But do you really think something valuable might be recovered? After all, it was falling uncontrollably, it probably shattered on impact with the water."

I tried to shrug indistinctly, but I winced at the unpleasant sensations. Okay, sure. We'd handle the fallen ship later. Now we had first-order business to attend to. First to talk with the hot-headed master of Earth Kung Waid Shishish, a Geckho known to despise delays. But before that most important conversation, I had to come to my senses. I tried to evaluate my condition.

Well, I could stand on my own two feet. And apparently also walk. I wasn't too confident with the result, but I tested putting elements of my Listener Energy Armor in their slots. It did work, but it looked funny. My armored metal arm was lashed down tight to my black matte body with plastic straps, leaving it half-bent. I had no way of using my left arm at all. Oh well, it would pass soon enough...

Minn-O La-Fin walked into the room with a huge lump on her forehead. The lump wouldn't have been so obvious on the Princess's ash gray skin if not for the thick smear of bright blue anti-inflammatory ointment on her forehead. My wife ran to me for a warm embrace, but she saw my injured arm and stopped short, limiting herself to just a friendly smile. Something was wrong with Minn-O, and it had nothing to do with the lump on her forehead. I spent a long time looking at my wife and couldn't understand what was bothering me. Then it suddenly hit me:

Gerd Minn-O La-Fin. Human. Dark Faction. Level-72 Cartographer.

"You became a Gerd?!"

"Yes!!!" my wayedda was delighted. "Grandpa Thumor-Anhu promised it would happen before I hit level fifty. My Fame was growing very quickly then, and it looked like he was right. But then you came along and I had that long string of failures. But my confidence gradually returned and my ease and my

Fame started growing again. Then a quarter hour ago, I left the starship and my subjects from the First Directory were receiving a shipment from our frigate. They saw me, recognized me, and were thrown off. A few even bit the sand. Then I finally got my status!"

I sincerely congratulated my wife and advised her to be very thoughtful about her new stat points because it might be a long time before she'd get the chance to improve her character like that again. What was most important for a Cartographer? Agility and Perception? I personally would have improved any statistics already leveled to 20+ so that every two points invested would give an extra one for free.

Then my thoughts shifted to a totally different topic. So then, Imran wasn't wrong, and the three huge antigravity thrusters really were going to the Dark Faction. Most likely, the three Sio-Mi-Doris were going to the Geckho spaceport for that exact heavy, bulky shipment. And thus, if negotiations with General Ui-Taka broke down, we'd have to activate the bombs and blow all three thrusters to hell!

Following Minn-O, somewhat limping, my companion Uline Tar came out onto the bridge with an electronic tablet in her hands. The Trader was clearly upset and, after making sure I was doing alright and paying sufficient attention to her report, started telling me everything that was damaged in the crash:

"Gerd Gnat, all four grav compensators have to be replaced, that is the biggest expense. They're sixty thousand crystals each. Eleven fuselage panels need to be either removed and repaired or also replaced. The

Engineer recommends replacing them because they'll never be as good as before. Plus the landing supports, bulkhead, computers, instrument panels, screens... All told the repair is gonna run us three hundred seventeen thousand crystals. And let me remind you right away we don't have that kind of money. At least the cargo, thankfully, was not damaged, but the buyers have already picked it up. We received payment for that, and we will be able to repair some with that. But unfortunately it is not enough..."

Three hundred seventeen thousand crystals... Sure, it was a significant amount no matter what, but easily manageable. I was not planning on hiding the fact that we got a large reward for the head of the dangerous pirate, but it was horribly bad timing. I didn't want to admit to our private and fairly delicate financial situation with others around. So I limited myself, saying it would be fair to put payment partially or even fully on the spaceport administration, given it had all happened because of their negligence. Uline first considered it, then was intensely inspired:

"You're completely right, Gerd Gnat! Go right to spaceport leadership and demand compensation, it's within your rights! Actually, not even. Take me with you! I know I can find the right words to get those do-nothings off their asses!"

IT WAS THE SAME old dispatcher's tower but for the first time I didn't go up the spiral staircase, but the normal high-speed elevator. Unfortunately, it only went as high as the restaurant (or maybe I didn't have authorization to go higher), so still I had to go the old-fashioned way up the stairs from there. For Imran and Eduard, this was their first time in the spaceport, a real curiosity. My companions stared wide-eyed at the plethora of starships (primarily cargo shuttles) and other crews on the landing strip. And easily visible from the tower, there was a long line of burnt grass from our crash landing.

An unexpected meeting took place on the restaurant floor. I ran into Geckho Diplomat Kosta Dykhsh having a lively discussion with some furry compatriots in identical light space suits. They must have been the crew of some ship. I greeted him politely and started to walk on as not to distract the Diplomat from the important conversation, but he asked me to come closer:

"Gerd Gnat, your counterpart Ui-Taka asked me to tell you that he might be a bit late to the start of negotiations, but he's doing his best. I saw him on an orange rescue raft in a raging sea and even offered to let him get on my antigrav, but he refused to leave his comrades. Their motor is working just fine, so they should make it in a quarter ummi. If of course the Naiads don't eat them first."

It felt like my eyes were opened in the space of an instant. So that was why those shot-down Dark Faction soldiers preferred to part with their armor to reach the raft. Their leader was there and they were obliged to defend him at any cost! Very good thing we didn't destroy the raft, otherwise the negotiations wouldn't have happened.

Taking advantage of the convenient moment, I asked Kosta Dykhsh about the episode my faction had recently been punished for and to tell me exactly how much they had left to pay.

"See, Gerd Gnat, I've known Ivan Lozovsky for some time and consider him a friend, but the law's the law! Your faction has another eighty-two thousand four hundred crystals left to pay."

I didn't argue and suggested the Diplomat come up one floor with me and my companions so I could get the cash out of a vending machine. Three minutes later, my faction's debt to the suzerains was completely paid off.

"I have sent a message to your capital node telling them not to bring any more lumber and ore to the dock to pay off the fine. Your leader is in a frenzy," Kosta Dykhsh told me secretly. "Ivan's Authority already took a dip today when you decided to negotiate with the Dark Faction without him. And now there will be another portion of Authority drops when his faction finds Gnat solved all the faction's problems by himself after all your directors together couldn't hack it. Ah, I suspect you and Ivan Lozovsky are about to have a serious conversation about leadership!"

Kosta Dykhsh left us and went back to his friends. Then all of us went up a floor. On the very top of the tower, on a floor that housed offices for the various spaceport services, my business partner quickly got her bearings and confidently dragged me and the others to the very end of the hallway.

"This way!" Without hesitation, the Trader threw open a set of plastic doors labeled: "Spaceport Manager," and ran inside.

I left Imran and Eduard to guard the doors, then walked in after Uline. As it turned out this was not the best time. Four Geckho laying back on the sofas in identical white uniforms were either having a late dinner or early breakfast, although the main "dish" on the table was a large number of vodka bottles. This must have been more of that swill "made by time-honored techniques" that my faction exported cheaply. I skimmed the information on all four of them, trying to determine which of these drinkers was in charge, but didn't have much success. Their levels were approximately the same: 142-149. And their classes of Supercargo, Financier, Engineer and Gunner did nothing to help me determine who was in charge of the spaceport.

Nevertheless, Uline Tar quickly made that determination with some clues only she understood and confidently headed toward one of the Geckho. Grabbing at his thick beard, the Trader gave a sharp downward tug, painfully and loudly slamming his head into the table:

"Scoundrel! Lazy bastard! Parasite! Coward! Clan Tar-Layneh will have to cover for your two-bit operation because you can't stay on top of your own duties!"

The level-147 Engineer by the name Vano-Ubish, and that was precisely who my companion was pummeling, was caught off guard at first. However, listening to his emotions, I very clearly realized Uline was seriously mistaken. Perhaps in other parts of the galaxy the influential and rich merchant clan of Tar-Layneh really could cause serious problems by slapping them with a delivery embargo to put the local traders out of business. But here on the edge of the Universe, they weren't the least bit afraid. And before Vano-Ubish came to his senses and put his great massive fists into action, drubbing the enraged female off him, I needed to intervene.

Psionic skill increased to level eighty-one!

"Uline, enough!" I forcibly pulled my furry friend off the huge Geckho who was already coming to his senses. "I have immeasurable respect for the most powerful and rich Clan Tar-Layneh, but they do not enter into this! This concerns only Kung Waid Shishish, for whom we were carrying an invaluable shipment. And the Kung would certainly be questioning all these Geckho if the pirates made it away with it. I'm afraid that the ghoulish fleet commander, not known for his peaceful ways, would make a wine glass from your skull, and ass cushions from your hides. And I'm not talking about the game here, this is in the real world!"

Mental Fortitude skill increased to level sixty-eight!

Mysticism skill increased to level twenty-nine!

Ah, it worked. And did it ever! With just one mention of the name of the hot-tempered master of

Earth, all four space port employees sobered up in an instant. I suspected my little speech made all four of them picture that scenario very vibrantly and in great detail, because this was the first time I had seen Geckho shivering in fear. I had to build on my success:

"I'm just about to have a long-distance call with Kung Waid Shishish, and I'm sure the topic of security will come up. What should I tell him? The truth, that clandestine Meleyephatian miners feel at ease in our star system, clearing out asteroids that belong to the Geckho? That Miyelonian smugglers can come land on our planet just four nodes from the space port as if they're at home? That pirates flagrantly attack landing starships right above the Geckho spaceport?"

Authority increased to 53!

I drove these harsh words into the frightened Geckhos' minds like red-hot pokers and the space port employees lowered their heads further and further. My spiny Analyst was not wrong. Pigheaded insolence was the best tactic here, and the chastised space-port employees were listening to me like some inspector sent by upper leadership. Finally, Vano-Ubish reached his limit:

"Gerd Gnat, that is all true, we are at fault. But security is not our responsibility! I assure you, the one responsible will be punished in the most severe fashion! I will shoot him three times myself!" the spaceport head assured me in a bleating tone. "As for what happened... I have funds set aside for building spaceport structures and urgent repair. It seems fair to me to spend those crystals on your starship, which fought so valiantly in an uneven battle with pirates..."

"Yes, it seems fair to me as well," I supported his right-minded idea. "And now, honored officials, I have to go negotiate. Can anyone tell me where to find the deep-space communication node?"

The three Geckho shot up all at once but the space port head Vano-Ubish told his underlings to all sit down with a gesture and assured me he would personally lead me to the negotiations. We had just reached the hallway when the disheveled Engineer, not at all ashamed at the soldiers accompanying me, tried to slip me a bag with monetary crystals clinking around temptingly, probably of quite high denomination.

"Gerd Gnat, there's no need to upset the Kung with such trifles on a distant planet when he's so busy..." he bleated timidly, shoving the money into my hands.

After that, his gaze caught on something and Vano-Ubish cowered, making him look even shorter. I followed his gaze and saw the winding missive on Imran's armored spacesuit saying that the armor was a personal gift from Kung Waid Shishish. I didn't know what clicked in the space port leader's head when he suddenly discovered how advanced my bodyguards were, but I got a double message about a boost to Fame and Authority.

I refused the bribe, assuring him the crystals from the construction funds would be plenty.

"But Uline Tar will make sure it's enough to repair my frigate first," I clarified so the space port head wouldn't try to pull one over on us. "And another thing:

in a quarter ummi I need a set table in the restaurant on the second floor for six people and one Geckho, Diplomat Kosta Dykhsh. Make it a fine, sumptuous table, worthy of deciding the future of this planet."

Authority increased to 55!

Attention!!! Your character has attained significant fame and authority and has now been assigned the rank Leng. You have received eight stat points.

Attention!!! Your character may now lead a faction. Choose one of the suggested options: Human-3, Human-6, Human-23, Human-25, La-Fin, Spaceport, or create your own faction.

"I'll do it all in fine fashion!" Vano-Ubish promised, unlocking the massive armored door with his crystal key. "Here is the deep-space negotiating chamber. Gerd Gnat... Oh! Leng Gnat! Congratulations on the promotion! And please send the great Kung my wishes of health and strength in the war!"

Chapter Thirteen

Negotiations, Negotiations...

THE STATUS PROMOTION came so unexpectedly I actually got thrown. So I was a Leng? I had basically been wanting and expecting this for a while, but still it knocked me off track. Especially when Imran said that the mini-map was no longer showing me as an ally, just a neutral player. Then I checked my own information:

Leng Gnat. Human. Faction [undefined]. Level-79 Listener.

What did that mean? Was I no longer part of the Human-3 Faction? And where would I come out of a virt pod in the real world? Especially if I chose one of the stranger options like Spaceport or La-Fin... After all, the Geckho's virt pods were clearly not on Earth. Like what if I found myself on one of the Geckho planets which, due to high gravitation, were not always a place humans could survive? Or in the magocratic world where, based on my wayedda's words, the heir to the huge La-Fin fortune wouldn't survive one hour due to the huge number of ill-wishers. No, I definitely shouldn't rush into a risky experiment and change faction! And the eight free stat points needed to be spent with my mind at ease, after careful consideration of all the possible consequences.

I left my companions and entered the negotiation chamber. I had seen such a circular room with mirror walls before in the depths of the Un-Tesh comet on the Geckho military base, but still I froze. It was just stunning to look at my innumerable reflections at various angles. The light went out and a hologram of the almighty Geckho started glowing in the air in front of me. He was wearing a luxurious suit of ceremonial armor and seated atop his throne. My ears laid back flat when I heard the thundering voice of the upset Kung:

"Finally! I guess you were in no rush to our meeting. I was getting sick of waiting, Gerd Gnat... Or is it Leng now? When did you have time for that?" his angry tone, clearly false and for show, changed to sincere and bordering on surprise.

Demonstrating submission and respect for the all-powerful sovereign of Earth, I got down on one knee:

"My Kung, I rushed to the comms point as soon

as I got medical treatment after a rough landing," I didn't delve into the details and tell the vaunted military leader about the security mishap on my peripheral planet.

"Yes, I can see you're injured. Alright, no matter. Have you got the delivery? Is it the exact thing you told the Trader?"

"Yes, my Kung," I pulled the heavy polished black stone out of my inventory and showed it to him with my good hand. "A map of all parts of the galaxy known to the Meleyephatians with a complete logistics scheme for their horde in maximum detail. It shows all space docks both in the game and the real world. It contains blueprints for starships and weapons, the coordinates of military bases, secret training centers, manufacturing facilities and mines of important resources. You can also find the coordinates of real-world data centers where their players' virt pods are located, and a full guide to the real Meleyephatian players behind characters in the game that bends reality. Plus there's lots of other stuff both on the Meleyephatians and the other races. Let your specialists sort it out."

I could see the gruesome fleet commander's eyes start to glimmer as his nostrils started flaring out in excitement. You don't have to be as wise as Solomon to guess just how valuable this all was to the Kung.

"What do you want for the drive, human?"

A seemingly normal question asked in a normal tone, however...

Danger Sense skill increased to level fifty-

five!

Danger Sense skill increased to level fifty-six?!

With a sudden attack of clarity, I understood that I would not be allowed to leave the negotiation chamber alive if I couldn't make an agreement with the commander. And they'd be able to kill me again and again because my respawn point was on the spaceport grounds and the Geckho knew that perfectly well. Since landing, I had spent all my time on land under their control. Fortunately, I was not going to test Kung Waid Shishish's patience and generosity even without those warnings:

"Let this be my gift to the great Kung! Everything that strengthens the Geckho benefits my race, so I will do anything to help my suzerains in the difficult war with the Meleyephatians!"

"You got that right, it is difficult..." the Commander of the Second Strike Fleet gave a heavy sigh and thought. But not long after he lit up: "Leng Gnat, it cannot be like that! Such a valuable gift demands equivalent gratitude on my part. Name your price!"

"Well, if my Kung insists..."I pretended to think even though the answer was on the tip of my tongue before I even entered the room. "I request this valuable information be copied and sent to the Commander of the Miyelonian Fleet Leng Keetsie-Myau!"

"I don't get it. Why should I make a competitor stronger?" The fearsome fleet commander grew severe again and even squinted.

I had to hurriedly explain my request before he flared up and said no:

"My Kung, the thing is that this information was obtained by Miyelonians, or more accurately an embedded agent of theirs. To cover their tracks, the data drive was sent through a long chain of middlemen of all sorts of races and, at a certain point, I became one of them. However, realizing the true value of the data, I decided to send it not to the commander of the Miyelonians, but to my Kung. And now I'm seriously afraid of consequences because Truth Seeker Leng Keetsie-Myau is not the kind of player you can just fool unpunished. What's more, the Miyelonians and Geckho are allies in this war, and helping your allies will be good for the Geckho. So that is precisely why I ask for this valuable data to be forwarded to Leng Keetsie-Myau and for you to say you got it from Gnat. That is plenty reward for me."

"So you're sure the Miyelonians will repay you so generously that you won't even need a reward from my race?!" I nearly went deaf when the Kung raised his voice.

Danger Sense skill increased to level fifty-seven!

To be honest, I didn't understand what made the fearsome commander lose it this time. Either Kung Waid Shishish's pride and ego were wounded by the fact that someone else was not bound by financial troubles and could possibly pay more than him. Or he simply didn't like my game and felt I was playing them off each other. It was probably the latter, although I purposely answered as if it were the first:

"My Kung, I never intended to wound the pride of the great Geckho race! It's just that I already own a starship and know perfectly how much it costs to repair. So I'm afraid to even imagine how colossal your expenditures must be to repair the Second Strike Fleet after the bloody battles with the Meleyephatians. And that means it would be utterly improper for me to ask the Kung for a monetary reward. The Miyelonians on the other hand haven't spent much on this war yet, so let them pay to repair the damage my frigate sustained in the landing!"

Here I plucked the right strings in his soul, I could sense that right away. The huge problems involved in repairing his severely damaged fleet had the commander worried, as did a lack of financing. The fearsome commander, covered in thick dark fur, stopped baring his teeth and finally shifted from anger to sweetness:

"Alright, have it your way, Leng Gnat! Especially because I already owe you one. Thanks to your timely warning, I managed to get half the garrison and two-thirds of the ships off the Un-Tesh base. So I'll send that along to Keetsie and tell her you asked me to do it. By the way, the Great One, as the Miyelonians call her, became a Kung not long ago, much the same as me. They say she even has a decent chance of becoming leader of the Union of Prides. So your reward..." Kung Waid Shishish went silent midsentence, watching my anxious face with a smirk, "now that you're a Leng and can have your own faction, is that the great Geckho race shall guarantee the absolute safety of one node of your choosing. Hell, make it three nodes! Anyone that attacks those nodes shall be an enemy of the Geckho and will be immediately destroyed!!! I've said all I have to say. Give the package to the Diplomat of my race, what's his name, that young clever fellow. Tell him to find a way to get it to me as fast as possible. And tell him as soon as he's done, I appoint him viceroy of the whole planet. As it is, with this space war I have no time to deal with the periphery myself."

"WELL, HOW DO I look?" Minn-O La-Fin was for some reason very invested in that question.

My wayedda, her lump gone without a trace, had changed out of her spacesuit and into a black and lilac dress of an unusual and I might even say old-fashioned cut with lots of skirts, lace sleeves and a high uncomfortable collar. And as far as I could tell, a Sio-Mi-Dori had been sent especially for that dress. One of the Dark Faction heavy assault antigravs quickly returned to the space port and a pilot girl with ash gray skin, bowing low at the waist to my wife, handed her a big packet of clothing.

Before answering, I scanned my companion's dress for any microphones or other surveillance equipment, as well as poison capsules or explosives. I remembered catching the Dark Faction red handed doing that before. Nevertheless, it was all clean.

"Idiotic cut, this dress hides your fantastic young body and doesn't work for you at all," I preferred to tell the truth rather than flatter my wife. "You'd never wear something like that unless it was truly necessary. I guess it's some kind of regalia to emphasize your status, right?"

The Dark Faction Princess was not offended, in fact she smiled:

"Exactly right, oh husband! This ancient style was laid out hundreds of years ago, and mine is in the coloring of a married woman of a ruling magical house. The shape of the collar indicates my status as an upper aristocrat, and lilac and black are the heraldic colors of the La-Fin dynasty."

"Oh my! I'll remember that. Okay then, emphasizing your high status will be worth something in the upcoming negotiations. But I really hope your laws don't require me to also change into something so pompous and uncomfortable."

"Oh they do," my companion smiled, "but you'd never agree to wear all the colorful pantaloons, frilly blouses and long robes, so I didn't even suggest it. What's more, in your black space armor you look very respectable even with a broken arm."

I gave her a kiss on the cheek and looked at the time. There were four minutes left until the start of the peace negotiations with the Dark Faction. I brought Gerd Minn-O La-Fin and my business partner Uline Tar with me. I brought my junior wife as a specialist in the norms of the magocratic world, a Princess of the ruling house of the First Directory and just as a translator of the language of her people. Uline then I needed as the owner of the starship, representative of the Geckho race and a member of the Tar-Layneh merchant dynasty to underline my profile among the suzerains of mankind. We had agreed to meet on the third floor of the dispatcher tower, then go down together into the restaurant.

"For some reason Uline is late..." my wife was nervous, clearly counting the remaining minutes.

"Our furry friend is dying patterns on her fur," I whispered to Minn-O, "for Geckho ladies it's basically like make-up. But the process of drawing the patterns is considered nearly intimate, only very close friends are allowed to help. So I'm just surprised Uline Tar entrusted that role to the Miyelonian Gerd Ayni. Ah, there is Uline now!"

The captain's assistant walked out of the elevator and, seeing Minn-O and I, came toward us in a quick pace.

"Hrmph, I barely made it! By the way, there were three people in the elevator with me who had the same skin color as Minn-O. One of them was basically naked, the largest and most muscular. I presume those are the people we'll be negotiating with?"

Basically naked? Strange. Although Uline's words were fully confirmed when we went a floor lower. There was a huge giant over six foot five with a shock of black hair and impressive muscles like a bodybuilder. He was wearing nothing but leather shorts with a wide belt which had empty holsters and knife sheaths on it. And good thing. Weaponry was not allowed at this meeting.

Gerd Ui-Taka. Human. La-Fin Faction. Level-63 Strategist.

Clearly, General Ui-Taka's rescue raft had just reached the shore, because my counterpart hadn't even found time to change clothes. Although it was also possible that Ui-Taka had purposely chosen this style of dress to display his power and unbridled strength. It really was impressive, what could I say...?

Mental Fortitude skill increased to level sixty-nine!

What was this? Was someone trying to attack me mentally?

"Hey, come on. No magic!" my shout of rage was aimed at the General's companions, two mages in identical black robes:

Gerd Avir-Syn La-Pirez. Human. La-Fin Faction. Level-109 Psionic Mage.

Gerd Mac-Peu Un-Roi. Human. La-Fin Faction. Level-96 Mage Diviner.

These were some no-nonsense dudes! And dangerous. Especially the first one: the wrinkly old man had smoldering blue eyes and I could feel with my skin the deadly hatred emanating from him. The second was a young man also with glowing magical eyes, but his gaze was not hostile, more studying like I was some rare and engrossing little animal. By the way, I now saw their faction as "La-Fin" rather than "Dark Faction." Was that because I'd become a Leng and was for now "out of the system," until I chose a new team?

"Grandpa Avir-Syn, magic is also a weapon and

is forbidden at negotiations!" the Princess reminded the geezer, and he threw his hood down low, covering his face and no longer boring into me with his smoldering gaze.

Astrolinguistics skill increased to level eighty-five!

Grandfather?! So this ghastly big old man was my wife's grandfather on her father's side?! Minn-O had told me about the tragic death of her parents in a terror attack, and her father's family did happen to be La-Pirez. Hrm, both of my wife's grandfathers, Thumor-Anhu and this Avir-Syn looked like they came out of a horror movie. Who was to say what dirty magical tricks this old man was capable of? So I quickly tossed all three free stat points into Mental Fortitude, raising it to seventy-two. After all, extra mental defense was always good when talking with a psionic!

"Yes, no magic!" Gerd Ui-Taka turned to his companions. "We're just talking. Where shall we go Gerd... Leng Gnat???"

I pointed to the farthest table, separated from the rest. Geckho Diplomat Kosta Dykhsh was already sitting there. We all walked closer. Wow!!! Even I was impressed, even though I was generally quite hard to surprise with luxury and abundance. It wasn't enough that the table was straining under the weight of the food itself, all the plates, platters and even glasses were made of red monetary crystals of various shapes and values attached together. I never suspected objects could be made of Geckho currency like LEGOs.

"Leng Gnat, admit it, is this your doing?" the

Diplomat asked strictly, pointing at his still empty plate which was worth around three thousand crystals.

Uline Tar answered instead, taking a big red salad bowl and studying it in the light with intrigue, staring at the dozens of skillfully interlaced crystals:

"No, we had nothing to do with this. This must be the administration of the local spaceport awkwardly attempting to make up for not providing security during landing."

"Yes we saw your... let's call it a landing," snorted the young mage, demonstrating a brilliant knowledge of Geckho.

He repeated it in his own language, and his two companions also broke down laughing. The general gave himself a generous splash of wine in a glass and pronounced a long phrase I didn't totally understand, so Minn-O had to help me with translation:

"Gerd Ui-Taka now thinks the starship will be out of the game for a long time because we don't have the money to repair it. And all this garish luxury on display now won't be much help to repair the frigate even if we take all the plates and glasses apart and use them as crystals."

And when I translated that to Uline Tar, it was our turn to laugh. To start the Trader showed the Diplomat then everyone else her tablet, showing an official contract with the spaceport administration saying they would repair our frigate. It gave a concrete timeframe for the repair as well: five days.

"And I hope the future viceroy," Uline said pointing at her furry compatriot, "will guarantee the quality of his underlings' work."

"Of course, now it's a question of honor," Kosta Dykhsh confirmed. "Leng Gnat can be sure that his ship will be ready within that timeframe."

Authority increased to 56!

"What's more," Uline put the tablet away, took an item from her inventory and demonstrated it in her open palm, "you don't know my human business partner well. Gnat has a knack for finding money everywhere, even on a pirate station or in open space. Just this journey he earned me... what did you call this Leng Gnat? An or-ranzh?"

"A blood orange," I corrected my friend. The "fruit" she was referring to was a highly valuable crystal, Uline's share of the reward for destroying the pirate frigate. Worth a whole million, it really was reminiscent of the red citrus fruit in size and shape.

"So you're deeply mistaken about the idea that we don't have money. But most importantly," Uline turned back to her compatriot Kosta Dykhsh and spoke passionately almost like an animal roaring as it tears into some meat, "future viceroy, tell these human aboriginals what my clan Tar-Layneh is known for."

The diplomat looked embarrassed and pushed his plate away, chewing the food in his mouth, then answered with clear deference to my partner:

"Clan Tar-Layneh controls a significant part of trade routes in the known part of the galaxy, more than five hundred starships and is considered one of the richest Geckho families and trading clans. Their financial reserves are basically unlimited. By the way,

Uline. It would be a great honor for me to speak with you separately after these negotiations."

"Endless financial reserves..." General Ui-Taka frowned, nervously tapping the tips of his fingers on the table and casting an extremely unhappy gaze at the Mage Diviner, which made the young wizard tense up in fear. "Sure. That doesn't play much of a role. In five whole days I can wipe the Human-3, Human-6 and even the distant Human-1 Factions off the face of the planet. Diviner, confirm!"

Astrolinguistics skill increased to level eighty-six!

Alright then, I understood that whole long phrase completely! Gerd Mac-Peu Un-Roi froze motionless, just his pupils were darting very quickly in his wide-open blue eyes. Ten or fifteen seconds passed before the young mage sharply exhaled and, trying not to look at the General, spoke without too much confidence:

"Something has changed in the lines of the future... Just three hours ago I saw a ninety-three percent chance of total victory over a coalition of enemies. And that was with Gnat in a starship in orbit. But now even with a defective frigate I see no chance for a complete military victory. Zero percent. I mean, we are still stronger and can dominate on all fronts, but I don't see total victory in any of the possible futures."

I couldn't understand everything there, but my wife translated. The Strategist then started nervously clenching and unclenching his fists. It seemed to me he was imagining breaking the young mage's neck because of his earlier inaccurate prognosis. Nevertheless, when Gerd Ui-Taka started speaking (with Minn-O translating), his ideas were completely sensible:

"An endless war of attrition without the possibility of final victory is not at all what we were after. And it is actually very good that all three of you are not directly in the Human-3 Faction and can look at the situation with an impartial eye and no fanaticism. I'm reporting the facts as I see them. In fact, the side I led was victorious..."

Here I wanted to object, but Geckho Diplomat Kosta Dykhsh suggested I first allow my opponent to finish his speech and argue only after.

"The enemy coalition has fallen apart. The Human-6 Faction lost its capital and is basically defeated. I specifically ordered not to destroy their coastal hexagons because living players have much higher prospects as vassals than the NPC's that would move into the empty territories. The Human-1 Faction... Yes, their arrival was a surprise and rolled back the timeframe of my victory, but they also took a big kick to the teeth and sent a Diplomat to agree to terms for freeing their many prisoners. And finally, the main enemy..."

The General splashed himself a bit more young rosé and, savoring the bouquet with clear satisfaction, continued:

"The Human-3 Faction's defenses have been destroyed both on the southern and northern fronts. The two southern hexagons are already lost and the cliff hexagon to the north only survived because I was in a good mood and announced the negotiations and ceasefire. I also allowed the Second Legion to escape a deadly trap after they were already crushed to dust. So show some appreciation for my mercy for the vanquished! But I don't think any of you will doubt that my army won this war. And thus I should be the one to dictate the terms of the peace!"

After making sure my opponent was finished, I asked the Geckho observer to listen carefully to my answer because a few parts might need confirmation. Kosta Dykhsh set his unfinished wine glass aside and told me he was listening carefully. Okay then, I was ready to respond. The only hard part was not to accidentally use magic. I really didn't want to be accused of breaking the rules.

"So then, incorrect initial data led General Ui-Taka to rushed and deeply mistaken conclusions. Let me begin with the fact you cannot possibly win now, which so surprised the experienced Mage Diviner," I pointed at Gerd Mac-Peu Un-Roi, who was listening to my words in the most attentive fashion. "Yes, it is impossible for our side to achieve a military victory! I have the right, given by the master of Earth Kung Waid Shishish himself, to select three nodes which the Geckho will defend as if they were their own."

"Impossible! The Geckho do not interfere in their vassals' squabbles, it's the law!" Psionic Mage Avir-Syn objected heatedly, to which I simply suggested that the Geckho Diplomat weigh in.

"Yes, Leng Gnat speaks the truth! He may select

three nodes for us to officially protect. Anyone who attacks them will be at war with the whole Geckho state," the suzerains' Diplomat declared, which caused an extreme flurry in my opponents' ranks.

Authority increased to 57!

"Beyond that, my starship will be repaired sooner or later. And that's where things get interesting... No, I'm not planning to break our agreement and destroy La-Fin Faction citadels. Instead I'll attack the nodes of the La-Varrez or La-Shin factions from space, the other corulers of your humanity! I'll attack the nodes of all other mages I can find! And I'll give these influential mages a choice: either their states declare war on the Second Directory or their factions shall be wiped out in the game that bends reality! A final death in the game is equivalent to dying in the real world, so the mage rulers will listen. They simply won't have any other choice."

Based on how the vaunted general lost control and started cursing ornately ("greasy hooker's ass" was nowhere near the limit here), this was an unexpected move. No longer hiding my satisfied smirk, I built on that:

"Oh yeah, I still haven't said the most important part! Before that, I'll make a speech to the magocratic world and, as head of the First Directory and legal heir to the La-Fin family, I will officially accuse the ruler of the Second Directory General Ui-Taka of the bloody terror attack at the funeral of great mage Thumor-Anhu La-Fin and the attempted murder of my wife Minn-O La-Fin! How many governments are now at war with the Second Directory? Four of thirty, I believe. Well, soon General Ui-Taka will have many, MANY more enemies!!!"

Chapter Fourteen

Claims Confirmed

AFTER MAKING accusations right to General Ui-Taka's face, I was expecting the sharpest possible reaction: denials, threats, maybe even physical attacks. But the huge muscular giant, not taking his piercing black eyes off me, sat back in his seat, crossed his powerful arms over his broad chest and... gave a loud laugh! And I could sense instantly that this was not mischievous or acrid laughter, it was purely good-natured:

"Oh boy we really did spook each other! It's nice to talk to a person that can't be scared with threats, and who comes back blow for blow! I love people like that!"

The Dark Faction Strategist took another little sip of wine and spoke to my companions:

"After all, Leng Gnat understands perfectly that I have nothing to do with what happened at the funeral. But he does see his enemy's pain points and hits them very hard as a true warrior should. It inspires unwitting respect and awe. In that regard, he reminds me of another Leng of the La-Fin dynasty..."

"Yes, I also pictured Coruler Thumor-Anhu La-Fin while Gnat was making his speech. My legs buckled in an inadvertent desire to fall to my knees before such fearsome power," the young Mage Diviner chuckled nervously, slaking his fears with more wine. "You are truly worthy to head the La-Fin dynasty!"

"What, have you totally gone blind?! This Johnny-come-lately is very far from the majestic and (unknown) Thumor-Anhu!" the old Psionic Mage Avir-Syn La-Pirez didn't agree one bit. "My late friend inspired respect and fear in all with his indominable magic powers. Gnat only inspires disgust with his pitiful vain attempts! He is unworthy to lead the La-Fin Faction, and furthermore he has no place in our world!"

What was this? The three Dark Faction speakers were not at all ashamed to discuss me aloud in front of me, as if I wasn't even there! What was more, Princess Minn-O La-Fin joined in:

"Grandpa, you're wrong! Yes my husband still has little experience in the magical arts, but he is definitely talented! Beyond that, very powerful rulers of the Geckho and Miyelonians know and respect him!

224

Gnat is worthy to lead the La-Fin dynasty and the whole First Directory!"

The decrepit mage, spraying spittle in fury, answered my wayedda with inexcusable harshness:

"Foolish whelp! Respect alone is entirely insufficient here! The head of a magical family can only be a mage! And the head of the most powerful La-Fin Dynasty with its ancient and glorious history can only be a very strong (unknown, probably a synonym of mage) — anyone else would be instantly torn to shreds by innumerable enemies and competitors! Gnat is completely not up to the task! But you have been blinded by your foolishness and love. To everyone else, it is obvious!"

"Wait, wait!" I jumped into the conversation not at all in my turn and in elevated tones. "I will not allow anyone to insult my legal wife, even if it is a very close relative! What's more, we are here in the Geckho spaceport to discuss terms for a peace between the La-Fin and Human-3 Factions, not my magical abilities or my relationship with the La-Fin Dynasty!"

"Well the first is inseparable from the second and third," Gerd Ui-Taka chuckled. "I am merely a steward hired by the undoubtedly great (same word, and again in the sense of mage or enchanter) Thumor-Anhu La-Fin to carry out a clearly specified mission: break through the enemy defenses, provide a military advantage and do everything in my power to lay the groundwork for a peace treaty with the most favorable possible terms for the La-Fin Faction. Despite the death of my employer, I am not accustomed to giving up on an unfinished job, or betraying people who trust and follow me. Now I have fulfilled my mission, but my subjects have already seen the one who came to replace their former leader. Just a bit more... Uh, what is that? A violation of the terms of the negotiations?!"

General Ui-Taka's last words were about Eduard Boyko, who came unexpectedly into the restaurant in a full exoskeleton suit. Something very serious must have happened. Like the rest of my crew, my friend had been given very clear instructions not to interrupt the important negotiations. But here he had broken the rule and come into the meeting armored and armed. I apologized, got up and hurried to meet the Space Commando before Geckho Diplomat Kosta Dykhsh accused our side of violating terms and slapped us with another heavy fine.

Eduard, nervously peering at the Dark Faction players, immediately explained why he'd come:

"Gnat, we just got a message from headquarters. While tallying the Second Legion soldiers after respawn, we discovered that one is missing. Well, you know her. It's their leader, Gerd Tamara the Paladin. She also hasn't come out under the Dome in the real world. The guys combed the swamp along the road very carefully. They figured she was lying wounded or unconscious. But she's nowhere to be found. The most probable explanation HQ can think of is that she was taken captive by the Dark Faction and stunned or has been anesthetized so she won't wake up and be able to say where she is. Commander, you know how much Gerd Tamara means to our guys. So they want you to ask the enemy and, if HQ isn't wrong, take measures to get Gerd Tamara back. And they also want you to ask about Anna the Medic."

I WENT BACK to the negotiating table and, without wheedling, demanded right to their faces to immediately tell me what had happened to Gerd Tamara, leader of the Second Legion. The three Dark Faction negotiators exchanged glances and the old Psionic Mage Gerd Avir-Syn answered:

"This is not the time for you to make demands of us!"

The ghastly mage looked me right in the eyes with clear mockery as if goading me to respond. Or might I risk challenging him to a mental duel?

Danger Sense skill increased to level fifty-eight!

Even without that message, I already knew this was not the time to be going head on and accepting a challenge that was sure to end in my defeat. Avir-Syn was an experienced mage who was a whole thirty levels higher than me, and he knew psionic mind-control inside and out. His skills there were much better levelled, he had more Magic Points. La-Pirez had at least an order of magnitude more experience than me in real-world mental duels as well.

Still, it also would have been wrong to pretend nothing extraordinary was happening. That ran me the risk of a serious drop in Authority. But what to do?

I didn't cross gazes with the ghastly old man. In fact, I turned away to a wide panorama window with a view of the space port. And playing right into my hand, there were three Sio-Mi-Dori assault antigravs right there. They'd already finished loading the new thrusters and were waiting for the end of negotiations to collect their leaders.

"Well alright then, if you won't understand the nice way... I'll have to be a bit mean and show you what gives me the right to make demands!"

One after the other at one-second intervals, all three assault-landing antigravs were engulfed in flames of bright explosion. The thunder-clap was audible even here in the restaurant, and a large piece of wreckage flew up to the dispatcher's tower, leaving a mark on the armored glass of the third floor.

Machine Control skill increased to level seventy-three!

Electronics skill increased to level seventy-four!

You have reached level eighty!
You have received three skill points.

Alright, good thing we hid those bombs! My opponents were shocked and more importantly impressed! Geckho Diplomat Kosta Dykhsh also gave a nervous jerk looking at the spiderweb cracks on the sturdy glass of the restaurant, but limited himself to a few words to nobody in particular: "after these negotiations, you will have to clean up the debris." That must have been directed at all people regardless of faction. I continued before my opponents' shock had passed:

"So then, as far as I understand there were five remaining Sio-Mi-Doris... Shall I find them and destroy them as well? Or are you going to tell me where Gerd Tamara is?"

"It's no use pressuring us, Leng Gnat. We don't have your commander! I swear on my honor!" General Ui-Taka said loudly and in no uncertain terms.

And so in the silence that fell, the words of the young Mage Diviner sounded out like thunder from a clear sky:

"The Paladin was separated from the other prisoners and immediately brought to the underground dungeon under the central hexagon citadel!"

Despite the more senior mage's outcry demanding he hold his tongue, Gerd Mac-Peu Un-Roi continued:

"I was ordered not to tell that to anyone, even faction head Gerd Ui-Taka. As far as I know, they intend to sell Gerd Tamara to our allies."

What??? Gerd Tamara really had been taken prisoner. And not all the Dark Faction negotiators knew about it. Plus there were some mysterious allies and they were planning to sell our girl to them!

"Who gave that order? What allies?"

The Mage Diviner wasn't fast enough to answer my question. He just went gray in fear as the senior Psionic Mage stood, sharply extended a hand in his direction and gave a command:

"Die!!!"

It all happened suddenly. Gerd Mac-Peu clutched his heart and fell right on the table, overturning salad bowls and glasses. And meanwhile the ghastly old man stood up and pointed a crooked finger at me with menacing decisiveness, saying loudly to the closely watching representative of our suzerains:

"Diplomat Kosta Dykhsh, I would like the record to state that Leng Gnat broke the ceasefire! He attacked our faction's aircraft and killed our people. And he is planning to kill me! The negotiations are cancelled!"

"Not at all!" I also stood up and my voice sounded no less loud and decisive. "It was a condition of this ceasefire that the Second Legion be allowed to leave unimpeded! And now it turns out that was not upheld!!! Diplomat Kosta Dykhsh, I wish the record to state that the Dark Faction violated the terms from the outset!"

Kosta Dykhsh was baffled and said nothing. But then the Psionic Mage suddenly wheezed and foam appeared on his lips. His eyes started to bulge strangely. The old man's mouth opened wide, trying to say something, then his legs gave out and he fell dead on the floor. Everyone looked at me for some reason but I just threw up my hands:

"No, I didn't do that! Notice, my level didn't change! If I had killed him, it would have given enough experience to level up a couple times at least!"

Yes it was an iron-clad argument in confirmation of my innocence. Once before I had proven my noninvolvement in the murder of the Great Priestess of the Miyelonian race the same way, so now

I instantly got my bearings and hurried to cut off any possible insinuations.

"Grandfather killed himself!" Minn-O declared decisively. "Every mage has an ampule of contact poison sewn into their robe which is activated by a key word or even mentally. That is why mages cannot be taken prisoner. They can always kill themselves and respawn somewhere safe."

"Hrm... What nice negotiations people have," Uline Tar, silent for a long time, couldn't hold back and let out a mean comment, releasing some nervous tension. "Is it always like this, Gnat?"

It was a rhetorical question and needed no answer. Unlike the next one asked by the Geckho Diplomat, who was clearly baffled and didn't understand what was going on:

"I can understand why Gerd Avir-Syn killed his ally: so he wouldn't keep talking. But why kill himself?"

I had an answer to that question:

"First of all, he was in a rush to get out of his virt pod to meet the young mage diviner in the real world. He needs to convince him to keep quiet or at least agree on a single consistent version of events. Second, such a theatrical death put me in a bad light, especially after the geezer said I threatened his life. Third, he was ending the important negotiations. For some reason, peace with my faction doesn't enter into Gerd Avir-Syn La-Pirez's plans."

After hearing out Minn-O's translation (in view of the death of his own Geckho translator, the Strategist had to fall back on my wife's services)

General Ui-Taka continued my speech:

"And fourth, it was the fastest way to get to the capital hexagon, where Gerd Avir-Syn La-Pirez's respawn point is. Most players, especially high-profile ones, leave their respawn points deep in the karst caves beneath the citadel for safety purposes. Down there, your faction cannot hit them with any kind of weapon, even nuclear."

I didn't inform him that my faction didn't have any nuclear weapons or at the very least I didn't know if we did. In fact, it was a military secret. Instead I noted that the captive Paladin girl Gerd Tamara was being held somewhere in those very catacombs, according to Gerd Mac-Peu Un-Roi. And so the old mage's urgent travel there may not have been a coincidence.

"Yes, you're completely right, Leng Gnat..." the huge muscular man stood up, looking through the window at the Dark Faction technicians fussing about with the spaceport workers to put out the flaming antigravs. "An idiotic situation... I always knew the mages of the La-Fin Faction might turn against me one day, so I always tried to stay on guard. But it never occurred to me that they might kill one another. Okay then, given the negotiations are over anyway, go rescue your vaunted commander before she is sold to another magical faction. Look, there's a small La-Fin Faction antigrav landing in the spaceport now. Gnat, go talk with the pilot. Convince him to take you to the first citadel."

What??? It was such a foolhardy suggestion I was taken aback. Go alone into the very den of my most dangerous and clever enemy, right into their underground prison even! Was Ui-Taka sane suggesting something like that? I would be killed as soon as I showed up! And that was in the best case. In the worst, they'd lock me up in that prison until the end of time!

"What, too scared?" Either my opponent really didn't understand or he was mocking me. "Leng Gnat, you said yourself today that you were the official ruler of the First Directory and, as such, leader of the La-Fin Faction. Are you really not confident enough in your powers that you are afraid of your own subjects? Take your wayedda with you then. Princess Minn-O can make it through any checkpoint in a ruler's dress like that. Apologies but I won't be flying with you. There's very little room in the antigrav, and I'm not going to sit on your lap. What's more, I'm very interested to see if you can manage. If you remember, I once went alone and unarmed to your capital fortress. Your warriors bowed before me even though I am their avowed enemy! You, Leng Gnat, are no enemy to these people but their rightful leader. Prove that elder mage Avir-Syn is wrong and you deserve to rule!"

I HAD ALREADY seen this high-speed antigrav before. It was how the majestic and terrible Thumor-Anhu La-Fin, leader of the Dark Faction, had flown in to free his granddaughter from captivity. A Pilot and Technician.

That was the whole crew of this small flying machine. Neither player had any questions and they both treated me with clearly demonstrated respect. Although maybe it was less for me than for my companion. After all, Minn-O La-Fin was their Princess and ruler no matter how you spun it. The Technician was a small squat girl with a cleanshaven head. She brought down the folding ladder and helped me and my companion come on board.

Inside was very cramped, I had to keep my legs folded up and my head hunched in nearly to the point it was between my legs. It was clear why the huge General Ui-Taka preferred other methods of transportation: he simply couldn't fit into this thing. I had to put my Listener Energy Armor into my inventory and sit Minn-O on my lap, then we both had to make like Indian yogis to fit into the very limited space. Whoever invented this thing did not have ergonomics or comfort in mind.

In many ways it looked respectable from the outside, even luxurious. Still the Dark Faction antigrav was quite similar to that old Starship Dmitry Zheltov used to drive around back in the day. It had a similar body made of welded lightweight pipes, the antigrav pancakes were just a bit larger and more powerful. There were just three seats not four, but outside the vehicle had millimeter-thick tin plating for better aerodynamics.

The main difference from the Starship was that this vehicle could actually fly rather than hovering just above the surface. We quickly gained height and raced off over the desert toward some snowy mountains on the horizon. The very highest peaks were already colored a slight crimson of the dawning sun. Through a transparent cap you could see dark sands, the odd dry bush and even a herd of either saiga or gazelle with their ears back in alarm and accompanying us with their gazes.

Cartography skill increased to level sixty-two!

Eagle Eye skill increased to level seventy-four!

That was all great of course, and that method of faster skill leveling was interesting, but I took a look at the map and asked the Pilot:

"Why are we taking a hook around the bay? Why not fly straight over?"

San-Doon Taki-Bu Human. La-Fin Faction. Level-89 Pilot.

The short pilot was wearing a soft helmet like a tank driver and a thick button-up jacket. He turned toward me:

"The previous Leng, Coruler Thumor-Anhu (unclear) to risk it. The vehicle is (unclear) fussy, sometimes one of the antigrav disks loses power or just (censored) malfunctions, requiring an emergency landing. So we (unclear) try not to fly over the sea."

Astrolinguistics skill increased to level eighty-seven!

Strange. In the space port, I could understand the Dark Faction negotiators nearly perfectly in their native language, but here I missed many words in just a few short sentences. Was this a different dialect? Or had I learned a strange accent? Nevertheless I assured my wife, who was shuddering and trying to get out of an uncomfortable pose, that there was no need for translation and answered the Pilot myself:

"Every second counts right now! So we're flying the shortest route. And try to squeeze as much speed as you can out of this clunker because right now we're crawling along like a particularly lethargic turtle!"

Authority increased to 58!

Woah! Now this was a totally different matter! I was pressed into the back of the seat. The pilot, inspired and clearly bored with these speeds and g-forces, squeezed the antigrav for all it was worth, just periodically giving the Technician commands to change the pancake settings and regulate the power loads.

I must have gone crazy to ask for this. Not only in the sense of the risky flight over the bay at high speeds, but this whole risky venture visiting the enemy capital. What happened at the negotiations could easily have been a temptation by the enemy leaders, demonstrating a false split in their leadership, but actually working together with the goal of catching another of the enemy's high-profile players. For example, the Mage Diviner might have read the lines of fate and seen that saying Gerd Tamara was in their prison could draw me into a trap, then mentally explained what to say and do to his two companions. After all, could the faction leader really not have known what was happening in his own holdings?

The more I thought it all over, the more worried

I felt. At a certain moment it all turned into a horror movie in my head and it got so bad I almost ordered the antigrav to turn around and go back to the spaceport. To distract myself from the taxing worries, I asked San-Doon a question:

"Say, what makes the Pilot class different from Starship Pilot?"

"Well for one thing the skills are totally different, Leng Gnat La-Fin," San-Doon answered me, not turning around and keeping a close eye on the instruments. "A Pilot has abilities for flying in conditions of (unclear, most likely 'insufficient' or 'limited') visibility and in bad weather. They have advanced piloting skills and skills for aerial and atmospheric combat, plus a Pilot can use some kinds of on-board guns. A Starship Pilot is totally different. The game offered me that class but faction leadership (unclear, probably either 'insisted' or 'recommended') that I choose simply Pilot."

Minn-O, forced to double over due to how tall she was and especially cognizant of the discomfort of the tiny antigrav, knew what I was after:

"My husband isn't asking just because. He needs a second pilot on the star frigate, he's looking at candidates."

"I would consider it my honor to serve you, my lord! But first you need to finish this whole (censored) war and intrafactional schism so they don't look at me funny. By the way, we're almost there. Behind that cliff you can see the central citadel and the main entrance to the underground dungeons."

In fact, beyond the sharp mountain peaks there was a squat structure stuck right into a steep slope. It had thick walls, a concrete dome, locators turning every which way and security towers with laser batteries.

"Permission to land granted!" The silent technician girl raised her voice for the first time since the start of the flight. "Garrison leader Gerd T'yu-Pan greets us and would like to personally come out to meet the new Leng."

"How do they know who's on board?" I asked, surprised and even more alarmed.

"Back at the spaceport both we and probably other groups sent messages about our unusual passenger."

The cleanshaven girl turned toward me and, gathering bravery, added:

"Leng Gnat La-Fin, everyone in the faction is sick to death of the endless drills, killings for the tiniest infractions and daily brainwashing. They're all desperately hoping the new lord from the other world will finally put a stop to this idiotic war!"

Chapter
Fifteen

Underground
Prison

HOW ABOUT that! Most of the Dark Faction didn't want to fight us? That was astonishing news because it went against the whole image in my brain. From my very first day in the game, my leaders had explained the Dark Faction as an aggressive and implacable enemy that wished us death. And a ghastly harsh one. I had heard stories about players from my faction they took captive. The Dark Faction torturers would stop at nothing to get information or recruit them. They used the most cruel and perverse torture methods, breaking prisoners both physically and mentally using drugs and a large share of psionic magic. And I was thinking about those horror stories during tonight's flight over the bay.

And now, in personal conversation with a Dark Faction player, I come to find out that they never wanted to fight, and their mage rulers were just forcing them? Very interesting! I just didn't know if the technician girl was voicing a common opinion or her personal views. And it was too bad but we couldn't keep talking because our antigrav was already coming in for a landing.

We were met by a group of soldiers in heavy armor. Not robot-assisted exoskeleton suits like Gerd Tamara and Eduard Boyko had, they were just encased head to toe in thick suits of metal. I was even afraid to imagine the Strength parameter needed to constantly wear these sturdy but insanely heavy pieces. My Gnat probably wouldn't be able to move in a tea kettle like that. Plus, the players also needed to carry weapons. Everyone I came across had a heavy plasma rifle of Geckho production. I had ordered ones just like it for my faction, so I knew perfectly that one of these rifles, which could go straight through a foot and a half of reinforced concrete, weighed forty pounds. Basically, the people who came out to meet me were titans, not humans!

I checked their names and levels, then correctly identified the group leader:

Gerd T'yu-Pan Yn-U. Human. La-Fin Faction. Level-104 Shocktroop.

Level one hundred and four! This guy was freaking awesome. T'yu-Pan clearly wasn't just wearing through his pants seat here in the citadel, he must have been very active in combat missions if he managed to level up that much. An intrusive thought told me this Shocktroop gained all that experience by killing my allies, but I chased it off. Yes, he was an enemy of my allies, a very strong enemy. But now that didn't matter.

Gerd T'yu-Pan tried to bow awkwardly, which was not easy to do in the stiff armor suit, then he extended a hand, helping the Princess and I down the gangway.

"My lord, what are your orders?"

He addressed me with all due respect, clearly accepting the new political order. Only after this did I calm down. Given Dark Faction players like him accepted Gnat as their new leader, that meant my claims to power were not unfounded and I would find support among the players. And really, why not? One mage-ruler of the La-Fin Dynasty was gone, and another mage from the same family had come to take his place. As far as a commoner from the magocratic world was concerned, that was the way things worked.

I asked the garrison leader if he knew about the captive paladin girl from the Human-3 Faction. A shadow of doubt ran across his face, the polite smile instantly crawled off his lips.

Successful Authority check!

The Shocktroop considered, but after a brief pause I did get an answer:

"Leng Gnat, there was a clear order from the mages around the former Leng not to tell anybody about this prisoner under penalty of death for the whole family in the real world. I can only say that a La-Varrez Faction tiltrotor is on its way here for her and will arrive any minute. There's an order to transfer the prisoner to them."

Very valuable information! So enemy mages would soon be flying in for the leader of the Second Legion with the goal of taking Gerd Tamara where we couldn't get her. That meant I had to hurry! Until then, I wanted to ask the garrison commander to take me to the captive Gerd Tamara, but now my plans had changed:

"Where is Gerd Tamara being kept? No, don't say it out loud! We won't be harming your family. Just look me in the eyes!"

I even raised my helmet visor to make full eye contact. Got it! A flood of thoughts from the huge and self-confident warrior flooded out onto me:

"Yes, that's the right move. Saves me breaking an order. I see our new mage ruler has a delicate touch. Okay then, let's see how good he is at this. After all, this is the same Gnat they used to scare all of us, the one who had a high price on his head. Hey, I don't actually remember that being called off. We'll have to protect the Leng. Otherwise who's to say what could happen. There are all kinds of freaks in the citadel right now. A few would cut up their own mother if the money's right. What's more the Leng is wounded, look at the sling on his arm. Although he is a mage, he doesn't need full range of motion. But it feels like he's been staring at me too long. Coruler Thumor-Anhu could have read

everything he needed five times by now. Gnat must have low experience. Very bad. If the mage rulers find that out, Gnat is a dead man."

This soldier had such "loud" thoughts they distracted and kept me from concentrating on what I wanted — information about the paladin girl. But in the end I managed! In my head, at first indistinctly, but growing in detail with every second, I received a three-dimensional map of the citadel with all its elevators and tangled corridors. And there was the place I was going! Nineteenth floor below ground, down in some natural karst caves. I broke the mental contact, trying not to show how much effort I was expending.

Cartography skill increased to level sixty-three!

Psionic skill increased to level eighty-two!
Mysticism skill increased to level thirty!

Oh yeah! On my mini-map I could see all the rooms and corridors of the huge Dark Faction fortress even though I had never been there before! I suspected it was the combination of reasonably well-levelled Cartography and Psionic skills that allowed me to receive the information like this. Now I definitely knew where to go. However, there was something I needed to do before heading off to rescue the girl:

"Gerd T'yu-Pan, you're exactly right! I really don't have much experience in wizardry for now, so meeting mages from the La-Varrez Faction doesn't enter into my plans. They must be delayed! And that isn't to say attack or arrest them. We have no need for a war with the La-Varrez Faction. We need to gingerly draw out time. Whoever comes in that tiltrotor, tell them that their flight was not coordinated with faction leadership so we'll need some time to check if they should really be here. Invite them to relax in a recreation room. That one in that building to the south there. Treat our treasured guests to whatever they like, make sure they're comfortable after the long flight. I need an extra quarter hour."

It was a difficult moment. Whose side would the garrison leader choose? The new Leng he'd just met? Sure I was the spouse of Princess Minn-O, but I wasn't even a member of the La-Fin Faction. And on the other side were the powerful mage-rulers from the inner-circle of previous ruler Leng Thumor-Anhu La-Fin.

Successful Authority check!

Successful Fame check!

The strong warrior straightened up to his whole respectable height, raised a right hand bent at the elbow and squeezed his fingers into such a tight ball that they cracked. That was the soldier's greeting in the magocratic world.

"Yes sir, Leng Gnat La-Fin! I'll delay our 'treasured guests.'"

JUST WITH MY wayedda, not bringing anyone from the garrison to protect us, I walked the unending hallways of the huge citadel. We met very few players on our way. That was evidence of both the late hour and the fact that the war with the Human-3 Faction was technically not over. Because of that, almost everyone capable of holding a weapon was still on the front. A thought even flickered by that a sudden landing party of a hundred of the highest-level soldiers from the First and Second legions could easily capture this fortress. And as this was the main citadel, the source of their claim to the level-four node, it would be a devastating blow. Immediately the Dark Faction would be down two thousand three hundred forty-nine players. Plus their huge stockpiles and months of dedicated labor would be out the window.

But all that could happen only if I told the Human-3 Faction it was possible, provided a star frigate for landing and shared maps of the tangled corridors and defensive structures in the underground citadel. But I wasn't going to do that. Yes, it was hard for me to consider myself a part of the La-Fin Faction, but I wasn't going to betray the people entrusted to me.

"That elevator there! Now we need floor minus nineteen."

Minn-O La-Fin stopped in surprise and looked at me doubtfully:

"My husband, I don't believe the shaft goes that deep. And there is no minus nineteen button on the panel. The deepest it goes is minus three. I have been on that floor. That's where the La-Fin Faction's secure respawn room is located. My point was set there for a long time."

"Nevertheless, on my map the shaft goes lower. And there must be some reason for this guard," I said, pointing at the young man listening to our conversation. Thankfully, he didn't understand a word of Geckho. Then I said to him: "Soldier, take us to minus nineteen."

Successful Fame check!

"Yes, my lord!" the guardsman took a card from his pocket, his hands shaking in panic, and placed it into a narrow barely visible crack under the normal sensor panel. In an instant, extra keys came on the panel and the guardsman obligingly selected "-19."

A minute later, Minn-O and I were on the very lowest floor of the fortress and looking down a corridor that trailed off in the endless distance. Based on my map though, there was an end: a door leading to the very bottom of a narrow mountain crevasse. And there, carved into the rock, were the very well disguised hangars for the Sio-Mi-Dori antigravs. So that was where the five remaining Dark Faction assault vehicles were hidden! But the antigravs themselves didn't concern me much, I hadn't come for them. I pointed my companion to an armored door in the corridor wall:

"That way!"

Scanning skill increased to level forty-three!

The only thing that made this door different from the hundreds we'd seen before were the automatic high-speed turrets hidden in nearby ceiling tiles and wall niches. I discovered them by complete coincidence when I activated scanning to see what to expect inside. In fact, there were turrets both in the hallway and in the room itself! I wondered what they were protecting against when they placed turrets inside a locked room? Dangerous escaped prisoners? Or was this not an element of defense but a way of getting rid of unwanted witnesses? Or even a guaranteed way of sending one's self to respawn if something went wrong? In any case, I found the one I was looking for: among the three player markers, behind some closed doors I saw:

Human. Level-102 Paladin.

Paladin was a rare class in general, so this was a sure thing. Other than Gerd Tamara, there was a level-89 Torturer and a level-84 Pyromancer Mage. However, I had a problem: the armored door was locked! Ugh, if only I had my trusty Annihilator, a little thing like a locked door couldn't stop me. Just shoot it off its hinges and it's open wide. Unfortunately though, the ancient weapon was still with Kirsan the repair bot. Modifying the relict artifact was taking a long time.

I had to find another way. So, first let's see how to control this door.

Mobile door control mechanism. Chance of making inoperable 37%. Total control chance 12%.

No, I was not going to break open the armored doors. Nor was I going to fry the electronics with a geological analyzer. I didn't risk trying to mind-control one of the two Dark Faction players either. With such a high-level mage I wouldn't manage, at least blind and without visual contact. But I could pull it off with the Torturer, even though I knew nothing about this game class. Their counterpart would probably not just stand by timidly and watch as they randomly got up to open the door, though.

So I needed to take control and force the door open. I only had a twelve percent chance, not great... I tossed the remaining skill points into Machine Control, raising it to seventy-six, but the chance only went up to thirteen percent. I tried a couple times but, other than a waste of Magic Points (and quite a hefty one at that), I got nothing. Seemingly the time had come to spend my free statistic points. I had been meaning to take a look at that in my free time and with a cool head, carefully weighing every possible consequence, but this was a time crunch and there was no other way to open the disobedient door.

So then, two points right into Intelligence. That should take that from twenty-three to... that's right, twenty-six considering the extra point for every two into a statistic higher than 20. Considering the two Intelligence rings I had on, I was now all the way up to thirty-one! Was that really not enough to open a door?

Mobile door control mechanism. Chance of making inoperable 72%. Total control chance 32%.

Thirty-two percent. Better now, even though it was nowhere near guaranteed. I decided to try a couple times and, only if it didn't work, put points into Intelligence. But I got lucky! I pulled it off on my first try!

Electronics skill increased to level seventy-five!

Machine Control skill increased to level seventy-seven!

Mysticism skill increased to level thirty-one!

The thick armored door opened silently and I immediately walked inside. It was a small room, almost all the space was taken up by a rectangular metal rack. Inside that resilient construction, splayed out with metal cables attached to cuffs on her wrists and ankles was Gerd Tamara, completely naked. Her life bar was down in the red and balancing at two or three percent. She was unconscious. They really worked her over! No part of the leader of the Second Legion's body was untouched. There were just innumerable bruises and bloody whip marks, as well as burns and electric-shock marks.

The whip just happened to be in the Torturer's hands as I walked in. She was a short but very muscular bald middle-aged woman and all she was wearing was a blood-streaked leather apron right over her naked body. Her partner was a tall and skeleton-thin young man in a red tunic, a striking contrast to the Torturer. The glow of his sparkling eyes revealed his wizardly nature, and the flickering sparks on the tip of his wand explained the electric shock marks on the prisoner's body. There were especially many below the stomach.

With extreme difficulty I overcame the desire to immediately kill both these sadists. All that held me back was that these two didn't even understand why I was mad. In the parallel world, there were no rules requiring humanitarian treatment of prisoners and the Torturer profession was both in demand and respected.

"So then... Who gave you the right to torture her?"

Both prison guards turned toward the voice and stared at me, batting their eyes in surprise. The Torturer came to first, leaning in a deep bow:

"My lord! My Princess! Gerd Avir-Syn gave the order to break the prisoner and prepare her for interrogation."

"And we were given very little time," the Pyromancer Mage entered the conversation. "They told us to hurry, because the Paladin would be picked up soon, so we got straight to business, and not always delicately. But there was no risk to life. We had everything under control."

"What's more, Gerd Tamara has great regeneration," the Torturer spoke up again. "Her life bar grows quickly; cuts heal over right before your eyes! You can torture her for a whole day without fear of accidentally killing her! She's just an ideal victim for levelling my skills!"

I didn't share the torturer lady's joy at all. I knew about that for a long time, Tamara told me about it herself. However, as it was turning out, high Constitution came with certain downsides...

"I've come for the prisoner. Set her free!"

Failed Authority check!

The prison guards exchanged unconfident glances, neither of them carried out my order. What was more, the Torturer put her whip away, clearly about to replace it with a more serious weapon.

Danger Sense skill increased to level fifty-nine!

I didn't ask what exactly the dangerous bald-headed woman had for me. Sharply extending my good hand in her direction, I gave a clear order:

"Die!!!"

Not very long ago, at the Geckho spaceport, an experienced teacher gave me a clear demonstration of how this was done. The muscular woman with ash-gray skin gasped, clutched at her heart and collapsed to the ground a lifeless doll. At the same time, Gerd Minn-O made two accurate shots with her laser pistol, sending the Pyromancer Mage to respawn.

Psionic skill increased to level eighty-three!
You have reached level eighty-one!
You have received three skill points.

What had we done? Why did we kill both prison guards? How would we remove the fetters from the prisoner now? In the silence of the cavern, my wayedda's voice sounded loud and sharp:

"My husband, may I shoot Gerd Tamara? I've been dreaming of it a long time. I'll enjoy it and she'll respawn in a safe place."

"Is that safe?" I doubted and stopped the Princess, who was already placing her gun to the splayed-out girl's forehead. "Most likely, Gerd Tamara's respawn point is in the Tropics node, which is now under control of the La-Fin Faction. I bet your allies will light up when the hated leader of the Second Legion shows up right in the midst of their camp totally naked and helpless. Beyond that," I pointed at the many empty syringes on the floor, "Tamara is on some kind of psychotropic. It is possible she was induced to change her respawn point to this room. No, we cannot kill her!"

Minn-O lowered her pistol and checked the corpses one after the next for fallen loot. She was looking for a key, but it wasn't there.

"Remember when you saw me for the first time?" my wife asked unexpectedly, walking a circle around the metal torture rack. "You know, in the mountain camp in your lands when I was lying on the ground naked and spread-eagled, and Gerd Tamara was standing next to me. If only you knew how I was bubbling with hate at that moment and hoping that, one day, everything would be the other way around! And now I got my wish. I don't understand why but it just isn't making me happy. By the way, you'll find this interesting! Or did you already see this cute little design?"

I walked a circle around the prisoner and saw where Minn-O La-Fin was pointing. On the small of the miniature dark-haired girl's back there was a small colored tattoo, barely visible due to the many electric burns. It was a cartoony design of a flying gnat carrying a bright flashlight and a sharp saber. And although the character was taken from the famous Russian cartoon *Mukha Tsokotukha*[2], it was clearly chosen for a reason. Hrm... I wasn't expecting that from the severe paladin girl.

---

[2] Translator's note: Originally a fairy tale by Korney Chukovsky rendered in English as *Little Fly So Sprightly*, it was adapted into a cartoon several times. The main characters are a little fly and a brave gnat who saves the fly from a bloodthirsty spider.

"Minn-O, we're wasting time, we need to do something!" I awkwardly tried to change the topic, but my wife just laughed in reply:

"She likes you, I can see it right away! Oh, look how red you got! Okay, okay, I'll shut up. I can try to put the pistol into constant beam mode and cut all the cables. But that is going to take some time."

"I've got a better idea! The locks are electromagnetic. Minn-O, look! The light is going out!"

I took out my Prospector scanner and a geological analyzer. It wasn't easy to do with one arm, so I had to sit on the floor and prop the Scanner up on my knees. Maybe I could get by without the "laptop" part, and just use an analyzer but I wasn't sure. Seemingly, the burst of energy was triggered only after the tripod synchronized with a scanner. I clenched the geological analyzer between my knees and spread the feet with my good hand. A sharp click rang out and the room was immersed in darkness. The only source of light left was the dim glow from my screen. That whole situation was painfully reminiscent of my first flight on the Shiamiru. All that was lacking was a shout of rage from Captain Uraz-Tukhsh: "Gnnnat!!!"

Behind me I heard a body falling to the floor. It worked!

Scanning skill increased to level forty-four!

But I didn't even have time to celebrate before I heard angry voices from the dark hallway. Then no more than a second later, the beams of bright flashlights started bouncing on the walls. I saw a few figures in the doorway which, due to the bright light in my eyes, I couldn't make out. But they recognized me right away.

"What a pleasant surprise, my dear mages!" And I shuddered to recognize the old-man's voice of the ghastly Gerd Avir-Syn La-Pirez. "We paid for only one prisoner, but now we get three at no extra charge!"

Chapter Sixteen

Moment of Truth

I DIDN'T EVEN understand how they did it. There was no eye contact, no words, spells or gestures but, just a few seconds earlier, I was standing just fine. Now I was sitting balled up on the floor not feeling strong enough to move my arms or even lift my head. My Magic and Endurance Points were both down all the way to zero.

Disoriented! Duration: 1 minute, 25 seconds.

Stunned! Duration: 7 minutes, 04 seconds.

Paralysis! Duration: 11 seconds.

Princess Minn-O La-Fin was lying next to me and howling in impotent rage, her mind under the control of the enemy mages.

"Gnat, your magic is even weaker than I thought!" came mocking laughter over my head from the old Psionic Mage as he came closer. "How can you be head of a magical house if you're so weak? Just so you know, Coruler Thumor-Anhu would have easily repelled a combined attack from three mages."

"Well, no one in their right mind would even try to attack such a fearsome wizard as Thumor-Anhu La-Fin," an unfamiliar woman's voice sounded from the corridor. "The head of House La-Fin wouldn't bear jokes and immediately killed anyone who was even slightly rude to him."

Mental Fortitude skill increased to level seventy-three!

Ah, now my defenses kick in? The pop-up message could be taken as little more than a mean joke. What the hell kind of raggedy defense was this? Enemy mages could just walk up and slam me to the ground! All my antimagic defense was torn into shreds in one blow. It was the same as trying to use a piece of notebook paper to block a shotgun shot. Hopeless. Nevertheless, I took the system message as something of a hint and put all three free points into Mental Fortitude, raising that critically important skill to seventy-six.

"He's resisting!" another mage came in after Gerd Avir-Syn and spoke with clear enjoyment. My attempts to defend myself amused him.

"Pitiful vain attempts, doomed to failure," the old Psionic Mage was categorical as ever. "Without magic and the chance to use his abilities, he's no one. He also can't kill himself. He's just about to lose consciousness, then we can load him up."

Mysticism skill increased to level thirty-two!

What was he talking about? Lose consciousness? I wasn't even paralyzed anymore. I could move if I wanted to. Yes, I was still stunned and poorly perceiving reality, but my mind was working full strength searching for a way out of this situation. And that said nothing about a possible loss of consciousness.

I could not kill myself? Arguable! I had four powerful fragmentation grenades in my inventory. That would be enough to send me and everyone else in this tiny little room to respawn. Just to be safe, I would actually have to first stash my Listener Energy Armor in my inventory, which had a shield that could absorb 12000 units of damage. Or maybe not. Then I would most likely be the only survivor.

"Grandpa, what are you doing?!" Minn-O somewhat found her feet and threw herself reproachfully on her forebearer. "Release my husband and me at once!"

A booming slap forced the girl to stay quiet, and the Princess began to sob, insulted.

"Foolish chicken! You'd better keep your nose out of serious games, and you'd really better not raise your voice to the person your life depends on! Minn-O this is your chance to lay low and keep your head down! What do you think I did after I killed myself in the Geckho spaceport? Do you know? Of course not! I left into the real world and ordered your virt pod destroyed!!! In my presence, its fragile plastic was stuck through with a dozen metal bars. Even if the mechanism wasn't fully broken, if you attempt to respawn in that capsule, you'll be killed instantly!"

"But... why?" I could hear unhidden horror in my wayedda's voice.

"Oh, for the mere reason," the ghastly old man suddenly began to shout, "that you were not supposed to survive Coruler Thumor-Anhu La-Fin's funeral!!! It was all planned down to the finest detail! We calculated the power and location of that explosion very carefully. All our competitors were to be elimintated in one fell swoop. And the people of the parallel world were to be officially blamed for the anti-mage terror attack. The La-Fin family estate was to be transferred to me as the closest living relative. I had even already come to an agreement with the most powerful La-Varrez dynasty to assert my claims in exchange for part of the inheritance. But you're just such a beanpole it only ripped your legs off while all those around you died!!!"

Mysticism skill increased to level thirty-three!

The pop-up distracted me from the old man's hysterical shouting. The skill responsible for mana-restore speed was growing very quickly. Maybe when my mana bar was almost empty, the narcotic intoxication had additional effect. After all, alongside the penalties to Constitution and Agility and especially to Endurance Points, I now had a huge 240% bonus to maximum mana and 67% bonus to restore speed for the same. I wasn't really sure what was going on but, in any case, all was not lost. My enemies mistakenly thought I was an empty husk and no threat. And meanwhile my magic was gradually refilling.

All the while, the ghastly old man continued sharing his plans:

"But when you survived that explosion, we decided to use that and play things differently. Still I really didn't like your headstrong and nasty character, so I destroyed your virt pod to make you obedient and silken once again. Now you'll go with the La-Varrez family mages and do everything they say! They will add you to their faction and you can leave the game in a different place. But before that you'll write a missive in which you recuse yourself from the status of junior wife of the idiotic dropout Gnat. In exchange for that loser, you'll be given a decent husband from the La-Varrez dynasty with proper magical abilities."

What lowdown bastards! I was just seething with hate when I heard the old man speak. I had a sharp change of mind about the fragmentation grenades. I didn't want to kill my wife. However other plans of action were coming to mind. The disorientation effect had faded and I managed to take a look around. There was still no lighting other than the flashlights in the hands of the mages. By the way, who specifically was here? I already knew the old Psionic Mage, but I quickly brought up the information about the other two:

Gerd Poll-Itra La-Varrez. Human. Level-111 Psionic Mage.

Rota-Uli La-Varrez. Human. Level-98 Telekinetic

Mage.

Another Psionic Mage, this one more experienced even than Avir-Syn? Not good. What was more I didn't know what the special features and strong sides of the Telekinetic class were, but this woman with short red hair was sucking all the Endurance and Magic Points out of me by periodically pointing her magic wand in my direction. Apparently she was having a hard time keeping my magic and energy stores emptied and it was tiring her, because the witch was doing it less and less often. In fact, the last few times she couldn't even burn up all my mana.

It took my great effort not to smile. After drinking with the Miyelonians, I still had serious debuffs to my physical characteristics, but was now stronger than ever in terms of Magic Points and their restore speed! The enemies couldn't have guessed that, otherwise they'd have come up with something a bit more effective than trying to hold my mana at zero.

Mental Fortitude skill increased to level seventy-seven!

Yes, the Psionic Mage Gerd Poll-Itra was stubbornly sizing me up and not stopping her attempts to take over my mind. For now it was not working. And if at first the Psionic Mage found my resistance funny, now she was just getting more and more peeved. But seemingly she also wasn't doing great with her mana stores because at a certain point the dangerous witch turned away and drank two elixirs in a row. I had something like that in my back pocket as well. Ever since the Medu-Ro IV station, I had been carrying two thermoses of Miyelonian cocktail in my inventory which could restore energy and magic. But I was in no rush to drink them. I wouldn't manage to do it without anyone noticing and that would be a clear sign that their control over my body and mind was not as complete as they thought.

And what would I spend this mana on anyhow? A direct mental duel with stronger and more experienced enemies? Not even funny. Last time they folded me in two seconds. No, that was definitely not an option. Take control of the turrets? An elegant move. But there was still no electricity and all four turrets were inactive with a zero percent chance of taking control.

However, there was a much more interesting target in the room to take control of. Every mage had a capsule sewn into their robe which could be activated by a certain signal and would kill the wearer if they were at risk of being captured. I couldn't see these capsules, but they were probably there. To see them, I'd have to activate the scanning pictogram. And so I laid down on the floor, imitating a stunned and paralyzed person while I patiently waited for the cooldown to trip so I could use it again.

Mysticism skill increased to level thirty-four!

Here a smile crawled onto my face and I couldn't hide it. Gerd Poll-Itra La-Varrez behind me was already cursing loudly before that, enraged by my stubborn resistance. What, did he not know a Listener was also a mage and that Gnat's main statistic was Intelligence? I suspected that my Intelligence was no lower than the self-assured Psionic Mage's, and his chances against me one-on-one were very small. Actually, while the Scanning skill reloaded, why not give him a little job! I set four points into Intelligence which, along with the other two bonus points brought that figure up by six points to thirty-two. And with the two Intelligence rings, I was now all the way up to thirty-seven! How do you like that, Gerd Half Liter?

Mental Fortitude skill increased to level seventy-eight!

Astrolinguistics skill increased to level eighty-eight!

My cursing and insulting vocabulary in the language of the magocratic world was noticeably richer and I suspected there were lots more four-letter words to learn. "Dried out blue whale penis jammed into the (censored) of a crested baboon," was not even the longest phrase I heard.

The Scanning icon finally changed color, reloaded. I had plenty of Magic Points and got right to work before the red-headed witch pointed her mana-burning wand at me yet again. So, what could I see? I had to zoom in the mini-map to get a closer look at the small objects. So then, here was what I was looking for:

Radio-activated poison ampule detonator. Chance of making inoperable 77%. Total control chance 59%.

As it turned out, the La-Fin Faction mages weren't the only ones who used these. By the way, old Avir-Syn didn't have one on him. He seemingly hadn't changed clothes since the space port.

Well, time to begin? I mentally ran through a plan in my head. Abruptly drink the two thermoses of alcoholic cocktail. Don't fall over from drinking too much (not all that easy with reduced Constitution and basically zero Endurance). Then wait a few seconds for mana to load up enough to use my Machine Control and try to take down the two mages. And hope all the while that all three enemies would just stand by silently and watch...

Hrm, that all sounded a rare kind of stupid. Let's start from the fact the thermoses contained two quarts of fairly strong alcohol and I just physically wouldn't be able to drink that much liquid fast enough. And meanwhile the guileful old man turned from Minn-O to me:

"Why hasn't Gnat crashed yet?"

The red-headed witch answered Avir-Syn, again pointing her wand at me and sucking out almost all my Endurance Points and most of my mana:

"I don't know either. In theory he should have lost all his energy long ago and fallen unconscious! Clearly Gnat's defense against magic is somewhat higher level than we thought. It'll take more time."

"Then quit talking and go harder! The last thing we need is for him to come around, take out his scary Annihilator and shoot holes in each of us, one after the next!"

Funny. If I had the Annihilator in the first place, I'd have sent these creeps to respawn long ago! But then I saw something even better than the deadly relict weapon. Gerd Tamara, forgotten by all, suddenly opened her eyes! Our gazes met and I didn't spare any of my few Magic Points, immediately reading her mind:

"Hold on, Gnat! I'm healing my joints right now. I just have to crawl over to a laser pistol someone threw on the floor over there."

Beaten half to death, her innumerable wounds probably causing ghastly pain, Tamara wasn't bellyaching or complaining but reassuring me, a person in complete physical health?! Unbelievable!

"I've got a better plan. Just defend me against magic attacks and I'll take care of the rest!"

Tamara closed and opened her eyes with exaggerated lethargy, showing that she understood. Three seconds passed and a brilliant warm wave of absolute harmony, happiness and complete assurance in my own safety rolled over me. It was hard to communicate these glorious sensations in words. I felt like a newborn baby in the arms of an endlessly loving mother.

Blessing received!

Immunity to fear. Immunity to magical effects. Immunity to psionic control.

Magic Points regeneration sped up by 713%!

Hitpoints regeneration sped up by 540%!

Endurance Points regeneration sped up by 830%!

Defense against physical damage increased by 13%

Defense against magical effects increased by 77%.

Duration: 1 minute, 24 seconds.

How about that! I didn't even suspect what the

paladin was capable of! I waited five seconds just to make sure I had enough Endurance Points then slowly stood up to the surprised gazes of all three enemies and, demonstrating a complete lack of haste, took out the thermos of Miyelonian cocktail.

"I don't like killing sober," I told my shocked enemies, taking a few big gulps of alcohol.

"Rota-Uli, wake up! Drain him!" Gerd Avir-Syn shouted.

The Telekinetic Mage came to life sharply and extended her magic wand toward me, but this time it had no effect. My mana and endurance were coming back faster than this mage girl could suck. Five seconds later, she herself was drained and lowered her hand, even forced to get down on one knee when she hit zero Magic and Endurance Points. I took a step, extended a hand and effortlessly plucked the intriguing magic wand from the enchantress's powerless fingers.

Wizard's Nightmare. Light magic wand * modified.

Burns through target's Magic and Endurance Points, spending those of the caster. Efficiency coefficient: 3.4 to one Endurance Point and 7.4 to one Magic Point.

Attention! This weapon contains the following modifications:

- *+20% Magic Points*
- *+1 Intelligence, +1 Constitution*
- *+140% critical hit effect, Stun on critical hit*

Attention! This weapon was named Wizard's Nightmare by its first owner. Name cannot be deleted or changed.

Statistic requirements: Intelligence 23, Constitution 23.

Skill requirements: Psionic 80, Telekinetics 80.

Attention! Your character lacks the Telekinetics skill.

Attention! Your character has insufficient Constitution to use this item.

An interesting item and, in magical duels, it would often even be indispensable. But unfortunately it was not for me. And although I could theoretically get Telekinetics to level 100, then spend a long time stubbornly leveling it to 80, the chance of getting Gnat's Constitution up by seven points... was slim. Should I really spend the two remaining statistic points now on Constitution and find a strong piece of "magic" jewelry to raise Constitution by another +2 or +3...? No, this wasn't worth my time.

"You're not big enough for such a dangerous toy!" I told the redheaded magess with a smirk, hiding the wand in my own inventory. "And next time, before you try to burn through another wizard's mana, make sure you've got enough to finish the job."

Mental Fortitude skill increased to level seventy-nine!

Mental Strength skill increased to level eighty!

I turned to the two Psionic Mages unhurriedly as they tried to take control of my mind with all their might or at least to mentally harm me in some way.

"Hey there, you should be ashamed to two-on one somebody, especially from behind! And it was very foolish of you to forget the first rule of Psionics: if your target's Intelligence is higher than yours by ten or more points, the success chance for a mental attack is precisely zero. I now have forty-two (this was a huge lie of course, but it's always helpful to stupefy an enemy). Are you sure you want to grapple with me?"

Authority increased to 59!

"Gnat, behind you!" Minn-O shouted, but I didn't have time to react.

Medium Armor skill increased to level fifty-seven!

Something gave a sparkle and my Listener Energy Armor forcefield sagged by three percent, then another two. I turned around, not even alarmed, more like surprised. I was wrong to count the Telekinetic Mage out. She was still on one knee but now shooting me with a Dark Faction laser pistol. I let her get a couple more shots off, watching the complete lack of success with interest, then I shook my head in reproach:

"Idiot! You're a mage, not a shooter! With such a pitiful pistol skill you couldn't even kill a mouse, which is to say nothing of an armored target! I don't think you're hearing me... Is my accent really that hard to understand? Okay, I'm sick of you! Die!"

Psionic skill increased to level eighty-four!
Machine Control skill increased to level seventy-eight!

You have reached level eighty-two!
You have received three skill points!

I managed to break the poison capsule, all while imitating a mental attack! I ended the Telekinetic Mage and turned to the remaining enemies. And just then, Gerd Poll-Itra La-Varrez's lifeless body hit the cold floor. What happened to him? I tossed a quick gaze at Tamara and Minn-O. No, they were not involved. The Paladin, her legs seemingly broken in a few places, had just started crawling towards the laser pistol, which was on the floor ten feet away. Minn-O then couldn't move until that very second. It must have been Gerd-Poll-Itra controlling her mind. The experienced mage could seemingly smell things heating up and hurried to kill himself before he was taken prisoner.

"Your last ally has fled in dishonor!" I turned to the ghastly old man. "But you and I are gonna need to have a very thorough conversation. As head of House La-Fin, I've just got too many questions for you. First off about the terrorism at the funeral, and working for a competing magical dynasty. And would you look here, a torture rack just got freed up!"

I extended a hand and tried to capture the old man's mind, but it didn't work. Nothing. Just an impenetrable wall. But my opponent was also apparently flummoxed based on the Mental Fortitude increase message that quickly flickered past, bringing it to eighty-one. And what now? Should I attack him hand-to-hand and try to take the old man down? Sure, with a debuff to Agility and Constitution, with a 90% Endurance Points penalty? I'd fall in the first two blows. Should I just use the Paralyzer?

By the looks of things, approximately the same thoughts were going through Gerd Avir-Syn's mind. But the Psionic Mage was much better prepared. Instead of the flashlight, now in his inventory, the ancient mage was suddenly holding a carved six-and-a-half-foot staff made of black wood and capped with a human skull. What a familiar staff! Known by the name of Wrath, I had once picked it up off the ground after killing Leng Thumor-Anhu La-Fin in the Harpy Cliffs node! I wondered where Gerd Avir-Syn got this item. The former Dark Faction leader was known never to part with it! The skull at the top of the staff lit up blood red and a blinding bolt of white lightning shot out, striking me right in the chest!

I stumbled back and could barely stay on my feet. My health went down by sixty percent. And meanwhile my armor suit's forcefield was still practically full! Did the damage pass through my armor, totally ignoring it?! And it did that much in one hit, even though I had 77% defense against magic?! I had to quickly take another sip of alcoholic cocktail to speed up regeneration and be able to survive a second identical attack. Although... no, I couldn't survive now: the short-term blessing had just passed and together with it the magical protection.

Gerd Avir-Syn seemingly was very surprised at my impressive resilience. Nevertheless he gave a mischievous laugh:

"Impudent whelp! You have a lot to learn about Psionics, and about what happens when you get a skill up to level 150!"

And of course his laughter stopped as soon as Gerd Tamara replenished my hitpoints:

Healing effect applied.

Your wounds have healed.

And then some flashlights started flickering from the hallway, voices approaching. Was this more enemies? Or friends? Seemingly, my opponent was wondering the same thing. Taking a step and kicking the floor pistol to the other end of the room (Gerd Tamara's fingers, stubbornly crawling toward the weapon clenched down on thin air), Gerd Avir-Syn spoke unhappily:

"It seems we will not be able to finish this conversation. But in any case..." the tip of the ghastly mage's staff lit up again, "you will never receive the La-Fin Dynasty inheritance, it belongs to me!"

The old man raised the staff with two hands and I winced, preparing for pain and death. But... lightning flashed and behind me Minn-O La-Fin fell, smitten. The ghastly wizard put the fearsome staff in his own inventory, took out a vial, uncorked it loudly and gulped it down. A second later, he fell to the floor next to his dead granddaughter.

Chapter Seventeen

Returning Under the Dome

I BELLOWED like a wounded rhinoceros and ran over to my wife's spell-addled body. Minn-O was not breathing, her heart was not beating, her health bar was completely empty. I tried to give her CPR and even unclenched her jaws and poured in a healing elixir. No effect. Garrison soldiers from the hallway, led by Shocktroop Gerd T'yu-Pan piled up in the doorway, looking at the bodies of the dead mage rulers from afar, then at the dead princess and naked girl holding a laser pistol as she sat on the cold floor. And they opted not to come in.

Authority increased to 60!

Mysticism skill increased to level thirty-five!

What were Authority and skill increases doing here?! My gorgeous wife had just died, that was all that mattered now! Minn-O didn't have a virt pod she could use to leave the game, so this was most likely her final death. I didn't give up though and attempted mouth-to-mouth resuscitation, but my hands and lips just went through her body. The game no longer considered it eligible for looting, so no longer allowed the body to be manipulated in any way. This was it.

I stood heavily and turned to the pile-up of La-Fin Faction players in the doorway. Probably, there was something off in my gaze, because the high-level players took a step-back in fear. Many even fell down on one knee.

"Garrison leader! Tell me, why did the mages of the outside La-Varrez faction make it in here?"

I didn't raise my voice, but still the huge Shocktroop fell to his knees and even started breathing less often, I could clearly sense his fear.

"My lord, I was unable to stop them! The mage rulers didn't even listen when I told them to wait. They just batted me off like a fly and headed straight for the citadel. What was I supposed to do, raise a hand to a mage?!"

For some time I glared at my subject with a burning gaze for failing my mission, then I waved a hand:

"Okay, no matter. I handled them..."

I fell down on one knee again next to the body of my late wife.

"Am I missing something here?" Gerd Tamara's surprised voice rang out behind me. "Gerd... Ah, no Leng Gnat, congratulations! What, is Minn-O La-Fin's respawn point far away? Why all this put-on grief?"

I realized that Gerd Tamara must have been out cold for most of that encounter. Plus she didn't know the language of the Dark Faction, so she didn't understand what me and the mages were talking about. I explained to the leader of the Second Legion what had just happened. Gerd Tamara put the pistol in her inventory, which looked quite strange given her current total lack of clothing or a bag. The weapon just disappeared and she pensively touched the dried blood on her broken and scabbed over nose.

"Well... I could try to resurrect her before the body disappears. But let me warn you that I've never brought a player back before! Only NPC's like dryads and Centaurs. So I'm not sure it'll work."

Minn-O could be resurrected? A spark of hope flickered in my depressed and dead heart. I raised my head.

"Yes, try at once!!!" I demanded.

"Okay, I'll try. Don't shout at me. But let me replenish my strength first because resurrecting any creature takes a huge amount of energy."

Need energy? I handed the paladin girl both thermoses of restorative cocktail, then got up and headed to the Dark Faction soldiers still frozen in the doorway.

"Gerd T'yu-Pan!" I addressed the still bowing head of the citadel garrison. "As far as I can see, you conduct video surveillance here. Tell me, are there any cameras in the secure rooms where the players set their respawn points?"

"Yes, my lord. There are cameras in all parts of the citadel right up to floor minus three," the huge Shocktroop confirmed.

"Great! Then send a brigade of builders there right away to Gerd Avir-Syn's res point! And make sure it's filled with a very dense grouping of tall and sharpened metal stakes ten minutes from now! Rebar, spears, water pipes... it really doesn't matter what they're made of! What matters is for that traitorous scum to never be able to enter the game again! And give an order to prepare a Sio-Mi-Dori. I'm escorting a prisoner!"

Successful Authority check!

The huge Shocktroop got up and bowed, then extended a hand for the radio on his belt and told my orders to his subordinates. Gerd T'yu-Pan wanted to leave on his own to personally check if his orders were being carried out properly, but I stopped him:

"That's not all! You must transmit a message from me to the people of the First Directory in the real world! Say that from this very minute, Avir-Syn La-Pirez shall be deprived of all titles and is now a criminal wanted for the bloody terror attack at the funeral of Coruler Thumor-Anhu La-Fin! He also stands accused of the murder..."

I fell silent and turned because I noticed

something moving with the corner of my eye. I looked in surprise as the Paladin girl tried to stand but fell to the floor with a pained cry. I wanted to help her, but Tamara showed with a gesture that everything was fine and my help was not needed. I turned to the Shocktroop again.

"No, correction. He is accused not of murder but of the attempted murder of Princess Minn-O La-Fin and for the attempted murder of myself! And thus, by my authority as legal ruler of the First Directory, I officially set a generous reward for the traitor's head! Whosoever kills the scummy old geezer and provides his head as proof, shall receive all the La-Pirez Dynasty's property as a reward! Castles, industry, bank accounts, everything! Right up to the last rusty nail and pair of underwear from their last wayedda!"

The Shocktroop couldn't hold back and whistled in surprise, then gave an emotional comment:

"The generosity of your reward is unheard of for one man, my lord! For that kind of reward, former ruler Avir-Syn would even kill his own reflection in a mirror. But most likely one of the old man's heirs will do it first. After all, none of them will want to lose all that property because the head of the family acted tyrannical."

I thought over the experienced veteran's words and nodded in agreement:

"Good, we shall give his heirs that ability. The La-Pirez Dynasty has twenty-four hours to provide me the head of the traitor in order to retain all their property. If they cannot do so, the offer will be extended to everyone else. And if in the end that lucky person has no magical abilities, my order is for them to be officially elevated in privilege to that of a mage with all the trappings."

Danger Sense skill increased to level sixty!
Authority reduced to 59!

I must have said something heretical, because the Dark Faction soldiers took a step back in fear and even began exchanging glances. One of them risked saying the reason everyone was so freaked out:

"Those are seditious and dangerous words, my lord. A simple person can never even dream of reaching mage-level privilege. Doing so is punished in the harshest manner! If anyone other than a mage ruler had said that, we would have already killed them for sowing unrest!"

Well, well! Was is it all that serious? I admit, I was somewhat discouraged by the sharply negative reaction. Could centuries of extremely harsh terror really have eradicated all desire among non-magical people to change the order of things? Or were they simply afraid to even think about having rights and freedoms in the presence of a mage? All that merited the most serious thought, but now was clearly not the time.

It wouldn't be right to insist. In fact it might be dangerous, so I was forced to cancel my previous order.

"Perhaps I don't know enough about your world, so I blurted out something foolish. Gerd T'yu-Pan, find me an advisor to correct me when necessary. That will allow me to avoid such incidents in the future. And you may correct me too, I give you that right!"

"Yes, Leng Gnat La-Fin!" the huge Shocktroop tried once again to bow in his heavy armor. "And as my lord has given me the right, allow me to give my first piece of advice. Given the horrendous crime committed by the head of the La-Pirez dynasty himself, all members of that family are legally subject to execution without exception, from the smallest to the greatest. That is the order Coruler Thumor-Anhu would have given, and all other great mages would do the exact same. Only fear can keep vassals in line!"

Strike down the whole family from smallest baby to the oldest geezer? Harsh... I was reminded involuntarily of the severe old Leng Thumor-Anhu. He always smelled of death and horror. He would have executed anyone involved in an attempt on himself or the members of his family. No exceptions. I was also reminded of a story Minn-O told me that her grandfather had ordered six million people executed in the Ninth Directory just to ease a famine. No, I was not raised like that. I could never do something like that. Did that make me not harsh enough for my subjects?

"And a second piece of advice, Leng Gnat. Put some clothes on your vaunted commander. As it is my people are embarrassed to look at her. Over here it's... not okay for girls to walk around naked..."

What was this?! The huge severe Shocktroop went red at these words and did his best to look away from Gerd Tamara. Now that was a surprise! With all the harshness of the magocratic world, moral precepts were also a bit stronger there. In my world, nudists and images of naked people had long ceased to shock or embarrass anyone. Nevertheless, I walked over to Gerd Tamara and gave her my track suit. Sure, it was too big for her, but still better than nothing. And a second later, the Paladin was dressed and smiling sheepishly:

"Yes, this is much better! I'm almost ready, Leng Gnat, my energy is full. Help me up. I need to be vertical for this. And let me remind you that I've never resurrected a player, so don't judge me if I don't succeed. Agreed?"

I nodded in silence and, supporting the miniature girl with my good hand, lifted her from the floor. Gerd Tamara took a deep sigh and spread both arms, pointing them up as if blessing someone in front of her. Golden sparkles started enshrouding Princess Minn-O La-Fin's body. My wayedda gave a jerk and sat up sharply with a scream. Then she jumped up off the floor and turned to me, her eyes wide in fear:

"My husband! What was that?! I could only look at the statistics of my last game session and the image was slowly going dim. Was that death?"

But I couldn't answer, because I had to hold Gerd Tamara, who had lost consciousness and was falling on the floor. It was very awkward to do with one hand.

"Hey, what is going on!?" I objected justly. "Are you two in cahoots or something? Can you both be in the game at the same time? Or do you only play in sequence now?"

Fortunately, Gerd T'yu-Pan hurried to help, grabbing the girl's body and picking it up.

"A powerful enemy! And yet she looks so

fragile..." he said, looking at Gerd Tamara with incomprehensible joy and even tenderness. "No one in your faction was such a thorn in the side of the mage rulers as her! I have simply lost count of how many times we met on the battlefield! I know I killed her eight times. And she killed me fifteen... or maybe she made it up to twenty. My lord, it would be an honor for me to carry such an illustrious warrior to an antigrav!"

"Yes, carry her! Minn-O, go after them!" I said, starting for the exit. However I stopped because the Princess was just still standing there looking all at sea, dumbfounded. Seemingly my wayedda hadn't even heard me. I had to repeat a bit louder. Minn-O La-Fin shuddered and turned. Woah! After dying and respawning, my wife's eyes had changed color. Now they were glowing and blue instead of dark hazel.

"My husband..." Minn-O was now in a state of clear amazement. "I have a magic bar now! And my game class changed from Cartographer to Aristocrat!"

A CAUTIOUS KNOCK at the door distracted me from contemplating the glass of cognac in my hands. Who could it be at such an early hour? I looked at the time. It was eight thirty AM. Well okay, I guess it was morning. I could calm down. I hadn't slept a wink last night, but sleep had been relegated to the back burner, pushed way onto the outskirts of my mind by a strong burst of adrenaline. Yes, too much had happened recently that required the most serious thought. And although I knew this would just make the exhaustion come back twice as strong, I didn't really feel like sleeping yet. I stood up and went to open the door.

In the doorway, embarrassed and shuffling from one foot to the other, was deputy director Alexander Antipov. Well, well! Unexpected. Last I'd heard of him, our house fed was in a coma after someone released deadly spores under the Dome. I walked aside, allowing the unexpected guest in and pointed at the armchair next to mine.

"I don't even know what to say, Kirill! On the one hand, you should probably be subject to immediate arrest due to your obvious connection to the Dark Faction. But on the other..." he didn't finish and just waved wearily.

Instead of answering, I splashed some cognac into a glass for him. Alexander Antipov drank it down mechanically, seemingly not even noticing the flavor of the noble beverage. He looked at me and gave a crooked smirk:

"Never do that again! And I'm not talking about drinking in the morning. I'm not your father to be teaching you how to live. You know. The capital node guards just about shit themselves when an enemy antigrav flew up to our main fortress then landed!"

"Well that means they were sleeping on the job!" I objected justly. "We went on the emergency channel as we approached the border to say who was on board and where we were headed. The soldiers had at least ninety seconds, so it's very strange that our coming to the central citadel caused such turmoil! What if it really was a Dark Faction invasion?!"

"Yes, conclusions will have to be drawn, and the magical butt-kickings will fly," the fed promised. "But you can also understand our troops: no one knew what to do. The ceasefire was theoretically over, so no one wanted to open fire and provoke another flareup. How long will this indefinite state last? The curators of the Dome project will shake Lozovsky down. But meanwhile our Diplomat might as well have resigned. He keeps saying the negotiations with the Dark Faction aren't being led by him, there's a higher-profile player, so leave him alone! He just gets mad at everyone, you see... Me too, the pouty little lady! Is that any way for a true leader to behave?!"

Alexander Antipov seemed to expect me to support his accusations of the excessively inert faction head, but I preferred to downplay the topic and speak on something else:

"There won't be a war for now. As Dark Faction Strategist General Ui-Taka said last night, 'a war without the possibility of final victory is not at all what we were after.' So everyone expects another round of negotiations to take place."

I gave another bit of cognac to my guest who was trying to just blow off some steam. I filled my glass again too, to the very brim. I needed it today, because I had pushed myself to the edge both emotionally and physically.

"Yes, Gerd Ui-Taka is a real badass! He fully

lived up to his reputation. But as for my personal opinion..." Alexander Antipov gave an unexpected chuckle and, setting the glass into his left hand, extended me his right for a handshake. "My thanks to you, Kirill! Above all for the ceasefire that allowed us to finish the Centaur Plateau node and turn on the new virt pods. It saved everyone who was in the medical center, even the most severe cases. And to put it briefly, now I'm a level-3 Inquisitor."

"Inquisitor?" I couldn't hide my surprise.

An inquisitor... well I'll be! That was first and foremost a priest, even if it did have the "bonus" features of an investigator and torturer for the good of the sect. The game wouldn't have offered Alexander Antipov such a profession if he wasn't personally very pious. I honestly didn't expect that from the severe fed.

"No one knows what that class is about," he said, either truly not knowing or somehow embarrassed at his choice. "The game also offered the class Torturer. But we've already got two of them, which is more than enough. What's more, I just can't bare executions or torture, so I went with the path less travelled."

I hid a wave of involuntary laughter under a fit of coughing.

"Interrogating and torturing all kinds of apostates is exactly what an inquisitor does, there's no escaping it. By the way, I met a Torturer from the Dark Faction. I think it was a lady. Is there a special word for a lady Torturer? Torturess? I could introduce our Torturers to her and our newly minted Inquisitor too for, let's say, an experience swap."

"I still don't know what she'll have to tell me. I can figure it out on my own. Anyway, I came to tell you that your wayedda Minn-O's request has been received. The faction head just has to confirm it. And now for the main question: who will be doing that? You or Ivan Lozovsky?"

That change of topic was somehow all too abrupt. Clearly, discussing his profession and skills hurt him somehow. Okay then, I had both seen this question coming for a long time and knew my answer. So I didn't delay:

"Ivan Lozovsky!"

"So then, Kirill, you'll be leaving the Human-3 Faction?" he asked, immediately coming to the right conclusion. "And where will you be going? The new Russian factions where the leader has less administrative work?"

"No, I'm not tempted to lead the Human-23 or Human-25 Factions. Or the German Human-6 Faction even though the game did offer it to me as well. I might take leadership of the Geckho spaceport. Or I'll take over the La-Fin Faction. That would be a guarantee of peace. But most likely I'll get together a team of friends and make a separate faction, maybe it won't even control a node on our planet. But in any case, I can only talk about all this after I finish negotiations with the Dark Faction."

The intelligence director set down his empty glass and gestured that he didn't want any more.

"Our guys will be really upset... They might even

start putting sticks in your spokes. Although personally I believe you have earned the right to take your own path. You've done so much for our faction! By the way, I forgot to say that Valentin Ustinov wanted to give you a big thanks from all our scientists for the alien technology. As far as I know, they've got weeks' worth of work left. But once they're done... It's a short trip from there to mastering space flight! And not only to Mars, Venus and the Solar System, even to distant stars!!!"

"I hope that won't be my last gift to them. As soon as I finish up here on the planet and fix my broken starship, I'm headed back into space. I need to establish contact with more alien races, find allies and business partners, study new technologies. And that's not some whim, some common curiosity or freakish obsession. It's vitally necessary for our humanity. After all, no matter how much we fight here in our sandbox, no matter how much we may swap ownership of game nodes on the planet, the Earth overall won't get any stronger. And when the tong of safety is up, we will be just as defenseless from outside invasion as we are now. And that is the situation I want to turn around."

"I believe you can do it. And you can count our faction to help in any possible way," Alexander Antipov decided to get a more comfortable seat on the sofa and, his interest suddenly piqued, pulled a black lacy bra out from under a sofa pillow. So that's where it was. Tamara was looking for so long this morning...

"Woah!" He picked it up and examined the trophy. "So, did I come at a bad time?"

"No, everything's fine. My guest has already left to get some sleep."

"One last fling before your junior wife comes here under the Dome and chases off all your admirers?" he laughed.

"Minn-O was aware of this visit," I surprised the director. "And although Minn-O and Tamara have a fierce mutual hatred, today in the antigrav, my wayedda whispered that Tamara and I were sure to have a romantic encounter, and that I shouldn't resist fate. And that isn't because Minn-O has a facile nature, nor to thank the Paladin for resurrecting her. It's just that her parallel world also has tales about kidnapped beauties and the gallant knights that rescue them. Well, over there its young mages. And the Princess knows perfectly well how all these stories end."

Alexander Antipov first whinnied like a mare, but suddenly grew sharply serious and thoughtfully said:

"I heard Tamara really got beat up in the prison. That's bad. Our psychologists already said the leader of the Second Legion made their hair stand on end. Now the test results will be..." he gave a pitiful sigh, "people have been taken to forced mental treatment for much less. Tamara has strong suicidal tendencies. And a panicked fear of becoming unwanted and abandoned. That's why Gerd Tamara rushes into the very heat of every battle, to prove her worth. Our Paladin has walked the blade of a knife so many times, being rescued from captivity only at the last moment. There's nothing surprising in the fact that she eventually got taken. Good thing you dragged her out. But let me remind you that we still have fourteen players in captivity with the Dark Faction. I suspect that their lives are not too sweet right about now."

"I'll be sure to raise that issue with General Ui-Taka," I promised the intelligence director. "And by the way, given it came up. I might not understand something, but I've wanted to know for a while: what is the point of torturing prisoners? Not in the sense of human rights, just on a purely technical level, game mechanics. After all, if it gets unbearable, the prisoner can just leave the game! So now I know you're an Inquisitor in the game, explain to me: what's the trick?"

"Leng Gnat, vanquisher of pirates and nightmare of the Dark Faction doesn't know such minor things?!" the newly-minted Inquisitor seemed to think I was mocking or testing him. "You're not making fun, you really don't know? Strange. I thought everyone knew. The Inquisitor and Torturer classes have a nasty little skill by the name of Imminence. When activated, their victim's game interface turns off for a certain amount of time. Their screen no longer shows game elements like health or progress bar. You cannot activate icons, abilities, use your inventory or look at stat windows. But the worst part is, you can't leave the game! At level one, Imminence only works for a couple seconds, but the duration goes up the more you level it. It also has an extremely long cooldown time, almost six hours. For those six hours, you have to use drugs to keep them in the game. If a person can't concentrate, they can't properly exit. Or you simply stun them."

Well, well! I really didn't know that. Apparently ignorance was bliss. If I had known that before tonight, I might not have been man enough to go try and rescue Gerd Tamara from the very lair of the enemy.

"I'll be sure to bring up our captive soldiers," I repeated my earlier promise. "And I'll also try to figure out the complex interrelations between the various Dark Faction subtypes. I'll try and find out what happened to Anna, too. It's very important for..."

I fell silent midsentence, because the door opened silently and Tamara entered the room. And the miniature girl was wearing black t-shirt that was far too long with the Second Legion's insignia. This morning I gave my floormate a copy of my room key, saying she could come in whenever she liked so the locked door didn't stop her. Alexander Antipov showed unusual delicacy and told the girl, who stopped unconfidently in the hallway, that we were done speaking and he was leaving. The deputy faction leader then shot into the hallway like a bullet and Tamara and I were left alone.

"I just can't sleep..." she complained, totally unashamed to pull the t-shirt off over her head and demonstrate a complete lack of underwear. "Let's not sleep together!"

Chapter Eighteen

Round Two

I MRAN THE DAGESTANI was stripped to the waist and walking on the sand. His muscular athletic body was glistening with sweat. Time was nearing midday and it was hot as ever on the Antique Beach pier.

"Ready, Gnat!" Two barrels of corned lamb were unloaded from the Peresvet and set in the shade. The Jarg was brought there as well. Our spiny Analyst had just about dropped dead from the heat, now his Miyelonian Medic was bringing him back to his senses. Three whole boxes of wine and vodka. Coal, tents, folding tables, we brought everything. However... it was obvious that he was too timid to ask a question. "You're an experienced player of course but are you sure that's the best way to prepare for negotiations with the Dark

Faction?"

I had changed my normal black armor suit for shorts and a light vest. With a happy smile I asked my friend:

"And I suspect you wanted to go to the enemy-held island draped in grenades and weapons like Schwarzenegger in *Commando*?"

"Well... basically yeah," the Dagestani replied, clearly embarrassed.

"See Imran, there are six hundred experienced troops there. There are only fifteen of us... and we come from four different races. Plus the Journalist who was attached to our group is a noncombat character. And a level-18 Bard won't be much help in battle either, but Major Filippov at least can use a machine gun and give out bonuses. But regardless we cannot defeat them in a contest of force. So we better not go brandishing guns and grenades, and instead take bottles and skewers."

I was twisting things a bit referring to our group's lack of teeth. Yes, we weren't taking any obvious weaponry with us to the negotiations. But first of all we had three mages: myself, Valeri-Urla and Minn-O La-Fin. Nothing much in the face of six hundred gun barrels, plus my wife had no experience in the magical arts yet, but still. Second, we had Little Sister with us. The deadly invisible shadow panther, Valeri's pet, was almost level one hundred. But our main trump card was the Small Relict Guard Drone, a metal object the size and shape of a basketball now levitating above my right shoulder.

Yes the repair of the ancient drone, which

Eduard had brought to me from the pirate store room on Medu-Ro IV in pieces, was finally complete and I managed to establish contact with it easily. The drone could be controlled both mentally and using the captain's tablet, plus it had a very expansive array of applications: from aerial recon and transporting small cargo to retransmitting and amplifying radio signals and destroying everything alive in a certain area. It wasn't much to look at and seemed slow at first glance. The flying metal ball didn't cause any fear in the uninitiated. In fact it was looked on as a mere curiosity. I had heard that a few Dark Faction mages used flying robot assistant drones that looked a lot like mine, so I was hoping they wouldn't ask any questions about my little helper. Of all my companions going to the negotiations, only Vasha and Basha knew what the Relict drone was truly capable of. But the Geckho brothers had been told the score and promised to keep quiet.

Uline Tar also knew about the secret, but my business partner was back at the space port today. She wanted to watch over the frigate repair and, as she put it, "make some business connections." Basically she wasn't acting one bit like the furry friend I once knew. Before, she was always eager to take part in any joint venture with the crew. But the Trader had spent half a day in her bunk today dying her fur orange, then purple and trying on and endless array of outfits and accoutrements. These "business contacts" must have had a very high value to her.

As far as I heard, Geckho Diplomat Kosta

Dykhsh was also not in his right mind for the second day in a row. He had already slept two nights away from his hut, spending all his time in the spaceport. And he was clearly relieved not to have to play Geckho observer at the natives' negotiations today. Seemingly, there was a connection between the unusual behavior of these two Geckho. Everyone was whispering about it except the repair bots.

"They're flying! There over the sea!" Tini my kitten pointed a clawed paw at a barely visible point on the horizon.

Eagle Eye skill increased to level seventy-five!

The point I tossed into Perception this morning, with the bonus, brought it up to twenty-nine, allowing me to see the distant flying machine in detail. The last of the eight free points from the rank-up, after long consideration, went into Constitution. Yes, you heard me right. Not Intelligence, which was most important to a mage, or Perception, which was required for many of my skills. I decided on Constitution. Why such a strange choice? Just because I was sick of constantly taking damage from high g-forces on take-offs and landings. I was the only person in my crew that happened to, which added insult to injury. My Constitution of 17 was still not so high, but better than 16.

"Yes, that is the Sio-Mi-Dori they sent out for us," I confirmed for Tini.

"And as far as I can tell, all the weaponry has been removed," Minn-O La-Fin also had impeccable

Perception and could see such details at a huge distance.

The Princess was wearing a light short tunic and looked unusual, but it was definitely a style that suited my wife, emphasizing her svelte legs and the feminine beauty of her body.

"I asked General Ui-Taka to do that," I explained to my wayedda. "The last time we landed in the Capital node in a Sio-Mi-Dori, they turned on emergency sirens in the real world, issuing a CtA (Call to Arms) to all players. So I asked them to remove all cannons from the aircraft this time so we don't test the nerves of the Human-3 Faction again."

"It looks so little. Are you sure we can all fit?" our faction journalist Lydia Vertyachikh was aware that I didn't want to take her to the important negotiations and was very worried that there would not be room in the antigrav for her specifically.

I kept silent so I wouldn't show my anger and annoyance once again. Yes, Ivan Lozovsky forced me into it. The faction leader was in a rut for a long time after I was promoted to Leng but he caught a second wind when he found out I was not going to replace him. And now, as if compensating for his passivity the last few days, he had been in an unusual flurry of activity planning for the second round of negotiations with the Dark Faction.

A message from General Ui-Taka proposed the meeting be held in an unofficial setting, as relaxed as possible, maybe even without the suzerains' diplomat. The Strategist also suggested we bring in more participants. For his part, the General promised to bring high-profile players from the La-Fin Faction who had already declared their loyalty to their new leader Leng Gnat La-Fin. He suggested that I bring my friends and starship crew so everything was as comfortable as could be.

Ivan Lozovsky insisted that I include Major Filippov and Lydia Vertyachikh among these "friends," though. First of all so the most experienced military specialist could see the fortifications the Dark Faction built on the island with his own eyes "just in case." And the Journalist so that Lydia as an independent figure, could make a highly detailed report for the whole faction. And though I wasn't particularly opposed to bringing the Bard along, I considered the Journalist unjustified. The faction leader could find out everything he needed from Imran, Dmitry Zheltov or Eduard Boyko just fine. Or even from me. I was not planning to hide anything, and especially not to deceive my faction.

Nevertheless, all the players I suggested were deemed "insufficiently neutral" by Ivan Lozovsky, plus they had been "gone a long time and had a bad understanding of the faction's day-to-day problems." I had to let him have that. I had no desire for a conflict with the Diplomat who really had no lost love for me. Especially now when my wife's fate depended on Ivan Lozovsky's permission to join the faction. Especially for such a minor reason.

But I really wanted to take Gerd Tamara to the negotiations. The Dark Faction knew her well and admired her. Plus the Paladin's presence was a guarantee that no one could mind control me or my friends. That was to say nothing of the fact that Tamara needed a change of scenery and to unwind instead of spending all her time cooped up under the Dome. Yes, it was strange, but after liberating the leader of the Second Legion, she had never once left the high-profile player residence, the inside of which had undergone a deep clean and was declared safe by CBRN experts.

For the most part, Tamara was locked in her own room, not wanting to see anyone except perhaps her deputy Roman Pavlovich. The huge gloomy veteran brought food to his adopted daughter, sent her messages and wishes for a speedy recovery from her Legion, and told her all the news. Sometimes without warning, Tamara would come to my room and immediately head into the bedroom with no prelude, getting undressed as she went. Her appetite for sex was insatiable, and one day she told me it was only these emotions and physical proximity providing her any fuel right now.

She just looked totally sunken. The imprisonment and harsh torture reflected extremely poorly on her. I mean, physically Tamara was in perfect health and in the real world her body didn't suffer, but psychologically something in her had broken... Tamara was always a bit strange, not at all like other girls, but now those quirks had grown much more distinct.

In order to help her quickly get over those days of cruelty, and to just change her mindset overall, I suggested Tamara fly with my group to the island. I thought that offer would get her interested. But the strict Paladin was categorical.

"No, Kirill! And don't even try to convince me, it's no use! To me, the Dark Faction and anyone who plays for them are enemies, and there can be no exceptions to that! Your wayedda Minn-O also was and remains an enemy no matter what faction she joins. Even you, Kirill, although I feel the warmest feelings for you, will be my enemy if you join the Dark Faction!"

"Why so categorical?" I had to admit, the Paladin girl was scaring me with her harsh edge and refusal to compromise.

"Because being so, as you put it, categorical, gives me strength and confidence! There is no such thing as half-truths. This world only has truth and lies. Black and white, no gray. It's a trick! Everything that is not white is black now. I am only alive because I believe such base truths to be inviolable. The world of magic is hostile to our usual one, that is the same kind of base truth. The end goal of the mages who live in that world is to destroy our world and that goal is what drives our enemy to such clever tricks. For example, sending you a beautiful wife from their world to put a crack in your firmness. Or loudly declaring that they were ready for a ceasefire. But all that is done only so they can destroy our world in the end!"

Hrm... Tamara was so confident that she was right. That and the unusual girl's unbending will were enough to defeat any challenger. I just couldn't disagree with her. It was not a magical or psionic effect, this was something of a different nature entirely, but just as crushing. It took me a lot of effort not to bend under the weight and to maintain my own personal but different opinion. I didn't know how right she was in her fanatic conviction, but bringing the Paladin to these negotiations with the Dark Faction would mean dooming them from the get-go.

But it wasn't only today's meeting with Gerd Tamara that had me upset and afraid. I couldn't ignore something else she said when we were lying in my bed and resting after our first very stormy encounter.

"Kirill, I have to tell you something. I'm a monster!"

Strange words for a pretty girl whose naked body I was stroking. What was she talking about? I tried to turn it into a joke, but Tamara was deadly serious:

"I was not made for love. My lot is to fight mages. That was the only reason fate gave me a second chance after so much time helpless in the dark. And the only thing people need me for is to fight the mages. If the war with the mages ends, I'll become obsolete! I am WAR itself. Living in peace will kill me. Even the soldiers of my own Legion, who now treat me like a goddess, will kill me as soon as there is peace with the mages. They will be unbearably ashamed and pained that they, a bunch of big strong guys, blindly obeyed a little girl. They'll dig up old offences, remember my strictness and uncompromising attitude. And they'll kill me. I know it!"

When Alexander Antipov came into my room that time, I was thinking tensely over these words. And I was holding them in my head now as I watched a Dark

his hand, calling someone from the antigrav.

A young dark-haired man in the traditional wizard's robe of a ruling house walked out of the flying assault vehicle and greeted everyone with a deep bow. The man was very tall, far over six and a half feet, thin as a matchstick and had big prominent ears. And although his eyes were the blue "magical" color, they didn't glow. Was he a mage? Was he just very weak?

Mark-Fes La-Pirez. Human. La-Fin Faction. Level-67 Psionic Mage.

Nevertheless, it wasn't his anatomical features or even his membership in the La-Pirez dynasty that drew everyone's attention but the ghastly object the young mage was carrying. It was the decapitated head of a gray-haired old man:

Head of Gerd Avir-Syn La-Pirez, level-109 Psionic Mage (trophy).

"My lord! I have carried out your order and killed the traitor! Grandpa tried to escape into the game but landed on a spear where my assistants got this trophy from," with these words the new leader of the La-Pirez dynasty laid the head of his insidious forebearer at my feet. "After that, I found the criminal in the real world next to his virt pod and defeated him in an honest one-on-one duel!"

An honest one-on-one duel? This snot-nose managed to take down a very strong psionic who was too strong even for my taste? Somehow I had a really hard time believing that. Either I was seriously underestimating Mark-Fes's magical abilities or this was a song and dance.

"Look me in the eyes!" I demanded, removing my sunglasses.

The man met gazes with me without reservation and I drowned in his thoughts and feelings.

Timidity. But no fear. Mark definitely didn't see any reason for guilt. His emotional state was more like relief that he was able to do this inside the assigned timeframe. And he was also extremely proud of the fact that he managed to do it faster than his five brothers, who were much more capable mages. But then I dug deep enough to find the facts on the real-world hunt:

"Greasy hooker's ass!!! You barely made it! The old man knew about the reward on his head in advance and managed to slam shut the lid of his virt pod. He fled into the game! No matter, if Malio-An my sister isn't lying, Avir-Syn won't be there for long. Now the most important thing is not to forget to switch your assault rifle over to constant beam. A lone laser pulse might not take down the old man right away. And that would be the end of me. Grandpa could kill me easily with his ghoulish magical abilities! He spent years leading Archmage Thumor-Anhu La-Fin around by the nose. The coruler never realized right up until he died but the man he entrusted his life and that of his granddaughter to was no friend, but a most hateful enemy. What? Is it just me or did the virt pod lid just rustle? Yes, exactly! Open fire!!! Cut the thin plastic with the laser! Yes! The scream of a dying traitor is music to my ears! I am the new head of the La-Pirez dynasty!!!"

As I suspected, there was no magical duel. The heir shot his grandfather with an assault rifle before he could get out of his virt pod. Nevertheless, it didn't violate my conditions, so it was all well within the rules of the game. That's how you treat a dirty traitor! I had everything I needed and broke the mental contact.

Mental Fortitude skill increased to level eighty-two!

Psionic skill increased to level eighty-five!

"Mark-Fes, by my authority as head of the First Directory, I hereby confirm you as the new head of the ancient house of La-Pirez! Congratulations! And let me personally express a hope that the new head of the dynasty will show better sense than to start making back-room deals with other corulers behind the back of the La-Fins."

"Yes, my lord! You need not doubt my loyalty!" the newly promoted mage fell to his knees and kissed my hand.

All that sounded and looked just too ostentatious, but I must have done everything right because I got a system message saying my Authority had gone up:

Authority increased to 60!

Minn-O La-Fin walked up and warmly greeted her second cousin, then with an air of disgust flipped the head on the ground. I told my wife about her grandfather's death not only in the game but in the real world as well. I was worried the Princess would be upset or even fall into hysterics, but Minn-O had a completely different reaction:

"He tried to kill me two times! And once he actually succeeded. I feel no sympathy for his death!

And you did the right thing my husband: traitors must be executed post haste! I suspect that Avir-Syn is only the first in a long line of enemies who tried to take a bite at the riches of the La-Fin Dynasty. As its head, you are obliged to punish that!"

Chapter Nineteen

Future Plans

T HE GIANT level-104 Shocktroop Gerd T'yu-Pan came. There was also level-102 Machinegunner Gerd Lang-Yu — a very young big-eared boy with an open and honest face. Surprisingly, he was commander of the most successful Dark Faction landing battalion. It was his soldiers who took the Rainforest node and, after forcing the Second Legion into that trap, just about took them out for good. Another was Gerd Alex-Bobl, a level-92 Drafter, the inventory of all Dark Faction armored vehicles, including the Sio-Mi-Dori antigravs and the Sio-Ku-Tati heavy tanks. There was also a young woman named Anni-Ir, a level-96 Agrarian whose job it was to keep her faction's many thousands of players supplied with food. And Gerd Mihoya-U, basically still a girl, this was the level-104 Dark Faction Scout, whose small squadron remained undetected in our lands for several months. In that time they crisscrossed the Human-3 Faction's whole territory, gathering data about troop movement and the coordinates of artillery batteries and strategically important facilities.

That whole group of celebrated players, all of whom had a hand in the Dark Faction's brilliant success and lightning-fast growth, supported me as the new leader of the La-Fin Dynasty. That was good. There was just the disconcerting fact that not a single one of them was a mage. After all, I knew perfectly well that the previous Dark Faction Leng, Thumor-Anhu La-Fin had a large group of mages of all kinds of specializations around him and many of them were Gerd status and past level 100. One of them, Psionic Mage Gerd Avir-Syn La-Pirez I had executed recently. But where were the others?

I was not feeling decisive enough to ask that question with everyone around. So I waited for a good opportunity when the high-profile players who had come to meet me went out to help put up canopies and set tables. Then I asked the General.

"One mage will be here soon. Gerd Mac-Peu Un-Roi is on his way here via Geckho ferry. He had some problems in the real world, and some technical issues with his virt pod..." the huge Strategist took a deep sigh. Then he made up his mind and laid it all out: "After the negotiations in the space port when the young mage got out of hand, old Avir-Syn ordered the guards of the digital facility to find and kill the Mage

Diviner at once. But it's not for nothing Mac-Peu Un-Roi is considered one of the best seers in our world. He saw the danger in advance and managed to escape the well-guarded facility, then hunkered down in a safe refuge. After Avir-Syn himself was declared a criminal, the young mage came out of hiding. But they had to change his virt pod. The old one was crammed full of spikes on an order from Avir-Syn. All the complex mechanisms were wrecked."

Well, well! That explained a lot really. I suspected that after everything that happened, the talented Mage Diviner was experiencing no warm emotions for the executed Avir-Syn and his associates, so I could count on his loyalty to me.

Successful Perception check.

"Get out of here! That is not for eating!" I gave a flawlessly accurate bop on the nose to the invisible Shadow Panther, who was sniffing Avir-Syn's head on the ground curiously. The creature gave a loud exhale and trampled grass flew into the air.

Little Sister appeared and, jerking her tail in offense, went off to complain to her master. The huge Strategist took a step back in fear when the creature went visible, a laser pistol instantly appearing in his hands. That told me he was very nervous although he was trying not to show it. And with surprise I also discovered that this muscular giant was afraid of me for some reason! Very strange. I reassured him explaining the panther and pointing to its master, the extraterrestrial lady Valeri. And she was tenderly stroking the glamorous if terrible predator staring at me with her huge eyes and shaking her head in dismay:

"Don't be mean to her, Gnat! Little Sister is still young and curious. She just wanted to investigate an unusual object, not eat it. Not at all. Little Sister keeps trying to steal up to you too to get to know you better, but you're always chasing her off!"

Psionic skill increased to level eighty-six!

I didn't see anything good in the fact that a deadly predator was sneaking up on me from behind "to get to know me better." If the panther wanted to be friends, she could come up in visible form, not keep testing my ability to detect her. Nevertheless, I didn't mentally answer Valeri and returned to my talk with the General, asking a question that had me very intrigued:

"As for Mac-Peu Un-Roi I understand. He'll be here soon. But what about the other high-profile mages from Thumor-Anhu La-Fin's circle? And really what is the situation with the faction's mages?"

Before Gerd Ui-Taka started answering, the way his countenance sharply grew sad clued me in to the fact that his answer was going to upset me. And I wasn't wrong:

"Not that long ago there were nine high-profile mages in the La-Fin Faction including Leng Thumor-Anhu La-Fin. After recent events, seven remain. I'm afraid, Leng Gnat, that only one of them is on your side: Gerd Mac-Peu Un-Roi the Mage Diviner. The other six mage rulers fled the First Directory and I seriously suspect that, in a few days, we'll be hearing about them in the La-Varrez or La-Shin factions, maybe even some smaller ones. And all players who have magical abilities are in approximately the same boat. Of one hundred seventy-two mages, forty-three died in the terror attack at Coruler Thumor-Anhu's funeral, and the majority of survivors went to join your competitors. Leng Gnat La-Fin, there are just eighteen wizards left on your side."

"I've also got Minn-O La-Fin. She's a high-profile mage even though she has almost no experience," I said, trying to perk myself up even though the picture being painted was not a happy one. Rats were fleeing my ship, which meant they had no faith in my ability to keep the situation under control. But one fleeting aspect in the general's words caught my attention:

"Hold up, what does that mean? Only the strongest mages from Thumor-Anhu La-Fin's retinue survived the terrible explosion at his funeral?"

The general just shrugged his shoulders indefinitely:

"Maybe power mages have a more developed sense of intuition and luck. Although I agree, it is a strange fact. It's almost like they were warned."

That was most likely the case. But I didn't discuss that with the enemy leader now. It was too unclear and slippery, so I changed the topic. I brought up the Human-3 Faction prisoners who were still stewing away in their dungeons. Fourteen soldiers. What would it take to get them set free?

"Ransom?" by the looks of things, the question surprised him. "Just take them! It's such a small thing that it's a shame to even waste time discussing it. I thought we came here to resolve truly serious issues.

First and foremost, a peace treaty and its conditions. I don't think there will be any problems with that. We'll come to an agreement quickly. Second, plans for the future. Now that really is important, and was the main reason I came here myself."

I stared at the giant, my eyebrows raised in surprise. I basically thought we were here only to settle a peace treaty and that we had a long way before we got there. The idea that it there wouldn't be any problems with that seemed unimaginable. But the Strategist gave a happy laugh and answered my obvious surprise:

"Leng Gnat, you're new head of the La-Fin Dynasty and leader of the First Directory. The players of the La-Fin Faction will obey you and only you. You're also the main Human-3 Faction negotiator. So technically, you're negotiating on behalf of both sides. So I bet you'll be able to reach an agreement with yourself. I'm just a temporary placeholder. My mission was to make sure the La-Fin Faction and my world get a fair shake in the peace treaty. What conditions do you have to offer, Leng Gnat?"

Unexpected! No really, I never would have thought that one day the responsibility to decide for both worlds would fall on my shoulders. This was like playing chess against myself. So then, if I thought about it, what conditions were fair? I was in no rush, gradually squeezing out phrase after phrase:

"The La-Fin Faction shall receive a Geckho guarantee for their capital hexagon and retain the captured Tropics node. There they may build a distant outpost and a seaport but only on the condition that they do not obstruct movement of goods between the H3 and H6 factions on the coastal rode. Also, their further expansion south shall be delimited by a node which shall belong to no one. La-Fin troops shall be withdrawn from Karelia and the faction shall renounce all claims both to that node and the one on the opposite shore of the bay. On the other side, the Human-3 Faction shall receive a Geckho guarantee on their Capital node and renounce all claims to the Harpy Cliffs. Again this will be on the condition that the road remains open for trade with the Geckho spaceport."

I fell silent, expecting commentary or arguments, but General Ui-Taka kept silent, listening carefully and allowed me to continue:

"The H3 Faction will remain under control of Ivan Lozovsky. And I transfer leadership over the La-Fin Faction to my legal wife Princess Minn-O La-Fin. I still haven't talked with her about it, but she is a mage and represents the ancient La-Fin Dynasty so our subjects should not have any objections. As for the island we are now on..." I gathered some air because the next demand was just pure impudence. "This island shall become my personal territory! My personal faction will be located here, composed of volunteers from both of the parallel worlds, as well as members of other space races. This island shall also be untouchable, as guaranteed by humanity's Geckho suzerains!"

I finished with my heart aflutter, awaiting a reaction. I figured General Ui-Taka could have very serious objections. After all, the Dark Faction had a serious advantage when combat ended and could have laid claim to more. But the huge muscular Strategist unexpectedly agreed:

"I accept, Leng Gnat! I told you, you're negotiating with yourself! The participants in the conflict are already disengaged. We now know that no matter how long this war goes on, neither side can fully destroy the other. And it seems that you are putting yourself forward for the role of humanity's future Kung. What can I say? It would be an interesting outcome. Now I need to get all that across to the others. Then, when the formalities are over, we can move on to truly serious matters!"

Snowy Mountains

Destroyed

Dark Faction

Desert

Harpy Cliffs

Spaceport

Karelia

Capital

Eastern Swamp

Antique Beach

Yellow Mountains

Jungles

Forest Spirits

Centaur Plateau

Destroyed

Antiquity

Dark Faction

Antiquity

Relic

H8

H8

"AND WHAT? You just up and agreed, just like that?" The faction Journalist couldn't believe the most important negotiations in the world were already over before they even got started.

"Yeah, right away. I mean, go ahead and write that we shouted until we got hoarse to keep the faction happy, of course. Say we just about killed each other fighting for more favorable conditions. But the reality is that the Dark Faction has just as little desire for a war of elimination as the Human-3 Faction."

I considered the explanation completely sufficient and, lowering my sunglasses, sat back blissfully in a folding lounger, planning to enjoy the bright sun and pleasant sea breeze. However, Lydia Vertyachikh didn't think the conversation was over. She even puffed out her cheeks in offense:

"Gnat, I cannot understand. What did I say? I don't think I've ever given you a reason to treat me the way you do. But you didn't want to take me to the negotiations, and now you're batting me off like some troublesome fly. Do you treat all journalists this way? Or just me?"

A tricky way of posing the question. Any short answer, either yes or no, would put me into an awkward position. So I had to go into detail:

"Lydia, I treat all journalists with decency, as I am treating you right now. What's more, in some measure I'm even somewhat grateful for your delicacy when it comes to Gerd Tamara. I was afraid that you were going to impose on the leader of the Second Legion with questions about her losing the expensive armor suit, her imprisonment and torture like the kind of reporter that swarms around any tragedy. I'm happy I was wrong."

"Then why are you acting so difficult?" the Journalist wouldn't let up.

No, with her around, I couldn't afford to let my guard down, concentrate on the bright sun, and enjoy the rare moment of relaxation. I stored my glasses in my inventory and, getting up, gestured broadly at the happy players, relaxing without a care:

"Look at them. Do you know the difference between you and everyone else on this peaceful green field?"

Lydia just shrugged, not knowing the answer.

"Good, let me tell you then. All these players, no matter what race they belong to, are members of my crew or loyal subjects of my family. The Geckho and Miyelonians, the Jarg and even the Dark Faction people will do whatever I order and follow me through fire and water. Except General Ui-Taka perhaps. He does not answer to me. But the General is bending over backwards to make sure there is a good relationship between me and the new La-Taka Faction. And now the Strategist has fulfilled his previous obligations and will leave the La-Fin Faction to join it very soon. And on the backdrop of this team of like-minded associates there is you, sent on an order from Ivan Lozovsky to spy on us and maybe dig up some blackmail material if possible. Yes, yes. Don't deny it. I read it in your thoughts. And I'm not the only one who could have."

"Yes, you be think too loud," Minn-O La-Fin walked up to us smiling with a glass of apple juice in her hand, unashamed to demonstrate that she was eavesdropping. "Journalist is many worry that no will be bad material for director Ivan. And now that we is conversation, tell your boss I is change mind! No is want now H3 Faction. Now am head of La-Fin Faction, my home. And they promise to fix me virt pod soon!"

Princess Minn-O was in an exceptionally good mood. I wasn't sure I'd ever seen my wife looking so happy before. When I suggested she head the La-Fin Faction, my wayedda was enthusiastic and delighted. Minn-O, a representative of a most ancient dynasty of mage rulers, who considered herself lesser for many years due to a lack of magical abilities, had a new lease on life. Now that she had Magic Points, she was vibrant, intense and proper. And still, I remained legal head of House La-Fin and leader of the First Directory. The Dark Faction players had confirmed me in that role. Having a mage wife only strengthened my authority as mage ruler, but she didn't eclipse me as dynasty head.

"I is happy today! Is want dancing!" The Princess's words confirmed my own observation.

"Then why are you drinking juice instead of wine?" I chuckled and a strange shadow ran over her face. I couldn't understand what she was thinking. Was she afraid? Trying to hide something?

"I just want to keep my clarity of mind on a day like today."

With a quick kiss on my cheek, Minn-O turned

around and hurried to the set tables, around which they were still celebrating the peace treaty. And Miyelonians and Geckho were taking part in the fun just as much as the people although I strongly suspect that most of my crew had no idea who was even at war on this planet, or what groups had just made peace.

Somewhat strange. Minn-O's behavior surprised me. Completely in spite of myself I tried to read my wayedda's thoughts and feelings. I must admit, it had become habit. I'd done so a few times before to better understand my wife. But this time it didn't work. Beyond that, the Princess's voice appeared in my head:

"Husband, you shouldn't do that! A woman must always have her secrets."

I didn't try to read my wife again, and turned to the Journalist standing next to me.

"It's hard to live when every other person is reading your thoughts like an open book..." Lydia noted, implying her case, but she completely randomly guessed at what had just happened between Minn-O and I.

Meanwhile, if the Journalist was embarrassed to have her private thoughts read, it wasn't for long. She even tried to go on the attack and cast aspersions:

"Kirill, when you said that only your subjects were gathered here, you were clearly exaggerating. At the very least Major Filippov does not belong to your team."

Authority reduced to 59!

I gritted my teeth in annoyance. How dare she cast a Leng's words into doubt?! Every day I had a better understanding of high-profile players who killed without warning for Authority drops. In fact, the more effort I expended, the more I realized this number was very hard to improve. Every time a common player disputed something I said, a few days' work went to down the drain! Should I shoot the Journalist or something? To teach her the game rules? Once upon a time that helped me, although it took me a while to appreciate the value of Gerd Tamara's lessons.

The small Relict guard drone, sensing my mood, came down further and focusing its innumerable data readers, locators and mobile video cameras on Lydia Vertyachikh, studying the suspicious being that had upset its master.

"No, please don't kill her!" I stopped my mechanical guard. "She is simply a fool, there's no treating it."

The drone lost all interest in Lydia and, obediently flying upward, got distracted by a seagull and followed it to some distant cliffs.

"So now I'm a fool all of a sudden?" the Journalist couldn't understand, also following the now distant drone with her gaze.

"Well because you're arguing with a Leng, which goes against the mechanics of the game that bends reality, and for that you *should* be killed. Yes, yes. I will forgive you, but just this once. Not least of all because you're the very last to hear the news, which is strange for a Journalist. But while flying in the antigrav, Major Filippov asked to join the crew of my Tolili-Ukh X frigate and was even hired to be the Jarg Analyst's assistant. Everyone but you already knows."

"How was I supposed to know?! You were speaking a language I don't know!"

I laughed happily, her justification seeming so ill-founded:

"Lydia, he's a level-18 Bard who just got into the game. Still he found time to study the language of the suzerains. Yes, his vocabulary is pitiful for now and his grammar makes them smile. His accent also gives him away for a native of Ryazan, not the planet of Shikharsa. But at least Major Filippov is trying! You're a level-53 Journalist, the one-time faction record-holder for levelling speed. You've been in the game almost as long as me. But you stopped growing a long time ago! Who were you even planning to talk to at these negotiations if you don't know the Dark Faction language, or Miyelonian or Geckho?"

Again the Journalist's abashment lasted just a brief moment, then she found a way out:

"Well, for example, what I'm doing now. Or with a new member of your team. By the way, where is he? For some reason I can't see the Bard in the clearing."

I turned and also furrowed my brow in thought. Major Filippov really was nowhere to be seen in the small clearing. By the way... someone else was also missing. I studied the crowd. Exactly! We were also missing Valeri the Beast Master. Did they go into the forest together? Weird of course, but anything was possible. Still better to check.

Scanning skill increased to level forty-five!

There they were! In fact, both AWOL players'

markers were together, but not in the forest. Valeri-Urla and Major Filippov were standing on rocks at the very edge of the surf. And next to them... my heart fluttered in panic because there were at least fifty red markers around my friends on the mini-map. That meant enemies. Naiads!!!

But that wasn't all I noticed. Next to Minn-O... and to be even more accurate inside her there was one more creature, reflected on my mini-map as:

Human. Level-0 Psionic Mage.

Chapter Twenty

Woe is Sea...

I JUST FROZE at the shocking news. My wife was expecting a child! How about that!!! And Minn-O was already pregnant when she was killed and respawned! Like ants in an agitated colony, thousands of thoughts ran through my head simultaneously. And most important was how to transfer a child from the virtual game into the real world? Minn-O once said it was possible. At the very least Coruler Thumor-Anhu La-Fin supposedly knew a way.

"What's the matter Kirill, can't keep track of your underlings?" the Journalist's acrid voice rang out behind me, jerking me from my thinking.

Authority reduced to 58!

No, she just never learned! I didn't even turn around, already knowing perfectly that the girl's lifeless body was falling to the floor behind me, her heart stopped cold. I hoped at our next encounter Lydia would learn to show respect to a Leng!

Psionic skill increased to level eighty-seven!
Mysticism skill increased to level thirty-six!

I heard shouts of fear. Everyone saw Lydia Vertyachikh dying at the same time. Meanwhile, no one stopped me or asked any questions, and most importantly didn't judge me. There was one upside to being high-profile. As a Gerd and all the more so a Leng, if I did something, that meant it was my right!

I walked up to the edge of the precipice, expecting to see anything: the Beast Master and Bard fighting off Naiads with the last of their strength, a pair of broken bodies. But the picture before me then was simply idyllic: Major Filippov was enjoying himself fishing with a spinning rod. And he was doing pretty well for himself. On the stringer tied to the fisherman's belt I could already see four medium-sized salmon. Valeri-Urla then, like a mermaid from an old tale, was sitting on a huge rock with her legs dangling down, sometimes lapped by the surf.

But where were the Naiads? I zoomed in the mini-map. The red hostile NPC markers were still there and very nearby, but underwater. Risking breaking my legs on the crumbly steep slope, I started down toward the water and at the same time called my drone just in case. Hearing the sound of rolling rocks, Valeri-Urla turned to me:

"Gnat, just be careful not to spook them!"

There wasn't even a shade of fear in the

Beastmaster's voice. It was more like annoyance that I was bothering her. As for "them," she meant the undersea creatures. I realized that instantly. So that meant my companion knew perfectly about the danger lurking beneath the waves? I asked that aloud.

"Captain, you are wrong there! Naiads are not dangerous if you don't harm them first. They told me that themselves. They have a very particular way of thinking. This is the first time I've seen such a thing. There are only two categories for classifying strangers who are not part of their underwater species: 'food' and 'do not contact.' And they have a photographic memory shared by the whole school. They remember everyone who ever harmed any of them. Anyone who does gets added to their 'food' category, and can never be moved back out."

By then I had already reached the water and was standing on a stone behind the alien girl. Instantly all the red markers on my mini-map changed to a neutral yellow shade.

"They changed to neutral. Your work?" I asked.

"No. I didn't tell them anything about you. The Naiads just came to the conclusion they had never seen you before."

Interesting. Very interesting. But then why did the caged Naiad kill Ivan Lozovsky right away before even giving the Diplomat the chance to establish contact? Valeri-Urla the Beastmaster immediately gave a totally plausible explanation for that also:

"Your former leader must have shown the Naiad a connection with someone who caused it pain and suffering. Maybe he gave a warm greeting to the players who captured it. Maybe he was just talking with or smiling at them. Also, the caged Naiad was starting to dry out, but its pain was just entertaining to those land-lubbers. So as soon as the captive got the chance, it killed its tormenter. And after that, all further attempts to establish contact were doomed to failure. Both with the still captive individual and its whole race. To all of them, the human Diplomat is now food, and you don't talk to food!"

I fell silent, thinking over the situation in the coastal waters around my island. The Miyelonians and Geckho were neutral to the Naiads. I wasn't sure about the Dark Faction people, but as for the Human-3 members, only Lydia Vertyachikh had ever been on the front lines of that war. The Journalist gave a report there and even held a gun in her own hands. Good thing I sent her to respawn!

"Is it possible to get the Naiads from neutral to friendly?" I asked the Beastmaster her expert opinion.

The huge-eyed girl turned and looked at me with a smile:

"Very good question, Leng Gnat. You think the very same way as me. But no, these ones cannot. They are simple everyday NPC's, very limited in their authority to make important decisions. Their leaders handle diplomatic negotiations, and one has already been sent for."

"Damn! Did you see that?! The one that got away was a lunker!!! I got it all the way up to shore and it jerked and stole my lure!" the Bard, five steps away, had a very emotional reaction to losing a fish.

By the way, Major Filippov's level had already hit 22! Not bad for less than an hour of fishing! I heard the game had suggested the career soldier an alternative profession as a Fisher, and clearly he had a knack for it.

"I was the one who asked Vasily to come here and fish," Valeri-Urla suddenly told me. "We needed to catch the Naiads' attention to get them closer to shore."

"Woah, holy crap!" the Bard, crouched down to tie on a new jig, took a step back in fear and even fell back on his ass when just one yard away a waist-high scaled creature with fish-like immobile eyes rose up out of the water.

Using its webbed hands, the Naiad lowered its trident in silence and pulled down a three-foot-long fish, setting it before Major Filippov. In its toothy maw, I could make out a bright yellow and blue lure with a bit of torn off line. Then, as silently as it arrived, the undersea native went under the water and dissolved in the depths of the sea. The Beastmaster commented on the entertaining episode:

"There's your answer about whether Naiads can be friendly. They want to be friends with people and do everything they can to butter you up. By the way, I'm gonna go for a swim. You coming, captain?"

The space girl, burned bronze, hopped off the wet wave-kissed boulder, scrambled up a bit higher, farther from the tide line and got undressed, unashamed and carefully folding her things on the stone. I lowered my eyes in embarrassment even though the naked extraterrestrial had a very attractive figure to my eye. All I didn't know was why Valeri-Urla wouldn't put her clothes in her inventory. Either the extra weight stopped her from swimming or she was just acting on an old real-world habit. Or was she teasing me?

Her hands extended, without the slightest splash, she entered the water head first. When she popped back up, she was already fifty feet from shore. Pushing the hair out of her eyes, Valeri-Urla laughed happily:

"How nice! You coming, Leng Gnat? It's hot out, the water is just so refreshing!"

At the same time as she said that out loud, she sent another message mentally just for me:

"Don't disappoint me, Captain! Confirm your reputation as a fearless adventure lover whose impressive feats are discussed the Universe over! Or are you afraid of the Naiads? Maybe you're just afraid of me?"

Damn! Damn! What an uncomfortable situation! Maybe she was just happy to be refreshed, but I remembered the game rules clearly: no Swimming skill meant you'd sink like a stone. And my Gnat didn't have that skill. I mean, I was a Listener at the end of the day, a mage specialized in controlling machines, not some marine or diver! Seemingly I had another Authority drop coming my way, third in a row...

"I'd love to swim with such a beautiful lady!" I didn't know when he'd made it down here, but the huge muscular giant Gerd Ui-Taka was looking at the beautiful girl frisking about in the water with clear interest. "If of course the Leng allows it."

The former Dark Faction leader's words wounded me with unexpected intensity. I turned around. On the high shore there were lots of people watching now both from my crew and the La-Fin Faction. I couldn't let them see me being cowardly! And that thought was the straw that broke the camel's back:

"No, General, I do not allow it! I'm diving into the sea myself!"

What was I doing?! Had I lost my mind? Out of concern for the opinion of a mysterious beauty from a distant planet called Tailax, I was going to lose ninety-two percent of my progress to level eighty-three? But it was the only proper decision, I knew it. If I didn't jump, Valeri-Urla would be disappointed and leave the crew. And along with her would go Denni Marko, the only one on my starship who could operate the cannons. And my Authority as a Leng would falter in my subjects' eyes.

But that self-serving interest was not most important now. I gathered my bravery and admitted honestly, at least to myself, that I liked Valeri-Urla as a woman. Although the space huntress already had a companion and her relationship with Denni had lasted for many years. Also I had my own wife. The beautiful and loyal Princess Minn-O La-Fin, future mother of my child. But still I was not willing to lose Valeri!

Not wanting to copy the sun-kissed huntress and put on my own striptease, I simply stashed my clothes in my inventory, leaving on just a swimsuit. I moved my respawn point to this stony shore as well. I would need it very soon. My three remaining skill points I set into Scanning, raising it to forty-eight. If I hadn't done so, the points would have just burnt up, because it had been more than 24 hours since I got them.

With a heavy sigh — ugh, bye, bye almost full experience bar! — and squinting, I decisively leapt head first into the deep blue water!

Fame increased to 74.

Authority increased to 59!

I didn't even have time to get scared before a huge number of webbed hands grabbed me and forcefully pushed me up to the surface. I took a greedy breath. Wow!!! I'm alive!!!

The strong arms of the underwater natives held my head above the water then, with a fairly haphazard poke in the ass, they pushed me onto something big, black and round. I didn't even know what it was at first, but it was a huge sea turtle drifting among the waves. Valeri-Urla was already there, straddling the unrushed animal like its master and laughing happily:

"That was funny! It looked like you were walking to your execution! Calm down, captain. There was no danger. I asked them to grab you if you dared to take such a suicidal jump. It was just a little test. And I have to admit, you impressed me. And not just me..." Valeri-Urla fell silent mid-word as if listening to something in her head. "I've just been asked to say that the prelates of the planet of Tailax would like to establish contact with you and your people, Leng Gnat."

IT WAS THE STRANGEST negotiation I'd ever had the ill fortune to take part in. An endless blue sea, only in the east at the very horizon could I see the rocky island. The sun overhead was scorching unbearably. The huge sea turtle under us moved its flippers phlegmatically. A whole escort of Naiads accompanied us and there were several subtypes. There were also sea monsters, some of which looked like they'd come right off the screen of a horror movie. And completing the surreal picture was the naked sunburnt girl next to me with huge anime eyes. She was pretty but her body was stuffed full of complex espionage equipment which her distant jailers used both to tell her what to ask me and hear my answers.

I learned a great amount. Above all else, what exactly would happen after the game's guaranteed tong of safety passed, and how a space invasion would look. Tailax had undergone one around three hundred years ago. Despair — that was the most appropriate word for the panic and anguish that took hold on their planet when the armada of the Meleyephatian horde, known as a scourge of every living thing, appeared simultaneously in the game that bends reality and the real world.

As it turned out, the "tong of safety" was exactly how long it took to sufficiently synchronize the virtual and real worlds. Attacking before then only in the game was basically pointless because it wouldn't capture the planet in the real world. And sending a fleet only in the real world was immeasurably difficult and, more importantly, an extremely drawn-out operation because travelling between stars in the real world frequently required thousands if not millions of years. Thankfully, in the game, the same stars were much closer at hand and could take just a few days to reach if not hours.

Tailaxian humanity's original suzerains were the Cyanians — a low population race of amorphous creatures that looked like bubbles. I'd once seen one of them on Medu-Ro IV going through passport control. In theory the Cyanians should have defended their vassals. In fact they had occupied a few territories on Tailax, rendering them off limits to the natives, supposedly for the purpose of building a planetary shield and other defensive structures.

In reality, the planetary shield was not finished in time. And one day, a never-ending flood of Meleyephatian horde space commandos just flooded out through portals built by the Cyanians themselves. They suppressed all resistance within two days. The forces were just too uneven and the orbital bombardment just too destructive, accurate. All those connected with the former authorities were exterminated without exception. The new authorities the occupiers put in place, made up of Meleyephatians and Cyanians set the laws Tailax was to live by from then on: a seventy percent tax paid to the

Meleyephatian horde for all resources, the use of local orbital docks to construct starships for their masters, and a yearly draft of recruits to fuel the further expansion of the horde. And even the slightest disobedience toward the occupying authorities was to be punished by killing every native of Tailax down to the tiniest mewling babe.

That heavy yoke hung on their peoples' shoulders for many long decades. Production expectations were constantly increasing, the horde needed more and more resources and starships for their expansion. Every year millions of young men and women were drafted into the Meleyephatian horde and flew off to unknown space. None of them had ever come back. The very idea of an uprising was cauterized with red-hot iron and by the planet's human natives themselves. The former ruling dynasties being wiped out, a theocracy was swept into power, leaving them under the thumb of the church of Survival. Centuries of oppression and isolation had made Tailax a very closed society in which church intelligence tracked every person via electronic implants.

A slight thaw came only two centuries later and the reason for the indulgence was that Tailax was running out of resources. The planet had lost its attractiveness to the Meleyephatian horde. The people of Tailax were allowed to add prelates of the church of Survival to the planet's ruling council. They were allowed to have their own space fleet, though exclusively noncombat ships. But most importantly, the restriction against further exploration of space was removed, so they could get back to that after almost two centuries of occupation. And although there were still fairly harsh restrictions on real-world space flight, they didn't apply to the game that bends reality and the virtual game had become Tailax's main source of information about the outside world. Furthermore, Tailax had come to surpass the great space races in the field of creating miniature devices to implant in human bodies which gather and transmit the full spectrum of information.

"But the biggest thaw came very recently, not even ten years ago," Valeri-Urla, lying on her stomach to tan her back, distantly commented on what her jailers were saying. "The planet of Tailax was given the right to conduct their own politics even if they contradicted the common thrust of the Meleyephatian horde. And just so Leng Gnat understands just how unusual that all is, the Meleyephatians have never made such indulgences to subjugated races before."

"Yeah?" I really was interested in this strange exception to the rules. "So why did they make an exception for Tailax all of a sudden?"

Valeri translated the question to Tailaxian for her masters. Nowhere near all of them understood Geckho. And she told me their answer:

"The prelates of the church of Survival believe that this unexpected thaw is connected with the Meleyephatian horde encountering a previously unknown but very tough enemy in the process of their expansion. Although the leaders of the horde conceal the precise nature of the problem, expansion in vector

8-9-17 ground to a halt long ago, and hasn't picked back up. What's more, we know there were some very extreme space battles in that sector of the galaxy two tongs ago. The horde suffered great losses."

"Is it known what enemy stopped the Meleyephatian horde?" I asked, not especially counting on a serious answer. And so it was all the more surprising to receive a response:

"Yes, it is. Humans."

Excuse me?! That was the last answer I was expecting. Humans? Another branch of humanity, which was apparently just scattered throughout the Universe? Not Earth, not Tailax, not the Gilvar Syndicate. Some totally different people!

"It's top secret information, the Meleyephatians will not share the details of the catastrophe with their vassals. All we know is that the horde's fleet was soundly defeated in a star system called the Aysar Cluster. No details. But regardless of what happened there, the Meleyephatians are afraid. And they're so afraid that, ever since, they've been trying not to provoke their galactic neighbors and have closed space flight vector 8-9-17 to travel. They even loosened restrictions for their human vassals!"

The Aysar Cluster... What a familiar name. I'd heard of that star system before... Oh yeah! A recent episode sprung up an my memory when I encountered the mysterious starship in hyperspace and it reacted brusquely to normal scanning, taking out my frigate's location and scanning systems. But hell knew where the Aysar Cluster was! A two-tong journey, if memory served. Did Meleyephatian space really stretch that far?

"The Meleyephatian horde has huge holdings that extend for many parsecs. But even they are not endless. Beyond is just undiscovered space, filled with mysteries and riddles."

"Earth's suzerains are not the Cyanians, but the Geckho a much more numerous and powerful space race. Are they capable of defending Earth?"

I froze, attentively waiting for the answer, my heart aflutter. Unfortunately, the answer was not what I was hoping for:

"The Geckho are strong, no argument. But their main territories are nowhere near your home planet, Leng Gnat. In that sector of the galaxy, Geckho positions are very thin: just one military base and a seriously ragged fleet. It is not enough to defend your planet. And you know that yourself, Leng Gnat."

I lowered my head because I really did already know that bitter truth. Kung Waid Shishish's fleet was Earth's only hope, but it was far away. And even if he reached the Solar System, he couldn't stay in orbit around Earth forever, because the Geckho had lots of colonies and vassals that required attention. But that wasn't the worst of it. Constant defense was impossible, I was sure of that. But us Earth natives had to regularly pay such impossible sums to the Geckho Fleet and its captains that we would have a very hard time coming up with resources of our own, so our chances were slim.

"There are no good moves here, Leng Gnat,"

Valeri transmitted the words of the prelates of Tailax. "Earth is doomed. As soon as the term of safety is up, alternative suzerains are going to be lining up, as they do for any planet that can support life. The Miyelonians or Trillians, Meleyephatians or some race from their horde... it makes no difference. And I mean, the Geckho themselves shouldn't be written off. They might demand your planet in repayment for defending it. In any case, there are predators lurking everywhere."

Mental Fortitude skill increased to level eighty-three!

Before that message popped up to warn me, I had already seen flaws in my counterpart's logic. The Miyelonians? Sure, the Tailaxians didn't know, but the commander of the Miyelonian fleet herself, Kung Keetsie-Myau had promised that her race wouldn't lay claim to Earth. The Trillians? Yes, that ancient race was widely settled throughout the galaxy, but they had no colonies or space stations in this sector. The Trillians couldn't hold a such a distant planet, so they wouldn't even try. The same could be said about the Geckho although the mysterious construction by the suzerains of some facilities on Earth, and the fact that some parts of earth were now off limits to earthlings had me on guard.

The only potential aggressor left was the Meleyephatian horde. And it just so happened that I was negotiating with a representative of one of their vassals just now, and they were most likely cautiously preparing me for an offer. I wondered what it would be.

I didn't have to wait long:

"Leng Gnat, you are one of the most famous people of Earth, and very respected. You have levers of influence in various factions. So we wanted to offer one way and possibly several of how to minimize damage to your kind after the end of the tong of safety, and we thought you were just the man for the job."

Mental Fortitude skill increased to level eighty-four!

You have reached level eighty-three!
You have received three skill points.

"I'm all ears," here I was bending the truth, in fact doing my best to concentrate.

The three points I threw right into Mental Fortitude without even thinking, bringing it up to level 87. They were trying to pressure me, maybe even openly trick me. I could feel it so there was plenty of reason to build on my defense.

"Leng Gnat, you have a fast starship, and it's Meleyephatian too. We have told you where to go. Yes, it will be a long flight. Very long. But you can find the power the Meleyephatians are so afraid of. And perhaps you can convince these powerful humans to intervene and save the other branches of the human race from occupation."

What? Were they being serious? That was ten to twelve years in flight one way and my chances of being understood, heard out, and even helped were transparently thin. And that was to say nothing of provisions and power for twelve long years, the fact I would be flying into restricted space, that my crew would not agree to such an insanely long flight...

especially the Geckho and Miyelonians. But even all that wasn't most important. Regardless, my frigate wouldn't make it fast enough and my desperate mission would never be able to save Earth. No, that was definitely not it.

My counterparts didn't argue or try and convince me. Seemingly they already knew I'd refuse, so they made a second offer:

"Okay, there's a more realistic way too. We give Earth's humanity some technology the Geckho would never give or even sell to you, and which would take your scientists centuries to achieve. Long-distance space communication technology. Subatomic energy technology. Nanoelectronics, powered by leucocyte decay. Hyperspace portal technology. Cold thermonuclear synthesis. Planetary shield."

It sounded very attractive. If head scientist Gerd Ustinov were in my place, he would be struck by the alluring perspectives. But how would we pay for all these riches?

"In some distant hexagons of the virtual planet, hidden from the Geckho, you build a few portal gates that allow you to open stable hyperspace tunnels. We will help and provide specialists to install them. Then you activate the gates on the very day planet Earth is no longer invulnerable, and let your defenders through. Naturally, I'm talking about the army of the Meleyephatian horde. Its mostly made up of Tailaxians anyway. Earth will peacefully join the horde without a bloody slaughter and, in most political matters, shall retain its independence. And you, Gnat, shall become the prelate of all Earth and one of the leaders of the Meleyephatian horde, an ancient and indefatigable force whose heavy footsteps make the whole Universe shake!"

Chapter
Twenty-One

Volcanic Island

I T HAD BEEN a long while since someone tried to entice me into betraying my faction so flagrantly. The last time I remembered was when Minn-O La-Fin tried on the Geckho ferry. Now my wayedda knew me much better and, surely would just laugh at herself. But back then Minn-O really believed that I could be scared and bought by telling me about the power of the Dark Faction and offering thirty pieces of silver. And here my current tempters had spent their whole lives in a very harsh state of total control. So they were totally sincere in their belief that a free person could be tempted by a softer collar and longer leash. No, it wasn't stupidity. Just a totally different worldview to mine, one held by natives of an enslaved planet where that offer probably looked more than acceptable, beneficial even.

What was more, I had no confidence that any distant all-powerful people who could stop the Meleyephatian horde existed. It might all have been a simple fairy tale to distract me. After all, the prelates understood perfectly that I would be heading on a super-long journey and they would never be able to check up on me. It was simply a prelude to the main offer: sell out the Geckho and voluntarily serve Earth up on a blue-rimmed platter to new masters from Tailax.

Agree just to keep up appearances? Advanced technology was the most expensive and valuable thing humanity could hope to get. It could advance our science by decades. But the prelates weren't just idiots who would pay without hard guarantees. They'd probably demand to implant spy devices into my body like Valeri's and some additional conditions of loyalty. No, I had to take a more subtle approach here...

"Send us one of those technologies now as confirmation that your intentions are serious. Then we can continue this conversation. But not the planetary shield, our scientists have already figured it out. We can come back to the rest later. Also, our planet is schismatic, space is bifurcated here, meaning we have two worlds. We would like to see that Tailax can help us with that problem as well. After all, no one wants to lose a world inhabited by billions of people just because its defenders are incompetent."

Astrolinguistics skill increased to level ninety!

Valeri-Urla, transmitting my answer to her jailers, spent a long time in silence. So long in fact that she got bored and took a dive in the blue sea, swimming a couple laps around the huge turtle. Finally, the space huntress crawled back on the shell and continued. First of all, Valeri-Urla told me the prelates had doubts that Earth's humanity already possessed planetary shield technology. The suzerains wouldn't have shared such a vitally necessary technology with new vassals. At the very least they wouldn't have until their control over the planet was confirmed, meaning after the tong of safety.

"We didn't get it from the Geckho, it was the Jargs, long-time Geckho vassals. They are interested in strengthening the Geckho military alliance so they sent me a crystal drive on Kasti-Utsh III. It contains some blueprints for combat vehicles but the main content is calculations for the power and construction of towers to support a planetary energy screen. According to our scientists, we don't understand everything in these calculations, but in combination with blueprints of the towers, which I obtained on the planetoid Ursa-II-II, we have enough to start building. What's more, a Jarg specialist has come to help Earth's scientists. I brought him on my frigate. So if Tailax also helps Earthen scientists figure things out, that would surely be perceived as a gesture of friendship between the branches of humanity. Anyhow apologies but, as you see, we wouldn't be able to consider that a fully-fledged gift of technology."

I was lying and bluffing confidently, mixing

easily checkable facts with flagrant lies and purposely lowering the value of the one technology my humanity needed most. And it worked, they believed me!!!

Authority increased to 60!

"Yes, the Meleyephatian horde is aware of the role of the Shiamiru crew and Gnat personally in the assault of the planetoid Ursa-II-II. We are aware of the TRUE story," Valeri-Urla said, emphasizing the word. "The horde is aware of other affairs as well which place the Free Captain's neutrality under serious doubt. In fact, let's take it a bit further. If Free Captain Leng Gnat had not expressed a willingness to work with us, he would have already been added to a list of enemies of the Meleyephatian horde. Then, any voyage he tried to take through space would be, to put it lightly, problematic."

Come on, they were threatening me again! Here I suspected for the first time that it wasn't the prelates of Tailax talking to me. Or more accurately, not only the prelates of the enslaved planet but also their true masters. They just knew too much and felt free to make comments and promises in the name of the whole Meleyephatian horde. And if I was not wrong in my suspicion, the offer to fly off in search of the force that the Meleyephatians were afraid of really was just a trick.

"Listen closely, Leng Gnat. As an advance, the people of Earth will be given long-distance communication technology plus detailed documentation on planetary shields. You can download the data in the nearest spaceport. All you need to bring is a drive of sufficient capacity. Valeri-Urla can tell you the package activation code at a vending machine. Tailax will in its turn find out the finer details of bifurcation of space then the prelates of the church of Survival will get back in touch with you. And at that we close the negotiations. And yes, Valeri-Urla, we are happy with you! Your prison sentence has just been cut in half."

The girl fell silent and spent some time just listening to her feelings. But then she clearly relaxed and even started smiling for the first time since the negotiations began:

"Okay, that's all. They hung up. Shall we go to the spaceport?" she suggested, seemingly suggesting we go straight there now on the turtle and without any clothing. It didn't seem to bother her one bit.

But I thought that was an unjustified rush and refused. First of all, I didn't want to offend Imran. My Dagestani friend had spent all day yesterday working with faction Mechanics to make "proper" meat skewers and a grill like back home in the Caucasus. He had also taken the Miyelonian kitten Tini as an assistant and stayed up deep into the night cutting and marinating meat in a special way, hoping to show the people and other races the proper, Caucasian way to make shashlik[3]. Second — I pointed at the Naiads who were still accompanying us — weren't we waiting for one of the leaders of the underwater folk to come here? Had their leader really not come yet?

---

[3] Translator's note: a regional variation on the shish-kebab.

Valeri-Urla grasped the pendant dangling between her breasts. The Beastmaster's eyes clouded over for a second.

"The Naiad leader arrived long ago. She's a female, very ancient and respected. She'll come up now."

Today I had already seen my fill of Naiads of all kinds. Black and silver, normal five-foot ones, and ten-foot giants. So I naively thought they couldn't surprise me now. I was wrong. When a toothy head the size of a compact car appeared from out of the water next to me, I took a step back and nearly screamed in fear. This gigantic predator was twenty-three feet long and weighed a couple tons at least.

Leng Veia. Oceanid. Ocean Faction. Level-174 Matriarch.

What was there to say here? With some imagination... well A LOT of imagination, a certain similarity could be seen with an overgrown mermaid. She had plate-eyes like a fish and a mouth full of teeth like a shark, adding some more to the picture. Veia's huge head was topped with a mother-of-pearl crown carved from a huge spiny shell. Standing up and bowing in respect to the undersea potentate, I tried to mentally speak with the Oceanid but came up against absolute lack of understanding. Just a solid wall. On the very edge of perception, I could sense some fleeting echoes of some of Veia's complex emotions but I couldn't get close enough to understand. Our consciousnesses were just too different. It reminded me of my unsuccessful attempts to mentally converse with

Little Sister. The Shadow Panther just didn't understand or accept me even though her master Valeri-Urla could converse with her pet no problem. In this case I also had to ask the Beastmaster for help.

"Valeri, translate my words for this queen of the sea. Tell her that I am the new master of this island, and have driven away its former, warlike inhabitants. I would like to propose a peaceful neighborly relationship and to guarantee that my subjects will not enter into conflict with her Naiads. We have something to offer the them as well. First of all, trade. We are willing to buy fish and seafood, paying with medicines for all kinds of ailments, as well as metal and weaponry made from it. Second, we are willing to employ Naiads for various kinds of labor. That means guarding the rocky shore and laying undersea cables as well as long-distance recon. But to start we need help from your marine folk to raise a starship that sunk in the bay. We are willing to pay handsomely, so the Naiads will not be left in the lurch."

Fame increased to 75.

Valeri-Urla said nothing aloud, but based on her tense face, the transmission of such a long message to the undersea NPC required serious effort from the Beastmaster. Finally, the space girl finished her work and told me the answer:

"Ruler of the sea Leng Veia greets you, ruler of the land Leng Gnat. The undersea folk know a place at great depth and in complete darkness where there lies a silver flying machine. It has broken into three pieces. The Naiads and sea monsters will raise all the pieces and bring them to the ruler of the rocky island. Our price is eight sharp knives made of shiny metal that does not rust under the sea and which people use underwater. Trade is also approved. The Naiads can provide Fish in any quantity. Veia also says that before the war people exchanged happy water and terrestrial fruits for pearls. She suggests renewing that trade. A basket of fruit for a handful of pearls."

Not a bad price. Of course I gave my agreement after which the huge Oceanid smiled, showing a huge maw packed with three rows of sharp teeth. Then she quietly slipped back underwater. Valeri commented on the successful end of the negotiations:

"It worked, captain! Although I admit, it was hard. At times I was afraid I wouldn't manage. Some words were extremely hard to explain. I had especially big problems with 'underwater cables.' How could I explain to an NPC Oceanid what that even was? All that came to mind was: 'a very long inedible worm which people want placed on the bottom.' Veia still doesn't understand why people would want something like that. In fact she thinks you're a weirdo and even a bit crazy, but still she gave her agreement."

"Great! Thanks, Valeri. Without you, all these negotiations would have been impossible. Tell me what you would like in return."

The space girl started smiling even harder, for some reason grew embarrassed but in the end refused:

"Leng Gnat, I have known since my very first day that you weren't taking me into your crew just because. A Beastmaster has no business on a starship. But you asked me a few times if I could speak with undersea creatures, so I guessed a long time ago what kind of work I'd have to do. You needn't give me any kind of additional pay. This was the very job you hired me to do. And don't you dare try and leave me on this planet now! Of course it is very nice here, and a happy hunting ground for a Beastmaster. But my strict masters want me to follow you."

At the same time as what she said aloud, a message rang out in my head just for me:

"Ever since that day, all my conversations have been closely recorded. Cameras and microphones capture everything I see and hear. I have been ordered to stay near you and track you, captain. What's more, in the local spaceport, I have been instructed to pick up a package with a set of miniature espionage devices, which I have been ordered to place on your frigate. So keep that in mind, captain. I ask you please not to stop me, otherwise my masters will realize that I warned you. And I recommend you have a few one-on-one conversations with me about Tailax, the Meleyephatian horde, invasion and other politics stuff. It will make things look authentic and raise my value in the eyes of my masters. After that I might be allowed to change faction and move my physical body from the Tailax prison. And if you come up with a way to get rid of all the bugs in my body, I will be eternally grateful!"

OVER THE REST of the day I had time to celebrate the

peace treaty and familiarize myself with my new territory, then have a talk with every high-profile player from the La-Fin Faction. But that wasn't the most important thing. I finally made up my mind about the choice the game gave me when it made me a Leng and I created my own faction, which I called Relict.

Why Relict? The explanation was very simple. When I chose the menu option "Found personal faction," I immediately realized the game wouldn't allow the new group to have whatever name I liked, it was just offering me a choice from among many available options. Among them were Gnat, Human-33, La-Fin 2, Tar-Layneh Double, Independent Island 1476 and a bunch of other names that were just as predictable and boring. I almost agreed to Gnat, although I considered naming a faction after myself improper and a very garish kind of bragging. But there in a long list of options I saw Relict, and I felt an electric shock.

I immediately decided that was the very name I was looking for because it was a great reflection of the thrust of my gameplay, studying the mysterious Relict civilization, their language and ancient artifacts. What was more, my character had a unique class, Listener, which originated among that ancient race. My Energy Armor occasionally contacted the mysterious Relict Pyramid, and even my main weapon came from a Relict outpost. And Gnat was of little interest to influential Gecko or Miyelonian players as a person. There were plenty of people in the game that bends reality as it was. But as the only Listener and one of the few players who knew the Relict language, I was of great interest.

So the faction name Relict was a great fit and emphasized my uniqueness. Beyond that... Logically I couldn't explain it but I knew it was the right path! I was used to trusting my intuition and so...

Relict Faction.

Current player capacity: 1 of 87.

ATTENTION!!! The name Relict has an ancient history, and your faction having this name could earn you both unexpected allies and surprising enemies. Are you sure (YES/NO)?

I seriously considered it. Unexpected allies were of course good. But surprising enemies... The first thing that came to mind was the Symbiote aka satellite, a mysterious ball of energy which had come near my frigate a few times in space. Kirsan the repair bot, who had been around since the time of the ancient Mechanoid race, called the satellite an "ancient enemy." The Relict drone the game had assigned me, which I had communicated with long-distance a few times, was also afraid of possible encounters with "Precursor defense systems" in space, perhaps meaning Symbiotes and the like. Would the satellite become aggressive on our next encounter? Sure, no one had seen one attack before (or so Ayukh the Navigator assured me), but no one in recent history had seen a Symbiote while being a member of an ancient faction! Nevertheless, I chose YES, confirming the foundation of a faction by that name.

Fame increased to 76.

Fame increased to 77.

Fame increased to 78.

A triple fame increase all at once? That actually scared me more than anything. The game had spread the fact that the Relicts were back, a most powerful force awakening from a many-century slumber. But there was nothing to be done. The choice was made.

For now my faction consisted of one lone player: myself. The faction didn't have its own Dome or corncobs. All faction members for now would be exiting the game into the same real-world locations as before. But I didn't see a big problem with that and hoped the situation would change eventually. The level-one island node afforded me eighty-seven faction members. Right at that picnic, I received some applications to join the Relict Faction too. From my crew: Dmitry Zheltov, Imran, Eduard Boyko and Vasily Filippov the Terrans; Tini, Gerd Ayni and Gerd Mauu-La the Miyelonians; Vasha and Basha Tushihh, Avan Toy and Ayukh the Geckho. They would all supposedly appear in the list of faction members in approximately three days.

I had heard Valeri's position as well and knew the Beastmaster was open to joining the Relict Faction, but before that she would need permission from her jailers. Denni Marko, as I immediately realized talking to him, wasn't attached to his present faction and would join whichever one necessary to stay with his partner Valeri.

The biggest surprise was that the Jarg wanted to join the new faction. The spiny armadillo, who alone took down nearly half of Imran's shashlik, even tearing a few chunks literally from the mouth of the panther, used the universal translator to spit out a stormy tirade, telling me and everyone around that he was willing to join the RELICT faction in awkward broken phrases. Of course, I didn't refuse the Analyst. He had already proven his worth.

By the way, the Jarg's name Uii-Oyeye-Argh-Eeyayo was no problem for the Miyelonians, but the other space races also found it a real tongue twister. No people or Geckho could remember or pronounce it without issue. The Jarg was also categorically opposed to shortened forms like just Uii and grew angry when he heard them, puffing up threateningly and showing a readiness to explode. So the spiny Analyst was simply called "Jarg," and that didn't bother him one bit.

After my negotiations with the key players of the La-Fin Faction, two of them immediately agreed to join the recently created Relict Faction. First was garrison leader Gerd T'yu-Pan. And I hadn't decided whether to take him with me into space or put him in charge of defense of the island. In that case I would allow him to choose the thirty or forty most capable soldiers of the Human-3 or La-Fin Faction to serve under him. But regardless the all-powerful level-105 Shocktroop was a very valuable acquisition.

The second high-profile player to join my side was Mage Diviner Gerd Mac-Peu Un-Roi. I chose the young talented mage as an advisor and, what was more, was planning to leave him in charge on the island in my absence. Most likely, I could have recruited others like him as well, but Princess Minn-O La-Fin in her usual half-joking half-serious manner announced that it was time for me to grow a conscience and that she as head of the La-Fin Faction would also need some of her key players. What was more, the La-Fin Faction had been bled dry after the desertion of leading mage rulers to competing cliques of the magocratic world, so every high-profile player had a huge value. It was the pure truth and so I stopped trying, simply enjoying the nice evening, outdoor picnic, pleasant company and surprisingly enjoyable singing of Bard Vasily Filippov.

After sundown, wanting to see my territory, I went up on the highest peak of the island and many players came with me. Of course, I didn't have to play mountain climber. We all could have just taken a Sio-Mi-Dori assault antigrav. I only took one of the five, leaving the four others with the La-Fin Faction. But there was a fairly well-worn and comfortable path leading to the top, which sentries used every day, and I wanted to walk it to get some fresh air for my tipsy head.

But it wasn't only a spontaneous desire to walk that got me out. It was a great chance to get my Mineralogy out of its dead stop at level one and I wanted to take advantage of it. The stalled skills problem actually went even deeper. Not only Mineralogy, also Rifles, Sharpshooter, Targeting and in some sense Medium Armor had me worried. They weren't levelling because I had no way to actively use them. And that affected how fast my character leveled, which was going quite slow at this point. The times had long passed when Gnat would grow ten to fourteen levels per day. It took me three days to hit level eighty-three and I didn't like that one bit. And so — into the mountains!

A night's walk between huge outcroppings of rock — what could be better for a Geologist! We all carried flashlights, which made the rocks shine back all kinds of colors as they slid over them. The rocks were clearly of volcanic origin. On my way to the top, I confidently recognized basalt, andesite and gabbro as well as a lot of other volcanic stones, raising my Minerology to 56, Eagle Eye to 76 and Medium Armor to 58. Just in that night the mountain trek brought my progress to level 84 up by a quarter!

But finally I reached the top, a bit winded but happy! A pitch-black sea on all sides, an even darker jagged rocky island underfoot and a distant shore in the East, territory of the Human-3 Faction. The Rainforest node to be more accurate. I stopped at a precipice and, taking in a full chest of fresh sea air, called out to my advisor Gerd Mac-Peu Un-Roi:

"What beauty! And absolute freedom! The Geckho guaranteed the safety of this island, so no outside conflicts can touch this territory. For that reason, one of Earth's planetary shield generators will be built right here on the island. Talk to the La-Fin Faction Drafter Gerd Alex Bobl. Have him bring the best workers in for the job. I will provide blueprints for the structure. I will also try to bring Engineer Gerd Ustinov's team in from the Human-3 Faction to help with the enormous project. But first of all we must find an appropriate place to build. There are cliffs all around, so that might be problematic. But we must manage. It is very important to earth!"

"Yes, my lord!" the young mage bowed mechanically, not displaying any emotions. Nevertheless I felt like he was mocking me somehow. Not surprising for my assistant's first day of work. I was holding out hope that, with time, this wary caution would all pass.

"Mac-Peu, after consulting with the Engineers and Drafters you will provide me a list of parts and materials necessary for construction, and I will buy them. I'll also need a list of personnel requirements by profession. Construction should begin in the next few days and end before the planet's term of safety is up. But powering the shield will take energy. Lots of energy. Mac-Peu, use your magical abilities, look at the possible futures and tell me what has greater potential: building a big power station here with our limited space or stretching an electric cable along the bottom of the sea from those lands over there," I said, pointing to the dark distant horizon.

"Yes my lord, it shall be done!" the Mage Diviner gave another mechanical bow, then finally showed some human emotion on his stone face. "Leng Gnat La-Fin, I must admit I am delighted! All mage rulers I have dealt with before as a diviner were only interested in war and searching for ways of eliminating competition. You're completely different. You aim to unite factions, not destroy them. And for the first time in many, many years, I've been asked to do something for creation, not destruction!"

Chapter Twenty-Two

Business Partner

I REACHED the spaceport far past midnight. First of all I of course, visited my frigate. It still looked pretty atrocious. It had huge ten-foot-plus gaps in the fuselage due to the still unreplaced insulation tiles and missing left stabilizer, which had been removed and attached to a special fixture to allow easier access. But the repair of my starship was going full pace even at night. There was no lack of either parts or working hands provided by spaceport head Vano-Ubish. The Miyelonian Engineer Orun Va-Mart, by the way, immediately agreed to join the new Relict Faction and assured me that within three days the Tolili-Ukh X frigate would be ready for takeoff. That was all great but... what was that thing? In the neighboring hangar, just six hundred fifty feet from ours, another starship was being assembled!

Kurimiru. Geckho cargo shuttle.

The most surprising thing was that bustling all around the thing was a group made exclusively of humans!!! And every last one of them came from the La-Shin faction! The thirty players of noncombat professions, climbing around the starship exterior like ants were repairing dents, switching out damaged armor panels and cutting and welding. An even larger number of players, all soldiers, were standing in a circle around the ship, fifty at least. It looked as if they were afraid someone might get in their way or try and stop them. And given the thickest part of the guard chain was facing our hangar, I suspected they were taking precautions against me and my crew precisely.

"It's rare to see old jalopies like that these days!" noticing my interest, Orun Va-Mart commented on the nearby spaceship. "The Geckho took the Kurimiru out of production fifty tongs ago, and even then it was very antiquated. Now the only place you can find a fuselage like that is a scrapheap. And the hyperspace drive just blew me away. I had to go take a closer look. It was from some ancient Cyanian frigate. Who could possibly want such museum pieces?"

"Someone who didn't have the crystals for a more modern starship," unlike the Miyelonian Engineer, I knew perfectly well what was happening here and I was sure I didn't like it.

This was one of the strongest factions of the magocratic world, the La-Shin Faction, and they didn't get along with the La-Fin faction and were hostile to my usual humanity. In the end, they got just enough crystals to purchase their own starship. And hearing they'd bought a seriously outdated model was paltry consolation. If the Dark Faction made it into space and thus around our suzerains' de facto technology and economic blockade, it would be a big breakthrough in their development. Then they could sell goods at a more or less fair price, without the Geckho's draconian fees. They'd have a source of space currency. New weapons. New technology. All that threatened to seriously throw the balance of power out of whack. It might even start a new war with the Dark Faction.

I couldn't allow my enemy to get into to outer space! However, I couldn't stop them from building this ship. At the very least my hands were tied here, in the spaceport, where the Geckho provided security. But out in space...

"Orun Va-Mart, we must complete construction and get into orbit before that washtub!" I told the Engineer, pointing at the ancient shuttle. "Speed it up, have the repair workers concentrate on the most necessary tasks. We can fix some things of secondary importance later, in space. Also I need constant surveillance over our neighbors. Let me know immediately if you think they're planning to attack or impede our construction! And talk with Uline Tar. Have her get the spaceport to provide extra guards for our Tolili-Ukh X! Actually, wait! I'll talk to her myself."

Uline wasn't on the frigate. I discovered that right away by scanning. Overall it wasn't a surprise. It was night out and, most likely, my huge furry friend had left the game into the real world. So I headed to the dispatcher's tower. There in a vending machine on the third floor I got the package from the Tailaxian prelates and immediately copied the invaluable data onto a fresh crystal drive I purchased as well.

Meanwhile, Valeri-Urla told me mentally that she had received her package and was prepared to begin placing the spy bugs on my frigate. She promised to give me a full list of what she installed where and I could check by scanning anyhow. Despite how unusual it was, I gave the Tailaxian girl my approval to install the bugs.

"Thanks, captain! Let my jailers think they're in complete control of the situation. At this stage it's in our shared interest."

The conversation ended. I went down the spiral staircase one floor... and unexpectedly met my business partner Uline Tar. The trader was in a state of deep thought, drumming her clawed fingers on an empty glass, was sitting alone in the empty restaurant. I walked up and sat opposite her.

"How was the date with Kosta Dykhsh?" It may have seemed a tactless question, but I knew my friend well, so I was sure she wouldn't get mad and it was better to ask directly rather than spend a long time talking around it.

"Ah you know..." Uline bared her fangs (a gesture that meant strong emotions in the Geckho, not necessarily hostile) and fell silent, not able to finish her thought.

"Did he offend you or something?" I also bared my teeth, showing her that I was taking her worries to heart.

At the same time, not trying to deeply read her thoughts, I took a look at the furry Geckho lady's emotional background. Melancholy. Love. Sadness. Thoughtfulness. She wasn't offended or even annoyed with the Geckho Diplomat. In fact, Kosta Dykhsh occupied the central part of Uline Tar's mind and sparked interest and especially positive emotions.

"No, Leng Gnat, come on!" The Trader flared up at the very idea he would have. "Viceroy Kosta Dykhsh was very gallant and polite. Half an ummi ago, he even made me an official proposal to become his legal wife..."

Legal wife? Wait! The viceroy?! That meant the drive with valuable information must have already reached Fleet Commander Kung Waid Shishish. But I tried to set those thoughts aside for now because I had seen my furry business partner gnawing on something. That meant she was very worried, maybe even suffering. And for some reason she couldn't or was ashamed to say the whole truth. I'd never worked as a psychologist for love-struck females of an alien race before, but you gotta start somewhere. And seemingly, I wouldn't be getting by here without a little mental influencing.

"And what did you tell the viceroy, Uline?"

The furry Trader averted her gaze assiduously, knowing about my abilities and not wanting to share her private thoughts. But she did answer eventually, and in fairly great detail:

"Well, what could I say? He's so handsome and charming, that young Kosta Dykhsh! It's rare that you meet such an educated and tactical Geckho. But there's some strange force behind him. After all, without the protection of influential patrons, the unknown youngster would never have been appointed Diplomat to a promising inhabitable planet. But who could it be? His clan Waideh-Dykhsh? Gnat, that name says nothing to me. I searched for information about his clan, but there was very little out there. It's strange. Either they're skilled manipulators who do everything through third parties without drawing attention to themselves or this has nothing to do with his clan. Anyhow, I couldn't give Kosta Dykhsh my agreement without first understanding who was behind him. But that wasn't even the most important part..."

The huge furry lady decisively raised her head, met gazes with me and I drowned in her bottomless lemon-yellow eyes:

"Gnat, look, I cannot agree to Kosta Dykhsh's offer! I represent an influential and rich clan of space traders, Tar-Layneh, I'm not some stray from an unknown tribe. My family has hundreds of starships, huge capital, and a bride of my stature simply must have a rich dowry to give, otherwise it cannot be. What's more, I accidentally bragged in front of my future groom, telling him about the success of our shared enterprise and showing him the one-million-denomination crystal. And after all that, to tell Kosta Dykhsh I have no dowry...

would be the kind of shame that doesn't wash out. Both for me and my entire family. Yes, I like Kosta Dykhsh, and he's a worthy groom — a planetary viceroy. I haven't given him my answer yet, but I'll have no choice but to refuse!"

Psionic skill increased to level eighty-eight!

Uline Tar turned her head and broke visual contact. After that she took a deep sigh as if about to dive into the water and blurted out:

"Leng Gnat, I really need some cash to leverage an important deal! At least five million crystals. But more would be better. I cannot ask them as a loan from anyone but you. My family and Clan Tar-Layneh won't give me any. I already told you that my relatives are upset with my behavior. First of all by the rift with Geckho hero Captain Uraz Tukhsh. So it's useless to ask them. But to me it is a very important deal. I'd even sell my share in the starship to get the money together if we can find it a buyer..."

Why was Uline afraid to mention the dowry out loud? Why was she trying to veil her request behind some trade deal? Most likely, the trader knew something. For example there could have been hidden microphones in the restaurant. I checked.

Scanning skill increased to level forty-nine!

Exactly! Every table contained a good amount of hidden devices, and quite often it was not some inoffensive thing like a gyroscope and antigravitation disk, providing for levitation of the table and fixing it firmly in one place. For example:

Hidden microphone, model OP-341. Chance of

making inoperable 97%. Total control chance 52%.

Code breaker. Chance of making inoperable 99%. Total control chance 84%.

Hidden video camera, model W-67. Chance of making inoperable 97%. Total control chance 52%.

Player inventory scanner. Chance of making inoperable 100%. Total control chance 88%.

Reader of electronic cards, wallets. Chance of making inoperable 99%. Total control chance 82%.

Portable drive data reader. Chance of making inoperable 94%. Total control chance 76%.

Holy crap! So many surprises for guests of the spaceport! Then the captains and crew members of starships trading with Earth would bust their brains over how money was taken from their wallets, and their trade secrets suddenly became available to their competitors. I suddenly had serious questions for the spaceport, because it was extremely hard to imagine all this equipment had been placed without their knowledge. And given it was all installed illegally I could afford to break it. No one would have any complaints. And proving a connection between Leng Gnat and the electronics suddenly going out of order would be factually impossible.

Machine Control skill increased to level seventy-nine!

Machine Control skill increased to level eighty!

Great! It was good experience for deactivating the spy equipment in the body of Valeri the Tailaxian.

"Uline, we can speak frankly. I just fried all the

spy devices in this room."

"So there was espionage equipment after all?" the Geckho woman squinted and groaned in dismay. "Gnat, I suspected that after the date with Kosta Dykhsh. Every time I searched the data network while in this restaurant he mentioned the thing I looked up: his clan, risky but potentially profitable trade routes, this planet's remaining term of safety... Somehow he always knew the answer to questions I wasn't even asking him."

What? Newly appointed Viceroy of the planet Kosta Dykhsh was somehow linked to the espionage equipment? I had to admit, it was hard to believe. Although... if I considered it, why not? I had noticed before that the Geckho Diplomat was greedy. I didn't know that Kosta Dykhsh sometimes pursued riches by illegal means though. Seemingly I had a new big topic for conversation with the newly appointed viceroy beyond the recently signed peace treaty and the Tailaxian prelates attempting to recruit me.

"Uline, about the dowry, I can assure you that I'll do everything in my power. I just don't have the money right now. I've got a million and a half but that isn't enough as far as I understand," seeing her head hang in shame, I hurried to continue. "But tomorrow, or at the very least the day after tomorrow, the Naiads will raise a cloaked frigate that fell into the sea which used to belong to the leader of the Miyelonian pirates. The starship broke up on impact, but we still have a decent chance of making out like a bandit. After all, that thing had laser cannons, a navigation system, shield generators, on-board computers, thrusters and a cloaking system... Something might be repairable, and every one of those parts is worth at least a hundred thousand crystals, more like millions. And I will give it to you as a gift. Let it be my wedding gift to you!"

Successful Constitution check!

Medium Armor skill increased to level fifty-nine!

Woah, I should have considered that the large strong Geckho woman might react emotionally and nearly strangle me in her embrace. Even my armor couldn't fully protect me from such a stormy outburst. I rasped with difficulty to let me down, and Uline immediately unclenched her bear's grip.

"Gnat, you're a real wonder of the Universe!" Uline told me, impossibly happy.

"I know," I chuckled, very flattered at her reaction. "But I do have one little condition. Before you promise anything to the viceroy and, all the more, transfer him the money, I need to have a talk with him. I want to make sure he isn't tricking you and that Kosta Dykhsh's intentions are pure. As leader of the Relict Clan, which is now funding the wedding of a gorgeous member, I have the full right to do so!"

Only there Uline Tar noticed that my faction name had changed in my character description. Momentary confusion gave way to a look of satisfaction:

"Great! I've been meaning to start playing differently for a long time. I'm sick of relying on the opinion of my relatives and leadership! Add me to your faction, Leng Gnat!"

I DIDN'T MANAGE to catch the Geckho Diplomat in the spaceport even though I was desperately seeking a meeting with Kosta Dykhsh. I needed to tell the suzerains as soon as possible that enemies of the Geckho had attempted to enlist me in a treacherous scheme. If I didn't, it could have the most serious consequences for myself and the whole earth faction I was associated with. Uline Tar told me I was too late and Kosta Dykhsh had flown back to his residence about a quarter ummi ago. But the Trader assured me the viceroy was still in the game because she was periodically exchanging messages with him via communicator.

I didn't wait for morning and went to the Capital node taking my wife Gerd Minn-O La-Fin with me and my advisor Mage Diviner Gerd Mac-Peu Un-Roi. We informed the Human-3 Faction of our purpose and flight plan before leaving the spaceport, so there was no panic or chaos when the Dark Faction antigrav showed up at the capital citadel this time. The Sio-Mi-Dori landed neatly in the center of the platform, which was marked with bright landing signals, and I was first down the gangway.

The twenty elite First Legion soldiers who had come out to meet our aircraft were frozen at attention. Leader of the Human-3 Faction, Gerd Ivan Lozovsky, a mountain of a man, stepped out in front. Behind his back, striving to keep up, there was a dark-haired plump lady I didn't recognize walking at a quick pace behind him in a strict business suit:

Gerd Eva-Maria Fischer. Human. Human-6 Faction. Level-73 Engineer.

A member of the Human-6 Faction? I didn't know what she was doing, although... why not really? The conditions of our peace with the Dark Faction and the future of Earth concerned the German faction directly, so I could easily explain their interest. Ivan Lozovsky, after greeting Princess Minn-O and giving a somewhat nervous sidelong glance at the Mage Diviner behind me, extended a hand welcomingly:

"Imran and Eduard already told me you concluded a peace treaty. And not only with the Dark Faction, the Naiads as well. Excellent work, Kirill! Now Eva-Maria would like to know when her faction will get their island back."

Holy crap, what a claim! I even froze in surprise. What was the most tactful way I could tell them the island belonged to me now and I was not planning to give it up? Anyhow... to hell with tact! It was a very convenient opportunity to demonstrate to everyone just how the political situation had changed:

"Ivan, Eva-Maria, perhaps my companions didn't quite tell you the conditions of the peace treaty clearly. Well, my advisor Gerd Mac-Peu Un-Roi will explain everything. Does Eva-Maria understand Geckho?"

The lady nodded in silence and young mage

Mac-Peu stepped out in front. Confidently and clearly, as if standing in a large room behind a tribune with a long-prepared speech, the mage began to explain:

"It's all in the terms of the peace treaty with the La-Fin Faction, which you know better under the name Dark Faction. As an aside, it is just one of the three biggest powers of the magocratic world. Anyhow, they agreed not to destroy the Human-6 Faction hexagons both on the eastern and western shores of the bay, and stop the invasion. The La-Fin Faction also agreed to never again lay claim to Human-3 or Human-6 Faction territory with the exception of the hexagons they already controlled long enough to produce a claim for: Tropics and Rocky Island. And at that both factions may transport any freight through La-Fin Faction territory with no limitations. An order to free the prisoners from the Human-1, Human-3 and Human-6 Factions was given yesterday during the day so, according to my calculations, they should all be back already."

Ivan Lozovsky gave a nod of approval, and the German faction representative did the same a second later. Gerd Eva-Maria Fischer immediately asked whether her players could now enter the game on the island, where Dark Faction security was previously executing them whenever they did. The advisor tossed an inquisitive gaze my way because he didn't know my plans. I continued on my own:

"The players stuck on the island will be evacuated in an orderly fashion in groups of fifteen. The Sio-Mi-Dori antigrav," I turned and pointed at the aircraft behind me, "will take you all to the eastern shore. My advisor will put together a schedule. And by the way, volunteers may remain on the island and join the Relict Faction. It's an inter-factional institution with the prime goal of defending our shared planet Earth after the tong of immunity expires. I am leader of that new force and am bringing together the most capable Builders, Engineers, Mechanics and members of adjacent professions on the island. I have some blueprints and I will use them to build a planetary shield generator for Earth on Rocky Island. If humanity, and I'm referring to both worlds now, cannot build at least four such generators and better six before the term of safety is up, our planet will surely be bombarded from space both in the virtual game and the real world."

Authority increased to 61!

After I finished, a long silence took hold. Clearly, my former leader was having a very hard time accepting the new reality of his former subordinate Gnat being fully independent from his faction. And I was discussing the kind of mass-scale projects and technologies the faction had never come up against before, which also seemed to irk him. The representative of the German Faction was just nervously biting her lip. I suppose she was hoping to the last to get the Rocky Island back.

A prophet is unrecognized in his own land. That was the very phrase that came to mind. After all, if I were any unknown high-profile Geckho or, let's say, the fearsome Dark Faction General Ui-Taka, my allies would have had a much easier time digesting the fact that a new power had come on the scene. The silence really did stretch on an indecent length of time. But my wife Minn-O jumped out ahead:

"I am now leader of the La-Fin Faction. And I am a bit bothered by the fact that the most important point hasn't come up yet. The leaders of the world where magic has atrophied have not confirmed that they accept the terms of peace. It is important for me to hear that unambiguously before I order my soldiers back from the fronts and for resources to be used on peaceful development instead of war!"

My wayedda's words acted as a catalyst and the pace of the discussion increased significantly.

"Princess Minn-O La-Fin," Ivan Lozovsky bowed deeply and respectfully, "I did not believe it was necessary to say because your spouse Leng Gnat was conferred total authority and had the right to make peace treaties in the name of the Human-3 Faction. But just so you don't have a single doubt I, head of the H3 Faction, officially confirm that we accept the peace treaty and it will not come under revision. Especially given our Geckho suzerains have expressed a surprising involvement in their vassals' affairs and guaranteed that some territories and borders are now inviolable."

"The Human-6 Faction does not dispute the terms of the peace either," confirmed the German Engineer. After some thought, she added: "Now we understand that an isolated island is not the greatest in terms of further development and logistics. But in any case, we lost a level-three node and our faction already has a catastrophic lack of players. In fact we have three times more than our maximum number of slots. Our players work in three shifts, cycling out for one another and that is not good for work efficiency. What's more, the players trapped on Rocky Island, and there are around three hundred of them, haven't been in the game for six days now. We found out from the Geckho that if a player doesn't enter the game for more than seven or eight days, their character first loses progress to the next level, then a few days later starts losing levels and skills. After that, they even start losing stats and health points. So we are very interested in getting our players off the island in the nearest future and are willing to transfer two or three hundred of our players temporarily or permanently to the Relict Faction."

"I don't think it'll be hard to agree there. We have the materials to develop the Rocky Island hexagon to level two, so it'll go up in the next couple of days. We'll be able to accept two hundred and fifty players then."

"Yes, I'm sure that won't be a problem," I confirmed my advisor's words. "Although it's possible that only those who fought against the Naiads remain on the island. In any case, we can discuss that tomorrow. Right now I have an important meeting with the viceroy of Earth Kosta Dykhsh. And I strongly advise the Human-3 and Human-6 Factions to get a crystal drive ready. I want to share technologies and blueprints that will be very interesting to you and humanity as a whole."

Chapter Twenty-Three

Web of Worlds

ULINE TAR wasn't wrong. The viceroy was in the game. Beyond that, Kosta Dykhsh seemingly knew I was coming, because he was waiting at the entrance to his metal hut.

"Kento duho, Leng Gnat," the huge furry Geckho replied to my ornate and warm greeting with the standard phrase, officious and cold. "Sorry, I can't invite you in. It's real bedlam in there, there's not even anywhere to sit. I'm folding and packing my things. Tomorrow morning I'll be moving into a residence more befitting a viceroy. Although it's something of a pity, I like it here. I always loved being secluded. You've got silence, no one coming around asking questions or pestering you. Just sometimes newbies would fall out of the Labyrinth afraid and confused. That always amused me..."

Kosta Dykhsh went silent and groaned in dismay because, from behind the slightly closed door, the metal hut, which was partially interred in the earth, something audibly fell and shattered. Apparently, the viceroy wasn't alone at this late hour. Did he have a nighttime guest? Perhaps a lady?

"I must have stacked some boxes wrong," Kosta Dykhsh tried sheepishly to justify himself. "I told you, I'm packing my things."

Excessive curiosity was not my style. I respected others' privacy and tried not to delve into their secrets. But this all just looked too piquant to let go: Uline Tar's groom, expecting a dowry of several million from her, had some stranger frittered away in his little hut in the woods. So I couldn't resist.

Scanning skill increased to level fifty!

I was expecting a marker for anything or anyone at all on the minimap. Anything but what the scan finally gave me:

Woman. Human. Level-62 Medic.

Uhh... Human medic, woman... And seemingly in hiding, because the Diplomat really didn't want to advertise her presence.

"Am I to understand Anna is in your hut?" I asked directly.

Instead of an answer, Kosta Dykhsh suggested we take a walk. What? Nighttime, a dangerous forest nearby with some creature regularly eating our lumberjacks which still hadn't been identified. The suggestion to leave the ring of bright lights and the security system around his domicile to go into the dangerous dark was so illogical and just bad... that I agreed. I just commanded my Small Relict Guard Drone to come down lower and protect me. We walked two hundred steps from the Geckho Diplomat's place before Kosta Dykhsh answered the question:

"Yes, it is Anna. From your faction. She is now considered a refugee from the Human-8 Faction."

Seeing incomprehension and many questions on my face, he continued:

"The human woman came to me two days ago. Afraid and confused, she requested asylum. Anna believes she was controlled by magic and used against her will for nefarious ends. She does not want to speak with any of the human factions. I know that in your world she has been accused of monstrous crimes, but here in the game Anna is under Geckho protection. Tomorrow I'll pick her up and take her with me to the spaceport. I'll get her set up in some starship or Geckho science laboratory on the planet. She'll be helped to change faction and her physical body will be transferred to a safe location."

Lots of questions suddenly bubbled up. But the main one was: how had Anna entered the game? The last time she had been seen was in the Canadian embassy in Moscow. Where had she found a virt pod? Based on the timeframe, Anna could easily have already travelled to the North American faction. But then why was her character here in the capital node? Still I understood it was useless to ask questions or argue. The Geckho didn't usually get involved in their vassals' conflicts, but when they guaranteed protection, whether for a node or humanity as a whole, it was not just empty words.

So I changed the topic and told them in all detail about the peace treaty and my talks with the prelates of Tailax. All that time, I didn't smooth over any sharp corners. I told them what the Meleyephatian vassals said about how, in the past, after the tong of safety was up the Geckho didn't always protect their vassals and sometimes just captured the planet for themselves if they took a shine to it. I also told them my fears about our planet being far from the Geckho's primary territories and thus harder to defend constantly.

"Well, Leng Gnat, as such serious and direct questions have come up, let's be honest. I will not comment on past examples. What's done is done. There have been many generations since those times. But Earth's situation now is worrying. The planet's term of safety is now half over. And the external situation is scary: there's a galactic war between the great space races, and the Geckho have fairly modest military positions in this sector of the cosmos. To our great fortune, the Meleyephatian horde has been forced to turn their attention to the Miyelonians, which has given the Geckho a chance to replenish their losses and reinforce."

Interesting, interesting. Kung Waid Shishish had gotten the reinforcements he requested, and the detailed map of Meleyephatian positions would clearly help the leader of the Second Strike Fleet. The Geckho fleet leader's issues were gradually smoothing over, which played into Earth's hand. But I didn't miss the chance to make a clarification:

"So the main battles are between the Miyelonians and Meleyephatians? Who's winning?"

The Diplomat groaned in dismay. My words were wounding him somehow:

"Battles are happening everywhere. The Geckho have many fleets, and Kung Waid Shishish's Second Strike Fleet is nowhere near the only one. In some places, the situation on the front is more favorable. In others less, but no one can say the Geckho are just hanging back and watching the war pass them by! The Meleyephatian horde has lost three times more starships to the Geckho than against all other opponents put together!"

I had to apologize and say I misspoke. The huge Geckho instantly became composed and answered my second question:

"For now the Geckho and Meleyephatians are just about on equal footing in terms of lost colonies and stations. Destroyed starships are also nearly even. But you're right in another way. The main winners in this war are the Miyelonians. The Union of Miyelonian Prides has captured more than seventy star systems from the horde at this point, and six of them are relatively near Earth. Your Miyelonian bride Kung Keetsie-Myau is just bathing in glory!"

"Bride?" I asked, the word having jumped out at me. "What makes the commander my wife all of a sudden?"

The Diplomat gave a loud rumble while bearing

his tusks, which was how his race laughed happily.

"When you performed the ritual Dance of Awakened Love with her, it was broadcast throughout the galaxy on every news channel! I know it was just a spontaneous decision caused by ignorance of Miyelonian traditions, but if you and Keetsie were of the same race, you'd already be considered man and wife! As it was, everyone thought it was merely something to laugh at."

"I just saw it as a convenient chance to talk with Keetsie where no one else could hear. It was over that dance that the Great One promised that the Miyelonians would not lay claim to planet Earth."

The viceroy immediately stopped bearing his teeth and turned more serious:

"Yes, Gerd Ivan Lozovsky told me after he heard the news from a different player. Good if so. But, you see, Gnat, you need something a bit weightier than a third-hand promise confirmed by nothing at all to call it a guarantee. Wait, stop," my mountainous companion stopped and started staring attentively into the darkness of the woods to our left. "I heard rustling in the bushes over there. Let's turn back."

I didn't see anything suspicious, although I was sure my Gnat had higher Perception than him. I lowered the IR-Lens over my eye and, in the infrared light, discovered a level-21 Fox hiding in the suspicious bushes, no danger. And there were no other large animals nearby, which I told Kosta Dykhsh. Nevertheless, the viceroy wanted to head back:

"Three days ago some creature came out of those

same hedges and ate me. I only saw a blurry movement then felt sharp teeth in my neck. But you, Leng Gnat, wanted to know about something totally different. Will the Geckho actually defend your home planet when it is no longer invulnerable? It is easy to boast of the greatness of the Geckho race, but will they really organize defense and bring sufficient forces to deflect an attack?"

Yes, I confirmed that was the question I wanted answered most of all. The hefty tall Geckho loudly sighed:

"I don't know the answer myself. Although, I'll be frank, not very long ago I would have said: 'no, they won't.' You understand, no matter what the Geckho say, my race doesn't have significant forces here other than one battered fleet. If a full-scale invasion were to take place, no one would bend over backwards for such a distant planet. Sure maybe there'd be some grumbling and they'd shake some compensation out of the invaders, but it wouldn't go further than that. Still, something is shifting imperceptibly. Lots of groups of taciturn Engineers and Prospectors are coming to the spaceport as of late, then they send them out all around the virtual planet. They're searching for something, building. This planet has an official viceroy. At the very least that means the Geckho rulers are no longer ambivalent towards Earth's fate."

Somewhat paltry conclusions, to be honest. I didn't hear any guarantee for humanity, just vague statements about a "changing situation." Seemingly, the prelates of Tailax were speaking the truth: the

Geckho were prepared to give up humanity as long as they got some compensation for our habitable planet. And that was probably exactly why the Geckho treated us aboriginals the way they did. Most of all it reminded me of how the greedy conquistadors treated the American natives. Judge for yourself: the robbery-level compensation they paid for our natural resources, imports from space were available only at the spaceport and for triple the normal price, we were isolated from the transportation network and subject to a complete blockade on information about events in distant space. I mean, come on. Geckho policy didn't exactly look like it was aimed at long-term development! It seemed more like an attempt to hurriedly unload as many of our natural resources as possible while they had the chance. In fact, Kosta Dykhsh's gray-market schemes for contraband metals and installing spy equipment in the space port restaurant all fit into the general concept of "scrape up crystals by any means because tomorrow it may be closed for business." But maybe that could all be changed?

What could people do to defend their homeworld? And would the suzerains support these measures? I asked Kosta Dykhsh. The furry fellow spent a long time thinking before starting to answer and I immediately could sense how carefully the viceroy was choosing his words:

"You told me about the technology and designs you got from the Meleyephatian horde. Yes, a planetary shield would help significantly to lower damage from orbital bombardment. But do you really think that I and the other Geckho haven't considered that? We haven't merely considered it. We've discussed it many times, argued and even made economic calculations! The problem is that it is a big challenge to build a planetary shield. You need an insane amount of materials, expensive equipment and a decent chunk of time. Each shield generator costs seventy or eighty million crystals at the very least. And to really work well, you need twelve! At the very least six or eight to hold fire from a couple of Destroyers until help arrives."

I shuddered despite myself, remembering the Meleyephatian Destroyer. It was a titanic ship that moved slowly and inexorably toward the Un-Tesh comet guarded by two thousand smaller starships. Destroyers with their colossal firepower were specialized in taking down defensive screens from planets, comets and other heavenly bodies. And in just half a tong these ghastly titans would be orbiting our Earth!

"Viceroy, the funds will be found! The human factions will invest as much as possible to defend of their home planet..."

"Do you really believe that, Leng Gnat?" he interrupted me fairly unceremoniously. "Your governments are disjointed, and your leaders continue to hide the truth about the game that bends reality from your people. The vast majority of humanity has no idea that your planet is under threat at all. I have spoken on this a hundred times with Ivan Lozovsky and the other diplomats of your world. I asked why your leaders were acting so irresponsible and I got all kinds of excuses, but never a promise to remedy the situation. And then I realized that nothing would get them off their asses until combat starships appeared in the sky, Miyelonian or Meleyephatian horde! And given your people don't want to save their own world, why should others do it for you?"

Near the end of his diatribe, the Diplomat was simply roaring his objection. After a short pause, Kosta Dykhsh calmed down somewhat and I answered his justified objection, saying the magocratic world was much better about secrecy. There, no one was surprised that the new head of the La-Fin dynasty was a native of a parallel world and had met Princess Minn-O in the game that bends reality.

"Yes, that is true," my furry companion answered, now in a decent tone. "That world is better prepared for fusion with the virtual. But it really is an interesting situation. It isn't every day you see bifurcation of space. That is of great interest from a scientific point of view. What will happen when the virtual and real worlds synchronize? Will just one planet remain, the one whose factions control more game nodes? Or will both planets appear in the real world? And if they do, what will be their positioning relative to one another? Will that not cause a space disaster?"

Ugh. So the prelates of Tailax wouldn't know either, given our Geckho suzerains couldn't give us a clear answer about what was coming next yet. And for the first time I was hearing Earth's various possible futures from the suzerains. Either only one of the parallel worlds would remain, the one with more progress in the game, or both would survive. And perhaps neither of them would survive if the two planets just collided. That wouldn't be good... I wondered what version of our planet would win right now.

"So is that what Geckho scientists are researching in the areas people cannot access?" I threw out a line and it clearly didn't land.

Danger Sense skill increased to level sixty-one!

Kosta Dykhsh stopped sharply, and a pistol suddenly appeared in his huge furry hand. Not a usual laser pistol, something with a bit more stopping power. Woah! I wasn't expecting such a simple seeming question to make him that angry. I instantly lowered my helmet's faceguard. A forcefield glimmered up around my Listener Energy Armor. I hadn't brought a weapon, but the Small Relict Guard drone came down and hovered a foot and a half over my left shoulder. Kosta Dykhsh sized up the drone with his gaze, looked at my ancient matte black armor and put his gun away.

"Leng Gnat, here's some advice: never ask that question again! Don't go sticking your nose where it doesn't belong! Humanity isn't meant to know what the great Geckho race is doing on your planet! Okay, conversation over!"

The huge Geckho turned around and headed to his metal hut, well visible in the beams of many flashlights. I just stood there in complete shock. What came over the viceroy? Why was humanity not supposed to know what the Geckho were up to on our planet? Plus... damn! I had never talked with Kosta Dykhsh about Uline Tar and her dowry! Should I go after the Diplomat? I understood that was a very bad idea. The representative of the suzerains had given me a clear signal that he didn't want to talk and insisting might come at quite a high cost to my faction both literally and figuratively.

Okay, to hell with the quick-tempered Diplomat. I looked at the time. It was just after four in the morning. Go back to the Human-3 Faction capital citadel? From there I could get an antigrav to take me to Rocky Island or the spaceport. Or (I remembered my very first day in the game), drop by the Firing Range, which wasn't far away. I'd been meaning to level my gun skills for a long time. I didn't think the Human-3 Faction would refuse me such a small favor. At the end of the day I could pay too, if they asked. Although... it was probably closed at night, and a member of a different faction breaking the locks to the armory would not look very good. I wasn't used to considering the Human-3 Faction foreign, I had to constantly mentally correct myself.

I didn't want to leave the game. So what could I do? Go hunt for the creature in the nearby forest that had chomped down a couple dozen people and the Geckho Diplomat as a snack? The fact that no one had discovered the monster yet was no impediment to me. Gnat had high Perception and the IR-Lens to search for warm-blooded creatures. Plus Scanning combined with the specialized Prospector equipment could be used to find anything in the universe.

What was more, unlike the other players after the dangerous beast, I had some idea of who I was looking for. After all, I had transported this creature to Earth in a heavy four-hundred-fifty-pound container after Fox the Morphian dragged to the pirate interceptor!

After reaching the place Kosta Dykhsh told me about suspicious rustling in the bushes I stopped and looked around carefully. Just a forest at night, nothing unusual. The fox had already run away. Nevertheless, my heart started seizing suspiciously, warning of a still unknown threat shrouded in mystery. The Scanning skill showed nothing. Seventy steps around me was just the same cold damp forest. Trees, bushes, little animals, midges... Overall, nothing unusual.

As not to wait a few minutes for the Scanning skill to reload, I sent the Small Guard Drone ahead for recon, sat on a hillock and took out my Prospector Scanner. I monkeyed with the settings, switching off search for metals, cavities, minerals and other things I didn't need, setting maximum intensity on organic, protein- and nonprotein-based lifeforms. Just the trees threw me. There were thousands of them around and they would fall under the parameters I set, possibly drowning out the whole signal.

Holding a Geological Analyzer at the ready, I was thinking whether it was possible to remove or at least reduce interference from the trees when suddenly I saw a fast, blurry movement fifteen steps to my right.

Eagle Eye skill increased to level seventy-

seven!

Danger Sense skill increased to level sixty-two!

I sharply turned my head to the right. I wasn't totally sure but I felt like one huge tree wasn't there before. And then I was struck by a premonition that disaster was inevitable. Already knowing that I had at most a few seconds left to live, I sharply unfolded the metal tripod and stuck the activated analyzer into the earth. But when I saw the Morphian changing form and moving, I didn't even have time to shout to him that I was not an enemy...

The world went dark, the mini-map disappeared along with the bars for health, hunger and various other game stats. After that, on a black background I saw a painfully familiar set of bright red words:

Your character has died. Respawn will be possible in fifteen minutes.

Would you like to review your statistics for this game session?

Damn! It was my fault, too. I knew it was dangerous here! In retrospect, hunting the unknown Morphian in the night forest did not seem like an intelligent move. I hadn't died for a long time, I overestimated my strength and paid dearly for it... I chuckled unhappily. At least now I wouldn't have to summon an antigrav to bring me to Rocky Island because my respawn point was still there from when Valeri-Urla and I went swimming. Just ten minutes on foot from the island fortress.

I refused a look at my statistics, and the virt pod

lid opened and slid noiselessly aside. I stood up and walked over the glass surrounding my virt pod room. It was partially dark under the Dome. The night lighting was on, and just a few of the street lights lining the park paths were on. I was unaccustomed to the empty view from way up here, no trees or grass. But they had to do it to sterilize the area.

At first I was thinking of just waiting the fifteen minutes and going back into the game right away but I felt very tired and was starting to yawn. I needed sleep. I managed to get down the stairs, but at to the exit I was intercepted by intelligence director Alexander Antipov:

"What luck you left the game, Kirill! I've got a job that's right up your alley! Follow me! It's very important!"

The fed was insistent and pulling me by the hand, but not toward the administration building, towards some security buildings, all the time repeating that it was a "wonderful coincidence" and this work was "right up my alley." I had to admit, it was nothing like Alexander Antipov's normal behavior. Strange thoughts flooded my head. Was this an attempted murder or kidnapping? But I saw strict-looking armed guards from the "external specialists" at one of the buildings, Faction leader Ivan Lozovsky, First Legion head Tarasov and a few other people I knew. Something really must have happened.

"This way!" Alexander Antipov opened the doors. "We don't have much time, but you might be able to get him to talk." "Let me through! Here is the very man we told you about."

The last words were directed at a group of armed people in the corridor and they parted to let us through.

But I was suddenly totally baffled. Get him to talk? What was happening? Anyhow, I soon saw for myself. In a room without windows where I was basically shoved, there was a dark-skinned dark-haired man cuffed to a chair and wearing a torn but clearly expensive suit. When I walked, he raised his head and gave an acrid chuckle through bloodied lips. I turned away as not to make contact with his glowing blue eyes and turned to my escorts, who were standing stock-still in the corridor:

"Are you out of your minds?! According to his documents, this man is an employee of the Canadian embassy!"

Chapter Twenty-Four

Closing the Breech

I WAS SEEING the strong severe man in a military uniform who answered me for the first time. He had no apparent rank but I immediately guessed the mustached officer was in command of the soldiers surrounding the building.

"This so-called 'embassy worker' was detained two hours ago in Moscow in a rented apartment. The biography in his personal file didn't add up: he has never lived in Bangladesh, never received Canadian citizenship, his documents are all fraudulent. Mr. Ahsanuddin Hussein Rahman was also nowhere to be found in the official Canadian embassy worker list, so he has no diplomatic immunity. How this guy got to Moscow, managed to legalize his migration status and enter a secure diplomatic mission unimpeded is a huge mystery. We're working with the Canadians now to figure it all out."

Woah! This really was a serious case if the Canadians wanted to work with us. The threat of using a biological weapon in the Russian capital was a critical situation for the whole planet and I imagined that helped them find the right words.

"We tracked him for a few days, listened to all his conversations and know for certain that when exiting the diplomatic mission, he had two capsules of the biological agent on his person. At the same time, a search of his apartment found nothing dangerous. Upon detention, Mr. Ahsanuddin Hussein Rahman resisted and somehow killed two of our men without so much as touching them. Then while in the vehicle he threatened that he could wipe out Moscow, New York, Beijing, Tokyo and several other large cities and would do so if he wasn't released at once. I have no idea how much what he said lines up with reality. He may be bluffing. Nevertheless, considering the biohazard capsules he has hidden in an unknown location, leadership decided not to risk it and bring him right under the Dome. First of all, no wireless devices work here. Second, assuming we've been properly informed, you speak with people like him here under the Dome and have a better understanding of the nature of this false diplomat."

Yes, that really was true. I and all the other

players under the Dome understood perfectly what ash gray skin and glowing blue eyes meant for this "Bangladeshi-Canadian." Obviously the man before us was a representative of the Dark Faction with magical abilities. And he was clearly not a small fry, because he could control peoples' minds and get through guard posts with such ease.

My heart gave a painful prick and I knew exactly what it meant. The handcuffed arrestee had just tried to kill me with magic. What a bastard! And if a normal person without wizarding abilities and magical resilience were in my place? Actually, I needed to make sure the others were safe.

"Get away, he's dangerous! Leave us alone!" I walked into the room over to the frightening arrestee and, scooting across a chair, sat opposite the enemy mage.

"Black sssunglasses, eh? Ssscared?!" asked false Ahsanuddin. And although he was speaking Russian he had a very strange accent, drawing out every hissing or shushing sound. And that was not, by the way, the usual accent of the language of the magocratic world. I suspected the arrestee could speak just fine, he was just trying to throw me off or scare me.

At any rate, his attempt to frighten the head of one of the three strongest dynasties of the magocratic world amused me.

"You La-Shin or La-Varrez?" I asked point blank in Dark Faction language, which clearly caught him off guard.

The captive mage stopped chuckling spitefully and gave me an in-depth explanation, now without any put-on accent:

"I don't know where and when you learned our language, but you're a dead man! I am Imeer-Toh La-Gorr from the ancient La-Gorr dynasty of mage-rulers! We are first-order vassals of Coruler Onuri-Unta La-Varrez!"

I felt another prick in my chest, telling me the enemy mage had attempted to stop my heart again. And based on the surprised and sour looked on Imeer-Toh La-Gorr's face, this time he had put a bit more effort into it and was counting on success. Naïve... I already knew I was the much stronger mage, and his fruitless attempts couldn't hurt me. I could easily kill him with a psionic attack, but I of course did not do so.

"I don't care what your real name is, because you're a dead man now no matter what you do..."

"Ha!" Imeer-Toh didn't believe me. "When I tell you the location of the spores, you will not only release me but also apologize and pay me very handsomely! I have all your governments wrapped around my finger! And you will do everything I say!"

Come on... Despite the fact this parallel-world mage was in handcuffs, he was being flagrantly rude and even threatening. Well, I would have to take a totally different tactic with a snot-nose like him. I'd have to change to a language he was more used to, force.

"Do you think I care a whit for the governments of this world? No, you're a dead man for a different reason, not because of the capsule of dangerous spores and not because you killed my people," I removed my dark glasses with exaggerated ease and set them on the table. "No, you must die now because you dared to attack me — Coruler Gnat La-Fin, leader of the La-Fin Dynasty and ruler of the First Directory! Such things are not forgiven!!!"

Boy did that ever do the trick! No matter how psychologically prepared and resistant to torture the enemy agent was, centuries of obsequiousness before the heads of the great dynasties worked their magic. All the piss and vinegar instantly drained out of him. Before me now was a frightened man, whimpering in fear and with a stinking dark spot spreading out on his light-colored pants.

"Listen to me very closely, worm! You have just one hour left to live. There's a clock on that wall, so you can see how long you've got left. Now I'm gonna ask you some questions. And you're gonna answer them honestly. When you do, I will tell your master Coruler Onuri-Unta La-Varrez that Imeer-Toh La-Gorr died honorably, as a proud mage of an ancient dynasty should. But if you try to lie or hide the truth from me even one time, you'll also die, but your master will be hearing that the La-Gorr mage shit himself in fear, betrayed him and is now working for the La-Fin dynasty. And you wouldn't be the only one hurt by that. I know exactly how Coruler Onuri-Unta La-Varrez's mind works. I'm sure that an hour later, there would be nothing left of House La-Gorr. Do you understand?"

Imeer-Toh his face black, looked away from the

wall clock and gave a downcast nod. I turned the table on the microphone on and the interrogation began.

FORTY MINUTES LATER, I stood up, tired and headed for the exit. I'd run out of questions much earlier, and I wanted insanely to sleep. In the end, I didn't cast any death spells. First of all, I didn't know any. Second, there was no need. Imeer-Toh La-Gorr was so convinced he would be dying soon that he would be dying in twenty minutes without any help from me.

"You can take it from here," I told a beefy mustached officer in the hallway. "Imeer-Toh is broken and answering questions honestly. Have you found the spore spreaders already?"

"Yes, both bombs have been found exactly where the arrestee said, and both have been disarmed."

The mage was not bluffing. There really were bombs. And if the signal from their master didn't come in time, a mechanism would trigger and the deadly spores would have spread through the ventilation of the Moscow metro. Potentially, that would have directly killed thousands and started the uncontrolled spread of a deadly infection.

But there were no bombs in other cities. For now. They were only in the planning phase, because the biohazard payload had not yet arrived from the game. By the way, the La-Varrez Faction had found and tested an interesting method for transporting items between the worlds. First you implant the item (hermetically sealed packets of spores in this case) into a player's clothes. Then change faction and, when the person left a virt pod a few days later in a different world, they carried the "contraband" with them.

Chaos, death, charges of using biological weapons and harsh wars between the countries of our usual world almost inevitably using our deadliest weaponry. Why did the La-Varrez Faction want that? An explanation was teased out of the captive's answers. As it turned out, head of the La-Varrez dynasty, great mage Onuri-Unta was firmly convinced that one of the two worlds was fated to disappear soon. I couldn't say what foundation he was operating on, but at every speech he gave, the great mage mentioned the idea that the factions of the magically imbued world needed to control more than half of the game hexagons of the virtual planet before the end of the tong of safety. To achieve that goal, Coruler Onuri-Unta was prepared not only to invest all possible resources in developing his own game faction and dozens of vassals. But also to poison his enemies against each other, and ideally destroy the world as we knew it. There was no peaceful way of negotiating with a fanatic like that.

There was also confirmed information that six high-profile La-Fin Faction mages, and another eighty normal players with magical abilities had already declared for La-Varrez and joined their new faction. That was bad, and not only because it made the enemy much stronger. The six Gerds who once occupied the inner circle of Leng Thumor-Anhu La-Fin were responsible for espionage and managing spy networks. Those deserter mages knew exactly which of the Human-3 players was working for the enemy! They knew how to get in touch with them, manipulate them and lots of other secrets as well. Now that dangerous knowledge was in the hands of the La-Varrez factions, and the recent story of Anya from First Med and the spores spread under the Dome showed how serious it all was.

I turned to leave, but the officer called out to me:

"Boy, I don't know who you are or what you said to Hussein Rahman, but it looked gruesome. I've never seen a person so afraid. But most importantly you managed to prevent a terror attack in the capital! As soon as that reaches my superiors, you can count on gratitude from the leadership of the country."

"As for me, I really hope that what Kirill said was not true," Ivan Lozovsky said, the only one there who understood Dark Faction language. "Both when he implied he didn't care about our world, and when he said Imeer-Toh La-Gorr would die soon. Anyhow, we'll find out int twenty minutes. In any case, Leng Gnat, I expect... no, I invite you to a meeting today at eleven in the morning. We need to decide what to do now with the Human-8 Faction now that it's been enslaved by the enemy. As for now, they're an uncontrollable hole into our world and a security risk for our planet."

I left the building and, accompanied by an escort of six armed guards, headed into the residential building. Despite the abundance of new information, which required the most serious thought, I could only bring myself to think about getting some rest. However... my room was not empty! I realized that back in the corridor because the guard and loyal assistant to the leader of the Second Legion Roman Pavlovich was sitting on his stool in front of my door reading something again. *Perimeter Defense. Sector Eight.* I caught a glimpse of the name on the cover before he put it away. Clearly, something about securing computer networks or maybe classified facilities.

Tamara greeted her adoptive father. I wanted to simply get through, but the gloomy military man stood up and blocked my path:

"Wait, Kirill. We've gotta have a chat."

And of course, I stopped. But Roman Pavlovich, pointing at the far end of the corridor, suggested I walk away from the door where Tamara could hear us. We walked over to the stairs, where he took a heavy sigh and told me:

"Last night, Tamara resigned leadership of the Second Legion. There will be elections for a new commander tomorrow. Most likely Rupor will get voted in. Although he isn't the highest-level player, he is talented and importantly has enough authority for the guys to follow him."

"What about you? You have higher authority than Rupor, and your level is just under a hundred."

The heavyset man shook his head:

"No, I'm also leaving the legion. I'll go wherever my daughter goes. Tamara is in a very bad way now. And she can't rest. As soon as she falls asleep, she wakes up screaming. Nightmares torment her. Talk to her. Try and calm her down."

I promised to try to help. I opened the door and entered my room. Tamara was wearing a white fluffy robe, sitting Indian style on a big soft armchair and watching a nightly news report. When I entered, she immediately turned her television off.

"You were the one who signed the peace with the Dark Faction." Instead of a greeting she met me with reproach.

"Yes, I did. We must move forward, prepare our planet to defend against invasion, and that unnecessary war has eaten through our forces and resources."

I sat next to her and tried to give her a hug, but Tamara twisted out of my embrace and sat further from me on the couch. Clearly, she wasn't in the mood. Then I noticed a pile of dirty dishes on the table next to the refrigerator. Yesterday in the morning it wasn't this messy. There was a maid who cleaned up all the rooms. Seemingly, Tamara hadn't even gone anywhere in the last day, spending all day and night here in the room. She saw me notice the dirty dishes and said:

"I would clean up after myself, but there's no dishwasher, or even sponge and dish soap. And Kirill, I brought all my things over here. There wasn't a lot, not even enough to fill one bag, so it won't get too crowded. I won't even go into my room anymore. It's empty and lonely there. My memories immediately shift to unpleasant things. Deathly sorrow and voices swallow me up. But the worst thing is the ghastly dreams sap all my strength. After one of those, all I want is to hang myself! So I'm staying at your place. Don't worry, I don't have much time left. I can sense it."

The former leader of the Second Legion trotted out the old song and dance about her being useless after peace with the mages. She said that to her peace was equivalent to death because her own soldiers would kill her. I'd already heard this a number of times but, just like yesterday morning, I was surprised she was so certain of her own death.

"Believe me, there will be enough war with the mages to last a century, and a Paladin will always be in demand," I tried coming at it from a different angle. "Tomorrow, or more like today, there's a meeting in Lozovsky's office. I was also invited, even though I'm not technically part of the Human-3 Faction anymore. I can tell you the topic already: they're planning to attack the two nodes of the Human-8 Faction, which has been subjugated by the Dark Faction. We expect strong magical resistance, so a Paladin will come quite in handy."

A little spark of interest was lit in Tamara's eyes, but it went out in a second:

"They'll manage without me... And I don't have combat armor anymore..."

"You're wrong about the armor!" I latched in there, because I thought it could perk her up at least a bit. "I spoke with Eduard Boyko yesterday... Well, not even that. He came to me right after the end of the negotiations with General Ui-Taka. The Space Marine offered his hard-earned exoskeleton armor for the now unprotected leader of the Second Legion. He said he'd buy himself a new one with his own money as soon as he gets to any space station with moderately acceptable prices. I am aware you are no longer leading the Second Legion, but know that you do have armor. And it's the same model you used to have even though the options are somewhat different."

Tamara, without answering one way or the other stood up from the sofa and walked over to the window to lower the blinds because day lighting had come on under the dome. And she spent some time standing in thought, looking at the empty space where the park had been torn up through the not fully closed blinds. Finally, she broke the silence:

"But that's a onetime reprieve. What about after that?"

I realized she meant the forthcoming attack and use of her specific character abilities. Now I was shaking Tamara out of her many-day malaise. She was starting to talk. I tried to build on my success:

"After all, we only signed a peace with La-Fin. Just one of the three biggest forces in the Dark Faction. There's also La-Varrez. They were behind the bio-attack here under the Dome and they were the ones who snuck a saboteur into our world. There's also La-Shin. Little is known of them, but that enemy faction is at the Geckho spaceport now preparing their very own starship for launch."

Tamara was listening carefully, and I was doing my best to keep her attention with all kinds of different options:

"Other than that, as leader of the Relict Faction, I have a great need for helpers that are resistant to mental control, and especially those who can protect others as well. And given you're no longer tied to the Second Legion, I invite you to Rocky Island! Sure, you can no longer interact peacefully with the Naiads in the sea, but as a Paladin you'll be priceless. There will be players from different factions and worlds. We're expecting a ton of difficult questions and your ability to protect other peoples' minds will come in very handy."

That was seemingly not the right idea, because Tamara cringed in dismay:

"I'm a combat character, not some administrator! I need battles and danger!"

"You want more action and danger? Then talk with Princess Minn-O La-Fin! She's the one who really needs defense against magic! Gerd Minn-O is the new head of the La-Fin Faction, but she's a very inexperienced and weak mage. In her world, it's not hard to find bloodsuckers a hundred times more dangerous than she is! Or I could take you with me into space. I'm gonna have a meeting with the Meleyephatians, who are known in space to be extremely powerful psionics."

Tamara suddenly turned around sharply:

"Kirill, what did you just say? Repeat that!"

"Meleyephatians are known in..."

"No, before that," the very agitated girl interrupted me impatiently. "Before. About your wife!"

Not understanding what had her so worked up, I repeated that Minn-O La-Fin really needed a companion who could defend her physically and against magical attacks. And that I didn't see anyone other than Tamara for that role.

"Exactly! That's the solution! The one I saw in my dreams! That is my path! Your wayedda will be under mortal danger in the next few days, but I can stave it off! To hell with the new armor, to hell with all the rest. That can wait. I need to enter the game right now and meet with Minn-O La-Fin! Tell me, where can I find your wayedda? It's important!"

"Minn-O is in the spaceport now and I suspect sleeping in her cabin on the frigate, still in the game. Her legs haven't come back since the terror attack, so Minn-O is trying to use the healing properties of the game to maximum effect and go into the real world as infrequently as possible."

"Great! Then I've gotta run!" Without even changing out of her housecoat and slippers into something more appropriate, Tamara dashed for the front door. But in the doorway she stopped, turned and said: "I am definitely not planning to miss the attack on the Human-8 Faction, so I'll see you in the game soon. But whether we'll see each other again in the real world... I'm not sure. In any case Kirill, I want you to know that you're the best thing that's ever happened to me."

What was happening to Tamara? I decided I'd have to catch up to her and ask. I quickly threw my t-shirt back on, pulled on my sneakers without even tying them but... in the entryway I ran into Ivan Lozovsky, who had come into my room with a big group of people. With him was the fed Alexander Antipov, and leader of the First Legion Igor Tarasov, even that mustached outside officer with a few of his own soldiers. And the looks on all their faces were decisive and unkind.

What did they need from me? Did Imeer-Toh La-Gorr die in prison? The faction leader's first words confirmed that:

"Kirill, hurrying somewhere? I'm afraid we're gonna have to detain you and ask a couple questions. First of all about the sudden death of a key witness."

I was still hoping to get rid of the badly time interrogation and catch up to Tamara, so I tried to limit myself:

"You had a whole hour to squeeze evidence out of him. Imeer-Tohh answered plausibly even to the most complicated and painful questions. But once his time was up, he killed himself. Was one hour really not enough for you? Who was stopping you from joining the interrogation earlier and asking your questions faster? And now you come complaining to me?!"

"But didn't you kill him?!" Lozovsky shot out in a rage. "After all, you threatened the detainee with murder in exactly one hour! And you killed Lydia Vertyachikh the exact same way in the game yesterday! Kirill, you're only a Leng in the game. You can only get away with anything there. This is the real world and you'll have to answer for what you've done."

They all looked at me and I couldn't hold back. Giving the mountainous faction head a condescending pat on the shoulder, I said reproachfully:

"Ah, Ivan, Ivan... How long have you been in contact with the Dark Faction? Five months? Have you really not noticed yet that mages can't kill someone they can't see? Even the great and terrible Leng Thumor-Anhu La-Fin couldn't do that, even though he was the strongest psionic of the magocratic world. By the time Imeer-Toh La-Gorr decided to shuffle off this mortal coil, I had already been in my room for ten or fifteen minutes and simply physically could not have killed him."

"But..." the faction leader tried to object but I stopped him:

"Don't interrupt! I hadn't finished my thought. Did you ever think about the fact that I tried very hard not to touch him even with a finger? Imeer-Toh is a vassal of the La-Varrez dynasty, a subject of the lord of Fourth Directory Coruler Onuri-Unta La-Varrez. I am lord of the First Directory, and war with the Fourth does not enter into my plans! Especially given that now there are so many bloodsuckers coming after Thumor-Anhu's estate! After all, all they need is the slightest excuse and they'll fly in *en masse* and tear me to shreds! So I could frighten Imeer-Toh, deceive him, pressure him with my authority, but never kill him!"

I admit, that wasn't even close to what I was thinking while I was talking to the prisoner. I thought up that explanation on the spot. But despite that, it sounded very plausible and did the trick! I could sense that based on how everyone's face changed. Or to be more accurate, the mustached officer and his soldiers seemingly didn't understand one bit of what was happening and were only more confused after what I said. But Alexander Antipov, Igor Tarasov and even faction head Ivan Lozovsky himself had heard everything perfectly and were now seemingly mad at themselves for accusing me. I had just a bit more to add:

"And now, if you don't have any more questions, I need to get some rest before a very hard gaming session. My Naiads haven't been fed yet. My starship is in repair. My wife is without magical protection. The island has to be brought up to level two and before that we need to evacuate the Germans still stranded there. My business partner is marrying the viceroy of Earth, and I need to somehow come up with seven million crystals for her dowry and fast. The prelates of Tailax are playing their own clever game and putting me forward for ruler of Earth. Then we've got the big construction of the planetary shield. I've got some tough negotiations with the Geckho coming up. Hopefully we can use their ferry to send a landing party to the nodes of the H8 Faction. And, as if I didn't have enough other problems, there's footage going around on galactic news channels of me performing a mating dance with a commander of the Miyelonian fleet, so the Geckho are picking on me!!!"

I had never seen such amazement on their faces before. The players of the Human-3 Faction knew so little about what I'd been up to that just running through my day-to-day tasks put them into shock! The uninvited guests, trying not to breathe unless strictly necessary, apologized for bothering me and went out into the corridor, quietly closing the door behind them.

Chapter Twenty-Five

Big Abi's Secret

ULINE TAR and I were standing on the very edge of a tall steep cliff and watching a truly colossal octopus drag the tail section of a Miyelonian Tikon-Mra V long-distance recon frigate onto the sandy beach. There were Oceanids fussing about around it and Valeri-Urla the Beastmaster was playing a construction worker talking to a crane operator, slightly adjusting where the giant left the debirs. The main complication was that the starship fragment was very large and heavy, and the octopus couldn't come on shore for some reason. I suspected it was so large that only underwater did it not feel the weight of its own body. But finally, the fragment was quite carefully laid on a trailer we brought into the water and a Sio-Tu-Tati tank, its engines roaring arduously, pulled it out then quickly brought the valuable spoils away from the surf line. By the way, the heavy assault tank was driven personally by its creator Alex Bobl a Drafter of armored vehicles for the Dark Faction, he'd offered to help when he saw the loading work and asked about the pieces of the space ship.

Okay, that was the last, third largest fragment of the broken starship. Before that, spooky black crabs pulled around fifty smaller pieces on shore, mainly bits of scattered armor plating. Valeri-Urla paid up with the Ocean Faction, giving them knives and underwater flashlights like human divers used. A minute later, only the Beastmaster was left on shore together with her pet Shadow Panther, and the only reminder of the hustle and bustle earlier was some tracks in the sand left by the treads and antigravitation pancakes. Seriously sunburnt, she wiped the sweat from her brow, glanced at the mercilessly burning sun and started pulling off her clothes, clearly intending to take a dip.

"Gnat, enough standing around looking at a naked human female! Let's go take a better look at our haul!" The Geckho Trader was burning in impatience, which was no surprise. Her marriage directly depended on whether there was something valuable among the debris.

Along with my furry business partner, I headed to the nearby hangars, where the players of three different factions were unloading and sorting through debris. There was an air of excitement, I heard shouts and swearing from the foremen, but when I came close the players fell silent out of respect. I went straight for Engineer Orun Va-Mart who was near the debris explaining something with Gerd Ayni's help to Human-3 Faction head scientist Gerd Ustinov. Like Gerd Alex Bobl from the La-Fin Faction, Gerd Ustinov was there on Rocky Island on my invitation as an expert consultant. When trying to decide on a location to build the planetary shield generator, we ran into lots of technical problems and we really needed experienced help. But once they both saw the debris we fished up, neither of them could resist.

Orun Va-Mart the big hairy tomcat walked over to Uline Tar and I, pointing at a starship wing, and said:

"Captain, this is even better than we could have hoped, considering the severe impact when the pirate frigate hit the water! Both laser turrets on the left stabilizer were saved. The model TR-3000 Assassins are better and more powerful than the cannons on our ship."

"Yes, Assassins are something of a 'gold standard' among Miyelonian pirates," Uline the Trader confirmed with a satisfied look. "They're reliable laser cannons, devastating and made of lightweight alloys. We'd save four hundred pounds per cannon too which, for a starship especially a light interceptor, is very significant. It'll be no problem to sell a cannon like this for eight hundred thousand crystals. If we put it up with pickup from the spaceport only, it'll be gone in an ummi. However..." my business partner faltered, as if reading my thoughts, "this is exactly the kind of thing we want for ourselves. If the value of the other stuff is enough for a dowry, I'd prefer to put the Assassins on our frigate and sell the old cannons!"

Yes, that was just the thing to do. I asked the Engineer to tell me more of what we'd found. The Miyelonian turned and pointed a clawed paw at Tini the kitten, who was using his thief's tools to open the frigate's airlock:

"Soon we'll see with our own eyes. For now all I know is what we can see outside. It hit the water just about flat with a little lurch to the right. The fuselage broke up along the stabilizer seams, you can see a fissure in the longerons. The nose section was most badly damaged. I'm afraid little could be salvaged there. Navigation equipment, communications systems and locators — don't count on any of that. I usually install a shield generator and cloaking system close to the middle of the starship, but with such a powerful impact, everything down below is also shattered. Anyhow, we'll see... But the tail section was well preserved, and the thrusters can be repaired. A hyperspace, main and both maneuver drives. A couple days' repair and they'll be good as new. As for the power unit, I'll need to see as well. I can't say right now."

"If the thrusters can be salvaged, that's already very good!" Uline Tar turned on her palmtop and started calculating. "Three and a half million, consider it in your pocket. Plus the million and a half crystals, Leng Gnat, that you are like supposed to have left after paying for paying to transport your former faction's troops by ferry." My business partner raised her head, expecting confirmation and I nodded in agreement. "And the broken Tikon-Mra V might give up a bit more, maybe another half million if we disassemble it and sell it for parts. At least it's enough for the dowry already. We won't even have to sell the Assassins. But still it would be nice to find another couple million..."

Gerd Ustinov walked over to our group, all red in excitement. Not one bit ashamed at my companions, the scientist said with great gusto:

"Gnat, what fantastic luck! A real spacefaring vehicle! I've taken pictures of the starship from all angles. I also photographed certain junctures and elements. The guards allowed me to even take samples of the insulation and armor paneling. It would be so cool if we could scan this mess with your tool. A three-dimensional diagram of a starship, even in such a dilapidated state is a real treasure! It would allow humanity to take another big step toward the stars!"

Uh, duh, didn't I already know that? Still I had to disappoint the scientist because I had a big problem with the Prospector Scanner...

Right after the meeting in Lozovsky's office where we were discussing the attack on the Human-8 Faction, I entered the game. Losing my progress to level 84 was upsetting, but I expected it. I was much more soured when I checked my inventory and discovered my scanner was missing. It must have fallen as loot after my character died. It was a very valuable item, especially the data contained in the scanner. So I got right to it and flew on the antigrav from Rocky Island to the Human-3 Faction capital until I found the place where I died. I discovered a spent Geological Analyzer there and lots of tracks from forest creatures. But as for the lost device, it was nowhere to be found. I didn't know who might have wanted it — only a Prospector or Listener could use such a specific device after all.

And again I sensed concentrated attention directed at me. And although it was a very bright day, and I had two armed pilot-escorts with me, I still felt uneasy. Scanning turned up nothing dangerous nearby, but I already knew that meant nothing. Then I straightened up and shouted into the forest, first in Geckho, then repeated the same message in Miyelonian:

"Oh wise Vaa! I am no enemy to you! I was the one who brought your body to this planet on a request from my Morphian friend so you could eat your fill here and come back from a two-year state of suspended animation. If you need details, come out and we can talk. I also came to say that I am flying away in two days. And if you want to leave this planet, come to the Geckho spaceport. I'm sure with your abilities it won't be any trouble to get there. And if you're the one who took my Prospector Scanner, give it back. I really need it!"

No answer followed, but the feeling of anxiety, like I was being watched disappeared. The Morphian heard me and probably understood, but didn't want to come out and talk. Okay then, that was its right. I waited a minute, after which I turned and walked the forest path to the Geckho Diplomat's hut. But I was too late. There was no metal hut where it once stood, just withered grass and an imprint in the ground confirming that a temporary structure once stood there. The viceroy had moved into a residence more befitting his high status. One of the residences built by the Geckho in the village adjacent to the spaceport. And the viceroy had brought Anna the refugee with him. Too bad, I wanted to speak with them so badly. I had a ton of questions for them both, especially the medic.

"Okay, I got it open!" Tini's shout of delight jerked me from my thoughts and memories. "The doorway is dented, so the door won't open all the way. But I can squeeze in."

"Good job!" I walked over and tenderly patted my ward on the nape of his neck. "I see your skills are growing. Well, shall we go in?"

I turned on the flashlight and was first to enter the crack. Inside it was wet and slippery. I just about stepped on a crab which skittishly ran out from under a broken panel. There was enough light even with no flashlight because sun came in through the many gaps in the fuselage. I tried to get my bearings. This was the corridor heading to the cockpit. Now it was twisted and blocked by sharp debris. Here, seemingly, was the gunner's seat. And the lounge room was located behind that accordioned barrier. Hrm... Quite a sight. It would have been absolutely impossible to survive that crash. But at least there were no dead bodies. In the game, they disappeared after a certain amount of time.

While I stood and looked around, Tini was scouring the starship, hurriedly sticking any little thing of any value into his inventory. It was all just personal items and light weaponry from the dead crew but still there was plenty of stuff lying around. Ayni the Translator was also filling her pockets. I didn't sink to such petty marauding although I was also looking around to see what I could maybe make a buck on.

"Too bad..." came the disappointed voice of the Miyelonian Engineer, sticking his whiskered nose into every nook and cranny. "Everything that could break did. The shield generator is in pieces. The power unit is beyond repair. That's bad... I won't even look in the cockpit, I already get the picture. So, what do we have here? Captain, look! This is a miracle!"

I didn't understand what Orun Va-Mart wanted to show me, pointing his flashlight at a bunch of cables and mess of plastic and metal debris. It all looked basically like a big heap of trash.

"Captain, that piece there," the Miyelonian impatiently cut the bunch of wires blocking his path with a knife. Then pointed its tip at a wet metal sphere approximately three feet in radius, which was hanging down off the wires. "This is the cloak generator! It survived all the chaos! By the way, the GGG-HI8 is a very good and expensive model. And compatible with our ship's hardware."

"Four and a half million crystals at least," came Uline Tar's voice, muted by the thin wall. The heavyset Geckho woman couldn't crawl into the broken ship but was carefully listening to our conversation. "Can you get it out at all?"

"Yes! We'll just cut a hole in the fuselage and extract it through there. There won't be anything else of value, so we can go the simplest and fastest way," Orun Va-Mart replied.

Nothing of value? Looking at the chaos and destruction around, it was easy to believe. However, before us was not some unknown frigate, but the ship of a very famous and successful leader of the pirate pride of the Bushy Shadow, Gerd Abi Pan-Miay. I was severely disappointed. Was there nothing special on the flagship of a pirate fleet? Maybe even something not so much of value, but at least of interest, something unusual? Some little knick-knack, a trophy from some massacre? But I didn't see anything like that.

"Where is the captain's bunk on these frigates?" I asked the Engineer, and Orun Va-Mart, thinking, pointed confidently at a dark gap going vertically up with the remnants of a stairway sticking out of the wall. We really hadn't checked that small dark room.

But how to get in there? I called Tini and pointed my kitten to the hole, which was potentially an interesting source of trophies. In two jumps, very gracefully off the walls, the Miyelonian teen shot upward and hooked his clawed paw into the edge. He contracted his body and climbed up. I wanted to praise my ward for his unbelievable agility when suddenly the orange Ayni next to me repeated the same trick, shooting up like a spring and landing right next to Tini. My jaw simply fell. I wasn't expecting that from the modest and bashful Translator!

From above, I heard Tini's voice almost at once:

"Gerd Abi's personal things are here. Mostly just trash, although there is a pair of blades that look pretty sweet!"

"And a very impressive collection of trophy tails on the wall, although now they're all wet and pitiful," Ayni added.

None of that really merited attention. I activated the scanning icon, zoomed in my mini-map as far as possible and looked at the captain's bunk. There it was!

Scanning skill increased to level fifty-one!

Eagle Eye skill increased to level seventy-eight!

"Tini, check the wall to your left. There are some niches a bit higher up. Based on my map, there is a suspicious cavity in the wall there."

Three seconds passed and an exultant double Miyelonian scream rolled through the ruined ship's hallways. And Ayni couldn't hold back her emotions, joyfully howling even louder than the teenage Tini:

"Captain, there's a hidden safe!"

The next fifteen minutes were spent trying to open the lock with picks and code breakers. And Engineer Orun Va-Mart lost patience long ago, suggesting we resort to radical measures and simply cut through the wall. But I asked them to wait a second. Tini was levelling up over and over again right before my eyes, practicing his thief skills and improving them. And my ward did it! But the contents of that promising safe were, to put it lightly, disappointing:

"Master Gnat, there's nothing here in the safe.

Or... Well there is a piece of white plastic with some numbers scratched in."

The kitten jumped down and handed me the broken chunk of plastic. At first glance it was trash. You see something like this on the ground, you probably wouldn't even pick it up. But on the surface of the ductile sheet, there was a whole system of interlaced rectangles etched in with something sharp. Miyelonian numerals. Lots of them. I had to crawl out into the sunlight to make sense of the cobweb of intersecting lines.

789609.960412 157890.233308 012500.3423-9

After that long series of numbers, it showed a date. Approximately half a tong ago in a time system that was accurate down to one ten thousandth of an ummi.

Intelligence increased to 33.

Astrolinguistics skill increased to level ninety!

I just about lost it looking at the endless rectangles! Even the game system considered my intellectual feat worth rewarding, giving Gnat a third boost to Intelligence, the last one I could ever get. I read the number aloud, but that didn't make things one bit easier to understand. What was this? Why was that Miyelonian Pirate storing a chunk of plastic with numbers in a secret safe?

"That's probably the number of a bank account and an access code," Ayni suggested, but the Trader immediately objected that the format didn't correspond to a banking number, and the time and date would be useless in that case.

"It doesn't look like coordinates either, too many digits," I said thoughtfully and the others agreed.

Still no one had any other ideas. What a shame. A huge one. But as much as it was, we were going to have to set the pirate captain's secret aside. There was zero time left, and I had a whole bunch of other stuff planned for today. I stored the mysterious item in my inventory and mentally shook myself, preparing for the burst of activity just around the corner.

"Uline, get our trophies to the spaceport and sell them. Orun Va-Mart will go with you and help with everything. Take as many people as you need. They're all," I said, making a broad gesture at all the many people gathered around the debris, "technically still part of all kinds of factions and even live in different worlds, but everyone here is actually my faction, Relict Faction!"

Authority increased to 62!

I looked up at the sun. It was almost touching the evening sea. Then I turned my gaze away to the team, which was preparing to leave with me.

"Okay, friends, let's go to the Sio-Mi-Dori! It's time to fly to Antique Beach. They should start loading Human-3 troops onto the ferry in half an hour. And ideally at least I will be there by then so there won't be any linguistic confusion between the people and Geckho."

I didn't say what I was thinking, but the main problem was nothing to do with lack of translators. I needed to have a talk with the leadership of the

Human-3 Faction for a totally different reason. The issue was that, at the same time as the first ferry, another ferry was supposed to be starting off with a landing party. That was Gerd Minn-O La-Fin kindly agreeing to help me out with three hundred of her best soldiers commanded by the best commander of the La-Fin Faction, a level-102 Machinegunner by the name Gerd Lang-Yu.

That wasn't exactly what I'd asked my wife for: I wanted a loan of her faction's four Sio-Mi-Dori antigravs. But the proud princess was unexpectedly stubborn and set two nonnegotiable conditions. First of all, her La-Fin Faction had to be able to take part in the combat operation. According to Minn-O, it would be a great chance for her to prove herself a successful commander before her subjects and to raise her Authority, while the whole faction had the chance to demolish the stereotype that they were merely an implacable enemy of my world. Second, the La-Fin Faction no longer had just four Sio-Mi-Dori assault landing antigravs, but six: two of the aircrafts had recently been repaired. Princess Minn-O La-Fin offered to use them all, but as a loyal wayedda she was supposed to also take part in the battle and fly off in the same vehicle as her husband.

I had to agree. And as for now, imagining Ivan Lozovsky's eyes going wide at the news that he would have to fight side by side with the Dark Faction, I didn't know whether to laugh or cry. It was all the harder to imagine the reaction of the Human-3 Faction rank and file, most of whom had a poor understanding of the politics of the magocratic world and didn't know the different dynasties. When they heard that they would be liberating the two Dark Faction-occupied North American nodes with the help of... "the Dark Faction," who could say what would happen.

Chapter Twenty-Six

Night Assault

A GROUP of seven Sio-Mi-Doris with lights off and locators inactive passed over the stormy night sea just skirting the high waves with its antigrav pancakes. To my eye, there was no need for so much risk, but Major Filippov who was leading the aerial assault, by the way now up to level-43, insisted we be as stealthy as possible. And that included complete radio silence, although the chance that the enemy might intercept messages between the landing groups was, to my eye, something from the realm of science fiction.

However, the level-61 Jarg Analyst was in enthusiastic support of Major Filippov's precaution so I didn't argue. The spiny armadillo had made more than one long-reaching conclusion and proven his advice to be effective and useful. What was more, my advisor Mage Diviner Mac-Peu Un-Roi had determined that all the antigrav pilots had sufficient skills and experience that the probability of all seven aircrafts reaching the enemy shore safe and sound was 94%. And from there, according to the diviner, the possible timelines diverged severely and, for now, he couldn't say for certain which we were heading for.

If the enemy was relaxed and careless as usual, then the active part of the operation could be over in eleven or twelve minutes, leaving us in control of both Human-8 nodes. We were expecting minimal losses. It was even possible we'd lose no one.

Mac-Peu was coming from the perspective that the Human-8 Faction was not at all militaristic and most of their players were of peaceful professions. We already knew a team of enthusiasts had founded the faction, mostly students at Canadian universities, and at first they used the game's capabilities to heal the hopelessly ill. Only a bit later did their activity catch the interest of the Canadian government (it would have been impossible not to notice the tall corncob-shaped buildings sprouting up on the campus of Quebec University), and the operation was transferred to a nearby military base. But even after they had soldiers playing full-time for their faction, most of them were still former chronically ill patients, which meant the vast majority of the Human-8 Faction were Financiers, Administrators, Engineers, Medics, and things of that nature. No more than twenty percent of them belonged to combat professions. And if that was all we were up against, three hundred Financiers who could barely even hold a weapon properly, our job sounded pretty easy.

But it if the enemy was somehow informed of our plans and prepared for defense, the picture changed completely. In that case, the lines of fate predicted horrible, bloody battles. The success of the operation as a whole was not guaranteed then. After all, in that eventuality, we could expect not only three hundred and six battle-ready Human-8 players (the total number of people in the infiltrated North American faction) but also a large number of La-Varrez faction mages, a small contingent of whom were there round the clock to keep watch. Then add to that some well-equipped and prepared combat subdivisions from the La-Varrez Faction and its ten or so vassals. That whole force might consist of more than fifteen thousand soldiers. Taking down all that power with six hundred commandos from a ferry and hundreds of landing troops from the Sio-Mi-Dori was unimaginable.

Meanwhile, that was the most negative scenario, and the Mage Diviner expressed a hope that we were heading into the more favorable scenario. Nevertheless, we probably would be encountering some mages on the occupied territory. According to Imeer-Toh La-Gorr, the number of these mage observers varied day by day from ten to twenty-five, but they were always strong experienced wizards who could control a crowd and suppress any attempts at disobedience.

Meanwhile, for the last four months there hadn't even been one attempted uprising, and it wasn't because the Canadian and American players lacked fighting spirit. No, it was much worse than that. Powerful psionics had manipulated the memories of their vassals, not only squeezing all kinds of information about our world out of them, but programming player behavior and planting false memories as well. So the Human-8 Faction had no memory of the fact that, four months ago, they lost a fast-paced war and ever since had been obediently carrying out their victors' will. The players didn't even suspect they had ever met anyone from the parallel magocratic world and didn't notice the strange people with ash-gray skin in their lands. However they did obediently carry out their every order.

It was fairly hard to believe the ghoulish story Imeer-Toh La-Gorr told about the psionic enslavement of the Human-8 Faction. However, unfortunately, the captive mage was telling the truth. The La-Varrez Faction mages came to the conclusion that the best chains for keeping slaves on the plantation, were those that they didn't even notice. Of course the defeat and war were the explanation for the Human-8 Faction's stalled development. The mage masters thought a large number of players would be hard for them to control, and having fifty free slots in the Human-8 Faction and empty virt pods in the corncobs on the military base in New Brunswick essentially gave them a highway into the parallel world.

So far they'd sent four agents into our world, all very skilled in psionic magic. One of them, Imeer-Toh La-Gorr had already been exposed and defanged but three were still at liberty and freely moving about the planet, easily passing any police document check or passport and customs control points. And not knowing languages was no impediment to them, because they could just communicate mentally. Anyhow, strong Astrolinguistics and high Intelligence allowed them to learn languages quickly and the agents had studied the most common languages of our world while preparing for the transfer.

Imeer-Toh had told me the names and descriptions of his coconspirators, but there was little to be gained from that. Every one of the dangerous mages was acting alone, operating only on instructions from their homeworld. All the agents were in the dark about one another's plans. So those three mages could be anywhere right now, from Los Angeles to Paris, from Bagdad to the Antarctic. Meanwhile, we had provided channels for communication between them. The Internet and advanced technology allowed us to communicate secretly with any part of the planet via messenger or satellite phone so, when needed, messages could be sent and received. However, the agents were only allowed to do that in extraordinary circumstances because it was thought to be too easy to trace. Imeer-Toh had given me contact information for the other mages in our world so now let our intelligence services bust their brains over how to use this information and catch the agents. Their biggest vulnerability was the fact that they had to return to a pod on a military base in Canada and enter the game at least once every seven or eight days. That gave our special forces good chances to track down and capture these dangerous enemies.

Cartography skill increased to level sixty-nine!

The pop-up message distracted me. Yes, tonight's antigrav flight was having a very positive effect on both Cartography and Eagle Eye, so my overall progress bar was filling fast. And in that it was expected to be a long flight — another hour and a half or so, I was hoping to get to level 84 before the Sio-Mi-Dori reached the shore. Princess Minn-O La-Fin sitting next to me was awake and staring pensively through a loophole-viewport. The Geckho brothers Vasha and Basha Tushihh weren't sleeping either, having unpacked their Na-Tikh-U board in the far end of the landing hold and once again trying in vain to best the Jarg. But all the others were getting some rest.

It was very unusual not to see the H3 Faction symbol on Gerd Tamara and Roman Pavlovich's armor as they slept. Plus their character descriptions looked strange:

Gerd Tamara. Human. Faction [undefined]. Level-103 Paladin.

Roman Pavlovich. Human. Faction [undefined]. Level-97 Grenadier.

Yes, to me it came as a great surprise, but the former leader of the Second Legion wanted to leave the Dome and our world forever and resettle in the First Directory. She had made an official request to join the La-Fin Faction, and its leader Gerd Minn-O La-Fin had already approved it. And now little Tamara had been working as my junior wife's bodyguard for the better part of a day, defending Minn-O from magical attacks. I had to admit, after Tamara said we might never meet again in the real world, I was expecting much worse, so this was perfectly fine with me. Reassuring even. Roman Pavlovich, as promised, came with his adoptive daughter and had also left our home faction. Both high-level newcomers had received exoskeleton armor suits from the La-Fin Faction. They weren't as huge as the refit Geckho armor, but they were very tough and functional.

"My husband, something isn't right!" Minn-O broke away from contemplating the night sea and shuddered in alarm, her eyes suddenly wide in panic.

I personally didn't sense anything unusual and certainly not dangerous, however, I was used to trusting Minn-O's presentiments. My wayedda's Danger Sense was much better leveled than mine. So I quietly stood up and headed for the cockpit past the peacefully sleeping friends on either side of the corridor.

The aircraft was piloted by Dmitry Zheltov, which was a bit strange because the main Sio-Mi-Dori pilot was San-Doon Taki-Bu, a highly experienced level-90 Pilot. He had many months experience ferrying Leng Thumor-Anhu La-Fin around on a high-speed antigrav, and was well versed in atmospheric flight. But still there was nothing extraordinary in handing the helm to the copilot. Dmitry was nowhere near a beginner in these matters. No matter how you looked at it, he was a level-77 Starship Pilot and could stand to level the specific skills for flying inside a planet's atmosphere. No, the cause of the trouble, and I had already begun to sense a growing panic myself, was something else.

Successful Perception check!

Eagle Eye skill increased to level eighty-one!

In the night sky, twelve miles to the left of our group, there were three barely visible spots moving in parallel to us. Unfortunately, they were too far away to identify but here over the ocean, one hundred twenty miles from the nearest shore, it was probably no coincidence they were here.

"Minn-O, wake the others!" I ordered, whispering for some reason as she came up quietly behind me. Realizing that I could speak at full voice, I loudly commanded: "Combat alert! Denni Marko to left gunner position! And the right..." I mentally ran through my options and realized I didn't have much choice. "Gerd Tamara to right gunner position! Dmitry, stay on main pilot. San-Doon Taki-Bu, I need you to get in touch with the Sio-Mi-Dori and warn them of the danger. To hell with stealth already! Enemy ten miles to the right! They're attacking!!!"

Whew! I realized after the fact I said these commands in three different languages, easily adapting depending on whom I was addressing. Cool, of course. Although ideally I would have my crew learn one common language at some point. For example Geckho, which was more relevant in space.

Danger Sense skill increased to level sixty-three!

Bunches of bright lines streaked off from the unknown aircraft in the night sky, headed in our direction. Rockets!!! And seemingly homing rockets based on how their trajectory shifted to match ours.

Surprising as it was, when he saw the oncoming death, our Pilot just gave a happy laugh and turned to his partner Dmitry Zheltov:

"Dmitrrr, how little they know of the Sio-Mi-Dori! Fools! We have excellent electronic warfare systems! Fighting your military, we had no other choice. You were constantly shooting smarter and stronger rockets at us. Like it or not, we had to adapt."

I couldn't say whether the Starship Pilot understood anything of the magocratic native's words but he did give a laugh as he watched the rockets rushing in. And in fact, before they made it a quarter mile, all thirty of the rockets exploded in midair without so much as grazing us. And the return fire from our seven Sio-Mi-Dori laser cannons, was more effective: two enemy aircraft caught fire and fell out of the sky. The last eventually came so close I could read its information:

Paeen-Ro. La-Varrez Faction atmospheric fighter.

La-Varrez. Our worst fears were confirmed. The enemy knew about our attack and had taken countermeasures, trying to intercept and destroy our aerial landing group before we reached their shore. Yes, the enemy had significantly underestimated the technical capabilities of the dangerous and well defended La-Fin Faction assault-landing antigravs. However I feared they would not make the same mistake twice.

The last of the three fighter planes tried to escape, hiding in the dense clouds. At the last moment, I managed to stick it with a targeting marker and belatedly sent the Small Relict Guard Drone off to chase it, but I wasn't especially counting on the drone reaching its target in the dense cloud cover and first rumblings of thunder. So it was all the more pleasant a minute later to receive another portion of messages:

Targeting skill increased to level thirty-one!

Machine Control skill increased to level eighty-one!

You have reached level eighty-four!

You have received three skill points (total points accumulated: six).

Great! Let that be a lesson to my enemies! I hurriedly tossed my six stat points where they needed to go. Three went into Mysticism, raising it to 39. Having more mana and faster regen was very important to a Listener. Another three into Mental Fortitude brought that skill up to 90. I could easily be walking into an encounter with enemy mages and increased defense against their attacks would come quite in handy. Just then, Major Filippov came into the cockpit, alarmed:

"Someone gave us up. I say we change our flight route, making it more unpredictable than a simple direct flight. Otherwise they might catch us in the air again and this time with enough forces to take us out."

"But we're going almost maximum speed now, and our flight time is synchronized to line up with the arrival of the two landing parties arriving by sea!" Dmitry Zheltov objected hotly.

The Military Academy graduate was accustomed to strict discipline. The very thought of deviating from upper leadership's plan for a combat operation plan horrified him. The experienced military strategist, although still just a level-43 Bard, answered gloomily:

"Dmitry, if we get shot down in flight, we won't be any help to our guys. So better to hold back a bit but get there alive than not to show up at all. Also... it's up to Leng Gnat here."

They both looked at me. I then kept silent in furious thought. The fact that the enemy knew about our route and even the approximate location of the antigravs was a very bad sign. It was evidence that the Human-3 Faction's mole was still active and had found a new handler. Or it meant there was just as serious a leak of secret information from the La-Fin Faction. And if the La-Varrez Faction was aware of the seven Sio-Mi-Doris, they surely already knew about the ferry landing party, so they would be disembarking into a fiery hell. Regrettably, the most negative possible line of fate had come to pass...

Could another hundred soldiers help change the course of the battle? A complicated question, but the answer was probably no. So then, what to do? Not, indeed, turn back. Although... Wait... The balance of forces was painfully reminiscent of the situation before Dmitry, Imran, Anna and I made our suicidal push into Dark Faction territory to distract their main forces. But this time it wasn't just four players on a flimsy

"Starship," but a full hundred soldiers with seven assault aircraft. And that meant we could choose more interesting targets than sown fields and comms towers. I could even choose a target that would make enemy leadership forget everything and urgently call all their troops back.

"Attention all! We're changing targets! We're going to the central node of the La-Varrez Faction!"

Major Filippov figured out my plan in an instant and in the silence that took hold, gave a demonstrative clap of admiration. But I had to explain it for the rest. Especially Eduard Boyko, who was screaming in hysterics: "We can't do that either, commander! In half an hour our brothers in arms will be dying and expecting help! And they'll never forgive us if we just abandon them like that!" But I managed to quickly reassure the Space Commando. Eduard even apologized for his lack of restraint. However, Gerd Mauu-La Mya-Ssa the Medic injected the warrior with something calming nevertheless. And the huge Space Commando sat back in his seat with a dumb and blissful smile on his face.

San-Doon Taki-Bu sent new coordinates and a strict order from the leader of the La-Fin dynasty to the other vehicles: "From this second, no one can leave the game. Any external contact is forbidden. Those who disobey will be immediately killed both in the game and the real world."

Yes they were harsh measures. But the success of our mission depended on the element of surprise. And I didn't know another surefire way to avoid another leak.

I had to talk separately with Minn-O. The Princess looked very upset. It was plain to see. And she quickly told me why:

"My husband, until now our actions could have been taken by the factions of my world as simply unneighborly, nothing beyond the pale. But a direct attack on the capital of the La-Varrez Faction with hundreds of soldiers, ninety percent of whom are from the La-Fin Faction... that's a declaration of war! And knowing the hot-headed nature of Onuri-Unta La-Varrez, war will be declared not only in the virtual game but in the real world! Our First Directory will have to fight with at least the Fourth, and most likely also the Seventh and the Eleventh!"

A very serious threat! At any rate, I assured my wife I was doing everything in my power to avoid open war between the great La-Fin and La-Varrez dynasties. But if I couldn't, I'd try to land a blow with such force that the La-Varrez Faction would need a long time to recover! Destroying a developed level-five hexagon, then restoring my starship and taking out all the other hexagons of the La-Varrez Faction would be a serious possibly knockout punch. They would be simply forced to make concessions!

"REMAINING FLIGHT TIME three minutes! I've got eyes on the enemy citadel!"

But I had already seen all that, watching the approaching shore through the IR Lens. It really was a very developed node. A sea of lights, just like a megacity. A large port, dozens of ships. Powerful on-shore artillery batteries capable of staving off an invasion by sea. High-speed roads with headlights running both directions. A coal carrier, working even at night. Lots of factories. Gardens, expansive sown fields. An airport with antigravs at the ready. And a huge dark fortress providing a reliable observation point over the ravine, which contained the only road leading to a neighboring hexagon.

I offered command to Major Filippov, but the Bard was categorically opposed. With such a large distance and in the dark he couldn't see much, so he simply asked to be assigned to give out bonuses. I had to take the Targeting System myself and show each division where to strike:

"Second vehicle, land a party right here," I placed a marker all my soldiers could see. "Get rid of the guards and blow up the crude oil storage. After that, take the aircraft out to port and sink ships, and have the soldiers fight their way to the citadel to help with the assault."

Authority increased to 63!

Targeting skill increased to level thirty-two!

"Vehicle three, I want your landing a party to block the highway. These bridges," I placed markers, "are to be blown immediately so the enemy can't send reinforcements. Careful! There's an anti-air base just over a mile away. I'm marking it too, just in case. You'll have to fly extremely low to the ground. After you complete the mission, go to the port. Fire at will. Destroy whatever you think necessary!"

Targeting skill increased to level thirty-three!

"Vehicles four to seven go to the citadel and land your parties at this point. After that, all Sio-Mi-Doris go to the airport and wipe it off the face of the earth. And have the landing party try to get inside the fortress at any cost!"

"And what should we do?" asked Dmitry Zheltov, still in the head pilot's seat.

I answered loudly so everyone in the vehicle could hear:

"We're gonna first pass over the factories and warehouses, sowing chaos and destruction. Tamara and Denni, to the side guns! San-Doon — you on the nose cannons! Open escape hatches on both sides. Basha, Vasha and Eduard turn on the rocket-propelled grenade systems and fire on everything that can be destroyed! Roman Pavlovich, T'yu Pan. You both do the same! But everyone buckle up so you don't accidentally fall. After the Small Relict Guard Drone destroys the enemy AA, we'll fly over there and attack that building," I placed another marker on the map.

"What's in the palace?" a few soldiers at once

asked in surprise.

I gave a predatory smile, taking out the Annihilator, which Kirsan returned to me yesterday, and installing a fully charged battery. Now not only had the effective firing distance of the ancient weapon grown, I could also use interchangeable rechargeable batteries instead of rare ancient Relict batteries. And I said:

"That palace, my friends, is where the head of the La-Varrez Faction lives, Leng Onuri-Unta La-Varrez! He is very cautious, so it's unlikely he went to the Human-8 nodes to help them. And I hope greatly the old mage is in the game. I've wanted to chat with him for a long time! But enough talking! Into battle!"

Oh it was unforgettable! The city was in flames. The boom of the exploding cisterns where they stored gas and combustibles laid my ears flat. The blaze of the petroleum-processing and nitrate-enrichment plants turned night into brightest day. Our aircraft weaved between the high towers and smokestacks of the endless huge factories, dodging large workshops and hangars, leaving behind us a trail of fire and destruction. And it wasn't so much that I loved destruction... though I did need to admit there was a certain attraction in decimating enemy buildings! I didn't have time to read all the skill-up messages for Targeting, Rifles, Sharpshooter, Machine Control and Eagle Eye.

But that wasn't the most important part. Five groups of landing troops had reached the central citadel, the source of the claim to the whole hexagon, and were getting deeper and deeper inside, killing the defenders and blowing up weapon and ammunition storage inside the building. The northern wing of the fortress was demolished and the central part of the building was just going up in flames. The node level fell from five to three causing lots of structures to collapse all around the city. And that wasn't the end because our assault was still underway!

Finally the Small Relict Guard Drone told me its mission was complete: all AA systems in the city were destroyed! And because the jet and antigravity fighters at the airport had already been taken out, our air superiority was now unquestioned.

Machine Control skill increased to level eighty-seven!

You have reached level eighty-five!

You have received three skill points.

What great timing! I immediately placed all three points into Mental Fortitude, taking it to 93. I had a sense that mental defense would be coming in handy quite soon.

"Dmitry, come up higher and fly to the palace! Other Sio-Mi-Doris, follow us! Oh! I see they're coming out to meet us. Hold your fire! I need to speak with them!"

Our aircraft took a bold turn and landed on a concrete platform in front of the building entrance, making sure all our cannons were aimed at the large group of people wearing mage cloaks. Yes, Dmitry Zheltov was a quick study and was already allowing himself little flourishes like that.

I jumped to the ground first and, gripping the Annihilator tight, headed forward unhurriedly. After me, shaking the earth with their heavy footsteps, the huge and skin-crawlingly fearsome Geckho brothers Basha and Vasha stepped out. The cannons attached to their exoskeleton armor could turn that whole crowd of mages to shreds. A bit behind the Geckho, brandishing blades, came three nimble Miyelonians. Gerd Mauu-La Mya-Ssa, Gerd Ayni Uri-Miayuu and Tini could instantly jump forward and chop the whole group of unarmored people to bits, while the mental defense provided by Gerd Tamara guaranteed the enemy psionics had no way of harming the Miyelonians back. The bloodcurdling and alert Roman Pavlovich, Valeri-Urla, Eduard and Imran completed our procession. I left the others in the vehicle. We needed our gunners in position, and there was no reason to show off our La-Fin Faction soldiers.

I walked forty steps toward the group of mages and ordered my companions to stop by raising a hand in the air. I went the rest of the way on my own. A tall old man wearing a gold embroidered luxurious black robe stepped out in front of their group. The staff in his strong, not at all old-looking hands, was somewhat reminiscent of Thumor-Anhu La-Fin's Wrath but, instead of a skull, it was topped with a stone dragon head.

Leng Onuri-Unta La-Varrez. Human. Dark Faction. Level-128 Psionic Mage.

Level one hundred twenty-eight?! Respectable. Very respectable. But how old was my opponent here?

He didn't look all that old, definitely not decrepit. It looked very much like Coruler Onuri-Unta had spent his extra statistic points not only on Intelligence, but also on Constitution and Strength. I noticed sparse gray patches in his long dark mage's beard and the fit of his mage robes hinted at a strong muscular figure. Curious. That meant the head of the La-Varrez dynasty had sacrificed magical strength for more youth and good health.

"Leng Gnat La-Fin!" the voice of the ruler of the Fourth Directory didn't sound old either. "I've heard a lot about you, most of it bad, and now I'm finally seeing you before me. What brings you to my city? What need have you?"

Somewhat rude, especially considering our equal status, but I was expecting him to start the conversation somewhat worse than that. We were left in complete silence, even the explosions in the city had seemingly gone quiet. I gave a slight bow, displaying appropriate respect to a Coruler of humanity and replied:

"Leng Onuri-Unta La-Varrez! I have come to discuss your servants crudely intruding in my affairs. Your underlings, hopefully without your knowledge, are keeping people from my world in mental bondage and threatening to use weapons of mass destruction in our large cities. Call these people off and give your word as a Mage that it will not happen again and this conflict will not lead to war between our dynasties. If you do so, I will leave here at once. You have my word as a Mage!"

I tried to phrase my offer in such a way that my

opponent wouldn't be damaged in the eyes of his subordinates if he agreed. And I was also sending a different message mentally, keeping my word to the captive mage Imeer-Toh La-Gorr and saying he died heroically.

He spent a long time in silence, perhaps speaking covertly with his retinue. Tensions mounted. I even ordered the Small Relict Guard Drone to come down closer just in case. And suddenly a huge series of flashes in the city showed that the level of the fortress had just fallen to two, which led to another large-scale destruction of buildings. This time, it was the ones that could only exist at claim three and above. Only after that did Coruler Onuri Unta shudder, wince painfully. However he responded very politely and even gave a slight bow:

"Coruler Gnat La-Fin, there must have been a misunderstanding. I will withdraw all my subjects from your world, and all those mentally subjugated will have their minds freed. I will order my servants to be more careful in the future. I hope such a minor incident will not impact the ancient and strong bond between our great dynasties."

From an outside perspective, it all looked very dignified, like two Corulers peacefully conversing about some minor friction then coming to an agreement. However my magical defenses were howling in strain. Mental Fortitude boosts flickered in one after the next. If not for Gerd Tamara and her magic protection spells, I'd already have been dead. Meanwhile, heard a mental message from Leng Onuri-Unta La-Varrez:

"This time, I admit. You outplayed me. Another half hour and there would have been nothing left of your sea landing party. But let's wait two days and see how you start singing then! I will summon the Council of Rulers to tell everyone the La-Fin Faction is working with our enemies and subverting the entire magocratic world! You will be dethroned as Coruler. Then we can discuss the fate of the First Directory and the La-Fin Dynasty!"

"CAPTAIN, THEY took off just twenty minutes ago!" Orun Va-Mart pointed at the empty neighboring hangar and circle of burned, still smoking grass.

"I found out from the dispatchers," Uline Tar instantly threw out, "The human La-Shin Faction's Kurimiru shuttle is now in orbit. They must be testing on-board systems before a long-distance flight."

Ugh, we had been beaten into orbit because of last night's attack! While the seven Sio-Mi-Dori returned from the long-distance raid, while I spoke with Ivan Lozovsky and explained why the Human-8 Faction stopped resisting, while all the logistic issues on Rocky Island were being settled, the little bird flitted away. "Anyhow..." I bared my teeth predatorily, "Occasions like this are why Captain Gnat has pirate status in the first place. If I don't wanna lose it, I've gotta cross the line sometimes." My whole crew was here at the spaceport, so there was nothing to stop us from a speedy take-off.

"Everyone to the ship! Dmitry, prepare systems for takeoff. UlineTar, handle the bureaucracy with the dispatcher service. We need immediate permission to take-off! By the way, did you get the dowry for your groom?"

"Yes, Captain Gnat. Eight million crystals, we didn't even have to sell the Assassins, which we installed on our frigate. Even without them, it made a respectable dowry. Viceroy Kosta Dykhsh was in utter delight! The wedding will be in twenty days right here on Earth. I invited my relatives, so it will get loud. And you're invited. Don't even think of refusing. I would just die! By the way, I almost forgot in all this rush..." my furry friend turned on her palmtop and read some information. "A medic has requested to join our crew. A human woman named Anna. She isn't in any faction. She said you personally invited her. Should I confirm? It's just we've already got one Medic, and he's pretty decent. Why do we need a second?"

A human Medic named Anna? I invited her? I hadn't talked to her since a good deal before she fled the Dome. And I don't remember inviting her to join my crew. Unless... Damn! That was right! I once really did ask Anya to come to space with me, back when I was heading to war in Uraz Tukhsh's Shiamiru. But she refused. Was she bringing that old invitation up now? Really?

When I ran a scan, it did show an outsider on the frigate:

Woman. Human. Level-62 Medic.

I went to figure it out and on the stairs I saw

Anya from First Med, who I first met so long ago. The long-legged blonde was wearing standard Human-3 light armor, but without a faction tag. She gave me a sheepish smile and handed me an item I'd recently failed to find:

"Leng Gnat, you asked for your Prospector Scanner!"

END OF BOOK FOUR

Want to be the first to know about our latest LitRPG, sci fi and fantasy titles from your favorite authors?

Subscribe to our **New Releases** newsletter:
http://eepurl.com/b7niIL

Thank you for reading *Web Of Worlds!*
If you like what you've read, check out other sci-fi, fantasy
and LitRPG novels published by Magic Dome Books:

Reality Benders LitRPG series by Michael Atamanov:
Countdown
External Threat
Game Changer
Web of Worlds
A Jump into the Unknown
Aces High

The Dark Herbalist LitRPG series
by Michael Atamanov:
Video Game Plotline Tester
Stay on the Wing
A Trap for the Potentate
Finding a Body

Perimeter Defense LitRPG series by Michael Atamanov:
Sector Eight
Beyond Death
New Contract
A Game with No Rules

League of Losers LitRPG Series
by Michael Atamanov:
A Cat and his Human

The Way of the Shaman LitRPG series
by Vasily Mahanenko:
Survival Quest
The Kartoss Gambit
The Secret of the Dark Forest
The Phantom Castle
The Karmadont Chess Set
Shaman's Revenge
Clans War

The Alchemist LitRPG series by Vasily Mahanenko:
City of the Dead
Forest of Desire
Tears of Alron

Dark Paladin LitRPG series by Vasily Mahanenko:
The Beginning
The Quest
Restart

Galactogon LitRPG series by Vasily Mahanenko:
Start the Game!
In Search of the Uldans
A Check for a Billion

Invasion LitRPG Series by Vasily Mahanenko:
A Second Chance
An Equation with one Unknown

World of the Changed LitRPG Series by Vasily Mahanenko:
No Mistakes
Pearl of the South

**The Bard from Barliona LitRPG series
by Eugenia Dmitrieva and Vasily Mahanenko:**
The Renegades
A Song of Shadow

Level Up LitRPG series by Dan Sugralinov:
Re-Start
Hero
The Final Trial
Level Up: The Knockout (with Max Lagno)
Level Up. The Knockout: Update (with Max Lagno)

Disgardium LitRPG series by Dan Sugralinov:
Class-A Threat
Apostle of the Sleeping Gods
The Destroying Plague
Resistance
Holy War

World 99 LitRPG Series by Dan Sugralinov:
Blood of Fate

Adam Online LitRPG Leries by Max Lagno:
Absolute Zero
City of Freedom

El Diablo by G.Zotov
(a supernatural thriller)

Mirror World LitRPG series by Alexey Osadchuk:
Project Daily Grind
The Citadel
The Way of the Outcast
The Twilight Obelisk

Underdog LitRPG series by Alexey Osadchuk:
Dungeons of the Crooked Mountains
The Wastes
The Dark Continent
The Otherworld

An NPC's Path LitRPG series by Pavel Kornev:
The Dead Rogue
Kingdom of the Dead
Deadman's Retinue

The Sublime Electricity series by Pavel Kornev:
The Illustrious
The Heartless
The Fallen
The Dormant

Citadel World series by Kir Lukovkin:
The URANUS Code
The Secret of Atlantis

You're in Game!
(LitRPG Stories from Bestselling Authors)

You're in Game-2!
(More LitRPG stories set in your favorite worlds)

The Fairy Code by Kaitlyn Weiss:
Captive of the Shadows
Chosen of the Shadows

More books and series are coming out soon!

In order to have new books of the series translated faster, we need your help and support! Please consider leaving a review or spread the word by recommending *Web of Worlds* to your friends and posting the link on social media. The more people buy the book, the sooner we'll be able to make new translations available.

Thank you!

Till next time!